MARA
AND
DANN

ALSO BY DORIS LESSING

MARA
AND
DANN

AN ADVENTURE

Doris Lessing

HarperPerennial
A Division of HarperCollinsPublishers

A hardcover edition of this book was published in 1999 by HarperCollins Publishers.

HarperCollins books may be purchased for educational, business, or sales promotional use. For information, please e-mail the Special Markets Department at SPsales@harpercollins.com.

First HarperPerennial edition published 2000.

Designed by Kris Tobiassen

The Library of Congress has catalogued the hardcover edition as follows:

Lessing, Doris May, 1919–
    Mara and Dann : an adventure / Doris Lessing. — 1st ed.
       p. cm.
    ISBN 0-06-018294-6
       I. Title.
  PR6023.E833M357   1999
823'.914—dc21   98-30782

ISBN 0-06-093056-X (pbk.)

HB 03.28.2024

Author's Note

One day last autumn my son Peter Lessing came in to say that he had just been listening, on the radio, to a tale about an orphaned brother and sister who had all kinds of adventures, suffered a hundred vicissitudes, and ended up living happily ever after. This was the oldest story in Europe. "Why don't you write something like that?" he suggested. "Oddly enough," I replied, "that is exactly what I am writing and I have nearly finished it."

This kind of thing happens in families, but perhaps not so often in laboratories.

Mara and Dann is a reworking of a very old tale, and it is found not only in Europe but in most cultures in the world.

It is set in the future, in Africa, called Ifrik because of how often we may hear how the short *a* becomes a short *i*.

An Ice Age covers all the northern hemisphere.

I cannot be the only person who, hearing that the most common condition for the northern parts of the world is to be under—sometimes—miles of ice, shivers, not because of imagined cold winds, since every one of us is equipped with that potent talisman for survival, It can't happen to me, making it impossible for us to weaken ourselves by brooding on possible calamities, but from the thought that one day, thousands of years in the future, our descendants might be saying, "In the 12,000-year interval between one thrust of the Ice Age and the next, there flourished a whole story of human development, from savagery and barbarism to high culture"—and all our civilisations and languages, and cities and skills and inventions, our farms and gardens and forests, and the birds and the beasts we try so hard to protect against our depredations, will amount to a sentence or a paragraph in a long history. But perhaps it will be a 15,000-year interregnum, or less or more, for our experts say that the next Ice Age, already overdue, may begin in a year's time or in a thousand years.

Mara and Dann is an attempt to imagine what some of the consequences might be when the ice returns and life must retreat to the middle and southern latitudes. Our past experiences help to picture the future. During the hardest of previous periods of ice, the Mediterranean was dry. During warmer intervals, when the ice withdrew for a while, the Neanderthals returned from exile in the south to take up life again in their still chilly valleys. If they did not see their sojourns south as exile, why did they always return?

Perhaps it is the Neanderthals who will turn out to have been our truest ancestors, having bequeathed to us our amazing diversity, our ability to live in any clime or condition and, above all, our endurance. I like to imagine them, with their great experience of ice, posting a watch for the advancing white mountains.

April 1998

The scene that the child, then the girl, then the young woman tried so hard to remember was clear enough in its beginnings. She had been hustled—sometimes carried, sometimes pulled along by the hand—through a dark night, nothing to be seen but stars, and then she was pushed into a room and told, Keep quiet, and the people who had brought her disappeared. She had not taken notice of their faces, what they were, she was too frightened, but they were her people, the People, she knew that. The room was nothing she had known. It was a square, built of large blocks of rock. She was inside one of the rock houses. She had seen them all her life. The rock houses were where *they* lived, the Rock People, not her people, who despised them. She had often seen the Rock People walking along the roads, getting quickly out of the way when they saw the People; but a dislike of them that she had been taught made it hard to look much at them. She was afraid of them, and thought them ugly.

She was alone in the big, bare rock room. It was water she was looking for—surely there must be water somewhere? But the room was empty. In the middle of it was a square made of the rock blocks, which she supposed must be a table; but there was nothing on it except a candle stuck in its grease, and burning low . . . it would soon go out. By now she was thinking, But where is he, where is my little brother? He, too, had been rushed through the dark. She had called out to him, right at the beginning, when they were snatched away from home—rescued, she now knew—and a hand had come down over her mouth, "*Quiet.*" And she had heard him cry out to her, and the sudden silence told her a hand had stopped his cry in the same way.

She was in a fever, hot and dry over her whole body, but it was hard to distinguish the discomfort of this from her anxiety over her brother.

She went to the place in the wall where she had been thrust in, and tried to push a rock that was a door to one side. It moved in a groove, and was only another slab of rock; but just as she was giving up, because it was too heavy for her, it slid aside, and her brother rushed at her with a great howl that made her suddenly cold with terror and her hair prickle. He flung himself at her, and her arms went around him while she was looking at the doorway, where a man was mouthing at her and pointing to the child, *Quiet, quiet.* In her turn she put her hand over his open, howling mouth and felt his teeth in her palm. She did not cry out or pull away, but staggered back against a wall to support his weight; and she put her arms tight around him, whispering, "Hush, shhh, you must be quiet." And then, using a threat that frightened her too, "Quiet, or that bad man will come." And he at once went quiet, and trembled as he clutched her. The man who had brought in the little boy had not gone away. He was whispering with someone out in the darkness. And then this someone came in, and she almost screamed, for she thought this was the bad man she had threatened her brother with; but then she saw that no, this man was not the same but only looked like him. She had in fact begun to scream, but slammed her own free hand across her mouth, the hand that was not pressing her brother's head into her chest. "I thought you were . . . that you were . . ." she stammered; and he said, "No, that was my brother, Garth." He was wearing the same clothes as the other one, a black tunic, with red on it, and he was already stripping it off. Now he was naked, as she had seen her father and his brothers, but on ceremonial occasions, when they were decorated with all kinds of bracelets and pendants and anklets, in gold, so that they did not seem naked. But this man was as tired and dusty as she and her brother were; and on his back, as he turned it to put on the other tunic he had with him, were slashes from whips, weals where the blood was oozing even now, though some had dried. He pulled over his head a brown tunic, like a long sack, and she again nearly cried out, for this was what the Rock People wore. He stood in front of her, belting this garment with the same brown stuff, and looking hard at her and then at the little boy, who chose this moment to lift his head; and when he saw the man standing there, he let out another howl, just like their dog when he howled at the moon; and again she put her hand over his mouth—not the one he had bitten, which was bleeding—but let him stare over it while she said, "It's not the same man. It's his brother. It's not the bad one."

But she could feel the child trembling, in great fits, and she was afraid he would convulse and even die; and she forced his head around, back into her, and cradled it with her two arms.

For days, but she did not know how long, the two children had been in a room in their own home while *the other one*, who looked like this man, questioned them. *The other one*, the bad man, and others in the room, men and women, wore the long black tunics, with red. The two children were the centre of the scene. All the questions had been asked by the bad man, whose face even now seemed to burn there, inside her eyes, so that she had to keep blinking to force it away, and see the face of this man whom she could see was a friend. The bad one kept asking her over and over again about her close family, not the Family, and in the beginning she had answered because she had not known they were enemies; but then the bad man had taken up a whip and said that if they did not answer he would beat them. At this, one woman and then another protested, but he had made them be quiet, with an angry look and a thrust of the whip at them. But the trouble was, she did not know the answers to the questions. It was she who had to answer, because the little boy had screamed at the sight of the whip, and had begun his clinging to her, as he was doing now, his face pressed into her. These bad people, who she was beginning to see were probably relatives, though not her own family—she seemed to remember faces—were asking who came to their house, who slept there, what their parents talked about with them, what their plans were. None of this she knew. Ever since she could remember anything, there had been people coming and going; and then there were the servants, who were like friends. Once, during the questioning, there was a confused, angry moment when she had answered a question with something about the man who ran the house and took orders from her mother; but the bad man had not meant him at all, and he leaned right down and shouted at her, the face (so like the face she was looking at now) so close to hers she could smell his sour breath and see the vein in his forehead throbbing; and she was so frightened that for a moment her mind was dark, and was dark for so long that, when she saw again, she was looking up at the man staring down at her; and they were all alarmed and silent, and he was too. She could not speak after that: her tongue had gone stiff and, besides, she was so thirsty. There was a jar of water on the table, and she pointed at it and said, "Please, water," using the politeness she had been taught; and then the bad man was pleased at the new good idea he had, and began pouring water into a cup, and then back again, making the water splash, so that her whole dry body yearned for it; but he did not give her any. And all that went on, the whip sometimes in the man's hand, sometimes lying on the table where she could see it, the water being splashed, and the man pouring it deliberately and drinking it, mouthful by mouthful, and asking, asking, asking the questions she did not know the answers to. And then there was a great noise outside of voices and quarrelling. The people in the room had exclaimed, and looked at each other, and then they ran off, fast, through the door into the storerooms, leaving the two children alone; and she had been just about to reach for the water when a whole crowd had rushed into the room. She thought at first they were Rock People because they wore the brown sack things, but then saw that no, they were People, her people, being tall, and thin, and nice looking. Then she and the little boy were lifted up and told, Quiet, be quiet, and they had travelled for hours through the dark, while the stars jogged overhead; and then she had been thrust into this room, the rock room, alone.

Now she said to this man, "I'm so thirsty"; and at this his face had a look as if he wanted to laugh, the way you laugh when something impossible is asked for. She knew exactly what he was thinking; her mind was so clear then, and she could look back afterwards and see that face of his, the good one—like her parents', kind—but on it that smile, *Oh no, it's not possible*, because everything was so dangerous and more important than water. But that was the end of the clear part, the end of what she remembered.

He said, "Wait." And went to where the room slab had been slid to shut out the night, full of enemies, pushed it along in its groove, and in a low voice said something which must be about water. How many people were out there? He came back with a cup of water. "Be careful," he said, "there isn't much." And now the little boy tore himself out of her arms and grabbed the cup and began gulping and snuffling the water down, and then ... the cup slipped, and what was left splashed on the rock of the floor. He wailed, and she put her hand on his mouth again and turned his face into her. She had not had even one mouthful but the man hadn't noticed. This was because he had turned away at the moment the boy was drinking to make sure the door slab was in place. Her mouth was burning, her eyes burned, because she wanted to cry and there were no tears there, her whole being was so dry, she burned with dryness. And now the man squatted in front of her and began talking.

And this was the part she tried to remember afterwards, for years, as she was growing up, for what he told her she most desperately wanted to know.

The beginning she did take in. She knew—didn't she?—that things had been pretty bad for a long time, everything getting worse . . . she must know that. Yes, she did, her parents talked about it, and she did know, as this man kept saying, that the weather was changing. It was getting drier but not in any regular way: sometimes it rained in the way it should and sometimes not at all or very little; and there was a lot of trouble with the Rock People, and there was a war going on between the different big families, and even inside the families—because, as she could see, his brother and he were on different sides and . . .

Her little brother seemed to be asleep, slumped there against her. She knew he was not asleep but had fainted, or gone into some kind of fit of not knowing, because he could not bear any more; and the few mouthfuls of water had been enough to relax him into a temporary quiet, though he jerked and trembled as he clung heavily to her, limp, his arms heavy and dragging. She felt she would fall. She had been like this for days, in that other place, her own home, where the child had clung and shivered and cried, noisily, then silently, when the bad man hit him to keep quiet. And now he was still there, against her, and she was staring over his head into the face of the man which, she could see because it was so close to her, was thin and bony because he was hungry, and full of pain too, for his back must be hurting. He was talking, fast, straight into her face; his mouth was moving and she could not stop looking at it: it was as if every word were being rolled around inside his mouth and forced out . . . He was tired, he was so tired it was hard for him to talk, and to explain all these things. It was about his brother, Garth, the bad one, and his friends. It was about her parents, who had gone away somewhere because the bad ones had wanted to kill them. And she must be careful to look after the little boy . . . She thought she was going to fall. She tried to speak but found her mouth was gummed up, there was only a thick gum in her mouth, and she looked into this man's face, the man who was saving her and her brother—she knew that much—and she saw a greying scum on his lips. That was why it was hard for him to talk. He was thirsty, like her. And now he grabbed her by both shoulders, and looked close into her face, and was demanding an answer—but this time not frighteningly, like the other one, but a kind of Yes from her, meaning she had understood; but she hadn't, she was thinking about water. It seemed that the sounds of water were everywhere, splashing on the rock roof and the rocks outside, but she knew she imagined it; and suddenly she saw from the dark, exhausted face so close to hers that he had understood. And she managed to lift a hand and point to her mouth. He looked for the cup and saw it lying on its side on the floor, and the stain of spilt water. He picked up the cup and got up, slowly, went slowly to the door, because he was stiff now from the wounds on his back, pushed the door along, said something, while he supported himself on the wall with one hand. A long wait. Then the cup was handed back in. He brought it to her. It was only half full. She said to herself that she would not gulp and guzzle as her brother had, but she couldn't help herself, and bent her head to the cup, hastily, greedily; but she did not spill any, not a drop, and as she drank the precious mouthfuls she saw the mouth next to hers moving, as his eyes watched every little movement of swallowing. He was thirsty, was desperate for water, but had given her those mouthfuls. And now he took the cup from her, slid it inside his tunic where the belt was, put big strong hands on either side of her, pressed her gently, and then gathered her, together with her little brother, into his arms and held them there a few moments. Never would she forget how she felt then, protected, safe, and she wanted never to move away from those kind arms. Then he gently released her and, squatting in front of her, as he had before, asked, "What is your name?" And as she told him, she saw his face change into a weariness and disappointment with her that made her want to clutch him and say, "I'm sorry, I'm so sorry"—but she did not know what for. He put his face close, so that she could see a little mesh of red veins in his eyes and the grime in the pores of his face, and he said, "Mara. I told you: Mara. I've just told you." And now she did remember that, yes, it was one of the things he had been telling her during the time she couldn't listen. He had told her to forget her name, her real name, and that now she was called Mara. "Mara," she repeated, obedient, feeling that the sound had nothing to do with her. "Again," he said, stern, and she knew he did not believe she would remember, because she hadn't, until now. "Mara. My name is Mara." "Good—and this child here . . . ?" But she could not remember what he had said. He saw from her desperate face that she did not know. "His name is Dann now. He must forget his name." And he went to the door, very stiff and slow, and there he turned and looked at her, a long look, and she said, "Mara. I'm Mara." He went out and this time the rock door was not slid back. Outside she could see the dark of the night and the dark shapes of people. Now she let her brother go loose and he woke. "That was a good man," she told him. "He is our friend. He is helping us. The one you are frightened of, he's the bad one. Do you understand? They are brothers." He was staring up at her, trying to understand: she was taller, because he was three years younger, four years old, and he was her little brother whom she had protected and cared for since he was born. She said it all again. This one was good. The other was bad. And her name was Mara now and he must forget her real name. And his name was . . . a moment's panic: had she forgotten it? No. "Your name is Dann." "No it isn't, that's not my name." "Yes, it is. You must forget your real name, it's dangerous." And her voice shook, she heard it become a sob, and the little boy put up his hand to stroke her face. This made her want to howl and weep, because she felt he had come back to her, her beloved little brother, after a horrible time when some sort of changeling had been attached to her. She did not know if he had understood, but now he said, "Poor Mara," and she clutched him and kissed him, and they were crying and clutching when two people came in, in the clothes of the Rock People, but they were not Rock People. They had bundles of the brown tunics under their arms and they took two, one for her and one for Dann. She hated the feel of the tunic, slippery and thin, going down over her head, and the little boy said, "Do I have to wear this?"

Now the man said, "Quick, we must hurry," and hustled them to the door. The candle was left burning; then he remembered, took it up and held it high, looking around the room to see what had been forgotten.

The little girl who was now Mara looked back too, so as to remember the room, or what she could, for she was already anxious because of what she was forgetting.

As for the little boy, he would remember later only the warmth and safety of his sister's body, as he pressed himself into it. "Are we going home now?" he asked, and she was thinking, Of course we are; because all this time she had been thinking, We'll go home and the bad people will have gone and then . . . Yet that man had been telling her, yes, he had been telling her—while he squatted in front of her, talking and talking, and she had not been able to hear because of her longing for a drink—they were not going home. This was the first time the little girl really understood that they were not going back to their home. Outside, in the darkness, she looked up to see how the stars had moved. Her father had taught her how to look at stars. She was trying to find the ones that were called The Seven Friends. And they were her friends, her stars. She had said to her father, "But there are eight—no, nine," and he had called her Little Bright Eyes. Where was her father? Her mother? She was just going to pull at the elbow of the tall man who had come in with the clothes, and ask, when she understood that she had been told and had not heard properly. She did not dare ask again. She saw four of the people go off quietly, quickly, hardly to be seen in the brown clothes. Two were left: the man and a woman. She could hear by how they breathed, too loud, that they were tired and wanted to rest and sleep—yes, sleep . . . And as she drowsed off, standing there, she felt herself shaken awake and in her turn shook her brother, who was limp and heavy in her grasp. "Can you walk?" asked the woman. "Good," said the man while she hesitated, and he said, "Then come on." Around them were other rock houses. They were all empty, she could see, while being hurried past. Why was the village empty? How could they, the People, just go into a rock house and walk through a rock village without guards?

"Where are they?" she whispered up at the woman, and heard the whisper, "They've all gone north."

Soon they stopped. High in the sky above her she saw the head of a cart bird turning and tilting to look down at them to see who they were. She was terrified of these tall birds, with their sharp beaks and great feet and claws that could rip somebody to pieces. But it was harnessed to a cart and she was expected to climb in. The cart was used on the fields, and was a flimsy thing that rattled about and only carried light loads. She could not manage it and was lifted in, and then Dann was beside her, and the whole cart creaked and seemed to want to settle to the earth as the two big people got in. The cart bird stood waiting. The slave who looked after the cart bird, who they called the cart bird man, sat just behind the bird, making it start and stop with a whistle she had often heard them make. The man and the woman wanted the cart to go forward and kept saying, "Go, go," but the bird did not move. Mara whispered, "It needs a whistle." "What whistle?" "Like this." Mara had not meant her little piping whistle to make the bird go, but that is what happened. The cart was rushing forward and the great feet of the cart bird were going down hard into the dust and lifting up and scattering dust back over them all. Where were they going? Mara was afraid that these two people who were trying to help them did not know, but they were saying to each other loudly, because of all the noise, "There's the big hill," "That's the black rock they described," "I think that must be the dead tree." Weren't they supposed to be keeping quiet because of enemies? Anyone near could hear the rattling of the cart, though the wheels were running quietly through the dust. The little boy was crying. She knew he felt sick, because she did. And then Mara fell off to sleep and kept waking to see the cart bird's great head jerking along against the stars ... And then, suddenly, the cart stopped. The cart bird had stopped because it was tired. It fell to its knees and its beak was open, and it tried to get up but couldn't, and sank back into the dust.

"We are there anyway," the man told the children; and the two big people lifted the children out of the cart, and were tugging them off away from the cart when Mara said, "Wait, the cart bird." And then, seeing these people did not know much about cart birds, she said, "If the bird is left tied to the cart and can't move it will die."

"She's right," said the man, and the woman said, "Thank you for telling us."

Now the two moved to where the rope from the cart was tied to the harness on the bird; but they did not know how to untie it. The man took out a knife and cut all the lines. The bird staggered up and to the side of the track, where it fell again, and sat moving its head around, and opening and shutting its beak. It was so thirsty: Mara could feel the dryness of its mouth in her own.

Now they were walking along a path, the kind the Rock People used: not straight and wide, like the real roads, but going through the bushes and grasses anyhow it could, and looping around rocky places. It was soft underfoot, this path: it was only dust. Several times she had to stop herself tripping, because her feet dragged in the dust drifts and she was pulling her brother along. The woman said something, and the man came back and picked up the child, who let out a wail, but stopped himself in time to prevent that hand over his mouth. They were trying to talk quietly, but the little girl thought, Our breathing is so loud, anyone near could hear it, and we are all too tired to walk carefully. Once or twice she drifted off to sleep as she walked, and came to herself at the tug of the woman's hand. Now it was light, Mara could see her face: it was a nice face, but so tired, and around her mouth was the greyish scum of being thirsty. The light was still grey, and across the great stretch of country from that reddening sky came that cold breath that says the sun will soon rise. Like the little cluster of stars, this early cold was her special friend, and she knew it well, for at home she liked to wake early before anyone else and stand by the window and wait for the sweet coolness on her face and then look out, watching how the world became light and the sky filled with sunlight.

Dann was asleep on the shoulder of the man carrying him, who was almost staggering with the weight. Yet Dann was not heavy, she often carried him. Now it was full daylight. All around was this enormous, flat country covered with grass, a yellow, drying grass that she could easily see over. No trees. Here and there were little rocky hills, but not one tree. The child could see that the woman, whose hand she was clutching, dozed off as she walked; and when that happened the big, dry hand went limp, and the child had to grab it and hold on. She felt she would soon start crying, she had to cry, she was so miserable and frightened, but she had no tears.

They were going down off a ridge and, look, there were trees, a line of them, and a smell Mara knew, the smell of water. She cried out, and then all four of them were running forward, towards that smell . . . They were on the edge of a big hole, one of a string of big holes, and at the bottom of this was some muddy water. Things flapped about down there. Fish were dying in that water, which was hardly enough to cover them, and there was a strong smell coming up, of dead things. The four jumped off the jagged edge of the hole into the dried mud around the water; but it was not water at all: it was thick mud and they could not drink it. They stood there, looking down at the dark mud where fishes and a tortoise struggled, and there was a new thing, a new sound, a roar, a rumble, a rushing, and the smell of water was strong . . . And then the woman snatched her up and the man picked up Dann, and the four were at the top of the edge of the big hole, and then running and stumbling as fast as they could, and Mara was saying, "Why, why, why?" gasping dry breaths; and they reached one of the little hills of rocks, and climbed a short way and turned to see . . . What the little girl thought she saw was the earth moving along towards where the waterholes were, a brown fast moving, a brown rush, and there was a smell of water, and the woman said, "It's all right, it's a flash flood." And the man said, "There must have been a cloudburst up north." Mara, no longer tired, her whole being vibrating with fear because of the nearness of the flood, could see only blue sky, not a cloud anywhere, so how could a cloud have burst? The brown water had reached level with them, jumping and tumbling past, but a wash of water was spreading out and had reached the little hill. Dann began struggling and roaring in the man's arms to get down into the water, and in a moment all four were standing in the water, splashing it all over them, drinking it, while Dann was like a dog, rolling in it, and laughing and lapping, and shouting, "Water, water"; and then Mara sat down in it, feeling that her whole body was drinking in the water; and she saw the two grown-up people were squatting to drink and splash themselves but the water was only part-way to their knees. It was up to her shoulders, and rising. Then the two grown-ups were standing and looking towards where the flood had come from and saying quick, frightened things to each other, using words Mara did not know. That water was short and everyone must be careful all the time, she knew, and could not remember now when things had been different. But she had not heard of floods, and dams and clouds bursting, and inundations. And then she felt herself scooped up again and saw how the man lifted Dann up out of the water; and they were halfway up the hill when there was another roar and a second brown flood came racing down. But now it was not just roaring: there were bangs and crashes and rumbles, and bellows and bleats too, for in this second flood were all kinds of animals, and some of them she had never seen before except in the pictures painted on the walls at home. Some were being tossed by the waves of the flood to one side of the main rush of water and, finding that they had ground under them, were climbing out and making for the higher ground. The big animals were doing well, but smaller ones were being swept past, calling and crying; and Mara saw one of them, like her little pet, Shera, at home, who slept in her bed and was her friend, riding past on a tree that had all sorts of little animals stuck all over the branches. Now Mara was crying because of the poor animals; but meanwhile others were running down from the higher ground towards the water, and straight into the flood to stand in it and drink and drink and roll in it, just as the four of them had done, for they were so thirsty. Mara saw the cart bird come staggering out of the grass, its feet going down wide because it was so weak, and when it reached the edge of the water it simply sank down and drank, sitting, while the water rose so that soon its neck was poking up out of the brown flood, like a stick or a snake. The water was now rising fast around the hill they were on. Where just a moment before they had splashed and rolled, it was so deep that a big horse, like the ones her parents rode, was up to the top of its legs; and then another wave came spilling out from the main flood and the horse stepped out and began swimming. Then the cart bird stood up, and now that it was wet all over, and its puffs of white and black feathers flat and thin, you could see it was all bones. Mara knew that animals were dying everywhere because of the dryness, and when she saw the cart bird, so thin and weak, she understood. She had a big book, with pictures of animals pasted in, and some she had never seen; but here they were, all along the edge of the water, drinking. Now she was watching a big tree rolling and tossing as it swept past, with animals on it; and as she watched she saw it rear up and turn over . . . and when it rolled back the animals had gone. Mara was crying, feeling on her palms the soft fur of her pet, and she wondered if someone was looking after Shera. And it was the first time she had thought that they, the People, had gone fast away from the houses, run away; but what had happened to their house animals, the dog and Shera? Meanwhile above her head the man and woman were talking in low, frightened voices. They were disagreeing. The man got his way, and in a moment she and Dann were lifted up again and the two grown-ups were in the water, which was nearly up to their shoulders now, so that the children were in it to their waists, and they were wading as fast as they could to another hill, much higher, less rocky, not far away. But it seemed very far, as the water was rising around them; and the tussocks of grass they could not see tripped them up, and the man once even fell, and Dann tumbled out of his arms and disappeared into the water, while Mara cried out. But the man got up from the water, picked Dann out of it, and when a roar from behind said there was another big wave on the way, he tried to run, and did run, making great, splashing bounds, easier as the water grew shallower; and they all reached this other hill just as the new wave banged into them, and their heads went under, and then they were up on the side of the hill, together with all kinds of animals, who were dragging themselves up, streaming water, half drowned, their open mouths full of water.

The children were carried nearly to the top of this hill, which was much higher than the one they had left. When they looked back they could see the water was already halfway up, past where they had been standing, and the animals there were so thickly clustered their horns and trunks were like the little, dead forest near home with its branches sticking up. Now the water covered everywhere: there was nothing to be seen but water, brown, tossing and flooding water, and all the hills were crowded with animals. Just near where the four people stood, the two children clutching tight to the legs of their rescuers, was a big, flat rock covered in snakes. Mara had never seen them alive, though she knew there were still some left. They were lying stretched out or coiled up, hardly moving, as if they were dead, but they were tired. And snakes were swimming towards the hill, through the waves, and when they reached the dry ground they slithered out and just lay, still.

"Some cloudburst," said the woman, and above them was a blue sky without one cloud in it, and the sun shone down on the flood. "I saw a river come down once, like this, but it was thirty years ago," said the man. "I was about the age of these children. It was up north. The big dam burst in the hills—no maintenance." "This is no dam," said the woman. "No dam could hold this amount of water." "No," he said. "I'd say the plain above the Old Gorge flooded, and the water got funnelled through the gorge down to here." "A pity we can't stop all this water flooding to waste."

Meanwhile Dann had found a hollow place in a flat rock where the water was trickling in, and he was sitting in the water. But he was not alone: lizards and snakes were there with him.

"Dann," shouted Mara. The child took no notice. He was stroking a big, fat, grey snake that lay beside him in the water, and making sounds of pleasure. "Stop it, that's dangerous," said Mara, looking up at the woman so she could stop Dann; but she did not hear. She was staring off in the direction Mara knew was north, and yet another wall of water was coming down. It was not as high as the others, but enough to push in front of it boulders and dead animals, the big ones with trunks and big ears and tusks.

"We can't afford to lose any more animals," said the man. And the woman said, "I suppose a few more dead don't make any difference."

They were speaking very loudly above the sounds of the water and the banging rocks and stones, and the cries of the animals.

At this moment Dann got up out of his pool, unlooping a big green snake that had come to rest around his arm, and climbed up towards them, careful not to step on a snake or an animal too exhausted to move out of his way, and stood in front of the two grown-ups and said, "I'm hungry. I'm so hungry." And now Mara realised she had been hungry for a long time. How long was it since they had eaten? The bad people had not given them food. Before that . . . Mara's mind was full of sharp little pictures she was trying to fit together: her parents leaning down to say, "Be brave, be brave and look after your brother"; the big man with his dark, angry face; before that, the quiet ordinariness of their home before all the terrible things began happening. She could not remember eating: food had been short for quite a long time, but there had been things to eat. Now she looked carefully at Dann, and she had not done that for days because she had been so thirsty and so frightened, and she saw that his face was thin and yellowish though usually he was a chubby, shiny little child. She had never seen him like this. And she saw something else: his tunic, the brown sack thing of the Rock People, was quite dry. The water had streamed off it as he had climbed out of the rock pool. And her tunic was dry. She hated the thin, dead, slippery feel of the stuff, but it did dry quickly.

"We don't have much food," said the man, "and if we eat what we have now we might not find any more."

"I'm so hungry," whispered Mara.

The man and the woman looked worriedly at each other.

"It isn't far now," he said.

"But there's all that water."

"It'll drain away soon."

"Far? Where?" demanded Mara, tugging at the brown slipperiness of the woman's tunic. "Home? Are we near home?" Even as she said it her heart was sinking because she knew it was nonsense: they were not going home. The woman squatted down so that her face was on the same level as hers, and the man did the same for the boy. "Surely you've got that into your head by now?" said the woman. Her big face, all bone and hollows, her eyes burning out between the bones, seemed desperate with sadness. The man had Dann by the arms and was saying, "You must stop this, you must." But the little boy hadn't said anything. He was crying: tears were actually falling down his poor cheeks now that he had drunk enough to let him cry properly.

"What did Lord Gorda tell you? Surely he told you?"

Mara had to nod, miserably, tears filling her throat.

"Well then," said the woman, straightening up. The man, too, rose, and the two stood looking at each other; and Mara could see that they didn't know what to do or say. "It's too much for them to take in," the woman said, and the man said, "Hardly surprising."

"But they have to understand."

"I do understand. I do, really," said Mara.

"Good," said the woman. "What is the most important thing?"

The little girl thought and said, "My name is Mara."

And then the man said to the little boy, "And what is your name?"

"It's Dann," said Mara quickly, in case he had forgotten; and he had, because he said, "It isn't my name. My name isn't Dann."

"It's a question of life and death," said the man. "You've got to remember that."

"Better if you could try to forget your real name," said the woman. And Mara thought that she easily could, for that name was in her other life, where people were friendly and kind and she wasn't thirsty all the time.

"I'm hungry," said Dann again.

The two grown-ups looked to see that the rock behind them did not have a snake on it. There were a couple of lizards and some scorpions, who did not look as if the water had discouraged them. They must have emerged from crevices to see what the disturbance was all about. The man took up a stick and gently pushed it at the scorpions and lizards, and they disappeared into the rocks.

The four of them sat down on the rock. The woman had a big bag tied around her waist. Water had got into it, but the food inside was so well wrapped in wads of leaves that it was almost dry, only a little wet. There were two slabs of thick white stuff, and she broke each slab into two so they each had a piece. Mara took a bite and found her mouth full of tasteless stuff.

"That's all there is," said the woman.

Dann was so hungry he was taking big bites and chewing and swallowing, and taking another bite. Mara copied him.

"Anything you don't finish, give back," said the woman. She was not eating but watching the children eat. "Eat," said the man to her. "You must." But he had only eaten a little himself.

"Is it the Rock People's food?" asked Dann, surprising his sister, but pleasing her, for she knew that he did notice things, remembered, and came out with it later, even when you'd think he was too little to understand.

"Yes, it is," said the man, "and you'd better learn to like it because I doubt whether you'll get much else—at least, not for a while."

"Probably for a good long while," said the woman, "the way things are going."

The man and the woman stood up and went forward to the very edge of a rock to take a good, long look at the water. It was still at the same height. And all the hills were crowded, simply crammed, with animals waiting for the flood to go down, just as they were. Down below, the great plain of brown water hurried past, still carrying bushes where little animals clung, and trees where big animals balanced; but now it seemed that there was less fret and storm in the water.

"It has reached its peak," said the woman.

"If there isn't more to come," said the man.

The sky was still a hard, clear blue, like a lid over everything. The sun was shining hot and fierce, and there were no new big waves from the north.

Dann had gone to sleep holding a half-eaten hunk of the white stuff. The woman took it from him and put it in her bag. She sat down and her eyes closed and her head fell forward. The man's eyes closed and he sank down, asleep.

"But we must keep awake," the little girl was pleading, "we must. Suppose the bad people come? Suppose a snake bites us?" And then she tumbled off to sleep, but later only knew she had been asleep because she was scrambling up, thinking, Where's my brother? Where are the others? And her head was aching because she had been lying in the sun, which had moved and was going down, sending pink reflections from the sky across the water. But the water that had covered everything had gone down and was a river racing down the middle part of the valley. Dann was awake and holding the hand of the woman, and they were standing higher up where they could see everything easily. This hill was now surrounded by brown mud, and the yellow grasses were just beginning to lift up.

"Where are we going to cross over?" asked the woman.

"I don't know, but we've got to," said the man.

Now the rocks around them did not have animals all over them, for they were carefully making their way back towards the high ground on the ridge. Mara thought that soon they would all be thirsty again. And then: We'll be thirsty too, and hungry. They had slept all afternoon.

"I think it would be safe to have a try," said the man. "Between the waterholes there will be hard ground."

"A bit dangerous."

"Not as dangerous as staying here if they are coming after us."

The dark was filling the sky. The stars came out, and up climbed a bright yellow moon. The mud shone, the tufts of grass shone, and the fast water that was now a river shone.

The man jumped down off the rocks and down the hill to the bottom, where his feet squelched as he took a few steps. "It is hard underneath," he said.

He picked up Dann, who was sleepy and silent, and said to Mara, "Can you manage?"

When Mara jumped down there was a thickness of mud under her feet, but a hardness under that. The moonlight was so strong it made big shadows from the rocks, and from the branches that were stuck in the mud, and sad shadows from the drowned animals lying about everywhere. The grasses dragged at their feet, but they went on, past the hill where they had been first, and where now there were no animals at all, and then they reached the edge of the river. The other side seemed a long way off. The man picked up one of the torn-off branches, held the leafy part, carefully stepped to the very edge of the water. He poked the branch in and it went right down. He went squelching along the edge and tried again, and it went down. He did it farther along and this time the wood only went in to about the height of the children's knees. "Here," he said, and the woman lifted Mara up. The two big people stepped into the brown water, which was racing past, rippling and noisy, but not deep, not here. The man went ahead with Dann, poking the wood of the branch into the water at every step, and the woman, with Mara, was just behind. Mara thought, Suppose the flood comes down now? We'll be drowned. And she was trembling with fear. They were right in the middle now, and everything glistened and shone because of the moon, which was making a gold edge on every ripple. The mud on the other side of the water was a stretch of yellowish light. They were going so slowly, a step and then a stop, while the man poked the water, and then another step and a stop. It seemed to go on and on, and then they were out of the water and on the mud. Close by were some trees. They had had water quite high up their trunks, though usually they were on the edge of a waterhole. They seemed quite fresh and green, and that was because they were here, not far from water, while the trees around Mara's home were dying, or dead. There were dark blotches on the branches. Birds. They must have been sitting here safely all through the flood.

Now they were well past the water. Mara felt herself being set down, while the woman's whole body seemed to lift itself up because of the relief of not having Mara's weight. And again Mara thought, She must be so tired, and weak too, because I'm not so heavy really.

They were walking carefully through the dirty and wet tussocks of grass, away from the water. They reached the rise that was as far as they had been able to see from the top of the big hill they had been on and, when they were over it, ahead were trees, quite a lot. So this couldn't be anywhere near their home—Mara had been thinking wildly, although she knew it couldn't be true, that perhaps they were going back home. She was trying to remember if she had ever seen so many trees all together. These had their leaves, but as she passed under them she could smell their dryness. These thirsty trees must have been thinking of all that water rushing past, just over the ridge, but they couldn't get to it.

The man stumbled and fell because he had tripped over a big white thing. It was a bone. He was on his feet at once, telling Dann, who had taken another tumble and was wailing, "Don't cry, hush, be quiet."

Ahead was another river, full of fast water, and the wet had reached all the way up here to the edge of the trees and had pushed away earth from under a bank, making a cave; and in the cave were a lot of white sticks: bones. The man poked his branch into the bones and they came clattering out.

"Do you realise what we are seeing?"

"Yes," said the woman, and although she was tired she was actually interested.

"What is it, what is it?" Mara demanded, tugging at the woman's hand and then at the man's.

"This is where the old animals' bones piled up, and the water has exposed them—look."

Mara saw tusks so long and thick they were like trees; she saw enormous white bones; she saw cages made of bones, but she knew they were ribs. She had never imagined anything could be this big.

"These are the extinct animals," said the man. "They died out hundreds of years ago."

"Why did they?"

"It was the last time there was a very bad drought. It lasted for so long all the animals died. The big ones. Twice as big as our animals."

"Will this drought be as long as that?"

"Let's hope not," he said, "or we'll all be extinct too." The woman laughed. She actually laughed; but Mara thought it was not funny, it was dreadful. "Really we should cover all these bones up again and mark where they are, and when things get better we can come and examine them properly."

He believed that things were going to get better, Mara thought.

"No time now," the woman said.

The man was poking with his branch at the wet earth, and it was falling away and the bones kept tumbling out, clashing and clattering.

"Why here?" whispered Mara.

"Probably another flood like this brought down dead animals and they piled up here. Or perhaps it was a graveyard."

"I didn't know animals had graveyards."

"The big animals were very intelligent. Nearly as clever as people."

"This is no graveyard," said the woman. "All the different species together? No, it was a flood. We've seen today how it must have happened."

The man was pulling from the mass of bones a ribcage so big that when he stood inside it the ribs were like a house over him. The ends of the ribs rested on the wet earth and sank in because of the weight. The big central bone, the spine, was nearly as thick as the man's body. If some of the ribs had not been broken away, leaving gaps, the man would not have been able to pull it: it would have been too heavy.

"What on earth could that have been?" said the woman, and he answered, "Probably the ancestor of our horse. They were three times as big." He went on standing there, with the broken ribs curving over him, the moon making another shadow cage with a blotch in it that was his shadow, lying near.

"Don't forget where this place is," said the woman to Mara. "We'll do our best to come back, but with things as they are who knows . . ." And she stopped herself from going on, thinking she would frighten Mara. Who was thinking, That means she doesn't know how frightening all the other things she has said were. And how could Mara remember where the bones were when she didn't know where she was going?

"Come on," said the woman, "we must hurry."

But the man didn't want to leave. He would have liked to go on poking about among those old bones. But he came out from the ribs of the ancient horse and lifted up Dann, and they walked on, Mara holding tight to the woman's hand.

Soon it was dry underfoot. They were back in the dryness that Mara knew. She could hear the singing beetles hard at it in the trees. She felt her tunic: dry. The mud on her legs and feet was dry. Soon they would all be thirsty again. Mara was already a bit thirsty. She thought of all that water they had left and longed for it. Her skin felt dry again. The moon was getting its late look, and was going down the sky.

It was hot. Everything was rustling with dryness: grass, bushes, a little creeping wind. Then, ahead, was a Rock Village, and the man said to the little boy, "Don't make a sound," and the woman said to Mara, very low, "Quiet, quiet," and they were running towards the village. It was not empty like the other one, for it had a feel of being lived in, and from a window in a house light came, just a little, dim light. And in a moment they had reached this house, and the man had slid the door along, and a tall woman came out at once. She put her hand on Mara's shoulder; and when the little boy, half asleep, slid down out of the man's arms, she put her other hand on his shoulder; and the three big people whispered over Mara's head, fast and very low, so she could not hear; and then she heard, "Goodbye Mara, goodbye Dann," and then these two who had rescued them—and carried them and held them and fed them, brought them safely through all that water—they were running off, bending low, and in a moment had disappeared up into the trees that grew among rocks.

"Come in," said this new woman in a whisper. And pushed the children inside, and followed them, and pulled the door across in its groove.

They were inside a room, like the other rock room, but this was bigger. In the middle was a table made of blocks of stone, like the other. Around it were stools made of wood. On the wall was a lantern, the same as the ones that were used in storerooms or servants' rooms, which burned oil.

On the walls too were lamps of the kind that went out by themselves when the light was bright enough and came on when it was dark, and dimmed and lightened as the light changed; but these globes were broken, just like the ones at home. It had been a long time since these clever lamps had worked.

The woman was saying, "And now, before anything else, what is your name?"

"Mara," said the child, not stumbling over it.

And now the woman looked at the little boy, who did not hesitate but said, "My name is Dann."

"Good," she said. "And my name is Daima."

"Mara, Dann and Daima," said Mara, smiling in what she meant to be a special way at Daima, who smiled back in the same way. "Exactly," she said.

And now, the way Daima looked them over made Mara examine herself and her brother. Both were filmed with dust from the last bit of walking and there were crusts of mud all up their legs.

Daima went next door and came back with a wide, shallow basin made of the metal Mara knew never chipped or broke or bent. This was put on the floor. Mara took off Dann the brown, slippery garment and stood him in the basin and began to pour water over him. He stood there half asleep, and yet he was trying to catch drops of water with his hands.

"We are so thirsty," said Mara.

Daima poured half a cup of water from a big jug, this time made of clay, and gave it to Mara to give to Dann. Mara held it while he drank it all, greedily; and when Mara gave the cup back to Daima she thought it could happen as it did yesterday—yesterday? . . . it seemed a long time ago—when Dann drank all the water and it was not noticed that she had not drunk anything. So she held the cup out firmly and said, "I'm thirsty too." Daima said, smiling, "I hadn't forgotten you," and poured out half a cup.

Mara knew this carefulness with water so well there was no need to ask. When Dann stepped out of the basin, Mara pulled off the brown thing and stood in the dirtied water. Daima handed her the cup to pour with and Mara poured water over herself, carefully, for she knew she was being watched to see how well she did things and was aware of everything she did. Then, just as she was going to say, Our hair, it's full of dust, Daima took a cloth and energetically rubbed it hard over Mara's hair, interrupting herself to examine the cloth, which was brown and heavy with dust. Another cloth was used to rub Dann's hair, as dirty as Mara's. The two dusty cloths were thrown into the bathwater to be washed later.

The two children stood naked. Daima took the tunics they had taken off to the door, slid it back a little and shook them hard. In the light from the wall lamp that fell into the dark they could see dust clouds flying out. Daima had to shake the tunics a long time.

Then they went back over Dann's head and Mara's head. She knew they were not dirty now. She knew a lot about this stuff the tunics were made of: that it could not take in water, that dust and dirt only settled on it but did not sink in, that it need never be washed, and it never wore out. A tunic or garment could last a person's life and then be worn by the children and their children. The stuff could burn, but only slowly, so there would be time to snatch it out of flames, and there would not even be scorch marks. There were chests of the things at home; but everyone hated them and so they were not worn, only by the slaves.

Now Daima asked, "Are you hungry?"

"Yes," said Mara. The little boy said nothing. He was nearly asleep, where he stood.

"Before you go to sleep remember something," said Daima, bending down to him. "When people ask, you are my grandchildren. Dann, you are my grandson." But he was asleep, and Mara caught him and carried him where Daima pointed, to a low couch of stone that had on it a pad covered with the same slippery, brown stuff. She laid him down but did not cover him because it was already so hot.

On the rock table Daima had put a bowl with bits of the white stuff Mara had eaten yesterday, but now it was mixed with green leaves and some soup. Mara ate it all, while Daima watched.

Then Mara said, "May I ask some questions?"

"Ask."

"How long will we be here?" And as she asked, again, she knew the answer.

"You are staying here."

Mara was not going to let herself cry.

"Where are my father and mother?"

"What did Gorda tell you?"

Mara said, "I was so thirsty while he was telling me things, I couldn't listen."

"That's rather a pity. You see, I don't know much myself. I was hoping you could tell me." She got up, and yawned. "I was awake all night. I was expecting you sooner."

"There was a flood."

"I know. I was up there watching it go past." She pointed to the window, which was just a square hole in the wall with nothing to cover it or stop people looking in. It was light outside: the sun was up. Daima pointed through it, past some rock houses to a ridge. "That's where you came. Over that ridge is the river. Not the place you crossed, but the same one higher up. And beyond that is another river—if you can call them rivers now. They are just waterholes." Then she took Mara by the shoulders and turned her round so that she was facing into the room. "Your home is in that direction. Rustam is there."

"How far is it from here?"

"In the old days, by sky skimmer, half a day. Walking, six days."

"We came part of the way with a cart bird. But it got tired and stopped." And now Mara's eyes filled and she said, beginning to cry, "I think it must be dead, it was so thin."

"I think you are tired. I'm going to put you to bed."

Daima took Mara into an inner room. It was like the outer room without the big table of rocks in the middle, but it had couches made of rocks, three of them, built against the walls. It wasn't thatch here but a roof of thin pieces of stone.

Daima showed Mara which shelf to use and a little rock room that was the lavatory and said, "I shall lie down for a little too. Don't take any notice when I get up." And she lay down on a shelf that had pads on it to make it soft, and seemed to be asleep.

Mara on her rocky shelf, which was hard in spite of the pads, was far from sleeping. For one thing she was worrying about Dann next door. Suppose he woke and found himself alone in a strange place? She wanted to wake Daima and tell her, but didn't dare. Several times she crept off this hard shelf that was supposed to be a bed and crept to the doorway to listen, but then Daima got up and went next door. Mara had time to take a good look at her.

Daima was old. She was like Mara's grandmothers and grand-aunts. She had the same glossy, long, black hair, streaked all the way to the ends with grey, and her legs had knots of veins on them. Her hands were long and bony. Mara suddenly thought, But she's a Person, she's one of the People, so what is she doing here in a rock village?

Now Mara knew she wouldn't sleep. She sat up and looked carefully around her. A big floor candle made a good, steady light she could see nearly everything by. These walls were made of big blocks of rock. They were smooth, and she could see carvings on them, some coloured. These walls were not like the ones in the other rock house, whose walls had been rough. Overhead, the big stone columns that held up the stone slabs of the roof had carvings on them. There were shelves made of rock, and in the corner a little room, sticking out, and opposite that a door into an inner room, with curtains of the brown, slippery stuff. This room had a window, but there were wooden shutters, not properly closed. People could see in if they wanted. Outside now, people were walking about; Mara could hear them: they were talking.

Now Mara was sitting up, arms on her knees, and she had never thought harder in her life.

At home there was a game that all the parents played with their children. It was called, What Did You See? Mara was about Dann's age when she was first called into her father's room one evening, where he sat in his big carved and coloured chair. He said to her, "And now we are going to play a game. What was the thing you liked best today?"

At first she chattered: "I played with my cousin . . . I was out with

Shera in the garden . . . I made a stone house." And then he had said, "Tell me about the house." And she said, "I made a house of the stones that come from the river bed." And he said, "Now tell me about the stones." And she said, "They were mostly smooth stones, but some were sharp and had different shapes." "Tell me what the stones looked like, what colour they were, what did they feel like."

And by the time the game ended she knew why some stones were smooth and some sharp and why they were different colours, some cracked, some so small they were almost sand. She knew how rivers rolled stones along and how some of them came from far away. She knew that the river had once been twice as wide as it was now. There seemed no end to what she knew, and yet her father had not told her much, but kept asking questions so she found the answers in herself. Like, "Why do you think some stones are smooth and round and some still sharp?" And she thought and replied, "Some have been in the water a long time, rubbing against other stones, and some have only just been broken off bigger stones." Every evening, either her father or her mother called her in for What Did You See? She loved it. During the day, playing outside or with her toys, alone or with other children, she found herself thinking, Now notice what you are doing, so you can tell them tonight what you saw.

She had thought that the game did not change; but then one evening she was there when her little brother was first asked, What Did You See? and she knew just how much the game had changed for her. Because now it was not just What Did You See? but: What were you thinking? What made you think that? Are you sure that thought is true?

When she became seven, not long ago, and it was time for school, she was in a room with about twenty children—all from her family or from the Big Family—and the teacher, her mother's sister, said, "And now the game: What Did You See?"

Most of the children had played the game since they were tiny; but some had not, and they were pitied by the ones that had, for they did not notice much and were often silent when the others said, "I saw . . .", whatever it was. Mara was at first upset that this game played with so many at once was simpler, more babyish, than when she was with her parents. It was like going right back to the earliest stages of the game: "What did you see?" "I saw a bird." "What kind of a bird?" "It was black and white and had a yellow beak." "What shape of beak? Why do you think the beak is shaped like that?"

Then she saw what she was supposed to be understanding: Why did one child see this and the other that? Why did it sometimes need several children to see everything about a stone or a bird or a person?

But the lessons with the other children stopped. It was because of all the trouble going on, and people going away, for every day there were fewer children, until there were only Mara and Dann and their near cousins.

Then there were no lessons, not even with the parents, who were silent and nervous and kept calling the children indoors; and then . . . there was the night when the parents were not there and she and Dann were with the bad man. The good brother was called Gorda. He was Lord Gorda, so said the two who had rescued them. She knew that there was a king and that her parents had something to do with the court.

She kept trying to put herself back into standing in front of Gorda while he was telling her things and she couldn't listen, but all she could see was that tired face of his, all bones, the eyes red with wanting to sleep, his mouth with the grey scum at the corners. He was so thin—just like the cart bird. He was not far off dying, Mara realised. Perhaps he was dead by now? And her parents? He had been telling her about her parents.

And now this place, this village. Rock People. In it a Person. She was sheltering them and she was afraid someone would come after them, but why would they want to? Why were Dann and she so important and, if so, who thought so?

And as she puzzled over this, the child's head fell on to her knees and she slid sideways and slept . . . And then Daima was bending over her and she could hear her brother's voice, "Mara, Mara, Mara."

There was a strong yellow glare beyond the window square. It must be the middle of the day. Outside now no voices, no people moving. Time to hide from the sun. It was cool in this room. Mara sat up quickly because of the shrillness of the little boy's "Mara, Mara," and was off the rock bed or shelf, and next door, as he rushed at her, nearly knocking her over—"Mara, Mara . . ." All the fear of the past few days was in his face and his voice and she picked him up and carried him to the rock couch, laid him down and lay beside him. Daima was sitting at the rock table watching how Mara handled the child, "There, it's all right, it's all right," over and over, while Dann wailed, "No, no, no, no."

Daima said, "Try to make him cry more quietly." And Dann heard, and at once his sobs and wails were quieter. This is what he had learned:

to obey fear. Mara held him, and he hid his face on her shoulder and sobbed softly, "No, no, no, no, no," and lay still there, but only for a time, because then it began again. All afternoon Mara lay there with him, and then Daima said, "I think he should eat something." Mara carried him to the table and he looked at the mess, so unlike anything he had ever eaten, and picked up his spoon and tried it, and made a face; but his hunger made him eat, at first slowly, and then it was all gone.

"Can I go out?" he suddenly asked.

"Not yet," said Daima. "We are going out at a special time, the three of us. It's important we do this. Till then, keep in here."

"Someone was looking in," said Dann.

"I know. That's all right. They'll all know by now that at least one child is here. Tomorrow we'll go out."

Again he needed to cling to his sister, so she sat herself on the rocky couch and he sat inside her arm and she played the game with him. "When we were on the first hill, what did you see? Then, when we got to the second hill, what animals were there?" As usual, she was surprised and impressed at what he had noticed. Insects for instance: "A great spider in its web between two rocks, yellow and black, and there was a small bird tangled in the web. And on the second hill there was a lizard . . ." At this Daima said, "What lizard, what kind of lizard?" Dann said, "It was big." "How big?" "As big as . . ." "As big as me?" asked Mara. "No, no, as big as you, Daima." And Daima was frightened, Mara could see, and said, "Next time you see one of those dragons, run." "I couldn't run anywhere because of all the water. It didn't want to eat me, it was eating one of the little animals. It ate it all up." "But when was that, when did you see it?" said Mara, thinking he was making it up. But no, he wasn't: "You were asleep, and so were the other two. You were all fast asleep. I woke up because the big lizard was making such a noise, it was going Pah, pah, pah, and then it finished eating and went off into the rocks. And then I tried to wake you up, but you wouldn't wake, so I went back to sleep."

Daima said, "You don't know how lucky you were."

Mara went on with the game. "And when we were going through the water, when we came down from the hill, what did you see?"

And Dann told them. Soon, Mara thought, she would say to him, "And what did you see . . . ?" taking him back to the room where the bad man frightened him; but not yet. He could not bear to think of that yet, Mara knew. Because she could hardly bear to think of it herself.

"Did you play the game?" Mara asked Daima. "I mean, when you were little?"

"I did, of course. It's how the People educate our children. We always have. And let me tell you, it's stood me in good stead ever since."

That *always* . . . Mara seemed to hear it for the very first time. It frightened her, a little. What did it mean, *always*?

The light outside was yellow instead of orange and hot, and the voices and movements were there again; and more than once a face appeared in the window hole and Daima nodded at them not to notice, just keep on doing what they were: Mara cuddling Dann and singing to him, Daima at the table. Then it was dark outside, and there were more of the lumps of white food, and this time with it some kind of cheese. The water in the mugs tasted muddy. The evening was beginning. Mara used to love all the things they did when the light went outside and the lights came up bright inside: games of all kinds, and then eating their supper, always with one parent there and sometimes both; and often their cousins stayed to sleep.

Daima was striking on the wall a kind of match Mara had never seen, and with it lighting a tall candle that stood on the floor, and then another, in a little basin of oil that was on a spike pushed in a crack between rocks. The light in the room wasn't very bright. Both flames wavered and fled about because of the air from the window. Some insects flew in, to the flames. And now Daima picked up a heavy wooden shutter and slid it over the window. The flames stood up quiet and steady. Mara hated that, because she was used to air blowing in the window and through the house.

Dann was on Mara's lap and she was beginning to ache with his weight. But she knew he needed this and she must go on for as long as he did. And now he began something he had not done since he was a tiny child. He was sucking his thumb, a loud squelching noise, and it was upsetting. Daima was irritated by it. Mara pulled the thumb out of the little boy's mouth, but he at once jammed it back.

"I think we should all go to bed," said Daima.

"But it's early," said Mara.

There was a pause then, and Mara knew that what Daima was going to say was important. "I know that you are used to a different kind of life. But here you'll have to do what I do." A pause again. "I was used to—what you are used to. I'm very sorry, Mara. I do know how you feel."

Mara realised they were both almost whispering. She had kept her voice low ever since she had come into the rock house. And now Dann said loudly, "But why, why, why, Daima? Why, why, why?" "Shhhhh," said Daima, and he at once began to whisper, "Why, why? I want to know." He had learned to obey, all right, and Mara's heart ached to see how he had changed. She had always loved the little child's confidence, and his bravery, and the way he chattered his thoughts, half aloud, and sometimes aloud, acting out all kinds of dreams and dramas that went on in his mind. He had never been afraid of anything, ever, and now . . .

Mara said to Daima, "Tomorrow, can we play What Did You See?"

The old woman nodded, but after another pause: she always thought things out before she spoke. Mara thought how everything was slow here, and she was used to everything quick and light and easy—and airy. It was stuffy now. The candles smelled hot and greasy.

"Tomorrow morning, when we wake up." Daima got up, and she was stiff and slow as she went next door. Mara could hear shutters being slid over there too, and could hear the match striking on the stone. A dull yellow light showed in the doorway. Daima came to lift Dann off Mara, saying, "Quiet, it is time to be quiet," and carried him next door, while he piped, "Mara, Mara . . ." She followed. Daima put the child where she had lain herself that afternoon. She did not take off his tunic. At home they wore little white shifts to sleep in. Daima said, "I wake when it is light. I'll wake you. Put out the light when you want to."

There was no door between the main front room and this one. Mara heard Daima moving about, blowing out the flames, and lying down. After a while Mara went to the doorway and looked in. She could just see from the light in her room that Daima was already asleep, lying heavy and still, her long, grey hair all over her head and face and shoulders, like a covering. Of course, she had not slept last night.

Mara went back into her room and found Dann asleep. Again she was saying, "I couldn't go to sleep so early," and certainly she was alert and awake, listening. Everyone seemed to have gone to bed or at least into their homes. Silence, everywhere. Mara began examining the walls. She could not make sense of it all. On one big block were carvings of people doing something that looked like a procession, carrying jars and dishes to a man and a woman who had high headdresses. But these people were nothing like the People, who were tall and thin with long, slippery, shiny, black hair. They were solid, with thick shoulders but thin waists, and long feet and narrow faces, and their hair was short, just below their ears and parted in the middle. They wore a tunic or dress that left one shoulder bare. They were not like the Rock People either. Who were they? On another block was a surface of fine, hard, white, and on that coloured pictures—red, yellow and green—of the same people. And now you could see their hair was black and the skin was a reddish pink, and the tunics were striped and tied with long sashes. But this picture was part of another picture, for only some was on this stone, and the edge of the stone interrupted the story. Other stones were blank, and even rough, and some had the figures going up towards the roof and were part of other stories; and the stones that had the white surfaces and the colours could even be upside down, so Mara stood with her head bent to see them. Why had she never seen anything like these people before? Where had all those bright, pretty clothes gone to? The cloth they were made of was finer than she had ever seen, and she could feel it soft and supple between her fingers when she closed her eyes to imagine it.

The candle that stood in a little shallow dish was sinking. Once it was out, Mara could not relight it. If she wanted to see she would have to slide the shutter along, but she was afraid of waking Daima. Then she saw a stick about the length of her finger near the candle, and she knew she must rub it on the wall to make a light if she needed one. She blew out the candle and rushed to her low bed where the slippery pads were.

It was completely dark. The dark seemed to be the same as the stuffiness. In her home Mara went to bed in a tall, light room open all around with windows, where she could pull the curtains back if she wanted and it was never really dark. The sky was always just there, outside, and the stars shone so brightly sometimes they woke her up.

Now Mara lay stiff, listening, alert with all of herself. This house was on the edge of the village. Not far away were some of the low, dry trees she had seen, and she ought to be hearing night noises: a bird perhaps, or the singing beetles who could go on all night when it was hot. But she could not hear anything. The air was heavy with the smell of the candle, and there was a little-child smell from where Dann lay asleep on his shelf. She had always loved burying her face in his neck, while he laughed and clung to her and she took in breaths of that warm, fresh, friendly smell; but he wasn't laughing now, but seemed to be dreaming, a bad dream, because he was whimpering. Ought she to be waking him, comforting him, holding him . . . ? She fell asleep, and woke to see Daima lifting the shutter down and letting in the morning light. And

Dann was already running across to fling himself on her—"Mara, Mara"—and she fell back with his weight, and then pulled herself up, holding him, and carried him, while he clutched her, next door, where the shutter was off and Daima's bed was tidied.

Later, this is what she remembered most when she tried to relive that time in her mind: the damp weight of the child, his face pressed into her shoulder, his clinging, and how her arms and then her back ached. And Daima watched and understood it all. Soon Daima would find ways of calling Dann away for a little, to go with her into another room or to help her, so Mara could rest.

Food was waiting on the table: bowls of the white lumps, this time with sour milk. Mara was beginning to hate this food, but she knew she had to eat it. And Dann was eating. Daima ate very little, watching them. Mara thought, That means food is short.

When they had finished, Mara asked, "May I see your house now?"

"Begin with this room."

Mara looked carefully around, and the first thing to notice was that there were no carvings on the rocks and no bright pictures. Over her head was thatch. It was a rough grass with some straws hanging down from it. All the blocks of rock were the same size, and smooth, and fitted together without the stuff that filled the spaces between the bricks she was used to. And they did fit, very well, but in some places there were cracks big enough to be useful, because the dish-lamp spike could go in. There were hooks, made of the same spikes bent, that had all kinds of things hanging on them: spoons and dishes and knives. All the things they used for eating were on the walls.

Mara went into the room she had slept in with Dann. She knew that room now, and about the lavatory in the little rock room, which was a deep hole going far down into the rocky soil. Near it was a box with earth and a shovel. There was a jug to pour water over yourself when you had finished, but nothing to dry with, and that was because of the slipperiness of the brown stuff that seemed to be used for everything when you wanted cloth. The air was so dry the wet between your legs dried quickly.

Dann came rushing after her—"Mara, Mara"—and grabbed her hand, and with Dann clinging to her hand, and Daima just behind, she went into the room separated from the sleeping room by a curtain. In it were only some stones in the middle of the rock floor. This was where Daima cooked. There were three stones, with ashes between them. All the

stones were blackened by smoke, and so were the pots and pans that
stood together along a wall. Above the cooking place was a hole in the
roof, which in this room was made of flat bits of stone, and there was a
rope to pull if you wanted to close the hole and make this stone go up
flat against the roof if it rained. There were old insect webs on the rope,
so the stone had been where it was for a long time. The rocks that made
this room were rough, and put together so you could see through them
in places to the outside. There were no carvings or pictures on the walls
here. There was a door into another room that had a heavy wooden
beam across it. The end of the beam had a chain, and Daima opened
with a big key where the chain fitted together. She lifted the beam
aside. They stepped into the dark. Daima struck a light on the wall and
lit a big floor candle, and then another. There were no windows. This
room was a big, square rock box, and in a corner was smaller rock box.
Mara could not see over into it, and tried to pull herself up with her
arms, letting go of Dann; and when she had got up, she sat on the edge
and saw that in it was water. There was another big rock box, and a
wooden chest of the kind she knew from her own home. Dann was tugging at her legs and whimpering, so she jumped down and took his
hand. Daima lifted up the child, and he let her. He was getting used to
her. He lay against her, and put his thumb in his mouth and sucked.
Suck, suck, suck. Daima did not stop him. Mara went to the other rock
box and found it full of white, floury stuff. This was what they were eating. She tasted it, but it did not taste of much.

"Is this a plant?"

"A root."

"Does it grow around here?"

"It used to. Everyone grew it. Not now: we haven't had enough rain."

"Then where does this come from?"

"People bring it from the north and sell it to us."

"What if they don't come?"

"Then we would be very hungry," said Daima.

Suck, suck, suck. The sound was driving Mara quite wild with dislike
of it, an irritation that made her want to hit her little brother, and she
was ashamed of herself and began to cry. She had hardly cried all this
time. Crying, she went to the enormous wooden chest. She could just
lift the lid. Inside were clothes of the kind they wore at home: delicate,
light coloured tunics and trousers and scarves. They were made from the
plants she had seen growing before everything got so dry, or of the stuff

worms made. Because she was crying, and she knew her hands were dirty, she did not touch them; but she wanted to plunge her hands into the clothes, or stroke them, then throw off the nasty brown thing she was wearing and put on these. She stood by the big chest looking, and wanting, and crying, and listening to how her little brother sucked his thumb. Then Daima took the thumb out of Dann's mouth, and he turned his face into her neck and howled.

Mara thought, Poor Daima, with two crying children, and stopped crying.

She wiped her hands carefully on her tunic and just gently stroked the robe that lay on top. It was a soft, glowing yellow. As she stroked, she thought that at home these clothes were in the big chests because they were precious and must be looked after. She knew now that these were carefully kept clothes from the past, and no one expected to have new ones.

She let the lid of the chest drop on the yellow, and looked at the grey rock all around. There were no pictures on these walls.

On a rock shelf lay bundles of the brown garments, lying anyhow. You couldn't hurt them no matter what you did.

She went to a door, this time a slab of rock in a groove, but it was too heavy for her, and Daima slid it aside. Dark—or almost, because light came in from the floor candles next door. This room was empty, but on the walls were the broken up pictures, like the brightly coloured ones on the hard, white stuff.

"You can come in and look at the wall pictures another time," said Daima.

She went through this dark room to another rock door, slid that back, lit a match, and in its flare Mara saw a rock room, empty, like this.

"There are two other rooms," said Daima. "Four empty rooms in all."

"Do they have the pictures?"

"Two of them do."

They went back the way they had come, and Daima slid the chain into place on the storeroom and locked it. In the room where the children slept she put the little boy down on the bed. He had gone to sleep. "It is a good thing he is sleeping. Perhaps he will sleep away the bad memories," she said.

The old woman and the child went into the room where they ate. They sat at the rock table.

"Do you want to start?" asked Daima.

Mara's mind was full of new thoughts and she almost said, Not yet, but said, "Yes." She began, slowly, thinking as she talked. "You have four empty rooms. That means the other houses aren't crowded, or the Rock People would come and live here. Have some of them gone away?"

"A lot died when we had the drought disease. And some went north."

"Then it's the same as in Rustam. It is half empty."

"Yes, I know."

"How do you know?"

"There used to be people coming through, both ways, going north, going south, and they told us what was going on. Now they hardly ever come. One was here two months ago. He said there was fighting in Rustam."

"Two months . . . I didn't know there was fighting."

"I expect your parents were trying not to frighten you."

"That means they thought the fighting was going to stop."

"No, Mara, I don't think they believed that."

Mara sat silent. She said, "I don't want to go on with that bit, I don't want to cry again." And her lips were trembling. She steadied herself and said, "You have your food and water in a room that has locks. That means you are afraid they will be stolen. But if all the Rock People got together they could lift the stones of the roof away and take the food and water. That means they still have food and water of their own."

"We still have enough. But only just. And if it rained properly here, we could grow a crop and fill our storerooms and our tanks."

"I could see it hasn't rained for a long time. I could see from how the trees looked. The trees we have left look worse than your trees, but your trees are dry."

Mara was thirsty, talking about rain. She was used to being thirsty. But she was licking dry lips, and Daima saw, and poured her half a cup of the not very nice water.

Mara went on, "This house wasn't built all at the same time. The rooms that have the stones with pictures were built first. The stones must have come from another house where the pictures went the same way."

"Good," said Daima.

"Some rooms were built on later. Like this room."

"Good," said Daima again.

"So once this village must have had a lot of people and they needed more room."

"It has far fewer people now than it had then. But that was ten years ago. It was before you were born."

There was a good long pause here while Mara tried to understand that *before you were born*, because her life seemed to have gone back a long way, beginning with little, bright memories, mostly of her brother.

She said, "The pictures on the stones are not Rock People or the People. Other kinds of people live around here."

"Lived here."

"When?"

"They think thousands of years ago."

"Thousands . . ." But Mara could not take this in. Only a moment ago she had been trying to work out: Ten years ago is three years before I was born, and the three years had seemed to her a very long time.

"They think as much as six or seven thousand years. They left old buildings up on that hill there."

Mara's eyes filled with tears: it was those *thousands of years*, like Daima's *always*, that made her want to lie down and sleep, like Dann, who had gone to sleep because everything was too much for him.

Mara went on, "You are a Person. You are one of the People, and you live here and the Rock People let you. That means they are afraid of you."

Daima nodded. "Good." And then, "But not as afraid as they once were."

Mara could not work this out.

Daima said, "You've done very well. I'll tell you the rest."

"No, no, let me try. You came here—the way Dann and I did. You had to run away."

"Yes."

"And that was before I was born?"

Daima smiled. "Well, yes. It was thirty years ago."

"Thirty . . ." And Mara really could not go on.

"I came here with my two children. My husband was killed in the fighting. We were travelling for many days, and we had to stop and hide because there were soldiers out looking for refugees. Twice I stole horses from the Rock People and we rode them for a while, and then let them loose so they could find their way back home. When we came to villages they wouldn't let us stop, but these people here did not drive us away."

"Why was that?"

"Because the year before the People punished them for attacking a sky skimmer that landed near here."

"Did they think you were going to punish them?"

"They thought I was a spy."

"I don't know that word."

"They thought the People had sent me so I could watch them and make reports."

"Then they must have hated you."

"Yes, they hated us. And the children had to be careful every minute of the day in case there was a trap. Once I had gone to the market—there was a market in those days—and left the children here, and they brought one of the dragons in. But the children locked themselves in an inside room."

"What did you do when you came back and found out what had happened?"

"Nothing. I pretended nothing had happened. I let the dragon out and it went back on to the hill there."

Mara could see from Daima's face how much she had suffered because of her children's being hated. "Where are your children?"

"That is what I hoped you might tell me. They went to Rustam."

"But that is where our home is."

"Yes."

And now Mara had to think for a long time. "So perhaps I know them?"

"You probably know of them. Moray and Kluart."

Mara shook her head. A long silence now, and then Mara said, "You'll have to say."

"I had to run away because your family threw my family out of our palace."

"Did my family treat you the way Dann and I were by that bad man?"

"That bad man is my cousin Garth, and so is the good one, Lord Gorda."

"Then it is all very difficult."

"No. There have always been changes in how the families are friends and enemies."

"Always," whispered Mara, holding back her tears.

"Yes. You must understand that, Mara. Sometimes one family is in power, and then another. But some of my family were good friends with your family and became part of the court. And your family heard I was here, later, and sent me presents."

"What did they send?"

"Money. Coins. There was nothing else of any use. I hid it. I'll show you where; but first I want to be sure no one is coming after you, because if they catch you they'll want to know if there is money and where it is."

Mara was trembling, afraid, reminded of the bad man, Garth, saying he would beat her if she did not tell what she knew.

"I know it is hard for you," said Daima. "But it is a good time to talk now, when Dann is asleep. Your grandmother was a cousin of my mother's. She always liked me. Once she even sent a message to come home, and said your parents agreed. But they had not sent the message. And besides . . ." she moved the brown stuff away from her chest and right across her old, wrinkled breast were scars where she had been beaten, ". . . I couldn't forget this. It was your father who gave the order for me to be beaten."

Mara was crying.

"It's no good crying about these things, Mara. Bad things. It's better to try to understand them. The next thing was, there were rumours about the one you call the bad one. I knew that Garth would try to make a rebellion. I grew up with him and I know him. He was always . . . you are right to call him bad. I'm not blaming him for wanting to take back what is our family's: the palace and the land."

"You could go back now, if Garth is your family?"

"No. I don't trust him. And besides, it won't last. There'll be another rebellion and more fighting. The worse things get with water and food, the more fighting. Besides, if he does manage to keep power then he will soon be hated, because he is so cruel. He won't last. I'm an old woman now, Mara. I've lived half my life here, in this village. I know these people. They aren't my people, but I've seen some grow up, and some have been kind to me. When I was ill, after I sent my children back to Rustam, one of them nursed me. She lives in the next house. Her name is Rabat. We help each other."

"Do the Rock People know about the beautiful clothes in the chest?"

"Yes. Rabat took my keys off me when I was sick, and she went in and looked at everything. I lay here in that corner and watched them all go in to find out what I had. They thought I would have more. They looked for the coins but didn't find them."

"They didn't take any of the clothes?"

"Yes, some. But they can't wear them. We are thin and tall, and they are short and thick. The children sometimes wear a tunic until they grow out of it—but our clothes are not meant to last." And now there were tears in Daima's voice. Mara thought, That's funny—she didn't cry when she remembered her husband's being killed, and being beaten and running away, but she wants to cry now and she's only talking about clothes. "Everything is so ugly, Mara. And it all gets worse because it's such a bad time. And there is a funny thing: all our clothes—the People's, I mean—and the dishes and the furniture and curtains and coverings, they are all beautiful and delicate and won't last. But everything here will last forever, and it's so ugly, so ugly, I can't bear it."

"Didn't the People ever want the things that last forever?"

"They were invented long before there were People."

"Invented?"

"You don't know the word because nothing is invented now. Once, long ago, there was a civilisation—a kind of way of living—that invented all kinds of new things. They had science—that means, ways of thinking that try to find out how everything works—and they kept making new machines, and metals . . ." She stopped talking for a while, seeing Mara's face, then put out her old hand and laid it over Mara's. "There was once a time, but it was a long, long time ago, when there were machines so clever they could do everything—anything you could think of, they could do it—but I'm not talking about then. No one knows why all that came to an end. They say that there were so many wars because of those machines that everyone all over the world decided to smash them. I'm talking of machines since then, simpler ones. And they invented this material that never wears out and the metal you see here that you can't break. There were whole storehouses of these things, but so deep in big forests no one had ever found them. Then the People came, and they wanted to prevent the Rock People from having them, to keep them for ourselves. But then we said it was not interesting, always having the same clothes and the same everything, nothing wearing out or breaking, so we took the old things and gave them to the Rock People, and went back to growing plants to make cloth, and making dishes and pots out of earthenware. But you might have noticed that in the kitchen at home there were some of the big vessels of this metal, because they are useful for storage."

Mara was silent, hoping she had taken all this in.

"Why are the special lamps here—look, like that one? At home only we have them, not the servants or the slaves."

"The Rock People raided once when there was a rebellion and fighting in the palace, and took away a lot of things. But it is a long time since these lamps worked. No one knows how they work."

"Why didn't you ask those people who brought Dann and me here where your children are?"

"There wasn't time."

"Who are those people? Why did they want to save us?"

"Gorda paid them to bring you. He probably thought there wasn't any other place that was safe."

"Are we safe?"

"Not very," said Daima. "But if my children could manage, then so can you."

"I'm afraid," said Mara.

"That's good," said Daima. "That means you'll be on your guard."

"I will try."

"And now, Mara, we should stop, and you can think about everything and we can talk again."

"And play the What Did You See game?"

"As often as you like. I would enjoy that, after all this time. And we must play it with Dann, because there aren't schools here and the children are taught nothing at all." She got up. "It is midday now. This afternoon everyone in the village will go over that ridge to the river, because there will still be new water there from the flood, and we will fill our containers. I'm going to take you and Dann so they can all see you. And remember, you are my grandchildren." And she embraced Mara, a good, hard hug, and she said, "I wish you were. I'm going to think of you as my granddaughter, Mara. You're a good girl. No, don't cry now; you can have a good cry tonight, but if we start crying now we won't stop. And I'm going to wake Dann, or he'll not sleep tonight. And I've got something new for you to eat."

She took a big yellow root from a jar and sliced it fine. She put the slices in three bowls, poured water over them and went to fetch Dann.

Mara tasted the water the sliced root was in. It was very sweet and fresh, and Mara did not find it easy to remember her manners and sit quiet, waiting for Dann. He came to sit on Mara's lap, and sucked his thumb until Daima told him to stop.

They ate up the root and drank the fresh water. Dann wanted more, but Daima said the roots in the jar were all she had until she could go out and hunt for more in the earth.

Daima then gave Mara a big jug and Dann a small one, and she her-

self lifted up four big cans that had set across their tops pieces of wood
to hold them by, tied two by two with loops of rope. She pushed the
door and it slid along in its groove, and the light and heat came in.
Mara's eyes hurt, and she saw Dann screw up his eyes and try to turn his
face aside, so that he was squinting to see. Then Mara was outside the
house, holding Dann's hand, and her eyes stopped dazzling and she was
able to see. There was a crowd of Rock People, all looking at her and at
Dann. Mara made herself stand still and look back, hoping they did not
see she was frightened. Now she was close to them for the first time in
her life, she could see their dull greyish skin and their pale eyes, like sick
eyes, and their pale frizzy hair, which stood out around their heads like
grass or like bushes. And they were so big. Everything about them
seemed to Mara unhealthy and unnatural, but she knew they were not
sick but strong people. She had often seen them carrying heavy loads
along the roads. A girl was in one of the People's tunics. It was torn and
dirty, but it had been a soft yellow colour once. She was splitting it
because she was so big.

Daima was saying, "These are my grandchildren. They have come to
live with me. This is Mara, and this is Dann."

Everyone was staring at these two thin, bony little children, with
their short black hair that should be shining and smooth but was stiff
with dirt.

A man said, "Yes, we know about the fighting in Rustam." Then he
said to Mara, "Where are your parents, then?"

"I don't know," said Mara. Her lips were trembling, and she stood biting them, while he grinned at her, showing big yellow teeth.

"This is Kulik," Daima said. "He is the head man here."

"Don't you curtsy to your betters?" said Kulik.

"Curtsy?" said Mara, who had never heard the word.

"I suppose she expects us to curtsy to her," said a woman.

Then another woman came out of the crowd and said to Daima,
"Come on, the water's going fast."

"This is Rabat," said Daima to the children. "She lives in this house
here, just next to us—remember? I told you about her."

Rabat said, "Pleased to meet you. I remember your parents when they
were little, like you."

Now all the crowd was moving off, and going to where the ridge was
and, beyond it, the river. Everyone carried jars and jugs and cans.

Rabat was just in front of Mara, who could see the big buttocks, like hard cushions, moving under the brown stuff, and sweat dripping down fat arms. Rabat smelled strong, a sour, warm smell, and her pale hair glistened as though it had fat on it—but no, it was sweat. And then Mara saw that the brown garments everyone wore seemed different. It was the strong light that was doing it: making the brown silvery, or even whitish, and on one or two people even black; but the colour changed all the time, so that it was as if all these people were wearing shadows that slipped and slid around them. Looking down at her own tunic, Mara saw that it was brown; but when she lifted her arm the sleeve fell down in a pale shimmer that had black in its folds.

Meanwhile Rabat had fallen back to Daima and was saying, very low, "Last evening four soldiers came asking for you. I was on my way back from the river and saw them first. They asked if you had children with you and I said no, there were no children. Then they asked where all the people were and I said at the river. I didn't say you were at home, though I knew you were there with the children. I was afraid they would go to the river and ask, but they were tired. I'd say they were on their last legs. One said they should stay the night in the village, and I was going to tell them we had the drought sickness here, but the others said they should hurry on. They nearly came to blows over it. I'd say they might have killed each other by now. They were quarrelling with every word. It seemed to me they didn't really want to be bothered with the children at all, they wanted to take the opportunity to run up north."

"I am indebted to you," said Daima to Rabat, in a deliberate way that Mara could see meant something special.

Rabat nodded: yes, you are. Then she bent down to Mara and said with a big, false smile, "And how are your father and mother?"

Mara's mind was working fast, and it took only a moment to see that Rabat was not talking about her real parents. "They were well," she said, "but now I don't know."

"Poor little thing," said Rabat, with the same big, sweet smile. "And this is little Dann. How are your father and mother, dear?" Dann was stumbling on, his feet catching in the grass tussocks and tangles, and he was concentrating so hard on this Mara was afraid he would forget and say, That's not my name, and Daima was afraid of it too. "I don't know where they are," he said. "They went away." And the tears began running down his dirty face.

Again Mara could not help seeing herself and Dann as all the others must: these two thin, dusty little children, different from everyone here except for Daima.

They were now going up the rise between dry trees whose leaves, Mara knew, would feel, if she took them between her fingers, so crisp and light they would crumble—not like the leaves of the plants in the house at home, soft and thick and alive, that had water put on them. These trees had not been near enough to the flood to get any water.

Now all the crowd stopped on the crest of the rise and waited for four of them to catch up. Again Mara was surrounded by the Rock People: these big, strong people, with their great balls of fuzzy hair that she could see, now she was so close, was not always the same paleness but sometimes almost white, and sometimes a deep yellow. If they wanted to they could kill Dann and her, just like that. But they hadn't killed Daima, had they? And Rabat was Daima's friend ... No, she wasn't, Mara thought fiercely. She was *not* Daima's friend, but only pretending to be.

In front of them the grass was covered with the brown dirt from the flood, which had been mud but was quite dry now. This was the slope down to where the water was—but surely this could not be the same river, for that had been so wide and this was just a little valley.

There were some trees marking where the water was, and a lot of animals of every kind clustered by the water, and that is why the villagers had to go to the water all together: for protection.

It was quite a short walk down, and the people in front were shouting and yelling to scare away the animals. They were mostly of the kind the People used for meat and milk—rather, had used. Some were smaller furry ones that tried to hide themselves in the grasses; and there were cart birds too, though Mara could not see if the one she thought of as her cart bird was there. All the feathers and fur were dry and you could not see how thin the beasts were.

And now Dann was tugging at Mara's hand: "Water, water," he was shouting.

"You'd better be careful," said Rabat to him, "or you'll get yourself eaten up by a water dragon." She said this with a smile, but it was not a real smile and Dann shrank away from her.

Now everyone was standing around the biggest pool and beating it with sticks, and there were all kinds of wrigglings and heavings under the water, and dark shapes appeared and sank, and then out came an enormous lizard, a water dragon, that lived in water and pulled smaller animals in to eat. The people stood back as it hissed at them, darting its tongue and banging its tail about, and whipping it from side to side. Then it turned and was off into the grass. "They are all going off to the big river," said Rabat. "There is a lot of water there and it is still running."

And Mara could see how the different kinds of animals were making their way from this smaller river up on to the ridge opposite and over it. She understood now. This was not the big river she had crossed—how long ago? it seemed a long time—but a smaller one that joined it.

The water of this pool was still being beaten, the sticks flailing about over the surface, and then there appeared a water stinger. Mara had never seen one, though she knew about them. It was very big, as big as the largest of the Rock People, and it had pincers in front that could easily crush Dann, and a long sting like a whip for a tail. This beast came straight out of the water at the people, its pincers opening and closing and its little eyes gleaming and cruel. The people did not run away but stood around it, so they were brave, and they beat the stinger with their sticks; and in a moment it had rushed through a gap in the crowd left for it to run through, and it went into a nearby pool with a big splash. The animals still around that pool sheered away. And now Mara saw that another water stinger, a smaller one, was by that pool and its tail sting was holding a quite big, furry animal—which was still alive, for it was bleating and crying as the pincers tore off bits of meat and stuffed them into the stinger's mouth.

The crowd were now all standing around the pool they had beaten. And then they all fetched their jars and containers and bent to fill them, and Daima did too, and Rabat, and Mara found a place low among all the big legs and filled her jar, and helped Dann fill his. Then, again, all the people stood around the pool, looking at it. Then, one by one, they stepped down into the water or jumped in. And Dann pulled himself off Mara's hand and was in, splashing and paddling like a little dog. "Hey, there," said Kulik, grinning, "look what we've got here," and he ducked Dann, who did not come up at once. Which meant that Kulik was holding him under. "Stop it," said Daima, and Rabat said nothing but climbed down into the water and pulled Dann up, coughing and spluttering. Kulik only laughed, showing those big yellow teeth. Now Mara was in, and Daima. Dann did not seem to know what had happened, for he was laughing and shouting and struggling to get out of Rabat's arms back into the brown water. But Daima took the child from

Rabat and went out of the water with him, though he was kicking and complaining. She never once even looked at Kulik. Mara quickly splashed herself all over, keeping close to Rabat, who stood near her, her brown tunic floating around her middle, staring hard at Kulik. Then Daima called, "Mara," who most reluctantly got out of the water, feeling it flow down off her and away from the stuff of her tunic, so that it was dry at once. Mara saw that Daima had called to her because a woman was bending down to take Daima's cans. As Daima took the cans from her, this woman giggled and smiled, just as if she had not been going to steal Daima's precious cans.

Rabat had got out of the water, and was standing with them, her tunic streaming and very dark, then lighter and then silver.

Everyone was getting out of the pool, and the animals that had not gone off to the other ridge were coming back and standing at the edge again.

Mara saw that Dann had had all the dust washed off him, but his hair was tangled and dull and her own felt stiff and nasty. Would she ever again have smooth, clean, shiny hair?

Daima, her hands filled with her four cans, and Mara, holding Dann, and Rabat went together away from the pool. Dann was tugging at Mara's hand, looking back over his shoulder at the pools and the animals and chanting, "Water, water, I want the water."

"You mustn't ever go there by yourself," said Daima, and suddenly Mara understood what a very big danger that was. If Dann got away from them and went to the water . . . She would have to watch him every minute. He could never be left alone.

Soon they were walking through the rock houses. Some were bigger than Daima's, some smaller, some not more than a room with a roof of rough grass. The stone roofs of some houses had fallen in. There were heaps of rock that had been houses. Outside every house was a big tank made of rock. There was one outside Daima's. All kinds of little pipes and channels led from the different roofs to the tank.

Rabat was saying things to Daima that Mara knew were important.

"I milked our milk beast," she said. "And I gave it food and water. I knew you were busy with your grandchildren." She did not make that last word a joke with her voice, but Mara knew she meant to tell Daima she did not believe her story.

"Thank you," said Daima. "You were very kind. I am in debt to you," she said, in the same special way.

"I took half the milk, as usual," said Rabat.

"I'm going to need milk for the children," said Daima.

"She is giving less milk than she was."

"Then I shall need all of it."

"You are indebted to me."

"You can put the debt for the milk beast against your debt to me for the roots."

"What about the soldiers?"

"That is such a big debt I don't think a little milk could match it."

"A quarter of all the milk," said Rabat.

"Very well," said Daima. Her voice sounded heavy, and angry. She did not look at Rabat, who was looking at her in a way that said she was ashamed. "They are such pretty children," Rabat said, trying to make up for insisting on the milk.

Daima did not say anything.

They had stopped outside the house next to Daima's. Suddenly the two women embraced, and Mara could see they hadn't meant to. Rabat was saying, "I have hardly any food left. Without the milk . . ."

"Don't worry about it," said Daima. "We'll all manage somehow."

Rabat went into her house, taking the water cans, and the others went on to Daima's house.

Mara stopped by the big rock cistern. "Is there water in here?"

"There would be if it rained."

Dann was jumping up like a puppy, trying to get hold of the cistern's edge so as to haul himself up. Daima took the cans of water into the house, rescuing Dann's jar, which was in danger of being kicked over. She came back and lifted Dann up and sat him on the edge of the cistern.

"There's a scorpion," he said.

"It must have fallen in, then."

Mara was trying to pull herself up: her hands could not get a proper grip on the edge, which she could only just reach. Daima lifted her up and she sat by Dann, pulling her legs up well away from the angry scorpion, which was trying to climb up the rocky sides, but falling back.

"Poor thing," said Mara.

"It's like the water stinger," said Dann, "only much smaller."

Daima fetched a stick, pulled herself up, sat on the edge of the tank and said, "Mind," reaching down the stick. The scorpion gripped it with its pincers, Daima lifted—and the scorpion let go. "If you don't hold on you'll die there," said Daima, but this time the scorpion kept its grip on the stick, and Daima lifted it out carefully. The three watched the beast scuttle off into the mats of dead grass.

"It's hungry," said Daima, "just like everything else."

It was so hot on the edge of the rocky box Mara's thighs were burning. She jumped down. So did Daima, and lifted down Dann before he could protest.

"How long since there was water in that?"

"We had a big storm about a year ago. The cistern filled up. I kept carrying water through to the tank you saw inside. And I've made that water last."

"Perhaps we will have another storm," said Mara.

"Sometimes I think it will never rain properly again."

Inside the house Dann began yawning. He ate some sour milk, making faces; and then Mara took him next door, to the lavatory, and then to his bed. He was asleep at once.

Mara thought, I want Dann to sleep, so as to sleep away the bad memories, but I want to remember everything. What is the What Did You See? game if it is not trying to remember everything? The light was going outside. Daima lit the big floor candle. This room was cool because of the rock walls, in spite of the warm air coming in at the window. Tomorrow the sun would jump up like an enemy and then soon it would be too hot to go out of doors.

Mara sat at the rock table with Daima.

"Is Rabat a spy?" she asked. "Does she tell the others everything about us?"

"She is a spy but she doesn't tell everything." Daima saw from Mara's face that she did not know what to ask. "Things are not simple," she said. "It's true that I shouldn't trust Rabat—isn't that what you are thinking?"

"Yes."

"But she did look after me when I was ill. And I looked after her when she broke her leg. And when my children were small she helped me with them."

"Didn't she have any children?"

"She did, but they died. It was when we had the little drought, and they got the drought sickness."

"Will she tell the others about the soldiers asking for us?"

"She might, but I don't think so. But it wouldn't matter. If the soldiers offered money for us, yes. But I think they were really running away as fast as they could. Rabat counts on me. She has very little food left. When the traders came last time I bought food for her because she had nothing to exchange. They give flour in exchange for the roots, but it is difficult finding the roots. Some people here grow a little poppy, but it has been too dry. The water in her tanks is finished, and I've been giving her some. And she does help me with the milk beast."

"Why doesn't she have one?"

"I said things were not simple. She had four milk beasts left. She and her husband gave me one for my children. It was her husband that was so kind: he was a really good man. And he died. One night some people on the run came through here and they stole her three milk beasts. So now she shares mine. It is only fair—I suppose."

"Do you always fetch water from the pool where we were today?"

"That little river has been dry for a couple of years. The big river has been nearly dry. I've got enough water in my tank in there to last us, if we are careful. I'm going back to the pool tomorrow when everyone goes. And I want you to keep Dann here."

"You think Kulik meant to drown him?"

"I don't know. Perhaps he began by a joke and then . . . It would be very easy to keep him under a little too long."

"Why did he want to kill Dann? A little boy?"

"Little boys grow up. And so do little girls, Mara. Be careful all the time. Not that you have to keep in the house. I'm going to teach you how to milk the animal, and how to let the milk go sour and make cheese. And how to find the roots too—and that is very important. You have to be out and about and do your share. I might die, Mara. I'm an old woman. You have to know everything I know. I'll show you where the money is. But remember: it is easy to slip a scorpion into a fold of cloth or throw a stone from behind a wall so that it looks as if it has come off a roof, or put a child in a cistern and pull the rock lid over. A child did die like that once. One of theirs, though. No one could hear it cry out because the lid was a fit."

"That means someone meant to kill it."

"Yes, I think so."

"That means that they fight each other—the Rock People."

"Yes, they do. There are families who won't speak to each other."

Suddenly Mara giggled, and Daima seemed surprised. Mara quickly said, "We haven't enough water. We only have a little food. But they quarrel." And looked at Daima to see if she had understood.

Daima said, very dry, but smiling, "I see you are growing up fast. But that is the point. The harder things are the more people fight. You'd think it was the other way about."

Next morning Daima said to Dann that he could go out and play just outside the doorway, where they could see him. He went out and stood poking a stick at the dust. He seemed half asleep. Mara thought that if their mother could see this dirty little child with his matted hair, she would not know him. Above all she would not know this listlessness. Soon there were footsteps, and voices, and two men came, and stopped a few paces away to stare openly through the doorway, where Daima and Mara could be seen sitting at the table. Dann was staring at them, and then began moving closer to them, step by step, his eyes going from one face to the other. The two men stood looking at him, surprised, then uneasy, then angry. They spoke to each other in low, angry voices. And still Dann moved towards them, step by step, staring. "Shooooo," said one man, and the other shook a stick at him, as if Dann were an animal.

"What's the matter with the child?" asked Daima. "Stop him."

"I know what's wrong," said Mara, and she did, though at first she hadn't. The faces of the two were so alike you could hardly tell them apart: two angry faces looking down at the child, their lips thin and tight with dislike of him. Mara ran out and grabbed Dann just as one man picked up a stone to throw at him. "Dann," she said, "no, no, no." And to the man, "No, please, don't." And still Dann stared, twitching with fear, his whole body shaking in his sister's hands.

"You keep those brats of yours to yourself," one man said loudly into the doorway to Daima.

And they went off, the two men, as similar from the back as from the front: heavy and slow, both with the same way of poking their heads forward.

Mara held the child as he sobbed, limp against her shoulder; and she said to Daima, past his head, that there had been two men with similar faces, and one had threatened to beat them and kept them without water, and the other was kind and gave them water—and now they seemed to Dann the same: the two brothers, Garth and Gorda.

Daima said, "Those two out there grew up with my two. I know them. They are bullies and they are sly. Dann must keep away from them, and you too, Mara."

And now Mara began explaining to Dann that two people can look the same but be quite different inside, in their natures, that he was con-

fused because of what had happened ... And as she talked, she was
thinking that all that had been less than a week ago.

While Mara talked, Dann was staring out of the door, where the two
men had stood. She did not know if he had heard her. She went on,
though, talking and explaining, because often he surprised her, coming
out later with something that showed he had understood.

"Let's play the game," she tried, at last. "What did you see?—" then,
at home, with the bad people? "What did you see?—" later, with the
man who gave us water? Slowly Dann did begin to answer, but his eyes
were heavy and his voice was heavy too. Mara persisted, while Dann did
reply, but he was talking only about the bad man, the bad man, with the
whip. At last Mara stopped. It looked as if the child had muddled it all
up: the scene that had gone on for hours, in their own home, when they
had to stand hungry and thirsty, being threatened by the whip, and the
other one in the rock room when Gorda came in. "Don't you remember
how he was kind and gave us water?" But no, Dann did not remember,
and he said, "Those two men out there, with the stick, why did they
have the same face?"

He stuck his thumb in his mouth and the loud sucking began, and
then he slept, while Mara sat rocking him and Daima went off to the
river with her containers.

When she came back she washed them both again, while they stood
in the shallow basin; and this time she washed their hair too, though it
would not stay nice and shiny for long, with the dust swirling about
everywhere.

Then Daima took the children out to where she said the milk beast
was waiting—she had told Rabat she would milk it. Dann was clinging
tight to Mara, so she could hardly walk. And she kept close to Daima
because the milk beast was so enormous, and frightened her. Its back
was level with Daima's head, and she was tall. It was a black and white
beast, or would have been if the dust wasn't thick on it. It had pointed,
hard hooves. Its eyes were clever and knowing; and Mara had never
seen eyes like them, for instead of a soft coloured round with white
around, these eyes were a strong yellow and had a black bar down them,
and long lashes. She thought the animal looked wicked, but Daima had
already slipped a loop of rope over its horns, and then the rope over a
post, and she was kneeling right under the beast's belly, where there was
a bag that had teats sticking out like enormous pink fingers. Daima had
a basin under the milk bag and she was using both hands to make the

milk come out. It shot into the basin, which rang out like a bell, and meanwhile the beast stood still, chewing with quick movements of its jaws. It turned its head and put its nose on Daima's neck, and then into Mara's neck, and she cried out, but Daima said, "Don't mind Mishka, she won't hurt you. Now, sit down here." Mara squatted by Daima, feeling Dann right behind her, because he was afraid of the beast but needed her more. "Use both hands on one teat," said Daima. The hot, slippery teat filled Mara's hands, and she squeezed, and a little milk came out; but Daima showed her how to do it and soon the milk was spurting. "There, you've got the knack," said Daima. "And she knows you now." Daima finished off the milking, until the bag hung empty, and the beast bleated and went off when Daima took the rope from her horns, picking her way among the humps and mats of grass to a group of milk beasts standing together under a thorn tree. They belonged to different people but they spent all their days together, and their nights too, in a shed, because the dragons came after them.

Daima had two cans of milk, one full and one partly full. They went to Rabat's house and gave her the part-full can. She looked sharply into the can to see if she had her promised share, then smiled in the way Mara hated and said, "Thank you."

Now it was the hot part of the day, and they sat in the cool half dark of the big room. Dann was sitting on the floor, his thumb in his mouth, pressed against Mara's legs.

Mara saw that Daima's eyes were full of tears, and then that tears were running down the creases in Daima's cheeks. "It is funny," said Daima, speaking as if Mara were grown up, "the way the same things happen."

"You mean, your children, and then Dann and me?"

"They wanted to play with the other children, but Kulik came and said, Keep your brats to yourself."

Mara left Dann, and climbed up on Daima's lap and put her arms around her neck. This made Daima cry harder, and Mara cried, and then the little boy began tugging at Mara's legs to be lifted up, and soon both children were on Daima's lap and they were all crying.

Then Mara said, "But your children are all right. They grew up. No one hurt them."

"Plenty tried to. And when I'd got them through it all, they went away. I know they had to. I wanted them to." Daima sat weeping, not trying to stop herself.

"I won't go away, I promise," said Mara. "I'll never leave you alone with these horrible Rock People, never, never."

"I won't go away," piped up Dann. "I won't leave you."

"I'll leave you first," said Daima.

Dann cried out, but Mara said, "She didn't mean that she would leave us. She didn't mean that."

And the rest of the day was spent reassuring Dann that Daima did not mean to abandon them.

Now Daima said it was time to show Mara how to do everything. How to look after the milk beast, Mishka. How to make milk go sour in a certain way. How to make cheese. How to look in the grasses for the tiny plants that showed where the sweet yellow roots were, deep below. Which green plants could be picked to cook as vegetables. How to make candles. And soon Daima said Mara should know where the money was hidden.

"If you were going to hide money, Mara, where would you put it?"

Mara thought. "Not in the room where the water tank is, or anywhere near where the food is. And not in this room, because people can come in so easily. Not in the thatch, because grass can burn. Not somewhere out of the house, because people would see when you went to look for it. And not in one of the empty rooms, because people would expect that."

A long pause.

"Where, then?" persisted Daima. But Mara could not guess.

In a corner of this room stood a bundle of big floor candles. The biggest ones were as thick as Mara's chest. One that looked just like all the others was quite smooth at the bottom; but when you scraped off a layer and pulled out a plug of candle, there was a hole, and in it a leather bag with coins in it. They were gold, quite small but heavy, and there were fifty of them. Mara remembered that at home the People wore big, heavy ornaments of this stuff, gold, and she herself had been given when she was born a bracelet made of these same coins, which she knew was very valuable. Where was it now? But her old life in the great, airy palace in its gardens seemed every day more of a dream and harder to remember. And she had had another name. What was it? She asked Daima if she knew what her name and Dann's had been, but Daima said no, she didn't, and anyway it wasn't a bad idea to forget them. "What you don't know won't hurt you," she said.

Often Mara climbed on Daima's lap, but when Dann was asleep, because she didn't want him to know that she often felt like a baby too. She hugged Daima, and felt the bones in the hard arms and the hard lap. Daima was not soft anywhere. Mara laid her face in Daima's bony shoulder and thought about her mother, though it was hard now to remember her face, and how she was soft everywhere and had a sweet, spicy smell, who had hugged her with arms that had bracelets on them, and long black hair where Mara could bury her face. Daima smelled dry and sour and dusty. Dust, the smell of dust, the feel of dust on everything: soft pads of dust underfoot, dust piling up in the grooves the door slid along in, dust on the rocks of the floor, which had to be swept out every day into the dust outside. Films of dust settled on the food even while they ate it, and often winds whirled dust and grass up into the air and the sunlight became spotty and dirty-looking.

"Perhaps it will rain," Mara implored Daima, who said, "Well, perhaps it will."

Soon Mishka began giving much less milk. Some mornings there was hardly any. There was something in the way Rabat smiled and looked that made Mara ask if perhaps Rabat was going out at night to steal milk. Daima said yes, she thought so. She said to Mara, "Don't be too hard. She has nothing to eat."

"Why doesn't she go out and dig up roots, the way we do?"

Daima sighed and said that it was no good expecting people to do what they couldn't do.

"Why can't she?"

Daima lowered her voice, though they were alone, and said, "She's a bit simple-minded." And then, lower still, "That's why the others have never wanted anything to do with her. And why she was glad to be friends with me." She gave the grim smile that Mara had learned to dread. "Two outcasts."

"Will Mishka give more milk when it rains?"

"Yes, but she is getting old and it is time she was mated. Her milk will dry up altogether soon if she isn't."

"Why can't she be mated?"

"Kulik owns the only male milk beast, and he won't let it mate with ours."

Mara was in such a tumult of feelings: she had just taken in that Daima's only friend all these years was a loony woman; and now, how cruel Kulik was.

She went off into the room where her rock bed was, and lay on it, and turned her face to the wall and thought hard. She knew she could not tell Daima what she wanted to do, because she would say no. She waited until Daima had gone out with Dann to take some water to Mishka, and then she went through the village, smiling politely at people, to where she knew most of the men were in the hot midday. Against a disused rock house was a long seat made of rocks, shaded by some old thatch that had slipped down the roof. Along this bench sat about ten men, their hands on their knees, apparently half asleep. Among them was Kulik.

It was difficult to walk towards them, seeing how their faces grew hard as she got near. This is the look she had seen on the faces of Rock People all her life when any of the People were near. Their eyes were narrowed, their mouths tight and angry.

She made herself smile, but not too much, and stood in front of Kulik. She said, "Please, our Mishka needs to be mated." In spite of herself, her voice was weak and her lips trembled.

First there were looks between the men, who were surprised. Then they laughed: ugly, short laughter, like barks. Then they all stared at her, their faces hard again. Kulik, however, had a grin on his face, and his teeth showed.

Mara said, her voice stumbling, "My little brother, he needs the milk."

Kulik narrowed his eyes, stared hard, kept his thin, ugly grin, and said, "And what do I get in exchange?"

"I don't think we've got anything. I could get some roots for you."

More laughter from the men.

"I wasn't thinking of roots," said Kulik. Then slowly, and with his face so full of hatred for her she could hardly keep standing there in front of him, "Down on your knees, Mahondi brat, down on your knees and beg."

At first Mara was not sure what he wanted her to do, but she dropped to her knees in the dust, and when she looked at him she could hardly see through her tears.

"Now bend right down, three times," said Kulik.

Mara had to think again, but she bent down once, twice, three times, trying to keep her hair out of the dust. On the last time she felt Kulik's big hand on her head, grinding her face down into the dirt. Then he let go. She straightened to her knees and, since he did not say anything, stood up. The dust was falling past her eyes from her head.

She said, "Please will you let Mishka be mated?"

And now a big roar of astonished laughter from all of them—except Kulik, who did not laugh this time but only grinned, and sat forward and said, almost spitting as he talked into her face, "You bring her when she is ready. I'm sure you know all about that from your hard work on the farms."

"I do know," said Mara. "I learned about how to mate animals."

"That would come in useful, to give orders to your slaves."

"Please," said Mara, "please."

"Bring your animal. But you must come alone. I'm not dealing with that old bag Daima. Alone, do you hear?"

Mara was angry that he'd called Daima an old bag, but she made herself smile. "Thank you," she said.

"And if the kid turns out to be male, I shall have it."

"Oh, thank you, thank you—" and she ran off.

She told Daima what she had done, and Daima caught her hand to her heart and had to sit down. "Mara," she said, "Mara . . . That was so dangerous. I've known Kulik kill someone who stood up to him."

"What is a Mahondi?"

"We are Mahondis. The People are Mahondis. Did he call you a Mahondi? Well, you are one. And me. And Dann."

"And he wants the kid if it is male. That means, we can keep it if it is female and have milk from her when she grows up."

"There are too many females," said Daima. "We can't feed what we have. He wants another male because his is old and he can keep control of who has milk and who doesn't."

"Perhaps Mishka will have twins."

"Don't wish for that. We would have to kill one. How could we keep them fed? You know yourself how hard it is to find food for them."

When Daima said that Mishka was ready, Mara put the rope around her horns and went through the houses to where the men sat.

She stood in front of Kulik with the beast and said, "Here is Mishka. I've come by myself, as you said."

"What makes you think I haven't changed my mind?" said Kulik, and went on grinning there, a long time, to keep her afraid in case he had changed his mind.

"You promised," said Mara at last, not crying, for she was determined not to.

"Very well, you come with me."

He got up, in his heavy, slow way—like an animal that has decided to tread all over you, Mara thought—and went towards the enclosure where his male milk beast was, all by itself. Mishka began to jump and rush about at the end of her rope.

Kulik turned his head to grin back and say, "Can't wait for it, can she?—you are all the same."

Mara had no idea what he meant.

At the entrance to the enclosure, which was a small one—just room for one animal and a bit over—he slid back a bar and pushed in Mishka, and then picked up Mara and lifted her over so that she was among the legs and the horns. Then he leaned his arms on the wooden rail, grinning, and watched while Mara dodged about, as the big male beast nudged and pushed and edged Mishka into position, and she sidled and evaded, and came back ... and all the time those great hooves were missing Mara by inches. Along the fence of the enclosure now were the men, standing there grinning and hoping that Mara would get a hard kick, or a poke from one of those sharp horns. It seemed to go on for a long time, the pushing and shoving in the enclosure, and Mara tried to get out through the rails of the fence; but the men pushed her back in, and this time she was just under Mishka's head. The male was on Mishka's back now and pushing Mishka down, but she was trying not to hurt Mara, keeping her head and shoulders away from the girl. At last it was done. The two beasts stood clear of each other. Mara was trembling so that she could hardly stand, and she felt her pee running down her legs. But she got the rope around Mishka's horns and stood with her at the place where the opening was. For a good long while Kulik did not take his arms from where they lay on the rail. Then he moved back, lifted off the rail and stood aside. Mara led Mishka out. She did not look at Kulik or at the other men, who were standing there grinning and pleased with themselves.

"Remember, it's mine if it's a male," said Kulik.

"I promise," said Mara.

"She promises," said the men to each other, in copies of her little voice, but lisping and silly, not as she spoke.

She took Mishka back to her place near the others, and stood for a time with her arms around one of the big front legs, because she could not reach any higher; and Mishka put down her soft muzzle and licked Mara's sweaty, dusty neck for the salt.

Then she went to Daima and told her. Daima only sat with her head on her old hand at the table and listened.

"Well, let's hope she takes," she said. And Mishka did "take": she was pregnant and she gave birth to a male. Dann could hardly be got away from Mishka and her kid. He adored the little beast, which would look out for Dann, who brought it bits of green he found in the grass, or a slice of the yellow root.

Mara said, "Don't love that little beast so much, because we can't keep him."

And Daima said, "That's right. He must know what the world is like."

"Perhaps it won't always be like this," said Mara.

And then the beast, which Dann called Dann, was taken away by Kulik, who chased Dann off and said, "I'm not having any Mahondi brats, get away."

Dann could not understand what had happened. He sat silent, puzzled, full of grief; but then it seemed some sort of change took place in him. "I hate Kulik," he said, but not like a little boy. "One day I'll kill him." And he didn't cry. His face was narrow and tight and suspicious and hard. He was not yet five years old.

2

On the low hill overlooking the village was a tall rock, precipitous on three sides and sloping steeply on the village side. There on the top of it sat Mara, looking down at a group of half a dozen boys playing a game of fighting with sticks. Dann was taller than any of them, though he was younger than some, at ten years old, and he was a quick, always watchful child, who dominated them all. Mara was almost grown, with her little bumps of breasts, and she was tall and thin and wiry, and could run faster than the boys, which she had learned to do from having so often to rescue Dann from danger. He seemed to have been born without a sense of self-preservation: would leap off a rock or a roof without looking to see where he was going to land, walk up to a big hissing dragon, jump into a pool without checking if there were stingers or a water dragon. But he was much better, and that was why Mara was up here, watching quite idly, not anxious and on guard as she had been every minute of her days and nights. Only recently had she understood that her long watch was over. She had been strolling from the hill to the village, listening to the singing beetles and her own thoughts, when she had seen Dann rushing towards her with a stick, then past her, and she had whirled to see him attacking a dragon that was following her.

"You should be more careful, Mara," he had chided, and not at all as if he were mimicking her constant, Be careful, do be careful, Dann.

She had gone in to Daima and told her, and the two had wept and laughed in each other's arms for the wonderful ludicrousness of it. And Daima had said, "Congratulations, Mara. You've done it. You've brought him through."

This was her favourite place. Nobody came up here: not Dann, who liked to be always rushing about; not Daima, who was too old and stiff; not the villagers, who said it was full of ghosts. Mara had been here at all times of the day, and at night too, and had never seen or heard ghosts. The danger was the dragons, who were so hungry they would eat anything. That is why she sat on a rock that on three sides they could not climb up, while in front she could slide down on her bottom and be off as soon as she heard the angry hissing. Or she could wait up here, safe, throwing stones down at the dragons if they showed signs of climbing up. This rock rose out of a tumbling and piling of small, rocky hills, full of clefts and crevices where bushes and trees grew, and caves and cliffs and pits that were old traps, and in some places heaps of old walls and roofs. When she had played the What Did You See? game with Daima, she liked best to do this hill, because she was always finding new things.

"And then?"

"The pits have black rings, with bits of chain on the rings."

"And then?"

"The rings are made of some metal we don't have."

"And so?"

"All the same, Daima, I think those pits are quite recent—I mean hundreds of years, not thousands."

When Mara said hundreds, she meant a long time; and when thousands, it meant her mind had given up, confessed failure: *thousands* meant an unimaginable, endless past.

Up on those hills—for behind the one near the village were piled others—forcing herself between bushes and saplings, squeezing through gaps in boulders, sliding down shaly descents in showers of stones, climbing trees to look over places she could not penetrate because of thick undergrowth, what Mara had slowly understood—and it had been slow, years—was that this was not just, as Daima had told her, a ruined city thousands of years old, or hundreds, or what the villagers saw it as—a place to get stones for building—but layers of habitations, peoples, time. She had been standing between walls still mostly intact, though roots had brought down part of one into a slope of blocks where little lizards sunned themselves, and in front of her was a great wall, many times her height, and wider than Daima's whole house, and there was not one rock missing from it. The whole wall was carved into stories and they were all about a war: the fighters in baggy trousers and tops and big boots, and they carried all kinds of weapons that Daima could not explain, saying only that once there had been weapons so terrible one of them could destroy a whole city. This wall was celebrating a victory: and certainly it was a description of how these ancient people had seen themselves and their enemies, for the faces of the victors were cruel and fierce and the defeated ones were frightened and pleading. At any rate, it was a story, on that wall, of how people had fought, and some had been killed. But on another wall in the same room, or hall, the blocks of stone were smaller and fitted closer, and were covered over with the fine, hard plaster, and the pictures were coloured. These were the same people, with their flat, broad shoulders and lean bodies, and narrow faces, and there was fighting again, but the weapons were different and so were the clothes. The same people, but from different times. That meant these people had been here for—hundreds?—of years. It meant that between the time of the plain carving of the stone and the time of decorating this smooth, crisp plaster with the coloured pictures, they had discovered the plaster and how to make it stick on rock, and how to mix colours that lasted for—how long? And on another part of the hill she found a part-fallen building with the inner walls carved, but it had earth halfway up the walls. Almost on top of these walls, as if the builders had tried to continue the old ones upwards, were other, newer walls, the white ones, with colours. This meant that the builders of the top building had not known of the building underneath. Earth had been washed away, so now you could see the two walls, one almost on top of the other. And this whole great area of hills and stones and rocks tumbling everywhere— Mara understood it all, quite suddenly. There had been a very big city of stone walls decorated with carvings. And there had been an earthquake.

And on top of and between the half destroyed houses and halls another city had been built, much more beautiful and finely decorated. And that, too, had been tumbled by a quake, but this time the people had not bothered to rebuild. Why hadn't they? What had happened to them? Where were they? Up here by herself, and even at night, though Daima hated her coming at night, Mara stood with these layers of the past all around her; and sometimes felt herself go cold and frightened, thinking of how they had lived here, all those people, building their houses when the earth shook and everything fell down ... And living there again, decorating walls with such care, mixing colours, putting pictures of birds and beasts and feasts, as well as fighting and soldiers, on their walls ... And then they had disappeared. People just like herself, she supposed: they had vanished, and no one knew about them. A little girl, over-whelmed by time, the weight of it, thoughts that crammed her brain and made it want to burst, she had climbed up on Daima and shivered and clung. "They've just gone, gone, gone, Daima, and they were here for so long ... And we don't know their names or anything."

But these days she did not cling or cuddle up to Daima, for Mara was as tall as she was, and much stronger. Now when she held Daima she felt as if the old woman were the child and she the mother, and she mar-velled that this huddle of thin bones held together at all.

Down below the little boys were fighting, a real fight. Often a play fight became that, the Rock People ganging up on Dann because they hated him, but so far he had not been hurt more than bruises and, once, a sprained arm. Mara watched and made herself stay still. "You must let him," said Daima. "You can't protect him any more. He has to fight his own battles." And perhaps letting him fight his own battles had led to his being able to say to Mara, like a grown-up, "You should be more careful." Now she watched how Dann was defending himself against the kicking, flailing boys, and it was almost more than she could do to stop herself from running down to stand by him and fight with him. It seemed to her even now that her whole life had been only that: Dann, Dann; and that for years all her body had been able to feel was his trembling need for her. Now the fight was a whirl of sticks and legs and stones, and then Dann broke free and ran into one of the empty houses, whose roof had gone, and shouted down at the others from the top of crumbling walls. It was dangerous. A bit of wall fell away from under his feet and he jumped clear. The others did not follow but went off, all together. Dann leaped down, and was off into Daima's house. He came out with two cans, and went running through the houses to where the milk beasts clustered under their old thorn tree. Their own beast now was not Mishka but Mishka's daughter, called Mishkita. When Mishka's milk stopped, Mara went to Kulik and asked that she should be mated again. This time he looked hard and long at her, and she could not read that look. Then he nodded and said, "Bring her when she's ready." Mishka was mated with her own son, Dann, and gave birth to Mishkita. Daima had said, "Don't go out by yourself at night, Mara. He's got a soft spot for you. That's even more dangerous." But Mara did go out at night, and when she saw Kulik smiled and nodded as if he were a friend and not an enemy, while all the time he was near her heart beat with fear of him.

Dann knelt under Mishkita, keeping a watch on those sharp hooves, and milked into the cans. He was quick and skilful. All the time he was looking around for fear of an ambush. He had once beaten up a whole gang of children teasing the milk beasts, and he said that if he ever caught them again they would find out what he could do.

This milk was all that Daima could eat now. If it didn't rain soon there would be no more milk.

There was only a little of the white flour left, because a trader had come but he had said he thought it wasn't worth his while if all they could give him was the yellow roots.

Mara had been making experiments. She found grasses that had small, lumpy seeds. She beat the thin, fragile heads of the grass on a stone, got out some grain and beat that on a stone. But for a whole day's work there was only a cup of flour. She had a stroke of luck when she found, while digging for the yellow roots, a big round root the size of a baby's head, which was filled with a dense white stuff. She cooked it and, risking that it was poison, ate, while Daima watched, ready with an emetic. But it was not poisonous and made a filling porridge. There were very few green leaves anywhere. They ate, though sparingly, the white flour, in case this was the last they'd see, the yellow roots, and this new white root. They ate sour milk and a little cheese. They were always hungry. Daima said that neither of them had had a square meal in five years and yet were shooting up like reeds after rain. They must be feeding on air, she said. "Or dust," they joked.

Two years after the children had come to Daima's house there was a big storm. Not a cloudburst far away, so that brown water rushed in tor-

rents under a bright blue sky. It was real rain. It was sudden and violent.
The cisterns outside the houses filled with water, and everyone shared
the water in the cisterns outside the empty houses. Daima and the children carried water again and again to the locked-up tank indoors. Soon,
there was another storm. The dried-up, yellowish earth and the dead-
looking grasses were bursting into life, and there were flowers, and the
milk beasts grew fat, and the people lost their dried, dusty look. The
waterholes became a river, and the wild animals stood about on the
banks at dusk and dawn, and there was a trumpeting and bleating and
howling and yapping from both rivers. All the villagers went up to the
ridge to look: they had believed there were no animals left. Certainly
there were only half of what had been. Because of the storm there were
some baby animals born. Kulik and his sons went out to catch the babies:
no one was strong enough now to hunt the big animals. They did not
share the meat with anyone else in the village. The villagers made a
channel for the water of the nearer river to flow into a low place, and
there a guard was set, day and night, so the stingers and water dragons
did not get into it; and in that pool everyone bathed every day, all at the
same time, for safety. There was even a little friendliness shown to Mara
and Dann, who took their turn, with Daima, guarding the pool.

And then—that was it. Because there had been two big storms in
that rainy season, everyone waited for rain in the next, with cleaned-out
cisterns and mended roofs. But there was no rain that season, nor the
next, nor the next. That good season with the two storms had been four
years ago. Again the waterholes were almost empty in the little river,
and the big river had stopped running. Everywhere the bones of animals
lay in the dead grass. Extraordinary events were reported. A water
dragon, almost dead with hunger, had been attacked by a water stinger
half its size; and when the villagers went down together to the waterholes they saw half a dozen stingers fighting over the half-dead beast.
And just outside the village a couple of the big black birds that normally
ate only seeds and berries attacked in full daylight a wild pig too weak to
run away, tearing from its shoulders and neck big beakfuls of flesh, while
the pig squealed. And these birds had taken to gathering not far from
the milk beasts, to stare at them, moving closer and waiting, and moving in again; and Dann had run out shouting and throwing stones at
them. They had flapped off, slowly, so weak they kept sinking and
wavering in the air, letting out hoarse, desperate cries. The milk beasts
were thin and weak and gave hardly any milk.

Perhaps this next rainy season?—everyone was saying. Or perhaps even another flash flood from up north.

There were fewer people. Only twenty still remained. Rabat had died. The old people had died, and three new babies. There was not one baby or small child in the village. Up north, so it was believed, things were better, even normal, and so many families had left or were leaving. Often the village was full of people, just for a night or two, because travellers from the south would arrive and simply take over the empty houses, demanding food from the villagers. They were mostly Rock People themselves with relatives, even distant ones, here, and so they could claim hospitality. But they found little food or water and went off again.

Once a gang forced their way into Daima's house and found the old woman lying—and, they thought, dying—on the shelf in the outer room. They drank all the water in the jars and cans in that room, but went off. The children were hiding in the empty rooms at the back. And now Daima told them that there must always be just enough of the roots and flour in the front room for any marauders to think that this was all there was in the house, and they must be careful to keep the inner doors locked and the keys hidden.

Then one midday when everyone was lying down waiting for the heat to lessen, a crowd of travellers came, about twenty, and they stood in a close group while the villagers came out to see who it was this time. And, gazing and examining, they became silent. These were certainly Rock People: squat, thick-built, greyish in colour, with pale masses of frizzled hair. But their faces were all the same. At first in disbelief, then in quiet horror, the people standing around the travellers looked from one face to another, and then again . . . No, it wasn't true, it couldn't be. Perhaps the villagers had become silly, their wits gone because of not having enough water and food . . . But no, it was true. Every face was the same, identical, with lumpy noses, long thin mouths, pale eyes under yellow brows, broad foreheads made lower still because of the frizzy bush above. The same in every detail. A moan, or groan, from the villagers. Then they began shouting. And then—Mara saw it while her heart went cold—Dann walked forward as if he were being pulled, one step after another, just as he had been when he saw the two brothers years before, unable to help himself, drawn by something he did not understand and did not know about. He came to a stop just in front of this little mass of people, which was also one person, or seemed to be, since their movements were the same and their faces each had the identical cold and hostile anger. And, as one, their eyes focused on Dann, the tall thin boy with the dusty black hair: a person so unlike them, and unlike anybody else there, that he seemed to them like an unfamiliar animal, a new kind of monkey perhaps. As if they were one person, their hands rose, and in the hands were sticks; and Mara raced forward and pulled Dann back, and the hands and the sticks fell, but slowly, and in the same movement. And now these people, who were like one person, were staring at the two children, who were not like any they had seen, being so knobbly and bony and staring back with frightened eyes.

Mara did not pull the boy into the house for fear this would bring this enemy after them, but stood at their door, behind some other villagers. She could feel Dann trembling, though now her hands were gripping not a little child but a strong boy whose head was nearly on a level with hers. He stood and shivered as he had years ago, shocked by a mystery: faces that resemble each other, eyes that are alike, while behind lie worlds as different as day and night. But here it was not two faces: there were many.

The newcomers went off, together, and the villagers dispersed, whispering among themselves as if afraid of provoking some new manifestation of this horror: people you could not tell apart, no matter how you stared and matched and compared. And Mara led Dann into the house where, like a small boy, he lay on his bed and hid his face.

Soon a neighbour came to say that these new people were going to stay for a while—"and that means until they have eaten everything we have got"—and she had been told to come to Daima's house to get food. And that meant, Mara thought, they were afraid to come themselves. And, yes, it was true: "They think you are ghosts. They think you are cursed."

Mara produced half a dozen of the yellow roots, shrivelled but still good. And then she went out to make sure the beasts were safe. The newcomers had taken over empty houses at the end of the village. Mara decided to stay with the milk beasts. Late, when the moon was making shadows around the houses, she saw the shadows thicken and then lengthen like drops before they fall and separate themselves. They were the same-faced ones, moving furtively, crouching and running, and she stood up and shrieked at them, stamping her feet and whirling about, and they went scrambling off, shouting with fear that there were demons in this place.

Dann could not be kept in the house. He was always watching the travellers: leaning against a house wall or even standing quite near them, staring, his face squeezed up and his eyes puckering with the effort of trying to understand. They pretended to ignore him, but they were afraid of him. And soon they left, partly because of their fear and, too, they were hungry.

This event had an effect on Dann. He was restless, but then lay on his bed for hours, staring. He put his thumb in his mouth and sucked it, with the old squelching sound that drove Mara wild with anxiety and irritation. He did not join in the other children's play, but did come up the hill to sit on the rock with Mara, when she asked him, to break his mood; but when there he only sat, staring down into the village. She said to him, "Dann, do you know why people who are alike make you afraid?" But he did not: in his mind was a door shut fast against memories, and all he knew—if he knew that much, and was not merely experiencing—was that the people who were alike haunted him, challenged him, frightened him. It went on for some days, this new behaviour of Dann's: listlessness, and a look of apprehension in those deep, dark eyes of his. He wanted to be with Mara, though he seemed not to know he had become a little boy again, reaching for her hand, or pressing close, when some thought she could only guess at made him tremble.

Then one evening two men came into the village, and they were Persons, People—Mahondis. They were directed to Daima's house by the villagers. But they had not come to see Daima or find the children, of whom they had never heard. They had walked from a long way south of Rustam, hoping to find shelter in that town, because their country was all dried up and dead. But Rustam was full of sand, they said: sand storms had blown over it, filling the houses and burying the gardens. No one lived in Rustam now: no people, no animals. And between Rustam and here, while things were better than in the South, it was dry and there were stretches of country where the trees were dying. Among these were new trees, of the kind that can live in semi-deserts. It seemed that the trees had known what was going to happen because they must have begun growing before the desert-like country appeared. When these two men came to the river and saw there was still some water, they had wept, because it was so long since they had seen waterholes that were not all cracked and dry.

Mara fed these men with sliced roots and milk and said they could use the bed in the outer room and her bed, and she and Daima went into one of the inner rooms for the night. They could hear the men's deep voices and Dann's excited voice, talking and laughing too: Dann did not often laugh but he was laughing now.

In the morning everything was quiet. Daima was asleep, and Mara went quickly into the room she and Dann had, and then the outer room; but the men were not there and Dann was not there. Mara ran out and through the village, looking for them. A woman said, Didn't Mara know? Dann had left with the men very early that morning, all three walking quietly, "as if they had stolen something." Dann had first run to Mishkita, pulling down her head to kiss her ears and her hairy cheeks, and then running back to the two watching men, crying. It was this—Dann's crying—that told Mara it was true: Dann had meant to leave, and for good.

Mara went into the house slowly, afraid she would fall. When she told Daima, the old woman put her arms around Mara and held her and rocked her while she wept.

3

It was almost dark in the room, because the door was shut and the window shutter left only a little slit for light. Through this slit fell dusty air. On the rock table sat a spindly creature: tall, with long, knobbly arms and legs, every bit of her skin covered with a brownish dust, and her hair hanging in long, greyish spikes. Her eyes were small and red in a little, bony face. Her brown, glistening garment seemed as fresh and new as at any time these last hundred or so years. This poor thing was Mara, and nearly five years had passed.

On the rock bed lay Daima, who was as thin and bony, but her hair was not in shags and rags because Mara combed it. Daima had by her a bag of the brown, shiny stuff, and she was lying on her side and taking out, one by one, all kinds of objects: a comb, a stone, a spoon, a dishevelled red feather, a snake's shed skin. She looked at them amazed, incredulous. "Mara, but there's nothing here, it's so little, is this all it is?" Mara did not answer, because Daima did this over and over again when she was awake. She was saying, Mara knew, Is this all my life has amounted to? At first, Mara had answered, "Everything is there. I've checked. Nothing is missing." But she could not go on saying it, she had so little energy left. Then Daima turned her old eyes on Mara with a close, intent, suspicious inspection; and it was as if she did not know who it was, though she did, for Mara understood that when Daima counted her life out in those possessions from the bag, Mara was among them, for she would touch a bit of cloth or the stone and say, "Mara, it is Mara." Mara made her face smile as she sat there, and turned her head so that Daima could see her, letting Daima look, and look, the close, deep stare, though she did not know what it was Daima searched for in her face. Perhaps she was making sure Mara was still there with her, for she was uneasy when Mara went out. While she did not know how bad things were out there, she did know it was dangerous.

It was midday. Daima was licking her lips, which were cracked and sore, and blinking her eyes to make some water, they were so dry. Mara went into the inner room where the pile of yellow roots was: only a few left now, only thirteen. She and Daima needed one a day to keep them as much alive as they were. Mara these days did not have the inclination to go out with her digging stick, or go to the waterholes, where there had not been water now for months, let alone climb up the hill to where the old cities were. Mara cut up a root into yellow slices and fed half of them to Daima, who even now when she was so feeble was trying to refuse her share so that Mara could have it.

Almost a year ago there had been another storm, not much of one, and they were just finishing the water Mara had collected then. Out on the plain around the village this rain had plumped the roots that lived many feet down in the earth. They had been shrivelling and were rather like wood: when Mara poked her digging stick into them they were not far off wood. But then the rain came and the roots were juicy again, and that meant Mara and Daima could live a little longer. The big white roots that seemed to absorb water were again like balls of hard, white pith.

Because of that rain, some people who had decided to leave stayed a little longer; but now no one was left, only the two women. Mara would have gone with the last group, even though Kulik was one of them, if it had not been for Daima, who could not walk.

When every one of the villagers had left, Mara had gone through the rock houses to see if anything had been left, and it was this that spoke most loudly and terribly of what had happened here. There was nothing in the houses. At least there had been a few utensils and some cans, and in each corner some of the yellow roots that were keeping them all alive, and a jar or so of water that they drank a sip or two at a time. But everything had been taken away.

As people died, and it was impossible to bury them in the hard earth because no one had the strength to dig graves, they were put in one of the empty houses and left, with the doors pulled tight shut. The air was so dry they shrivelled into mummies, so light you could pick them up like pieces of wood. But then the big lizards and the dragons, hunting everywhere for food, came into the village and tried to push the doors aside, or force their way through the windows, and one of them even climbed up on a roof and went down through the thatch. Once, these beasts had eaten only vegetable stuff, but they had long ago forgotten they were herbivores and ate anything they could find. They had lain in wait by the waterholes, when there was water, and fought with the water dragons for a share of any meat there was. Mara had come into the front room one morning to see the head and shoulders of a big lizard pushing through the aperture of the window, hissing, its tongue flickering. It wanted Daima, who was asleep on her shelf. Mara had hit the thing with empty water cans, and at last it went out backwards and waddled through the village looking for a way into a house.

That was why the rock doors were always shut now, though Mara believed there could be no lizards left, they must be all dead. But perhaps not. She had not been up to the hill cities for some time, because she was afraid, so she did not know if lizards and dragons were still there. Up in the oldest part of the ruins, Mara had found storerooms deep in the earth; and while there was nothing left of what they had once held—weapons? gold? ornamented dishes and basins and trays, like the ones pictured on the walls?—there had been water. It was old water that tasted bad because of what had fallen into it, but it was real water and for a while she had gone up to collect it. Twice she had scared away the big lizards drinking there, one of them actually standing in the water, so at first she had thought it was a water dragon; but it wasn't, it was a land dragon. That water had not been replenished by the storm of a year ago, so it must have forced its way up through the rocks from deep under the hills. But the last time Mara saw it there was only a damp stain on rock with scorpions over it, perhaps hoping the water would well up again. From where? These days Mara saw what she looked at differently from how she once had. Hills did not stay the same, she knew that: she had seen the boulders come crashing down hillsides when lightning cracked them open. Waterholes sometimes were dusty pits and were sometimes rivers. Animals that had eaten plants learned to chase humans for their flesh. Once, digging for a root, she had found a small stream running through a rocky place underground; but when she looked for it later it was dry. Who knew what rivers moved under the earth, or had moved and were now dried up? Under the hills up there had been cities upon cities, and the people must have drunk water, so perhaps rivers once ran there that had gone long ago? Everything changed: rivers moved, disappeared, ran again; trees died—the hills were full of dry forests—and insects, even scorpions, changed their natures.

The scorpions were in the village. Mara had to watch every step. They had come in for the dead people. She had watched them trying to squeeze in through the cracks in houses, or down through the roof stones. And they did squeeze through. You could hear them scuttling and rattling about in the houses, eating up the corpses. Then the villagers had begun something new. Instead of finding an empty house and putting their dead into it, they fitted corpses into the cisterns that stood outside the door of every house. Sometimes the dead person had to be put in bent double. Then the heavy stones were put back on. The scorpions could not get in, because the lids always fitted perfectly to keep the dust out of the water. As you walked through the village, the scorpions clustered on the tops of the cisterns ... Waiting? For what? And then they died. There were dead scorpions everywhere. But there were scorpions that had not died, that were able somehow to live—eating what?—and they were bigger than the old ones had been. It would be easy to think that there were two kinds of scorpion, big and little ones; but no, some were growing larger, and very fast. Once, Mara would have kicked a scorpion out of the way, but she would be afraid to now, for these new beasts could take a hand off, or a big piece of flesh out of a leg.

Mara sat on the rock table, with her feet pulled up, just in case there was something she had overlooked—a scorpion or a smaller, half-grown lizard that had hidden in the empty rooms—and she had long, interesting thoughts while she watched over Daima's sleep. Perhaps one day, as far into the future as the old cities in the hills were in the past, people would find this village half buried in dust, or perhaps deep under the dust, and the bones in the cisterns, and they would say, "These ancient people buried their dead just outside their houses in rocky graves." They would find the bones of big lizards in the deep rocky pools in the hills because—who knew?—the water might start filling the pools up there again, and they would say, "There were two kinds of lizard, or dragon, and they both lived in water." They would find the pig bones scattered about over the plain and see the marks of bird claws and beaks and say, "These birds killed and ate pigs."

But what was worrying Mara now was that they might also be able to say, "In those days there were insects, earth insects, the size of a thumb." When Mara looked out over the plain where she had dug for roots she could see everywhere circles showing pale on darker old grass. The under-earth insects whose tall homes dotted the plain—though they hadn't when Mara and Dann first came: these great hard-earth heaps were new—came up from their tunnels at night to chew up the dry old grass with jaws like the pincers of stingers, though not as big yet, and the fragments of grass made these whitish circles. They must have watercourses running deep under their heaps for the earth of their galleries was wet. The villagers had even thought of how they could dig down through one of these insect cities until they reached water; but not only were they afraid of the insects that thought nothing of eating up a small animal in a few minutes, they did not have the strength left to dig, nor did they have anything better than wooden sticks to dig with.

These insects were rapidly growing larger. So far they did not seem to want to move far from their homes, but Mara had watched a column of them marching towards the hills of the old cities—so many of them you could not think of counting them: brownish, glistening, fat insects with their pincered heads—and she had simply run away. Every day she expected to see their brown columns trickling through the houses.

While the milk beasts were still alive these insects had been the villagers' greatest worry. A guard was put on the beasts, day and night, to watch the grass tussocks for the scorpions and the lizards and then, when they noticed how the earth insects were growing large and bold, for their columns.

One night this problem was solved for them. Travellers had come through, pushed the weakened villagers aside and driven off the milk beasts. Mara cried as she had not since Dann went away. She loved Mishkita, and now there was nothing left for her except Daima, who she knew would soon die. And yet quite soon they would have had to kill the milk animals, for they gave so little milk now and there was nothing to give them to eat. Mishkita's teats had been red and sore from being squeezed to get milk. And Mara had seen something that had made her frantic with the sadness of it. Mishkita had spread her legs and bent her head under her body, careful that her horns would not poke the flesh, and sucked at her own teats. She was so desperate, for she was given only two or three of the yellow roots every day and it was weeks since she had been given a drink of water—it was when Mara had found the old water up in the hills. Mara had found herself thinking, as she stood with her arm over the beast's back, and Mishkita's nuzzle in her neck, licking, licking, because of the salt, Perhaps poor Mishkita will not be sorry when her life is over. And that made her think of her own: would she, Mara, be pleased if one day she were surprised by one of the big lizards, or found the earth insects scrambling over her as she slept? She thought for a long time about this. Every day was so hard, such a struggle, and she was feeling so weak and often so dizzy—and yet she thought, No, I don't want to die yet. When Daima dies I'll go north by myself and then . . .

There had been another worry, the biggest of them all. One day, when there was still a little water left in the waterholes and she was not as thin as she was now, she saw a red thread of blood on her skin, on the inner thigh, and she thought, Something has stung me. But no, the blood was flowing from inside. She was at the waterholes when this happened. She went carefully back through the houses, holding the water cans so no one could see; but Daima had noticed and said, "Oh I hoped this would not happen. I thought perhaps you are too thin, there's no flesh on you." She then told Mara what she needed to know. But what concerned her most was that Mara should never, ever, let a man near her, because for her to get pregnant was the worst thing that could happen. It would be the death of her—she was too undernourished, and the child would die too. Since then Mara had looked newly at every male, and at their instruments for making children, but she could not imagine not being able to defend herself. But while Mara thought about it, deciding there was nothing to be afraid of, with all the men so weak and hungry, she did keep an instinct of alarm alive for Daima's sake. For she had been so apprehensive, so frightened for her—Mara could not remember Daima's ever being so anxious.

Meanwhile, while the blood did flow there was a problem. The brown material did not absorb liquid. The mosses the village women used were all dust. Daima told Mara to tear up one of the beautiful old robes in the chest to use as pads, and Mara did, though it hurt to do it. She used secretly to let her mind linger over that chest of coloured garments, when the ugliness of everything around seemed to be dragging the life out of her.

The blood ran for two or three days, stopped. It came again. And Kulik, who had had too many problems of his own to notice Mara, sensed what was happening. He was thin, he was gaunt, but he was not weak, and Mara found herself looking out for him. When he saw her he came up, grabbed her by the arm, grinned right into her face and said, "What are you waiting for, a Mahondi husband?"

She tore herself free of him and ran, but then the blood stopped, and he seemed to know that too.

Kulik had had two sons. One was killed by a water stinger, not at the waterholes but just outside the village. The young man's bones was all that they found. The other son went north with some travellers passing through. And then, but not long ago, Kulik went. He was the last to go from the rock houses.

Recently Mara had been thinking that if she did have a child—if the blood did come back—it would be something to love. For sometimes her arms ached to hold somebody. It was her little brother her arms remembered, she knew that, and now it was Mishkita, for she had so often gone to stand with her arms high around the beast's neck, her head on its shoulder.

Suppose—Mara thought—that she had become too weak to leave? She had never had this thought before: it had always been, *When* I leave. This frightened her.

On this afternoon, as Mara sat on the rocky perch, she heard the light, rasping breaths from the dusty shelf where Daima lay and she thought, I have heard that breathing before, when someone is not far off dying.

Mara longed to be out of this dark, hot place where she and Daima were like two prisoners. She was dreaming of water on her face and on her arms, and running over her body. She took up a can, from sheer habit, from the line of cans near the wall and went out into the glare, though it was less now, being afternoon. She could hardly see the plain with its pale dryness, where some dust devils circled lazily in the haze. There was a fire somewhere. In the dust were little flecks of black from dead, burning grasses. They were bitter on her tongue. One fell on her and she rubbed and, because it was still warm, greasy marks were left on her skin. The fire smoke hung in dark clouds away beyond the hills of the old cities. If the fire reached them, that would be a real conflagration, for there had not been a fire there that Mara could remember, and there were all those dead trees and old scrub.

The spaces between the houses of the Rock Village were bare. The heaps of dust had been swept away by hot winds. Mara walked past the house where Rabat had died and where she now lay on her rocky shelf. Drying out had twisted those falsely smiling features into an angry sneer. There were scorpions on the roof but they could not get in. Mara went on slowly, listlessly, knowing she was straying about, not going directly forward. She could hardly keep her feet on the path to the ridge. No, she thought, she could not leave here; this is where she would die. It took a long time to reach the ridge from where she could see down to the lines of dead trees along the empty waterholes. She stood there resting, panting, her tongue dry between dry lips. Then she staggered down through the dead grasses. Among them were bones, but most of the bones were over the second ridge, on either side of the main watercourse. That is where the dying animals made their way, hoping there might be water left there. Every kind of bone was scattered about: big ones from the great animals that had died first because they needed so much water, to the little furry animals that had sometimes come up to the houses begging for water, before they died.

Mara did not stop at the first dry waterhole, the one where long ago Kulik had almost drowned Dann, nor the second, where lay the carapaces of two big water stingers, and the shells of turtles, and the bones of water lizards. Beyond was a stretch of clean white sand. She set down the can, which had not held water for months, and took off her tunic, and knelt on the sand. She came here, when she felt strong enough, to this bright, clean sand, to try to free herself of dust. For a long time she knelt there, running the fine white sand over her legs, then her arms, seeing how the dirty surface of her skin came away, leaving cleanness, and then she rubbed handfuls over her neck and her cheeks. The greasy lumps of her hair disgusted her, but she could not do anything to improve them, for the sand only stuck there. Pressing her eyes tight shut she rubbed sand over them and her forehead, again and again, and then lay on the sand and rolled her itching back and shoulders in it. She was rolling as she had seen animals do it, and at the thought she quickly raised her head to see if some scorpion or big bird, with its great talons and beak, or a lizard, had come for her; but no, the banks were empty.

And now she knelt and looked down between her thighs to see if perhaps that trickle of red blood was back, but the lips of her slit were
pulled tight and wrinkled with dryness. Where she should be peeing was
a burning that she had become so used to it seemed only part of the
angry, hungry, itchy desperation of her whole body for water. She peed
so seldom, and when she did it was dark yellow and so strong she could
not drink it, though she had tried, thinking that here was some sort of
liquid going to waste. She had watched the dark drops being sucked into
the dust and at once drying, leaving a few rough edges around the little
pit, like an anteater's hole.

She was kneeling there, rocking back and forth as Daima did, or had
done—for pain and grief, eyes shut—when she heard thunder and
opened her eyes to see clouds that were not smoke clouds. They were far
ahead, on the horizon; but up there, in the north, was water, was rain:
she was sure she could smell it. Slowly she climbed out of her little
sandy desert and stood on the bank above the dried watercourse to look
at the clouds: it was so long since she had seen lightning dance in banks
of black cloud. Her skin craved and ached—soon, soon, drops of rain
would fall and hiss on her parched skin ... But she had done that
before, stood waiting and watching rain on the horizon, but no rain had
come. The clouds were growing bigger, gaining height over her. Was the
thunder louder? She thought, If there are any animals left, they will be
thinking as I am, and running as fast as they can to get here. But she
could see no animals. Then she saw, as she had as a child, what seemed
like the earth rolling down towards her, a brown avalanche; but now the
flood was a low, brown creeping, and not very fast, not roaring and raging and throwing animals and trees and branches about, but it was coming, and would soon be here. At last she could drink her fill and fill the
can and take it back to Daima, who had not felt water on her tongue or
her lips, only the juice of the yellow roots, for days now.

The flood had reached her, and was slowly spreading out, but low
down, filling the waterholes which bubbled and hissed, drinking in the
wet, and billows of white foam almost reached Mara's legs, and she
stepped back. This was nothing like the floods she remembered, when it
had seemed the whole world had become water; but it was a flood, this
was water, and she knelt at the edge and plunged in her face and arms and
then her whole body, rolling in it as she had in the sand. And then there
was a great clacking and clattering and the surface of the flood was carrying a white load, which was bones, the bones of so many dead animals.

She had to move quickly back, for now there were trees too: not the green, fresh trees that had tossed and bounded on the surface of other floods but the dead, white, fragmented trees of the drought. It was dangerous to be in the water or even too close. She stood back and waited for the water to carry the bones and trees past her. Then she saw, farther down, a big tree had stuck itself in a bank, and another came to rest against it; and behind this barrier were piling bones, loads of bones—a mass, a multitude—and she remembered how, long ago, she had seen the bones spilling out from under the bank on the big river she had come through with the two rescuers she had never seen again, or heard of. "Remember," the man had said to her, "remember where this is." But she had never been back to see if the bones were there or had been washed away again. Yet that place was no farther away than the short walk it had needed for the two strangers and Dann and her to get to the village. And now here was a new mountain of bones, with brown water rushing through them making them knock against each other. When the flood went down they would remain and the dust would blow over them and they would be hidden. People would think, This is just a river bank, until another flood ... The clacking and clicking seemed to be less and the brown water was running more slowly. Up north the sky was blue, the hot, bright, antagonistic blue of drought, and soon the water would be gone. Desperate, she stepped into it, risking blows from the last of the bones, and splashed herself and drank and drank. It was muddy water, but she could feel her body soaking it in. Soon she was standing by water running low again and shrinking back into the waterholes; and her body was fresh and cool, and the filthy, dry paste of dirt had gone, leaving on her a film of the dust the water carried, a greyish film. She thought, I'm the same colour as the Rock People, but did not care. For she was thinking of Daima, and how she had not yet felt the water on her face and in her mouth. Mara was stronger now. With the sun setting in a blaze in the again hot, dry sky behind her she went home, walking well, looking at every step for insects or scorpions or anything at all making its way to the waterholes. And she did see some scorpions, the big ones, going in lines towards the water.

In the dark, hot room Daima moaned, and her breath was hot and heavy. Mara took down the shutter and opened the door a little, and gave Daima a drink, and said it had rained up-country and there had been a small flash flood. But Daima was too ill to care now, and Mara washed her all over, slowly, for a long time, so the water could sink into that drying, cracking skin; and she rubbed cloths over her hair. And made her drink, again and again.

When the morning came, Mara would go up to the waterholes again, and perhaps over the next ridge to the river, to fill the cans and bring them back, to get more water into the cistern that was in the house, though no longer locked up, since there was no one to steal it. She would make the journey again and again till the cistern was full—but then Mara thought, What for? Daima will soon die and there will be nothing here to keep me. Mara was awake all night, standing at the door, looking into the dark and at the sky, where all the stars were out, washed clean and glittering. The very moment the light greyed she took up cans and shut the door tight, and went on, the only moving thing in that hot landscape, up the ridge to its top, and stopped to see what she could see. The flood had gone, leaving a film over everything, greying the white bones heaped up against the dead branching trees. The waterholes were filled, and around every one were scorpions, and beetles and spiders. Where had they been hiding all this time? She had not seen anything but scorpions for a long time. The stretch of sand where she had rolled yesterday was there again, a white glisten over a dark dampness. On the dead white trees along the watercourse the branches seemed clotted with dark crusts or bumps. Insects again, all kinds of them. Had they drunk what they needed and fled up the trees to get away from the scorpions?

Mara was hungry. Now she had drunk enough so that her whole body was sated, and the many aches and sorenesses were not one pain all over her body but could be felt separately—her stomach was shouting, was screaming, at her that she must eat, she must . . . But what?

Mara went on up the second ridge, and when she reached the top saw more or less what she had expected. There was a running brown stream, low down under the dead white trees with their white branches, like arms: Please, please, give us water. There were bones in piles on both sides of the water, but not very far up, and on the bones sat all kinds of insects and scorpions. She went slowly, watching every step, between the bones to the water's edge. It was a slow, sinking stream with wet, whitish clay all along it, which would soon be hard crusts and ridges—as hard as the surface of the white on the walls of the old buildings of the dead cities in the hills. Mara had not come here very often, because when the waterholes nearer the village were dry this river was too. Why had she come here so seldom? For one thing she liked better than anything going to the old cities. And then, when the villagers were still here, she kept her distance and none of them would go near the old cities: they liked the water holes. Her life had steadily narrowed, even before she had become too weak to go to the hills.

The mud the water had carried down had sunk down to the bottom of the pools. She could see clear down through the water. Her ears were ringing. The singing beetles were there on the branches. She had not heard them for . . . She could not remember when she had heard them last. Another sound . . . surely not . . . it was not possible . . . Yes, there was a croaking from the edge of a pool. Some toad or frog had lived through the dry years under the hard, dry mud, and now, the water having softened the mud, the creature had climbed up through it and there it was, sitting on a stone. There were several. When the water went down—and it was going down fast—goodbye, that would be the end of them. The end, too, of the singing beetles. There would be silence again.

Mara stripped off the brown tunic and knelt by a pool. Slowly she sank into it, and rolled in it and lay there absorbing water; and then, when that pool was muddy, went to another pool and squatted, looking in. She could see herself, so thin, only bones with skin stretched over them. Her eyes were deep in her face. It was her hair—those greasy, solid clumps—that she hated. She could hardly bear to touch them. She was staring down at herself there in the water, and saw that next to her was someone else. For a moment she thought her reflection was doubled, but she raised her head and saw on the other side of the pool a youth, who was staring at her. Deliberately, he cupped his hands, dipped them in the water, and drank, keeping his gaze on her. He was naked. She saw there between his legs what Daima had told her she must be afraid of: the two young, round balls in their little sac, and the long thick tube over them—nothing like the wrinkled old lumps Mara had seen so often when the Rock People bathed. This youth was not as thin as she was. There was flesh on him. It had been a long time since she had seen skin fit so nicely over the bones of a face, or arms and legs that had a smooth softness to them. There was a quickness and lightness about him as he squatted there, balancing on his heels and letting the water trickle through his fingers. She was thinking, I ought to be afraid of him. She was thinking, He isn't one of the Rock People . . . And then she knew it was Dann and, moreover, had known from the first. She reached her arms out towards him across the water, but let them fall, and smiled, and said, "You've come back."

He did not say anything. He was looking at her as she was at him, at every little bit, taking in, finding out ... But why didn't he say anything? He did not smile, he did not seem to have heard. He only frowned and examined her. Five years he had been gone. He had been ten years old, and now he was fifteen. He was a man. The Rock People married when they were thirteen or fourteen and could have children by Dann's age.

"I heard you were still here," he said. "Before that I thought you must be dead."

"Everyone is dead, except for me and Daima."

He stood up. He took up from the ground a whitish rough tunic of the kind servants had worn back home. He shook the dust out of it and slid it over his head. For the first time, it occurred to her that she was naked. She put on her brown tunic, hating it, as she always did. And he was making a face as he saw it. He was remembering that—and what else?

She wanted to ask, "What did you see?"—but you asked that about a place, a feather, a tree, a person, not five years.

"Where have you been?" she asked, and he laughed. That was because it was a stupid question. He had not laughed or even smiled till now. "Have you been here all this time?"

"Yes," she said.

"Just here, nowhere else?"

"Yes." And she knew that part of what she wanted to know had been answered. His smile was scornful, and she was seeing her life as he did when he smiled: she had done nothing, been nowhere, while he . . .

"Who told you I was here?"

"Travellers said."

She thought that he was speaking Mahondi as if he had forgotten how to. She spoke it with Daima, so she had not forgotten.

"You haven't been meeting many Mahondis," she stated.

That laugh again: short, "That's it, yes. Not many."

"I'm going back to see how Daima is. She is dying." She dipped her cans and began walking back. She did not know if he would come with her. She could not read his face, his movements; she did not know him. He might just walk off again—disappear.

They went carefully past the fast drying waterholes of the smaller watercourse, where the scorpions were fighting, and where from the trees insects were dropping to the earth to get to the waterholes—where scorpions tore them apart with their pincers.

"All the insects and the scorpions are getting bigger here," she said.

"And everywhere. And down South."

The phrase *down South* did not go easily into her mind. She had often said, "up north," "down south"—but south to her had meant their old home and her family. She was thinking that, to him, who knew so much more, south must mean much more. Nearly everything of what she said or thought was from their old home, from the What Did You See? game, from Daima's memories. It was as if she had been living off all that ever since.

They took some time to get to the village. It was because she was slow. He kept getting ahead of her, stopping to wait for her, but then when they set off in no time he was ahead again.

In the village she told him which houses had the dead in them, which cisterns had corpses—but they must be dried up now, or skeletons.

At Rabat's house he stopped, remembering. He slid back the door, peered in, went to the corner where Rabat lay, and stood looking down. Then he lifted the corpse by its shoulder, stared into the face, let Rabat drop, like a piece of wood. Except, thought Mara, any piece of wood we found we'd treat more carefully than how he has just handled Rabat. And she had learned another thing about him: the dead were nothing to him; he was used to death.

At their house Mara slid back the door and listened. She thought at first that Daima had died. There was no sound of breathing, but she heard a little sigh, and then a long interval, and another sigh.

"She's going," Dann said. He did not look at Daima but went into the inner rooms.

Mara lifted water to Daima's lips but the old woman was past swallowing.

Dann came back. "Let's go," he said.

"I'm not going while she is alive."

He sat down with his arms folded at the rocky table, put his head on his arms—and was at once asleep. His breathing was steady, healthy, loud.

Mara sat by the old woman, wiping her face with a wet cloth, then her arms and her hands. She kept taking gulps of water herself, each one a delicious surprise, since it had been so long since she could simply lift a cup and take a mouthful without thinking, I must only take a few drops. Mara thought, If I don't eat soon I will simply fall over and die myself. She left Daima and went to the storeroom. There were still some roots. She sliced one, licking the juice off her fingers. Then she reached up out of the dry cistern a can that had some of the white flour in it, which she had saved so that one day she would have the strength to leave. It had been three seasons since anyone had come with flour to barter. It smelled a bit stale, but it was still good. She mixed it with water, patted it flat, and put it out on the cistern top, where she knew it would cook in that flaming heat in a few minutes. When she went back to Daima, the old woman was dead.

Dann still slept.

Mara put her hand out towards his shoulder, but before she touched him he was on his feet, and a knife was in his hand. He saw her, took her in, nodded, sat down and at once drew towards him the plate of sliced root, and began eating. He ate it all.

"That was for both of us."

"You didn't say."

She got another root, sliced that, and ate it while he watched. Then she brought in the flat bread from the cistern top, broke it in two and gave him half.

"This is almost the last of the flour," she said.

"I have a little with me."

When he had finished eating he went to bend over Daima, staring. She probably hadn't changed very much since he left, except that her long hair was white.

"Do you remember her?" she asked.

"She looked after us."

"Do you remember our home?"

"No."

"Do you remember the night Gorda rescued us and arranged for us to be brought here to Daima?"

"No."

"Nothing?"

"No."

"Do you remember the two people who brought us?"

"No."

"Do you remember Mishka? And her baby, Dann? You called him Dann?"

He frowned. "I think I do. A little."

"You cried when you had to say goodbye to Mishkita."

And now he sighed, and looked long and hard at her. He was trying to remember? He didn't want to remember? He did not like it, her trying to make him remember?

It was painful for Mara: her body, her arms—her arms particularly—knew how they had sheltered Dann, how he had clung and hugged her, but now he seemed to remember nothing at all. Yet those memories were the strongest she had, and looking after Dann had been the first and most important thing in her life. It was as if all that early time together had become nothing.

But she thought, If I did let my arms reach out now it wouldn't be Dann, but only this strange young man with the dangerous thing between his legs. I could not just hug him or kiss him now.

Then just as the sense of herself, Mara, was fading away, and she was feeling like a shadow or a little ghost, he said unexpectedly, "You sang to me. You used to sing to me when I went to sleep." And he smiled. It was the sweetest smile—not a jeer, or a sneer—and yet what she felt was, the smile was for the songs, and not for her, who had sung them to him.

"I looked after you," she said.

He really was trying to remember, she could see. "We'll tell each other things," he said, "but now we should go."

"Where?"

"Well, we can't stay here."

She was thinking, But I've been here, and Daima too . . . She wanted to give him something good out of those long years and said, "Up in those hills there are the old cities. You never really saw them. I could show you, when the fire has died out."

"There are old ruins everywhere. You'll see."

Mara and Dann stood on either side of the tall stack of rocks that was a table and looked at each other as strangers do who want to please each other, but thinking, I can't read that face . . . that look . . . those eyes. And both sighed, at the same moment.

Dann turned away from the strain of it. He began looking around the room, with sharp, clever eyes: he was planning, Mara could see. What was going into those plans she could not even guess at. For she had been here, all this time, knowing nothing but this village, while he . . .

"Water, first," he said. He took two of the cans that had the wooden handles set across the tops, put loops of rope into the handles, tested the loops, slung the cans on a thick stick. Then he took them inside to the cistern. He did not have to tell her why: the mud in that water would have had time to settle.

He brought the cans back. "A pity we can't take all the cans."

"Don't they have them—where we are going?"

"Hardly any. Not of this metal. All these would keep us fed for a year. But never mind. Now, food." He put on the table a leather bag and showed her the flour in it. Enough for a few pieces of bread. Mara brought ten yellow roots from next door and a bag of the white flour traders had once brought.

"Is that all we've got?"

"That's all."

"Get some of these things." He indicated Mara's brown garment.

She grimaced, but went into the storeroom and fetched back an armful.

"We can get food for these," he said. He bundled them, three and three.

She went back in, and fetched some of the delicate old garments from the chest full of them, and spread them out. He picked up one, frowning: his hands were unused to such fragile cloth.

"Better leave these," he said. "If people see them they'll think we're . . . we're . . ."

"What? But we are. We wore these, at home. I don't want to leave them."

"You can't take them all."

"I'll take these two." The soft folds, pale rose, and yellow, lay glowing on the dark rock.

"Perhaps someone'll pay for them. Or give us something."

Now they set two sacks side by side on the floor and began packing. First, into hers, went a roll of the torn-up material that she used for the blood flow. She was embarrassed and tried to hurry and hide what she was doing, but he saw and nodded. This comforted her, that he understood what a problem it was for her. She put in next the two delicate dresses, rolled up. Then the three brown ones. Then five yellow roots and her little bag of flour. Into his went, on top of an old cloth that had in it an axe, five roots, his bag of flour, three of the brown tunics. "Let's go," he said.

"Wait." Mara went to Daima, stroked the old cheek, which was chilling fast, and stopped herself crying, because tears wasted water. She thought, Daima will lie here and go as dry as a stick, like Rabat, or the scorpions will push the thatch aside and come in. It doesn't matter. But isn't that strange? I've spent every minute of my time worrying about Daima—what can I give her to eat, to drink, is she ill, is she comfortable?—and now I say, Let the scorpions eat her.

"Have we got candles?"

She indicated the big floor candles. Among them was one half-burned. Forgetting what it concealed, Daima had set it alight one evening, and it was only when an acrid smell of burning leather reminded them that they put out the flame. Now Mara took up the stump, turned it upside down, dug out the plug at the bottom and pulled out the little bag. She spilled on to the old rough rock a shower of bright, clean, softly gleaming gold coins. Dann picked one up, turned it about, bit it gently.

She could have cried, seeing those pretty, fresh, gold rounds, dropped in there from another world, like the coloured robes—nothing to do with this grim, dusty, rocky, cruel place.

"I don't think anyone would want these," said Dann. "I don't think anyone uses them now." Then he thought and said, "But perhaps that's because I've just been . . . I've been with the poor people, Mara. This is what I've been using."

He took from the inside pocket of his slave's garment a dirty little bag and spilled out on to the rock surface beside the scatter of gold some coins made of a light, dull greyish metal. Mara picked up a handful. They were of no weight at all, and greasy.

"This is the same metal as the old pots and the cans."

"Yes. They're old. Hundreds of years." He showed her a mark on one of them. "That means five." He counted on his fingers. "Five. Who knows what five meant then? Now they're worth just what we say."

"How many of them to one of the gold pieces?"

And now he laughed, finding it really funny. "So much . . ." He spread his arms. "No, enough to fill this whole room . . . Leave them. They'll get us into trouble."

"No. Our parents . . . our family, the People, sent them to us. To Daima." She scooped them up, counting into the little bag, which was stiff with the candle wax, the pretty, bright little discs of gold, each the size of Dann's big thumbnail, twice as thick and surprisingly heavy. Fifty of them.

"Fifty," she said; and he said, "But keep them hidden."

And that was how they could have left behind the coins that would save their lives over and over again.

Because of this little fluster and flurry over the gold, which really did seem to steal their minds away, they forgot important things. Matches— that was the worst. Salt. They could easily have chopped a piece off the bottom of a floor candle, but they didn't think of that until too late. Mara did just remember to take up a digging stick, as they went out, which she had used for years and was as sharp as a big thorn.

What they were both thinking as they left, slinging the carrying pole between them: We have the most important thing, water.

4

The two stood at the door and looked into the glare and the heat and the dust. Black flecks were floating about. Red flames could be seen beyond the hills. The wind was coming this way. As they thought this, a spurt of flame appeared at the top of the nearest hill and at once ran up a dead white tree and clung there, sending up flares of sparks.

"If the wind doesn't change the fire'll be here in an hour," said Dann.

"It can't get inside the rock houses."

"The thatch will burn over Daima," said Dann.

Well, thought Mara, haven't I just decided it doesn't matter what happens to dead people? She felt sad, nevertheless, and angry with herself. She thought, If you're going to feel sad every time someone dies or goes away, then that is all you'll ever do . . . But she was wiping the tears away. Dann saw and said nicely, sorry for her, "We'd better go if we don't want to be roasted too." A thin line of flames, almost invisible in the sunlight, was creeping towards them in the low, dry, pale grass.

They walked, then ran, though Mara was pleased she had the stick to hold on to, through the rock houses, up the first ridge, down past the already half-empty waterholes, each one clustered with spiders and scorpions and beetles—some dead, some alive—up the next ridge and down to the stream, which was running so low that it was only a string of waterholes with wet places between each.

Dann set down his can, told Mara to do the same, and caught two frogs, killed them with his knife, which he took from under his tunic, and skinned them—all in a moment. She had never seen anything so quick and so skilful. He gave her some pink meat to eat. She had not eaten meat, or could not remember doing so. She watched him chewing up pink shreds and felt her stomach heave, and he said, "If you don't, you'll starve."

She forced the meat into her mouth and made herself chew. This hurt, because it was tough and her teeth were loose from starvation. But she did chew, and swallowed, and it stayed down. And now, for the first time in so long she could hardly remember, she needed to empty her bowels. She went off a little way into the grass, squatted, and the stuff poured out. Last time there had only been pellets, like Mishka and Mishkita's black, round pellets. She was losing water to the earth. This was how people began the drought sickness, wet shit pouring from their backsides.

"Perhaps I have the drought sickness," she shouted to Dann from her place behind tall grasses; but he shouted back, "No, you aren't used to enough water."

He made her kneel by one of the holes and drink, and drink again. Then he drank. They stayed there, side by side, feet in the water, their flesh soaking up wet. She was feeling her hair with both hands, wishing it away, knowing that if she put it into water the stiff, greasy clumps would not change. He watched. Suddenly he took his knife, said, "Bend your head." While she was thinking, Oh, he's going to kill me, she felt the knife blade sliding over the bones of her skull and saw the horrible lumps falling into the sand. She kept quite still for fear of being cut, but he was skilful and there wasn't a scratch. "Look at yourself," she heard, and bent close over the water and saw that her head was as smooth and as shiny as a bone or a nut; and she began to cry and said, "Oh thank you, thank you."

"Thank you, thank you," he mocked her gruffly, and she saw that thank-yous had not been part of his life.

She thought that her face, all bones, all hollows, made her smooth head look like a skull, and she again drank, wishing the water to fill out her face, her flesh.

"We'd better get a move on," he said.

The sky behind them, where the village was, was black with smoke, and greasy burnt bits were falling everywhere around them.

She was thinking, I can't move, I can't. Running here from the village, up and down the ridges, had worn her out. Her legs were trembling. She was thinking, Perhaps he'll just go off and leave me if I can't keep up. He had gone off with those two men, hadn't he?—without a thought for her, or for Daima?

"What happened to those two men you went away with?"

He frowned. "I don't know." Then his whole body seemed to shrink and shiver. She could see little Dann, whom she had held trembling against her. "They were . . . they beat me . . . they . . ." Dann could have sobbed, or cried out, she could see.

"How did you get away from them?"

"They tied me to one of them with a rope. I couldn't keep up with them. Sometimes I dragged behind them on the earth. One night I chewed through the rope. It took a long time." Then he added, "Perhaps it wasn't so long. It seemed long. I was just a child. And then I was starving. I came to a house and a woman took me in. She hid me when the men came to look for me. I stayed there—I don't know how long."

"And then?"

She could see he would not answer much more—not now, at least. "I travelled north with some people. We came to a town that was still—it had people in it, it had food and water. And then there was a war again. I would have been a soldier, so I ran away again . . ." And he stopped. "I will tell you, Mara. I want to know about you, too. But come on, we must go, quick."

Again she was pleased that she had the stick between them, shoulder to shoulder, to steady her. They walked along the big watercourse, not close to the water, where the bones were heaped up, but halfway up the ridge. From there they could see the big flames leaping and climbing and dancing all over the hills where the big cities were. Well, those hills must have burned before, and often, and still the old walls stood.

"While you were travelling," she addressed Dann's back, "did you find out about . . ." But she hardly knew what she wanted to ask, since there was so much she needed to know. "Has there been this kind of drought before? Or is it only here?"

"I'll tell you," he said, "but let's keep quiet now. We don't know who might be around."

"There's no one. Everyone's left, or they're dead."

"There are people on the move everywhere, looking for water or for something better. Sometimes I think that all the people alive are on their feet walking somewhere."

It was mid-afternoon, the hottest time, the sun beating down and the earth burning their feet. Mara's naked head ached and throbbed as she walked with her free arm across it. The air was full of dust and of smoke. The sky was a yellowish swirl with dark smoke full of black bits pouring across it, and the sun was only a lighter place in the smoke. She wanted to lie down, sit down; she wanted to find a rock and creep under it . . .

"We must keep moving, Mara. Look back." She screwed up her eyes to look where they had come and saw that smoke was rising from where the village was, and farther on too—the flames were racing to the watercourse, and soon would cross that, in a jump, and reach the one they were walking along. Would those piles of bones burn, putting an end to memories of so many animals? Dann saw how she held her arms across her pate, and found a bit of cloth in his sack and gave it to her to drape across her head and make a bit of shade. She saw that sweat poured off him everywhere, felt it running down her too. She was afraid that the water she felt running down her legs was wet shit. She quickly looked, but no, it was sweat. She was afraid because of losing all that water, and went to a waterhole to drink, with him. They drank and drank, both thinking that they must while it was there. Then he said, "Come on: if the wind changes, the fire'll catch up with us."

She was so glad of her end of the pole: otherwise she would be staggering and falling. She was walking in a kind of half-sleep, or trance, and wondered that Dann could still move so lightly, that he was so alert, turning his head all the time, this way, that way, for danger. They went on, and on, their shadows at first small under them, but then black and long on the flat places between rocks, but jumping and changing when they went through rocks. She felt she must fall, but knew they had to go on. Every time she turned her head she could see how the smoke clouds were darkening and how they hung well beyond this second watercourse: the flames must be into the plain beyond the rivers. Where she had never been. Stumbling there in her half-sleep, burning up because the sweat had run itself dry, she thought, What a little life I've been leading. I wasn't curious enough even to cross over the rivers to the western plain . . . And there it was again, a word in her mind and she had no idea where it had come from: west, western. Like north, which everyone used. What was North, where was it?

Just when she thought she could no longer move one foot before the other, they were walking on burnt earth. The fire or another recent one had come here. The low, black grasses still kept their shape, as if they had grown out of the earth black and so fragile they crumbled into bits at a touch, and would blow away at the first strong wind. An old log burned, a red glow deep in grey ash.

"We'll be all right now," he said. They were still on the ridge with the watercourse down on their left, big pools from the flood. He lifted the pole off her shoulder, and went leaping down, and she followed, carefully holding herself upright. Just like farther down there were bones here, old bones and new ones, and the insects clustered and clotted on them and on the dead trees. Dann had flung off his garment and was in a pool like a big rock basin. She slowly took off her slippery skin and joined him. They drank and splashed water over their heads and shoulders and lay in the water, their heads resting on the edge. From there they stared straight up into a sky full of smoke and, turning their heads, saw columns and towers of smoke—probably the dead trees by the waterholes.

The fire would kill the scorpions and the singing insects and the new frogs. It would make the water in the holes steam and sink quickly down into the mud, which would soon be dry and cracked. It would burn the smaller bones. And the earth insects, which had to have grass to live? When the fire had passed over the plains, burning up everything, even the earth in some places, would the grass grow again? If not, the insect cities would die, their towers would stand dead and empty, and then . . . there would be just dry earth everywhere, and the dust clouds would blow about and slowly the Rock Village would be filled with dust and sand.

"Come on," Dann said, as he leaped out and pulled on his white garment. Oh no, she was thinking, I can't go on; but he had not meant that: he was looking for a safe place for them to spend the night. She climbed out of the water, put on her tunic that was like a snakeskin, and helped him search among the rocks. He was looking for a place that was hidden, but high enough for them to look down and around from. And there it was: a flattish rock on the top of a little hill, with still unburnt bushes and grass around it. There was something that looked like a barricade or a wall of small stones: yes, this was a wall, joining bigger boulders, and it had been made for defence. People before them had thought this place a good one. When she looked she could see the little rough walls here and there, some of them tumbling down. Quite a long time ago then, not recently, this hilltop had been fought over by—well, who?

The yellow glow in the sky that was the sun behind smoke and dust was lower now, but it was very hot, and the flat rock pumped out waves of heat. Mara took some of her white flour, mixed it with water and made cakes which she laid on the rock. Meanwhile Dann was moving away stones from where they could sit, their backs to a big boulder.

He sat with his legs stretched out, and she by him, thinking, Now perhaps he'll talk, he'll tell me ... And then she was asleep, and woke to see that the whole sky seemed on fire, the clouds and billows of smoke full of light, and rays shooting right up towards the sinking sun. Dann was looking at her. She thought, I'm so ugly. He must think I'm like a monkey—but he has never seen a monkey I expect. But where did I see them? Oh yes, it was home, there were monkeys in a big cage. I know what I look like, and my head ... She was so hungry. The flour cakes she had put on the rock?—he had eaten some. She would have gone to get herself some but she felt she could not move. His gaze did not leave her face. He was examining her, as Daima had looked at her before she died, as if her face—Mara's—held some truth or secret. Oh, she was so hungry. As she looked at the cakes, wanting them, Dann leaped up and fetched them, putting them carefully into her hand. And then he watched her eat them, slowly, a bit at a time, as she had learned to eat, food being so short, every crumb, every tiny bit held in the mouth to get all the goodness from it. Besides, her teeth hurt.

She did not feel uncomfortable that he was watching her. She was happy he was there, but she did not understand him. Nothing he did was what she expected, nor much of what he said.

She said to him, "If you hadn't come then I would be dead."

"Yes."

"I was dying and didn't know it."

"Yes."

"And when that fire started I think I would have decided to stay with Daima and let it burn me."

He said nothing, only gazed at her face, and her eyes.

"There would have been no reason for me to leave. Nowhere to go. And I was too weak anyway."

He said, carefully—and it was because he didn't want to offend her—"Didn't you ever go anywhere else? Only the Rock Village?"

"Only out to find the roots—and there were seeds, too."

He put his knuckles to the earth and leaped up, and stood staring away down the side of the hill. She knew it was because he did not want her to see his face. He was shocked because she had not made any effort to go anywhere else. But you didn't know how it was, how difficult, she wanted to say to him. But she was ashamed. She had lived all that time, knowing nothing—*nothing*. While he . . .

He was taking from his sack one of the yellow roots. He cut it and gave her half, sat by her, looked over to where the sun was going down, a red, burning place among the dark clouds.

"When you went off with the two men did you come this way?"

He shook his head. A long silence now. A real silence. Long ago, at this hour, the sun going, there had been all kinds of animal noises, bird sounds, and the singing insects were so loud they split the ears. Now, nothing.

"Where are we going?"

"North."

"Why?"

"It's better there."

"How do you know?"

"People say."

"Have they been there?"

"The farther south, the worse. The farther north, the better. There's water up there. It still rains there. There is a big desert, they say, and it is drying everything around its edges, but you can go around it."

"There is going to be a desert here."

"Yes."

"We use words like south and north and east and west, but why do we? Where do they come from?"

He said with a laughing sneer, as if he had suddenly become another person, "The Rock People are just stupid. Stupid rock rabbits."

"All these words come from somewhere. I think from the Mahondis."

He jeered again, "The Mahondis! You don't understand. They aren't anything—we aren't. There were people once—they knew everything. They knew about the stars. They knew . . . they could talk to each other through the air, miles away . . ." His mood was changing: he seemed to be wanting to laugh, but properly, then giggle . . . "From here to the Rock Village. From here to—up north. To the end of North."

And now she found herself giggling too.

"You're laughing," he said, laughing. "But it's true. And they had machines that could carry a hundred people at a time . . ."

"But we had sky skimmers."

"But these could go on flying without coming down for days . . ."

And suddenly they were laughing aloud, for the ridiculousness.

"And they had machines so big that—bigger than the Rock Village."

"Who told you all this?"

"People who know what's up North. There are places there where you can find out about the old people—the ones that lived long ago. And I've seen pictures."

"The pictures on the old walls?"

"No, in books."

"When we were little there were books."

"Not just paintings on leather and leaves. They used to have books made of . . . It's a very thin, fine stuff, white, and there can be a hundred pages in a book. I saw some pages from an old book . . . they were crumbling . . ." His mood changed again. He said furiously, "Mara, if you only knew . . . We think the Rock People are just—rabbits. But those people, the ones that lived long ago—compared to them we are beetles."

Now the dark was coming up through the rocks. He said, "I'm going to sleep. But you must stay awake. Do you know how to? When you get sleepy, then wake me. Don't wake me suddenly or I'll hit you. I'll think you're an enemy—do you see? You slept a bit earlier." And there and then he lay down on the rock and was asleep.

And now it was really dark. There was no moonlight: the moon was almost full, but the sky was too full of smoke and dust to see it, or the stars. Mara sat with her back against a rock and her head whirled with everything she had been hearing. She wanted to cry, and would have cried, but stopped herself, thinking, Bad enough to lose all that water in sweat, but I can stop myself crying. She thought of her life all these years with Daima, who told her tales, full of all kinds of things the little girl had thought were made up—just stories—but now Mara was wondering if Daima's tales were true after all. But mostly they had played What Did You See? And what *had* Mara seen! The inside of a neighbour's rock house. The details of the scaly skin of a land lizard. A dead tree. "What did you see, Mara?" "The branches stick up like old bones. The bark has gone. The wood is splitting. In every crack insects are living." But they aren't now: the flames have killed them, every one. "The birds come and sit in the dead trees and go off, disappointed. There are birds' skeletons in the trees. When the skeletons fall to the ground you can see they are like us. They have legs and feet and their wings are like

arms." "And what else did you see, Mara?" "The dead wood of the different trees is different, sometimes light and spongy and sometimes so
heavy and hard I can't push my thumbnail into it." "And what else,
Mara?" "There are the roots deep in the ground that I dig up." And that
was what she had seen, all those years. The village. The Rock People.
The animals, always fewer and then gone. The lizards and dragons—but
they had gone too. Mishka, darling Mishka, who had licked her face
clean, and then Mishkita. And the earth insects . . . insects, scorpions,
insects, always more of them . . . Well, even the scorpions would have
been burned up by now, probably.

And that was all. She had not gone farther than the dead cities in
the hills. "What did you see, Mara?" "I saw pictures of people, but they
were not like us, but a different brown, with differently shaped bodies,
painted eyes, rings on their hands and in their ears. I saw . . ." Perhaps
those were the people that Dann said had been so clever that they knew
everything?

Mara was staying awake easily because of her sad and ashamed
thoughts. Then she wanted to pee and was afraid to move and wake
Dann. She crawled away, trying not to make a sound, and squatted
paces away. There was a lot of pee now, and her pee place was no longer
sore. Her body was not burning and aching and itching and crying out
for water. When she crawled back she saw Dann's eyes were open,
watchful gleams in the dark.

"Did you hear something?" he asked.

"No."

His eyes closed and he was instantly asleep. A little later he rolled
towards Mara, and was hugging her. "Mara, Mara," he said, in a thick
voice, but it was childish, a little boy's voice. He was asleep. He snuggled up to her and she held him, her heart beating, for she was holding
her little brother; but at the same time he was dangerous, and she could
feel his tube thick and hot on her thigh. Then his arms fell away. He
was sucking his thumb, suck, suck. Then silence. He rolled away. She
could never tell him that he had sucked his thumb. He would probably
kill her, she thought. Then was surprised at the thought, which had
come so easily.

Before Dann fell asleep, while he watched his sister, he had been
thinking, Why am I here? Why did I come for her? She's such a poor,
sick, feeble thing. But all he knew was that ever since he had heard from
travellers that there were people alive in the old village, he had had to

come. He did not know why, but he was restless, he was unhappy, he could not sleep. He had to look for her. She was mistaken, thinking he had not seen monkeys. He had, in cages—and people too, in cages. He thought she looked like a little monkey, with big, sad eyes and a naked head. But she was already fattening a little. She was no longer just a skeleton with a bit of skin over the bones and enormous dry, hungry eyes. And that was in only two days. At the waterhole he had seen something he first thought was an animal, with its long claws and filthy mats of hair on its head; but now he knew her again, for certain looks of hers, and movements, and memories, were coming back. They were all of warm arms and a soft voice, of shelter and comfort and safety. He was trying to match what he saw: the little, spindly creature, all bones, with the memories his limbs and body held, of soft, big, kind arms, everything big and soft and warm.

When the light began, Mara saw that all over her were bits of the black, greasy stuff from the fire. So the wind had shifted. She said, "Dann," and he was at once on his feet and looking at the black bits on him. The fire had burned to the edge of the older fire, and gone out. There was smoke everywhere, but it was thinner ahead, where they were going. He took up the water cans, and put the pole on his shoulder, and went bounding off down towards the nearest waterhole; and then he shouted to her and she went to the edge of the little hill, the rock already hot under her feet, and saw him point down. The black from the fires seemed to have over it greyish-yellowish streams, like liquid: earth insects, like a flood, going down to the watercourse. But that was not their destination: the streams were already on their way up the farther ridge. "Quick," he said, and bounded down, though keeping a distance between him and them; and she followed, shivering now not with weakness but with fear, and plunged after Dann into the biggest waterhole. There they washed the black smears off them, and filled the cans right up, and drank and drank, always watching the earth insects; but saw that the mass was spreading out sideways, towards their waterhole. She wanted to scramble out but he held her, and then, as the insects fell over into the water, he grabbed them with his quick fingers, pulling off their heads and cramming the still squirming bodies into his mouth. He ate several, then saw her face and stopped to think what to do. She was not far off fainting with horror. Along the edge of the water now was a fringe of drowning insects. He stepped through the water to the bank, reached for his big sack, took from it a smaller one, filled it with drowned insects, and then nodded at her to get out of the water. She was afraid, for the insects seemed to be everywhere. But he stepped up and out, carefully, putting his feet between the trickles of insects which, if they had a mind to, could eat him and her to bones in a moment. But no, the insects were going as fast as they could through the waterholes to make new cities for themselves in a part that had not been burned. Yet there was nothing to be seen but the black of the fire, so they would have a long way to go, carrying everything they had: bits of food from their underground farms—which, Mara could see, seemed dry and shrivelled instead of plump and fresh—their babies, and their big mothers, each the size of Mara's hand, white and fat, and who even as they were being carried along were laying eggs that fell from them like maggots and were gathered up by the insects and carried in their mouths. This was a people moving from one home to another, as the Rock People moved into an empty house if they liked it better than their own. Mara watched Dann step carefully among the insects, who were now more like a flood, a flash flood, when it seemed as if the earth itself was on the move; and she went after him afraid she would set her feet down on them because of her faintness. But soon they were through the insects and going along the ridge again, above the watercourse where the holes were already only half what they were yesterday. Looking back they could see more and more of the insects coming; soon there would be none left in the tall earth towers that were like cities. Up the two went to the place between the rocks, and Dann put the drowned insects on the hot rock, and in a few moments they had lost their juicy, glistening look and were like little sacks of skin. And now Dann gave Mara one of them, looking hard at her, and she put it in her mouth. It tasted on her tongue acid, and pulpy; she pretended it was a bit of fruit. Dann handed her another and another, and she ate them, until she was full. Then off he jumped down back to the swarm, and she saw him scooping the insects out of the rivers of them, putting them into the bag, and in a moment was back, and as he took each one out of the bag he nipped off its head. The insects were hissing and fighting inside the little bag. His hands had been bitten, they were red and swollen. But he went on, beheading them and laying them out on the rock, which was by now almost too hot to touch. He ate them as they cooked, and handed her one after another, and she knew that he was measuring that bony little body of hers with his eyes and thinking, She's fatter, she's better. "Eat, Mara. Eat, you must," he commanded.

By then it was mid-morning. Again they were going to travel through the hottest part of the day. They went parallel to the watercourse. There was no shelter, only rocks and dead trees, their branches reaching up like bones. The fires were behind: ahead the sky was full of dust but not of smoke. Mara longed to give up for the day, go down into the water and lie there, because it was sinking so fast that some of the waterholes were already only mud.

She was walking with her eyes kept lowered because of the glare, holding tight to the pole where the water cans hung. Then Dann said, "Look ahead, Mara," and she did try to unscrew her eyes to see that ahead the ridge went sharply up and into a high country, and down it fell a trickle of water, which was all that was left of the flood of four days ago. But the fall of water was between sharp rocks, and she knew she could never climb there to drink. "We'll stop soon," he said. She thought that he sounded as she must have done, talking to him when he was a child. He was coaxing her on. "It's better up there, over the escarpment. You'll see. Tonight we'll stay halfway up and tomorrow we'll be up."

In the late afternoon they made their way down to the water, which here was not waterholes, had been a really big river, and still flowed slowly from the fall, before it ran farther and became sand and rocks and the sparse, drying holes. Bones everywhere. Big, branching, white bones and, among them, horns and tusks. As they walked to the water's edge they had to step in the spaces between bones: ribs, and skulls and teeth and little bones that the sun was crumbling into chalky white earth.

She was afraid there might be stingers or even a water dragon still alive and so, evidently, was he. He stood by the side of the shallow stream and poked everywhere into it with the carrying pole, but there was no creature in it, nothing broke the surface. This water was flowing only because of the flood, and the stream had been dry so long nothing had lived, not even a frog or toad. Again they bathed and splashed and drank and filled the cans, and went up among rocks high above the ridge, some distance from the fall, which was whispering its way down—though once that waterfall had been half a mile wide, for where they stopped for the night the stains of water were on the rocks around them, and were so smooth from old water they had to be careful not to slip on them. The light had not yet gone. They sat looking down over where they had come, and saw how the fires were raging away, but going south, away from them. She could not see the village, though it could not be very far—they had been walking slowly because of her weakness. It was all blackened country, and smoke was rising in places from a slow-burning log, or from a pile of bones. She tried to see the hills near the village where the old cities were but they were only a faint blue line away in the smoke. The wind had changed again: no black smuts were falling on them.

She mixed flour with water and again cooked cakes on the rocks. Then they ate another root. Very little flour left now, and eight yellow roots.

"Up on the top there's more food," he said. And he took out his little bag of greyish coins and laid them out and counted them. "We won't be able to buy much with that," he said. And then he stayed, squatting, brooding over the coins, resting lightly on his knuckles, his other hand stirring the coins around. "I've been thinking, Mara. It's that gold. The trouble is, how are we going to change those coins? Let's have a look at them." She brought out her bag of gold coins and spread them out on the rock.

"You know, I've never heard about these except as a sort of joke. 'As good as gold.' 'More precious than gold.' 'It's a gold mine.' But the more I think about it, I remember that it is used. But only by the rich people and that's why I didn't think at first . . ." He sat stirring his fingers now in the gold coins. "They'd kill us if they knew we had these," he said.

"If we can't change them, then how are we going to eat?"

"I didn't say we couldn't." He sat, frowning, thinking.

The little coins lay shining there, and when she touched one it was already hot from the rock.

"With one of these you could buy a big house," he said.

"Oh Dann, let's buy a house and live in it—somewhere where's water all the time."

"You don't understand, Mara."

Well, she knew she didn't, and she felt she must have heard this many times already: *You don't understand.* "Then begin telling me," she said.

They were crouching face to face, coins, the gold ones and ugly, thin, grey ones, on a big stone between them, and even up here on a dried up hillside that seemed quite deserted, he lowered his voice.

He took up a big stick and began drawing in the dust between stones. He drew a big shape, longer than wide, and on one side it bulged right out, so that it was like a fat-stemmed throwing stick.

"That's the world," he said. "It is all earth, with sea around it."

"The world" floated up easily into Mara's mind from long-ago lessons with her parents. "The world is bigger than that," she said. "The world has a lot of pieces of land with water between them."

He leaned forward, peering into her face. He seemed frightened. "How do you know? Who told you? We are not supposed to know anything."

"We were taught all that. I was, but you were too little. Our parents told us."

"But how did they know? Who told them? *They* don't tell us anything. They want us to think that what we have is all there is. Like rock rabbits thinking their little hill is everything." The sneer was back in his voice.

"It's this shape you've drawn. I remember it. It is called Ifrik. And it is the piece of earth we live on. Where are we on it?—that's what I'd like to know."

He pointed in the middle, well below the bulging out bit.

"And how far away is Rustam from here?"

He pointed a little distance down, and then put two fingers, almost together, one where he said they were and one where Rustam was.

She felt that she had really become as small and as unimportant as a beetle. In her mind the journey from Rustam was a long one, a change from one kind of life to a completely different one; and now all that had become—because of those two fingers of his, held with a tiny space between them—nothing very much, and she was nothing much too.

But she held herself steady and said, "I remember they said that Ifrik was very big. And where are we going tomorrow?"

"Tomorrow and the next day and the next . . ." He held his fingers the same tiny distance apart, but now on the opposite side of where he had said they were.

"And that is north?"

"It is north. But the real North is . . ." And, excited, he pointed to the very top of the space or shape he had drawn.

"If it has taken us so long to come such a little way then how long to get North?"

"Why long? It's been two days."

"But . . ." she was thinking of that journey by night away from Rustam and knew that he wasn't. And probably couldn't.

"From here, going north, it will get better."

"And if we were going south, instead, it would be worse?"

"Worse, until we got to the very bottom, here . . ." and he pointed to the bottom of Ifrik. "There are high mountains, and then there is water and green."

"So why aren't we going south?"

"We'd die trying to get there. Besides, when everything started to dry up and the deserts began, then a lot of the people travelled south, crowds of people, like those earth insects today; everyone went down and down and then through the mountains. But the people there didn't want them, there wasn't enough water and food for everyone. There was a war. And all the people from the high, dry lands were killed—because they were weakened by the travelling."

"All killed?"

"So they say."

"And when was this?"

"Before we were born. When the rains began to stop, and there was no food, and the wars began."

"Daima ran away from a war. That was a long time before we were born."

There was a silence then, with the sun going down in its dusty red, the shadows dark and warm between the rocks, the little tinkling of the waterfall.

"I don't see how we are going to stay alive," she said.

"I've stayed alive, haven't I? I know how to. You'll see. But we have to be careful all the time." He looked again at the gold coins, thinking. Then he said, "Give me two of those strips of cloth you have."

She fished them out of the bottom of her bag, wondering, sadly, And when am I going to need these again? He was watching her, and she thought, He knows what I am thinking: he's kind.

He divided the coins into two heaps of twenty-five and tied them, one by one, into the strips of cloth, with a little knot between each. So they wouldn't clink—she understood; and began to help him. There were soon two knotted cords of twisted cloth lying on the rocks.

"See if you can tie one around you—high up, above your waist."

She lifted her tunic and tied one of the cords where he had pointed. The trouble was she had no breasts at all, she was flat. When she showed him, she was ashamed, because across her chest under the flimsy brown the knots of the cord were visible, taller than her little nipples.

The tears splashed off her face on to the stones.

He smiled, and put his hand out, taking a little pinch of flesh where her neck was bare above the tunic. "Poor Mara," he said, gently. "But you'll be a girl again soon, I promise you." And he rocked her a little with his hand, while she smiled and made herself stop crying. "All right, take it off." She slipped the cord down under her tunic and gave it to him.

"We'll get you something to wear that's thicker and then no one will see what you've got under it."

"I wish I could have something different, soon." And she took up handfuls of the stuff of the tunic, letting them spring back into shape, trying to crush it, destroy it. "I do hate it, Dann. I wish I could wear the same as you've got on."

He said nothing and his face changed: he was angry.

"I know it is a slave's dress," she said. "Our slaves used to wear them."

"I don't remember." But he was remembering something bad.

"Anything would be better than this," she insisted, and then he smiled at last.

Now it was dusk, the material of her tunic was not brown but a soft, glistening black.

"It's such funny stuff," he said, fingering it and hating it. "It changes colour. Sometimes in the strong sun I think it's white, and then it's brown again."

"Where can I get one like yours?"

"We'll have to buy one. And we don't have enough of the little coins. So we'll have to wait until we can change a gold one." He dropped one of the strings of twenty-five coins into his sack, and one into hers. "And now you sleep and I'll stay awake."

Mara lay down between the stones, her head on her hand, and was at once asleep, and woke to know Dann was not there beside her. Then she felt his hand over her mouth and heard his whisper, "Quiet, there are people." Feet moved among stones just below them, closer to the waterfall than they were. Clumsy feet: stones slipped and bounded down off the rocks. The light was in the sky again. The two peered over the edge of a rock and saw a man and a woman clambering down, who stopped, consulted, lay down where they were and slept. "Very tired," Mara breathed. Then she watched Dann creep down towards the travellers. He was among boulders, and in the dim light could be thought of as a boulder, for he stopped to wait, crept on, stopped . . . She saw him stoop down near the two sleeping bodies and was back with her at once, with a bag in his hand. They emptied it on the ground. Not much in it, only a little dried fruit and some pieces of flat bread. Dann at once divided the fruit and began eating his share. She thought that the two travellers had come from beyond the Rock Village somewhere, and down there was no food at all. "They'll be hungry," she whispered, and saw Dann lean forward to stare into her face. When he did that, he was trying to work out what she was feeling, and what she was expecting him to feel. Then he whispered into her ear, "Eat, Mara. If you want us to stay alive, then we have to use our wits." She ate. The pieces of bread went into her sack.

Dann slung the cans back on the pole, careful they didn't clink, and pushed the stolen bag deep into his sack. She slid her end of the pole on to her shoulder, and together they moved on up the sharp ridge, full of rocks. By the time they reached the top the sun was up and they looked back from this higher place at the black from the fires, the smoking logs here and there, and far away the fires themselves, burning slowly down into the south. Between where they were and the fires, nothing green was left, only grey rocks and stones here and there in the black. They went on up and over the escarpment and along the river that was falling behind them in the trickle she had seen from the plain. Mara was walking well, was keeping up easily with Dann. She was sure that her limbs were plumping out, with all the water she had been lying in, and drinking. But when she pinched her thigh through the tunic, and then her forearms, there was still only skin there, not flesh. But she was feeling better.

Now, ahead of them, was an enormous basin of land, with mountains all around it. The river came from a small lake. And the story was the same: once there had been water, big water, probably filling the basin right up to the mountains; but now cracked old mud, which was in places dust, spread out from the edges of the little lake. They were walking over hard, dry mud and bones.

In the lake, which was more of a large pool, she could see movement and said, "Are there still water dragons?"

"No. They have died. But there are water stingers."

"Then we daren't go in the water."

"No. When I was coming to you I walked along here. I thought the water was safe. I put a foot in to test it—and I only just got away. It was a big stinger."

Here, on this side of the mountains, the air was cleaner. The sky was yellowish with dust, and low down, and the sun was making thick, regular rays through it, but it was not smoke. Soon they came to a village. The houses were not made of rocks but of big bricks, with roofs of thatch. A fire had been through here, but not recently, for the black had mostly blown away. The thatch had burned: the houses stood roofless. The inhabitants had left. The two went carefully through every house, room by room, and in every room Dann leaped up to see the tops of the walls, for he said people hid things up there and might have forgotten them. A likely story—both were thinking—with everything so scarce. There were jars in every house for water and food, but no rock cisterns. The jars were very big and it was not possible to carry them away. There was no food, not until the very last house, where Dann had to frighten away scorpions clustered around the door, and there they found in a jar some tightly packed down dry leaves. Dann filled one of his smaller bags with them: he said they were nourishing. While they were doing this they heard voices and hid, and peered out to see going past the couple they had robbed up in the hills. These two were a kind of person Mara had never seen, with great bushes of black hair and almost black skin. But they were so thin, and so weak, it was not possible to say whether really they were solid and strong, or wiry.

Dann pulled himself by a door to see all around the top of the wall. Only part of the thatch had burned here. He let out a shout, and reached out, and threw down a thin roll of cloth, which had inside it a garment like Dann's. The cloth was a little scorched but not the robe. Mara took off her old skin-like tunic, which she had worn day and night for years, and was in this robe or dress that was made of a vegetable fibre, a soft, coarse cloth. She was actually crying because of her joy. She was about to throw the old brown garment—though it was as good as new, with not a mark on it, not a tear—away into a corner, goodbye, goodbye, you horrible thing, when Dann caught it up and said, "No, we can sell it." And stuffed it into her sack. Now they had seven of them.

With this new robe, which had been white once but was now a light brown, from dust, she felt she had thrown off her old life and was wearing a new life, though there was another person's smell on it, and she knew that it was stained with that person's sweat. But she could wash this dress and make it hers. And now Dann pulled out of her sack her cord of knotted coins, and she tied it just above her waist, and it could not be seen under the thick material. The cloth the dress had been rolled in would come in useful, for something.

The two went back to the edge of the lake, or pool, and stood looking at it. Mara wished she dared wash her dress there, and let it dry on her. Dann was silent. Mara saw on his face something she had not seen before: it was anger, or pain, or fear—but she could not decipher it. He only stared at the dirty little lake, and at the dried mud, and then over the lake to the mountains. She was afraid to ask, What's wrong?—but he turned his head towards her, and she understood that if he could cry, could sob, could allow weakness, then that is what he would be doing now. It was pain she was looking at. "Why?" he whispered. "Why? I don't understand. It was all water. When I ran away that time, it was water from here all around to the mountains. Why should everything go dry, why does the rain just stop, why?—there must be a reason." And he came stepping across the hard mud ridges and took her by the shoulders and peered deep into her face, as if she must know the reason.

She said, "But those cities, the ones near the Rock Village, they had people in them for thousands of years, Daima said, and now they are just nothing." And as she spoke, she thought that she used the word thousands because Daima did, yet she still did not know more than the ten fingers on her hands, the ten toes on her feet. Long ago she had been taught more than that, in the school at home, but in her mind it was the same as if she said hundreds or thousands, and yes—there was another word—millions. He let his hands fall and said, "We walk over all these bones, all the time." She knew that tears wanted to come into those sharp, clever eyes of his, which were beautiful when he sat thinking, or had just woken; but his mouth was tight. "When I came this way to get you I saw skulls, people's skulls, piles—I couldn't count them." And now his face was so close to hers she could feel the heat from it on her cheeks. And his eyes seemed to press into hers. "Why is it happening, Mara? Why don't we understand anything? No one knows why anything happens."

And then he let her go, turned away, picked up the end of his pole and waited for her to lift hers. "There was a boat," he said. "That was only a week ago." His voice sounded ordinary again. They went on, carefully, well beyond the edge of wet, for in both their minds was the thought that if a water dragon or a lizard had survived it could be up and out of that water to get one of them. The water stingers rattled as they moved, so you could hear them. She was thinking, I say words like day or week, or year, and never think what I am saying, but behind these words are what they are. I know what a day is because the sun shines in it, and then there is dark, and I say night. But why a week, and why a year? She was tormented, haunted, by memories that refused to come properly into her mind: she had been taught these things, she was pretty sure. And now she did not know what a year measured, or why the rain fell or did not fall, or that the stars were . . . Of course she had known about the stars: she remembered her father holding her up to look at them, and saying, "That one there is . . ." But she had forgotten all the names.

They were at a place where once there had been a wooden jetty; but now the wood had rotted and all wood was so scarce that it was of stone that the causeway was made, leading to the water's edge. A boat was coming. Mara had never seen one. It was a fisherman's boat, Dann said, a big one, and a crowd of people were approaching over the dried mud, about twenty of them. Two men had long oars, and stood at the front and at the back of the boat. She and Dann went on with the others. There was a rail around the boat and she held on tight. They were all standing close together, and the smell of the crowd was thick and sour. The boat was low in muddy water. At the last moment a man and a woman came stumbling to the boat. They were the couple who had been robbed last night. It seemed they hadn't found food anywhere else, because they were hardly strong enough to stand. Dann glanced at them indifferently, as he did at the others. Water stingers were watching them, their eyes and pincers sticking up out of the water. Everyone kept and eye on them: a stinger could knock someone in with its tail. Now the boat was in the middle of the little lake, and from down here the mountains seemed high. Yet the ones behind them were where Dann and she had come in a morning.

Mara had not known there could be so many different kinds of people. There was a woman with a thick body like the Rock People, but her hair was a frizzle of bright red. She was with a man who was yellowish brown, a thin, sick man, and his hair was in shags of white, though he wasn't old. There were three that could be Mahondis, tall and thin, but their hair was like the Rock People's, a pale mass. She and Dann were the only Mahondis, but no one seemed to notice them or mind, and this was because, they decided, they both wore the long, loose, once white robes that everyone knew were slaves' or servants' dress. What would Mara and Dann's parents think if they could see their children now? Would they even recognise us?—and Mara tried to remember her mother's face, and her father's, but could not. Their voices—yes, and

they laughed a lot, she was sure. And they smelled: her father had a
warm, spicy smell she had thought was the smell of kindness, and her
mother a teasing, sweet smell ... Meanwhile Mara was standing in a
press of people who smelled of dirty sweat and feet. The water was
muddy. The boat was hardly moving. The boatmen were shouting at
Dann to use his carrying pole to push the boat along. Then they passed
an oar through the crowd to her. They thought she was a boy, being so
thin and bony inside that robe, and with her still bare pate. Only the
men were being given oars and paddles. The sun was scorching down. It
was midday. Over the mud shores the heat waves oiled and shimmered.
As the oars and poles plunged into thick water, bones were disturbed
and appeared for a moment, and sank, and, worse, corpses of beasts
came up, emitting the most fearful stench, and went down, leaving the
air poisonous. But the boat was making progress. Soon they were out of
the lake and into the stream that fed it—a narrow, shallow flow that
had once been a big river—and the boat had to be pushed along with
poles. It was farther to the mountains than it had seemed from where
they embarked, and by the time they reached them it was mid-afternoon.
There was a jetty of rotting wood, and the boatmen ordered everyone
off. Grumbling, the people got on to the shore. The boatmen held out
their hands, and into them were put a fruit, a little bag of flour, a flap of
bread. Mara and Dann offered two yellow roots, which the boatmen
turned over and over, not having seen them before, apparently. To save
argument the two jumped quickly on to the jetty. Mara was beside the
woman they had robbed. She saw the mass of black hair just in front of
her eyes and thought, But that's like the fur of a sick animal. It should
be standing out and strong, but it was limp and dull. The woman was
swaying, she could hardly keep herself up. Mara pulled out from her sack
one of the yellow roots and held it out to her. She was thinking, But
she'll need a knife—when Dann was there, with his knife, and was cutting the root in two. The movement was so quick, and Dann's eyes narrow and sharp—she looked and saw the crowd was pressing in around
them, all eyes on her sack, and on Dann's, and on his knife—which was
why he had been so quick to cut the root in half: he wanted everyone to
see the knife. The woman began sucking at the juice, moaning and crying, and her companion snatched at the other half and chewed at it.
Dann pulled Mara away, and they ran up into the mountain, not stopping until they were among rocks. Mara was thinking that Dann
believed they were going to be killed, because of the sacks, and the

water. And she waited for him to scold her, or say something, but he didn't. And she was thinking, Those two, when Dann was stealing their little bag, if they had woken up and seen him, would he have killed them—all for a little dried fruit and a bit of bread?

Dann said, "You must have a knife. And make sure that everyone sees you have got it."

They climbed to where they could look down on the lake, and the river running in from this end and out the other side, and the great basin of dried mud and dust. The mountains on the other side where they were yesterday stood up high and blue and fresh. "That cloudburst must have been there," she said, "somewhere in those mountains. And the flash flood went down the other way, it didn't come this side. Otherwise that lake would be bigger. And it would be fresh."

"It hasn't rained here for a long time," he said. And the sullen, restless note was in his voice again. And she was thinking, If that cloudburst had happened just a little way this side of those mountains, the flood would have come this way, not down past the Rock Village, and I would be dead now. And Dann said, angrily, "Everything is just chance. It's just luck—who stays alive and who dies." And then, again, "You must have a knife."

They searched until they found a place where they could lie among rocks and look out. Several times they heard people from the boat go past, farther down. "They think the stream goes on and they can follow it," said Dann.

"And it doesn't go on?"

"No."

She wanted to ask, What will they do? And what will we do?—but Dann had dropped off to sleep, just like that. She kept watch until he woke, and then she slept while he kept watch. When the light came they drank water, but he said they should be careful, water was going to be short; and they ate the bread they had stolen, and a yellow root each. Now had practically no food left. The dried leaves were so bitter Mara could not eat them, but Dann said they had to be cooked. There were no matches.

"We'll get some food today," he promised. And he smiled, a stretching of his lips, cracked and a bit swollen from the sun, and he quickly put his hand on her shoulder, but let it drop again, because he had heard a sound from down the hill. The hard, suspicious stare was back on his face, and he sent quick glances all around at the rocks and the dead or dying trees, and when a stone fell clattering down among rocks he was on his feet, his knife in his hand.

Then, silence. He pushed his knife back into the slit in his robe, where there was a long, narrow pocket to hold it, and crouched down over their sacks. He pulled out the bundle of brown tunics, and laid two out on the rocks. One had come off Mara's body yesterday. They stared, for again it had sprung into its own shape and lay fresh, glistening, unmarked, though it had been on her day and night for months. It was repulsive, that unchanging, slippery brown skin, lying there on the rock, with them leaning over it, both so dry and dirty, their skins scaling and flaking dust. "How could they do it, how did they?" he asked, in that voice that meant he could not bear his thoughts. "They made these things . . . and those cans that never break or mark or change. How did they? How, how, *how*?" And began twisting the thing in his hands, trying to make it tear; and he pulled at it to make it split, but it resisted him, lying there whole and perfect on the rock, shining in the sunlight.

He sighed, and she knew what it meant, for she was feeling what he felt through her whole self: here they were, these two hunted and hunting creatures, and in their hands, their property to use as they liked, these amazing and wonderful things that had been made by people like themselves—but they did not know how long ago.

And now he pulled out the knotted cord of coins from the bottom of his sack, and in a moment had untied a coin and pushed the cord back, all the time glancing over his shoulders in case someone was watching. The slim, bright gold circle lay on the old grey rock. They sighed, both of them, at the same time. How long ago had that coin been made? And here it lay: the brightest, freshest, prettiest thing for miles around.

"If we can change even this one coin, then . . ." He put it down the long tube of cloth inside his robe that held the knife. "I'll say you're my brother," he said.

"So what's my name?" she whispered, and her mind was full of that scene where Gorda had told her to forget her name. And she had: she had no idea what it was. She was going farther away from her real name now, when she said, "Maro. Dann and Maro."

They set off downhill, united by the carrying pole where the water cans swung. The trees here were not all dead. Some must have roots down into deep-running water, for they stood strong and green among the tree corpses. There was a bad smell, sweet and disgusting, as they came to where the hill flattened into another plain. That smell . . . She knew it, but not as strong. Dann said, "They made a big grave over there." He pointed. "Hundreds of people."

"Was it the water sickness?"

"No, there was a war."

"What about?"

"Water. Who was to control the water from the spring that makes the stream that feeds the lake we were on."

"Who won?"

"Who cares? It is all drying up anyway."

As they walked away from the hill, the smell lessened and then it had gone.

Dann walked lightly, warily, his eyes always turning this way and that, his head sometimes jerking around so fast because of a sudden noise, or even a gust of wind, that she thought his neck must ache. She tried to walk as he did, his feet seeming to see by themselves where there was thick, soft dust or some rocky ground where they would make no sound. She knew they were nearing a place where people were, and when she saw his eyes she felt she ought to be afraid of him, they were so hard and cold. Ahead was a town, and these houses were bigger than any she had seen, though she seemed to remember her own home had been built high, windows above windows, and these were like that, of brick, but nothing like as graceful and delightful. They were walking along a street between ugly houses. There had been gardens, but in them now were only scorpions and big yellow spiders that coated every dead bush or tree with webs as thick as the material her robe was made of. Some spiders were the size of a child—of Dann, when she first had charge of him. She was afraid, seeing their glittering eyes watching them go past. There seemed to be no people.

"Did they all die in the war?" she asked, in a whisper, afraid the spiders would catch the sound, and a web near them began vibrating and jerking as the spider climbed to see what had made the noise. He nodded, watching the spider. No people, nobody. Then she saw sitting in the open door of a house an old woman, all bones and eyes, staring out at them, and in the path between her and them were clustering scorpions, and she was flicking them away from her with a stick. But as they landed on the earth, they scuttled back to where they had been, their pincers all held out towards her. Quite soon she would not care: she would let that tired old wrist of hers rest, with the stick lying in front of her, and would wait for the scorpions.

"I don't like this place," Mara whispered. "Please, let's go."

"Wait. There's a market here. If it is still here."

They came into an open place of dull, yellowish dust, with some trestle-tables in the middle, and one man guarding them all. Around the edges of this space, along the walls of the houses, were scorpions. On the two dead trees were the spiders' webs, and there was a big dragon, lying out in the sun as once dogs had done.

Her brother was standing in front of the man, staring hard at him, and the handle of his knife was showing: his right hand was held ready near it. On the wooden slats of the trestle were a few of the big roots Mara had not seen for a long time now, bags of dried leaf, a few pieces of flat bread, a bowl of flour, and strips of dried meat. What meat? It did not smell: it was too dry.

Dann took out the brown garment they had examined on the hill that morning, and she saw the man's eyes narrow as he peered at it.

"Haven't seen one of those for a bit," he said. "Have you come from the Rock Village? I didn't know anyone was still alive."

"There isn't now," said Dann. "So this is the last of these you'll be seeing."

"You aren't Rock People," the man said. What he was really saying was, You are Mahondis.

Dann ignored that and asked, "What will you give me for this?" He held tight to one end of the tunic.

The man looked steadily into Dann's face, his teeth bared, and put on the board, one after another in front of Dann, six of the food fruits. He added a bag of dried leaf, but Dann shook his head and the bag was put back beside the other bags. A pile of the flat bread—Dann nodded. And waited. The two men stood glaring at each other. Mara thought they were like two animals about to attack each other. Past the man's shoulder lay the dragon, apparently asleep. It was only a few paces away.

"Water," said Dann.

The man lifted on to the board a jar of yellowish water. Dann slid their two cans off the pole, and was topping them up with water from the jar when the man said, "I'll take those cans." Dann did not respond, went on pouring. "I'll give you these dried fruits for them."

Under the trestle was a sack full of dried fruits. Dann shook his head, put the cans back on the pole, where they swung between him and his sister.

"We need more for this tunic," he said. "Matches?"

The man sneered, then laughed. "I'll give you a bundle of matches for the two cans."

"Forget it," said Dann. "Have you got candles?"

The man produced some stumps of candle. At Dann's nod, he laid them beside the big fruits and the bread.

The two glared at each other again. Mara thought that if it came to a fight Dann would win, because this man was as thin as a sick lizard and his hair had the flattened, lifeless look—pale, fuzzy hair. Starving children's hair sometimes looked like that.

"More bread," said Dann.

The man counted out from his pile one, two, three, four, five, six pieces of bread and pushed them forward.

And to Mara's surprise, Dann let go the end of the garment and the man snatched it up, held it up, gloated. Mara thought, Something I've worn for years and years—it is worth some food fruits, a little water, and some bread. And stumps of candle.

"Have you got another?" asked the man, carefully pushing the garment into a sack and tying it tight.

Dann shook his head. Then—and Mara could feel Dann's trembling, in the stick that lay from shoulder to shoulder—he said, "I want to change a gold fifty."

At this the man's face came to life in an ugly laugh. "Oh you do? And what do you want to buy with that? You can have one of the houses here for a few matches."

"Are you going to change it?"

"Let me see it."

Again the precious, shining gold piece seemed like a message from another time, or place. Dann held tight to one edge while the other stared at it. He sighed. Dann sighed. So did Mara.

The man's eyes were glittering and he was very angry. "You could try your friends up there in that house. Wait till dark. You don't want to be seen."

Dann quickly put the bread, fruit, candles into Mara's sack, and the two went away, as quickly as they could, and as far from the fat dragon as they could.

Dann began peering into the doorways of houses, but from each room came hissing, the sound of scales on dust or stone, the clattering of scorpions. Then there was a room that seemed to have nothing in it. The two went in, and Dann's eyes were moving everywhere: up in the rafters, in the corners, behind the door. Was that a sound above them, in the room over this? There was something up there. Mara was frightened, but Dann took a big stone and jammed the door that led from this room into the rest of the house. He said, "Nothing can get in here." In the middle of the room, their eyes always on the door out into the market place, they squatted and drank water from a can, and ate two pieces of bread each. It was after midday, and the afternoon heat was yellowing the sky. Mara wanted to sleep, but Dann's eyes were restless and suspicious: he was afraid. Several times people went past, stopped to glance in, and then went on. Then Mara did sleep, for she woke to see Dann at the door, watching some scorpions. It was getting dark.

Dann took one of the stumps of candle and fitted it into a hole in the wall. Mara was thinking, But we have no matches, when he pulled from the pocket that held the knife a single long match, and slid it back. "Last one," he said. "We mustn't waste it." She had not known he still had a match. He hides things from me, she thought. Why does he? Doesn't he trust me? Dann saw the look on her face and said, "Suppose someone said to you, 'What does Dann have in his sack?' Well, if you didn't know, you couldn't tell them, could you?" He laughed. And now what he saw on her face seemed to disturb him, for he said, "Oh come on, Mara. You don't understand." There it was again, and she had no answer to it. He waited, watching her until she smiled, and then he gestured her to the door, and they went out, carefully, and stepped quickly past the scorpions.

They walked in the dusk up a path towards the lights of the house they had been shown. It was a house like the one she remembered from long ago: a tall, light, pretty house, and there had been a garden and trees.

They went up stone steps, and were outside a room that was lit by tall floor candles. Mara remembered furniture like these chairs and tables. A man came forward, smiling. Mara thought, He knew we were coming. And then, Of course, in a place where there are only a few people, everyone knows everything.

He was a Mahondi. The three of them were alike: tall, slim people with black, smooth, long hair. But he could not know that Mara's black, fuzzy stubble was really hair like his.

"I have a fifty gold," said Dann.

The man nodded, and Dann took out the coin. He gripped an edge tight, and held it out.

"You'll have to let me see it properly."

That voice: waves of remembering went through Mara. She had become used to the heavy, rough voices of the Rock People. Dann let go of the coin. The Mahondi took it to a candle, turned it over and over, and bent to bite it. He straightened and nodded. Dann was trembling again. The man handed him back the coin and said, "What do you want for it?"

Dann had expected to change it, but now it was evident there would be no change. "We want to go North," he said. The Mahondi smiled: You don't say! "How far could we go for that?"

"Your brother and yourself? A long way."

Mara could feel the carrying pole trembling again: Dann was full of fear, frustration and anger. It was because he did not know how much to ask, was afraid of being cheated. He asked, "Do you have transport? Can you arrange it?"

On the wall was an enormous coloured picture. Mara remembered it. It was a map. It was like the one she remembered from the classroom long ago. And it was the same shape as the one Dann had drawn in the dust for her. The Mahondi stepped to the map and pointed to a place in the middle. He meant: we are here. Then he pointed farther up the picture, to a black spot that said MAJAB, in large letters. It was a span of about three fingers' breadth.

"When can we go?" asked Dann.

"Tomorrow morning."

"We'll come back here," said Dann.

"You'd do better to stay here. We'll give you a room."

Who was *we*?

"How are we going to get to Majab?" asked Mara. Dann and this Mahondi both looked impatiently at her for asking the question.

"Well, of course," said Dann, "sky skimmer."

Mara had not known they still existed.

The man said again, "You'll be safe here." All of Mara longed to say, Yes, yes, yes, thank you; but Dann shook his head and then jerked it towards Mara—Come.

"Then be here just after sunrise." And then they heard, "You shouldn't go back into the town with that on you." Dann was walking away, not replying. "They know you've got gold. It's dangerous."

The last light was in the dark of the sky, a red flush. The two could hardly see the path. The man was watching them go. "He thinks we won't be coming back," said Mara. "He thinks they'll kill us down there." Dann said nothing. At least he didn't say, You don't understand—when Mara understood very well. It's a funny thing, she thought, knowing something about someone, like why Dann is afraid of that Mahondi, but he doesn't know. I don't think I can explain it to him, either.

She could hardly bear to walk down into that town. In the market place the stallholder and some other people stood around the trestles eating. There was some bread and fruit there. All of them turned to watch Dann and Mara go past. Their faces were hard and cold. They had not expected to see the two again.

A woman said loudly, "Their own kind won't have them."

Those faces: Mara was looking at a hatred worse than anything she had known, even in the Rock Village. She whispered to Dann, "It's not too late, we could go back up there." He shook his head. "These people want to kill us." But she could see he knew that.

They were returning to the house where they had been. The door was open on to the square: it had been closed when they left. Inside the main room some light came in from the twilight, not much. "The moon will be up later," he said.

"It's going to be quite dark until then," she pleaded, expecting him to ignore her; but he looked at her—that long, intent look—and took out the precious match, rubbed it on the wall, lit the candle stub. A thin light wavered over the dark room. Now he went to the inner door and pulled aside the stone that held it. They heard hissing. It was a lizard's hiss. She was frantically trying to pull Dann towards the door into the square, but he said, "Wait. We must look." He pushed open the inner door and beckoned. There was another room, and along a wall a half-grown lizard was dying, and hissing at them, but only feebly. Stairs went up. Dann leaped up the stairs and nodded at her to come too. There was a big empty room up there. Beyond it another room. Dann opened that door and quickly stood back. She went to be with him, thinking this was the same as when he was small, when he would jump off a rock or into a pool hardly looking to see if there was danger. There was a great hole in the roof here, and the sky showed a couple of still pale stars. This room was full of spiders: not the yellow and black ones but enormous, brown spiders that were everywhere on the walls and the floor. What did they eat?—she was wondering, and at once knew the answer: they were eating each other, for as she looked a great brown spider, the size of a big dog, leaped on a smaller one and began crunching it up, while the victim squeaked and squirmed, and others came scrambling to join in the feast.

Mara said, "I'm not staying in this house."

She had never said no to him, had let him take the lead. And he stood still, those intent eyes of his on her face: *What am I seeing now, what does it mean?* How strange it was, the way he searched faces, wanting to know what people were feeling. As if he didn't feel himself—but that wasn't true. And why was he not afraid now? The spiders knew they were there and would surely attack them? And suddenly Mara understood. Dann was afraid of people, only of people . . . But she was already off down the stairs, while he came leaping after her. She had picked up her sack and was out into the dark, and stopped, because of the scorpions. But they were not there, had gone off into their holes and hiding places because they did not like the cold. And the people had gone off too. Dann stood looking this way and that way and then he ran across to the trestles, and jumped up on the biggest of them. She followed. He was right: better to be well off the ground. But where was that big dragon? The light had gone, and the stars were coming out, dusty, but friendly to Mara. The two sat back to back, their sacks and water cans near them, she with the long carrying pole close to her hand, he with his knife pulled half out of its pocket. They ate one of the food fruits that were like bread, but this one was not soft and rich, as it ought to be, but was dryish and tasteless from lack of water. They drank a little of their water, not much. "Who knows when we are going to get some more?" Dann whispered. And Mara thought, Those people up in that house, they would give us water.

And now the moon came up, as heavy and solid as a food fruit, but it was not a complete round. Its bright yellow had an edge that looked as if it had been gnawed. They could see everything. Both looked for the great dragon: where was it? And the yellow and black spiders in their thick webs: did they know the two were there, so close? Soon, it was sharply cold. She felt the heat from Dann's back in her back, and wished that she had, like him, long black hair that she could pull close around her shivering neck. Instead she wrapped her naked head in the cloth that had held the slave's dress that Dann had found at the top of the wall. Neither slept. They were in a half-sleep, or dream, watching how the black shadows of the houses moved towards them across the dust. And they saw something else: a movement in the shadow near the door of the house they had left. Then someone, crouching, ran back towards houses that had flickering lights in them. Here they burned candles all night, for protection: how did they dare to sleep at all, the people of this horrible town? The very moment the sky greyed, Dann was stretching, peering about, on guard. Again they hastily ate a little, one of the yellow roots, and drank a mouthful or two. They were waiting for the sun to show itself, and soon there it was, a hot red burn over the hill they had been on yesterday. The scorpions came running around the edges of the houses and took up their positions. The stallholder from yesterday came into the market, but stopped when he saw them. He seemed surprised. He went to the door of the house they had been in, opened it, and out waddled the dragon. The man had led the beast into the house when it was dark and had expected it to attack them. He had not seen them there on the trestles. The dragon came fast across to the trestles, its mouth open, hissing. The man took out a piece of meat from a jar and threw it to the dragon. His angry, hating smile at the two said clearly: I thought the dragon would not need feeding this morning. The dragon lay down where it was yesterday, in the sun. It was a guard for the stallholder, perhaps even a pet.

The two went quickly away out of the market and again up the path to the house on the rise. On the way Mara went aside to pee. It ran clear and light yellow into the soil, which hissed gently, from dryness. She was not sick any longer. She thought, I'm well; soon I'll be as strong as I ever was. And she looked at her thin, stick-like legs, lifting her robe to see them, and thought they were already more like legs. She put her hands on her buttocks to feel them: but they were still just bones, no flesh there yet.

Just inside the door of the front room, they stood side by side, each holding an end of the carrying pole and a sack in their hands. The man from yesterday came in, and Mara saw his smooth, shining skin and his clean, shining hair, and thought how she and Dann must seem to him, with their dirty robes, and their dust. They had brought dust in with them: dusty footprints on the polished floor, and dust fell from them as they stood.

The man held out his hand. Dann took the yellow coin from the pocket that held the knife, and put it into the hand.

The man stood looking closely at them, Dann, Mara, Dann again, and asked, "Did you come from Rustam?"

Dann said, "I don't know."

The man looked enquiringly at Mara. She almost said, Yes, but was afraid. He said, "You look very much like . . ." and stopped. Then, "Do you know how to ride in a skimmer?" Surprising her, Dann said, "Yes." To Mara the man said, "You must keep very still. If the skimmer has to come down, get out, wait until it begins to lift, and jump in. They have very little power now."

"I had a job working skimmers, on a hill shuttle," said Dann. Was that actually a smile? Was he trusting this Mahondi after all?

"Good. Then if you are both ready, we'll go . . ." And at that moment another man came in, a Mahondi, and Dann's mouth was open; he stared, and was trembling. The two men were alike. But, thought Mara, frantic, already knowing what was going to happen, Mahondis are alike. These two men just look like Mahondis—that's all.

Dann was letting out gasping, feeble sounds, and the two men, frowning, astonished, turned towards him, presenting their faces to him, close, leaning forward. Dann gave a shout, said to Mara, "Come on," and ran, the two cans on the carrying pole over his shoulder, his sack in his hand. Her first thought was, And now I shall have no water.

The two men were looking at her now: *Why?* She could not speak, for her throat was thick with the need to cry. She knew why, but how could she explain it to them? "What's the matter with him?" asked the man who had just come in.

Mara felt herself sway, and was able to reach a chair where she sat, eyes closed. When she opened them, the two were staring at her.

"Your big brother is rather strange, isn't he?" said the first man.

And now she had to smile: little Dann, her big brother. But they were still staring: were they seeing something they hadn't before? She thought, In a moment they'll whisk up my robe to have a look. And what they will see first is the rope of coins knotted around my waist. She stood up. They were looking at her chest. She thrust it out so they could see its flatness.

"How old are you?" asked the second man.

"Eighteen."

The two looked at each other. She did not know what that look said. A long pause. Then the first man said, "We'll take you, if you like."

First she thought, Oh yes, yes, anywhere away from here. Then she thought, But Dann, I can't leave him; and she said aloud, "I can't leave my brother." She had nearly said, My little brother.

"You'll be by yourself. It's dangerous," said the man she now felt was her friend, and whom she did not want to leave.

She did not reply. She could not. Her throat was thick again, and she was thinking, If I cry the way I'd like to, they'll know I am a girl. And meanwhile there was a new thought in her mind. She wanted to ask, Please may I have a bath?—but this was ridiculous, so dangerous . . . But she was remembering, because of the faces of these two, which were so familiar to her, so near—like her parents, like all the people she had known as a child—how one could stand in a big basin and water was splashed all over you, cool water; and then there was a soft, sweet-smelling soap, not like the fatty sand she had used to clean herself at the waterholes. She longed so much for this water that she was afraid of saying anything at all, because it was dangerous . . . Of course it was, for she would have to take her clothes off and then . . .

The two men stood side by side and looked hard at Mara, trying to understand.

"What's your name?" asked one suddenly.

A name came pushing into her mind from long ago; yes, she thought, that's my name, it is my real name, my name—and then she saw Lord Gorda's face, tired, thin, kind, so close to hers. Remember, you are Mara, your name is Mara.

She nearly said, Mara, but said, "Maro."

"What is your family name?"

And now she could not remember. Everyone then had had the same name, and she never thought about it.

"I don't know," she said, and she was even thinking, Perhaps they'll know and they'll tell me. And she was still thinking, I'll ask . . . they're kind . . . and I can wash this robe and make it white instead of dusty brown and wash out the smell of that other person.

"Then if you're not coming, I'll give you back the fifty," said the first man, holding it out.

And now she was pleading, "Oh no, no, please, let me have it in small coins, please."

And now another long look between the men. Then the man she thought of as her friend said, "But Maro, the change for this would fill your sack. You couldn't carry it. And besides, no one has that amount of money these days." And the other man asked, "Where have you come from, Maro?"—meaning, How is it you don't know this already?

She said, "The Rock Village."

Again they looked at each other, really surprised.

To avoid more questions she said, "I'll go." And held out her hand for the gold. The coin was put into her hand. Then her friend went to a chest, pulled out a bag of the light, flimsy coins, poured some into a smaller bag about the size of her hand, and gave it to her.

She said, "Thank you." And again, "Thank you, thank you." She longed to say, I've changed my mind, please take me in the skimmer away from here, but she could not.

"Keep that money out of sight," her friend said.

And the other, "Don't go back into the town."

5

She walked away from the house, and never in her life had she felt as she did then, as if her heart would break: she was going away from what she really was—that was how she felt.

At the foot of the rise she turned: they were still in their doorway, watching her. She lifted her hand: Goodbye. And thought that in her other hand she still held the gold coin and the little bag of coins. She dropped both into her sack.

She would rather have died than go back into the town. She felt sick with fear even thinking of it. There was a dusty track leading away from the town, going north, and she began walking along it, alone. She thought, I won't last long without Dann. They'd kill me for this sack, or for this robe I have on.

She kept glancing back along the track to make sure she was not followed. On either side was the landscape that by now she knew so well: dead and dying trees, like sticking-up bones, whitish drifts of dust, the sky yellow with dust and, dotted about among the drought-killed trees, the occasional strong, fresh, green trees, their roots going far down. She walked on, the sun burning her pate through the thin cloth she had draped there, and she was thinking of how, deep in the earth, streams of clean water ran, making pools and marshes and falls and freshets and floods, and into them reached the roots of these few surviving trees. And why should these few have fought to reach the deep water, and the others given up? It was midday. Ahead she saw a thin crowd of people. She was at once afraid. More afraid than she had been of the spiders or the dragon? Yes; and she understood Dann. She was walking faster than they were: soon she would catch up with them. What ought she to do? When she was closer she saw they were the mix of peoples that was usual now: every kind of shape and skin colour and hair colour and kind of hair; but everything was dusty: dust on them and on the clothes they wore, which mostly were trousers and tunics that she knew were worn farther south than the Rock Village. When she came up with the end of the straggle of walkers, she saw the two people Dann and she had robbed—and was it really only two nights ago? Both were on their last legs, almost staggering, their eyes glazed. These two took no notice of Mara, but others turned to look, but were not interested in her. She went on behind them, more slowly, because a lot of people walk slower than one or two, and because it was very hot. The front of the crowd could hardly be seen through blowing dust: the wind was getting up, and dust clouds were swirling about and through them. She tried to make out the faces nearest to her: some she thought were from the boat. It was important to recognise faces, friends or enemies. She was stumbling along, thinking that she longed for a mouthful of water, and she had none; that if Dann were not as he was, then they both would now be travelling north in the skimmer, would be far away from this dying land . . . Someone was walking up behind her . . . was level with her . . . had moved ahead; and it was Dann, who did not smile or greet her, but only adjusted the carrying pole so that it again rested on her shoulder and the two cans swung between them. She said, "I have got to have some water." He said, "Wait, or when they see you're drinking they'll grab it all."

They walked all through the hot day, while the pale dust clouds swirled about them, and when the red sun became a big reddish blur low down, the whole company began moving up into a low hill beside the road: they were all staying together, for safety. And while they were doing this, their attention distracted, Dann quickly rested the pole and handed Mara a can of water, standing close to her, shielding her from curious looks, and she drank . . . and would have gone on drinking, but he said, "Stop, stop, that's got to last us."

The smell of the water seemed to have reached some stragglers, who turned to look, but Dann had the cans back on the pole, and his knife was in his hand. On the top of the low hill, they found a big rock to protect their backs, and crouched there, close, the cans between them, while she whispered that the two men he had been afraid of had given her the little bag of coins. He was at once suspicious. "Show me," he said, and she did, and he let the thin, light stuff run between his fingers on to a rock.

"It looks all right," he said.

She asked, knowing it was useless, "Dann, why did you run away? They were friendly. They wanted to help us." And she saw, astonished, how his eyes moved fast from side to side, heard his fast, frightened breathing, watched him hunch up, protecting his head—little Dann, in that long ago room on that long, hot night.

"Bad," he said. "Bad men."

He put the bag of coins back in her sack and looked for something that would burn. He found bits of old bark in a crack in the rock, and pulled down a bough from a dead tree. He went to his sack, was about to take out his axe, saw that if he did it would be the only one here, and he wouldn't keep it long. He broke up wood with his bare hands, built them a fire, lit it with a brand taken from the nearest fire. He didn't ask, just took it. A dozen small fires burned on the big flat rock that topped this rise, and around each huddled a few people, guarding their food and their water containers. One group had a pan and were cooking the dried leaves: the smell of the leaves, a memory of fresh green, blew about and around the hill, together with the dusty smoke.

Mara and Dann ate flaps of bread and shared a yellow root. Not far away the two whose last food they had taken sat with their backs to a rock. Mara asked Dann with her eyes if he would let her take them a root, but he shook his head.

And then everyone was lying down, and the fires were burning low. Dann was listening. He stood up and listened, went to the edge of the rock and listened again. Then he said loudly, "Someone should stay awake, someone should be on guard. And we should keep the fires going. There are lizards and dragons just down there." People sat up to stare at him: it was because he had called them *we*, had suggested they might help each other. Some lay down again and even turned their backs: Leave us alone. Others stayed sitting up, poked their fires, and one went to the edge of the hill, as Dann had done. Mara thought he looked like Kulik, and then that he didn't. There were movements down the hill, something big and dangerous.

Dann said to Mara, loudly, meaning it to be heard, "Move in, the dragons will get the ones lying at the edge." Again, some took notice and moved in, so the fires burned between them and the edge, and others stayed where they were. The moon was up, large and yellow, and the shadows were thick and black from the rocks around the edge. Dann said to Mara, "Something could jump down on us from the top of this rock." And they went farther in, having kicked the fire close to the rock, so the heat and flames went up its face to the top.

"I'll sleep first," he said. Both were longing to sleep. Last night—was it really only last night?—they had sat half asleep on the market trestles, and since then they had been walking for hours. As always he was asleep almost before he had finished speaking, lying so the water can was against his body. All of these people had their most precious thing, water containers, against their bodies, between their legs, or in their arms.

Mara sat listening. Into her mind came the words, I am listening with every cell in my body—and was at once jerked full awake. Cell. All these words that she knew, but did not know why. Probably Daima said it: she often used words that went by Mara. Again Mara was seized with the hunger to know more, to understand: *she wanted to know* . . . And even while she was thinking that this hunger was like the need for water or for food and as strong, and always stronger, she was staring hard into the shadows that edged this place where everyone was asleep. All but one: a man sitting up beyond the last of the fires. There was something familiar about him, but she could not see him clearly. In the middle, lying between two adults, was a child. Mara thought that she hadn't seen a child for . . . it was certainly months. She knew this child would not live—how could it? There were heavy movements in the rocks beyond the edging shadows. She looked quickly up because of a movement and saw the sharp head of a big lizard poking over the rock under which they had set the fire. The head disappeared, because of the smoke. She broke up more wood and fed the fire. That rock was not as dark as it was because of this fire but from earlier fires. She and Dann were not the first to have thought, This rock will make a safe place for our backs . . . then, later, that, An enemy could jump down on us from its top.

How many others? How far back? She did not know for how long people had been leaving their homes to move North . . . The man beyond the far fire was on his feet, leaning forward, listening. She thought he looked like Kulik, except that he was so thin. There was a moving and shoving in several places below them now. The moon was directly overhead. The dead white trees glistened. Rocks sparkled a little in the moon rays. She saw that a long shape, half in and half out of the shadows, was a lizard, and she leaped up and yelled as the man who might be Kulik whirled around, flailing his stick; but the lizard had taken up a sleeping woman in its mouth and was waddling off out of sight. She did not even scream. They could hear the crunching sounds of her being eaten, and the hisses and grunts that meant other predators were wanting their share. Even now not everyone was awake. Dann was. He stood up and said, "We should all get into the middle and make a big fire." The people awake looked at him but no one moved. They were all thinking, If we are crowded together it will be easier to steal from each other.

Dann said to her, "Back to back." Again they sat, like last night, back to back, he with the knife, she with her stick. She felt from the relaxing of his hard, bony back that he had gone to sleep again. She was not tired, but alert. It was foolish for her to sit staring out in only one direction, and she gently slid away from Dann, let him fall sideways; and now that he was asleep, her little brother, she could kneel by him, and feel how her love for him wrapped him around, just like long ago, when he was a baby, and then a small child. She also watched the man who might be Kulik walking up and down and around. He had a big stick. She saw him use it to lift up a water can from between the legs of a sleeper, but she coughed, and he let the can fall back. The sleeper did not move. She thought, That man is my enemy now. He went on walking, around and back and forth, sometimes glancing at her to see if she was watching.

She was fingering her upper chest. There was a little pinch of flesh there. She thought, But when my breasts come back, then I'll be in danger. Then she thought, But if the trickle of blood comes back what shall I do? I shall have to be afraid of every man who comes near. Then: I am sitting here worrying about the monthly blood but a woman has just been eaten alive by a lizard. And I don't care. Some of us are going to die or be killed, and there is nothing we can do.

She remembered the grave that held hundreds of people, near the hill of two nights ago. Hundreds, Dann had said. She began counting in her head: ten fingers. Then: ten toes. She knew that five twenties made a hundred but after that everything became difficult: only words, words that she used without understanding. It was silent now down the sides of this little hill. She was sleepy. Dann jerked up and said, "Sleep." She curled up and wished she could fall asleep the way he did, a closing of his eyes and—out. She heard sounds, knew that a wind had risen, and what she had begun to think was hunting lizards was the wind worrying and whining among rocks. She saw Dann standing over her, his knife in his hand, looking out at the dark. In the strong moonlight he seemed smaller, and easy to attack. The other man was staring at him past the fires. Was he thinking that Dann was only a boy and could easily be overthrown? Or was he Kulik and recognised Dann? But how could he? Mara had only just recognised him. And as for her, she still had breasts when he saw her last, and was a girl whom he tried to surprise behind walls and in corners. The wind was lifting the dust about and when it was blown into the low fires it burned, sending up sparks. The dust was what was left of plants, trees—or perhaps the bodies of animals. And people. Mara slept and woke with the light warm on her face. The fires were all out and the travellers on their feet, picking up their belongings. Dann put a piece of bread into her hand. She gulped a mouthful of water. Kulik—but was it he?—was watching them both. When everyone began filing down towards the track, he went first to make it clear he was the leader, and looking at Dann to challenge him; but like yesterday Mara and Dann came last. Near the track was a mat of dusty brown hair from the woman the lizard had eaten, with blood on it. The two robbed by Mara and Dann were not far from the end, walking stiffly, one foot after another, and seemed to be asleep with their eyes open. Mara thought, They had so little food left that what we took wouldn't make all that difference, but she knew the two would not be walking like that, on their last legs, if they had eaten the food that was now making strength in Dann and her.

They all walked on, slowly, while the sun rose up, hot. Then Mara saw beside the road the little straggle of half-dead leaves on a brown stalk that told her that under it was a clutch of yellow roots. She showed Dann; but he did not remember how they grew. If these two fell out and were alone on that track it would be dangerous, yet all around now she could see the brown stalks and leaves. She called loudly, "There's food here." Some people turned, turned back, indifferent. Others stopped. Mara took her digging stick from her sack, and dug with it in the hard earth, while Dann stood guard, and the others were stopping and coming back. She hoped that the roots would not be deep—sometimes they were as deep in the earth as she was tall. She reached the first roots at the depth of her arm, and pulled out the dusty brown balls, used Dann's knife to cut one, and showed how the yellow liquid dropped from it. At once all these people were scrambling around among the dead grasses, digging with anything they could find. Into Mara and Dann's sacks went ten of the roots, five each, after they had eaten as much as they could.

Mara saw the two robbed ones, who were dying, simply sitting by the road: they did not have the strength to dig. Dann knew what she wanted to do, and this time did not stop her: everyone was so preoccupied with their digging they wouldn't notice. Mara gave the two a root each, cut open, and saw that they had hardly the strength to suck them. Although it was Mara who had seen the tell-tale vines and alerted everyone, now she was being pushed out of the way and kept at a distance from them.

The man from last night was organising the effort, allotting the vines and the sharing out of the roots. He hardly looked at Mara and Dann standing by, watching, but when it was over, and the travellers were on the move again, he stood staring at them, glaring. He hated them. Whether he knew who they were, or didn't; whether he was Kulik, or wasn't . . . he loathed the two youngsters and intended them to know it.

There was a coughing, grumbling roar and from behind them came a skimmer, low over the track, turning up dust and chaff, and the raw earth from the root diggings that looked as if miners had been prospecting there. Everyone scattered off the track, and there were mutterings of hate, then shouts of rage, as the machine came level. In it were five Mahondis, all looking very serious, worried—but Mara could not see if her friend was there. The machine was low: if the travellers had wanted they could have pulled it down on to the ground. She knew the skimmer should be much higher, about treetop level; she knew that inside it must be comfortable seats . . . How did she know these things? She only just remembered travelling in them. It took a long time for the clouds of dust to settle: on either side of the track were drifts of pale, thick dust. As a child she had looked out from the windows of the skimmers at the Rock People and never thought how they felt about the dust, or how much they must hate the skimmers and everyone that travelled in them.

They all walked on, hardly visible to one another in the dust, and then up a rise, and saw that down the other side the skimmer was on the track, the dust already settling around it. All the crowd ran up to it: inside the Mahondis sat, frightened to death, afraid to get out and lighten the machine. If they did, they would be killed, they knew. And then the pilot struggled with his levers and gauges and got the skimmer up quite high, well above their reaching arms. It trundled on, making grinding and creaking noises, and then it fell—it crashed. At once all the travellers rushed up, peered in, reached in. Some of the Mahondis were dead, but not all; there were groans and cries and blood, but what the travellers were after were the provisions they carried. What food there was soon found itself distributed among the travellers—kept by whoever had grabbed it. Containers of water came out too, but there were only two small ones. And then the machine exploded, and the people near it were killed, together with anyone left alive inside. The skimmer lay in pieces all over the road and on either side of it, and black smoke went up. Ten of the travellers had been killed. The rest, thirty or so, stood shaking their fists and cursing the machine and the Mahondis. Mara knew she could have been among them: it might have been her head, or her arm, lying there in the dust. If she had accepted the invitation of the two men to travel with them, then she would be dead now.

She was waiting for Dann to say, Mara aren't you glad I ran away? Aren't you glad I said no?—But while he stood there, as always alert on his two feet planted slightly apart, gripping the pole on his shoulder with one hand and his knife with the other, he did not seem to be thinking anything of the kind. He did not respond to things as ordinary people did. Surely he ought to be thinking now of their escape? She said to him, pleadingly, "Dann—Dann?" But he turned to give her his close, acute look, and then his narrow smile—and he was already moving away from the crash. Was it that he had been near death so often that he did not care about it?

Dann waited until all the travellers were back in their places: Kulik or, at any rate, the leader, at the head, the rest in their families behind, and then he and Mara at the very end. Behind them they could see that, across the space between here and the hill they had spent the night on, lizards and dragons were waddling. Big, fat, bulging-with-flesh beasts, the size of a big man. They had smelled the blood.

Now they were walking through flat country and the big, green trees were few, so the underground rivers must be dry or perhaps had never run here. Everywhere stood the pale, dead trees. At sunset, the time to stop, there was no hill or high place. They would have to stay the night in the open, with miles of emptiness around them, the moon showing where they were. It was still a bright moon, though only half of what it had been.

Kulik—but Dann said he thought it wasn't Kulik—told everyone to get into a big circle, with their faces outwards and their sticks and weapons ready. He was taking command because he thought that last night Dann had been trying to be a leader, and he kept giving Dann hard stares that said, Don't you try to challenge me.

There was nothing to burn, only a little grass. They would have to forget fires for that night. They did not listen to Kulik, because they could not trust anyone, and were again in their little groups. Near Dann and Mara were the couple that had the child, who looked about four but was really ten years old. It was very still in its mother's arms. Her face was hard and angry. She carried the dead child well away from the crowd, which was already settling to sleep, and laid it on the earth. At once everyone was shouting at her, "Do you want the dragons and lizards to come for us?" So she fetched it back, and sat over it while it lay on the earth with its eyes staring up from a dirty little face.

The yellow half-moon rose high up and the dark forms of the people lying on the earth seemed small, and like a scattering of boulders or low bushes.

When the sun rose the mother again carried the child far away from the travellers, almost out of sight. She came back running, stumbling, weeping. Mara wanted to say to her, Don't waste water on tears, and was shocked that she could be so cold. If there are no children left, she thought, then what will happen? Perhaps I will have a child one day? But that seemed ridiculous, when she thought of her bony boy's body. The staring eyes of the little child that had died of hunger haunted her, and she knew that she did not want to be like that mother, with a dead child in her arms.

That day was like the last, but there were no roots, and they did not see a river, not even a dry one, nor a muddy waterhole, nor any sign of water. That night they lay in the open again. The moon was now much smaller. Mara did not like to think of the dark of the moon, just ahead. In the morning the two people Dann and she had robbed were dead. The travellers simply walked away from the corpses, leaving them on the road. Three more days passed and three more people died. There was little food left. The yellow roots had been eaten, and the water was almost finished.

It was ten days since Mara and Dann had left the Rock Village: ten days' walking and nine dangerous nights.

When they all stopped for the tenth night, before they slept, Dann told her to make sure the bag of coins that had been given to her was at the top of her sack, easily reached, and said, "This is our last night on the road. There are skimmers ahead—no, they don't fly, but you'll see." In the last light from the sunset he knelt and drew a rough map of Ifrik in the dust, a shape that seemed to move and flicker in the firelight, and made a mark for the Rock Village, and measured a width of three fingers north of it. Mara knew he was exaggerating their progress to comfort her, and when she smiled at him to say she knew this, he did smile back, and they laughed. "But you'll see," he said again, and they lay down to sleep, back to back. In the night she woke to see Kulik—and it was he—bending over her. Now she understood why he had been so hard to recognise. On the right half of his face were two scars, not yet healed: one from his nose, just catching the corner of his mouth, and lifting it, down to his collarbone; the other from under his eye to under his ear. He was not merely thin, his big bones showing, but yellow and sick looking, even in this bad light. He had been just about to flick up her robe with his stick. She did not know if this meant he had suspicions about her, as a boy, or if he thought she might be Mara, or if he had somehow caught a glimpse of the knotted cord around her waist when a gust of dusty wind had blown her robe up. He saw she was awake, and grunted and moved off. He did this in the way they all used: he was unapologetic, not guilty, not even concerned that she had seen him. They could thieve from each other, threaten, even kill, and the next minute could be walking along the road a pace apart, or lie down to sleep within touching distance, if the danger was enough.

Dann was awake and whispered, "Don't worry, we'll get away from him today." "It's Kulik," she whispered. Dann said it wasn't. She said he hadn't seen Kulik for five years. He said he could never forget that face: he even had nightmares about it. She said, "Then you'll have worse nightmares now."

Next morning they each had a mouthful of water. The others had taken to staring at the two water cans hanging there on the pole, and Dann put all the water they had left into one can, which they hung on the pole, and the other can went into Mara's sack. As they walked, the water slopped around in the can, and the people ahead kept glancing around to look at the enticing can. Both knew they would soon be attacked for the water, but at midday there appeared a skimmer on the crest of a rise, and around it were a group of ten youths, armed with knives and sharpened staves. The travellers moved off the road to keep well clear, but Dann signalled to her to hang back until the others had gone out of sight over the rise. Then he went up to the group, and the youth who seemed to be the leader let out a shout, and in a moment Dann and he were hugging each other, talking and hugging again. Of course: Dann had said he had worked with skimmers. Now the two men went off a little way and conferred. Dann came back to take the bag of coins from her. He counted out coins into this new—or old—friend's hand. Dann motioned to her: Get in. This little machine was smaller than the one they had seen crash and burn. It had four seats. It was like a grasshopper or a cricket. Dann got into the pilot's seat. Ahead the road dipped down in a long but steep slope to a string of pits that had once been waterholes, and rose up again to the next crest. At the bottom the group of walkers, who probably had not even noticed that Dann and Mara had not kept up, were plodding heavily on. The youths pushed the machine, which did not attempt to fly but only rolled down the slope, getting up a considerable speed. The youths pushed until they could not keep up, then went back to their station on the crest of the rise. Dann's friend waved at the two, and then the others did too. Because the machine was making no noise, with its engines silent, it was only at the last moment the travellers knew it was there, and they jumped off the road, cursing and shaking their fists; and when they saw Mara and Dann in it, they ran forward to grab it, but the skimmer was going too fast by then. The impetus from the long run down got them to the top of the next rise, where another group of youths stopped it. Mara and Dann got out; Dann conferred with these youths, saying that he had paid for eight skimmers. It was clear they were not altogether happy with this, but they allowed the two to transfer to the next waiting machine. The one they had come this far on, would return with one of these youths as pilot.

Again, this group pushed them off, down another and this time steeper decline, and again the skimmer reached the top of the next rise, and was brought to a stop by another gang of youths. This was a relay service, using skimmers whose engines no longer worked, for travellers who still had the means to pay. How did they live, then, these bands of young men, each with their skimmer?—but Mara knew the answer. They lived by robbing travellers—how else? They took food, and water, and anything else they fancied—and Mara wondered for how many stages of this shuttle the authority of that first youth, Dann's friend, would command respect. Soon, she knew. When this skimmer reached the third rise, the youths there demanded more payment. Dann still had a little clutch of the coins as a reserve, and he wasn't going to part with them. And the gold coins were each many times too much. For the ride from the third stop to the fourth Dann paid one of the brown garments, which had the young men exclaiming and marvelling so much they took little notice when Dann and Mara got into the skimmer, and had to be summoned by a shout from Dann. Down they went, and up they went. All this part of the landscape was a system of valleys between crests, each ride from ridge to ridge about

two miles. At the fifth stop they parted with another brown tunic. There
were now four left. Dann said that the youths were getting far more than
they deserved, for these garments earned in the markets to the east a small
fortune each. What markets, what do you mean, the East?—Mara wanted
to ask, but they were in the noisy machine. At the sixth stop the youths
wanted the two to turn out everything they had in their sacks. They were
not impressed with the name of Dann's friend, nor that he had once been
one of them. In the end they did not insist on their opening the sacks, but
accepted the water can, which, again, they found such a wonder that it
was only after some time Mara and Dann were pushed off from the ridge.
This was a long, deep descent, and the machine rocked because of the
speed, and Mara held on while the landscape rushed past on either side:
the same old brownish grass, the same dead or dying trees. At the seventh
stop the atmosphere was more friendly, for no reason they could see, and
the youths were satisfied with a couple of the food fruits—the last. And
now the last long dip down and then up, and at the top the youths were
truculent and surrounded the couple with a circle of staves and knives and
angry, threatening faces. There had been no travellers through that day,
nor the day before, they said. The stations farther back grabbed all the
good things—and now what were they going to be given? To say that the
two had paid for this last stage would be asking for more trouble. These
youths wanted food. There was no food. Then they said they would take
the can and its water. They actually had taken it off the pole when Mara
piped up, "There isn't enough there to give you even a sip each, but it's life
and death to us." At this they forgot Dann and turned on her, jeering and
laughing. "Listen to the kid." "What a pipsqueak." "He's got a loud voice
for such a little squit." And so on. They began jostling and shoving her—
and pushed Dann aside when he tried to protect her. Then one said, "Oh
leave him," and they all stood back. And then, just at the right moment,
when the youths were wondering what to try next, Dann said, "I've got an
axe." Now, axes were rare and precious. "Show us," cried the youths, and
when Dann produced the axe were silent because of it. It was very old: the
man Dann had got it off had said it was the usual "thousands of years old,"
made of a dark, gleaming stone, and with an edge that left blood on the
thumb of the youth who tried it. It was, like the gold pieces when they
were allowed to see the light of day, made with a craft and a care and a
knowledge that no one knew how to match. It was worth—well, it was
worth Mara and Dann's lives.

The young men no longer cared about the two, and hardly noticed when they set off down the long descent. They were handling the axe, silent with awe of it.

The laborious walking down, with ahead of them a long ascent, told the two just how much the skimmers had saved them every day. The distance covered in the skimmers amounted to two or three days of the slow walking that was all the travellers could manage now, being so exhausted. Mara and Dann were in better shape than most of the others because they had had more water and a little food, but they were learning today that they were reaching the end of their strength. Then Dann said, "Wait, wait, we're going to see something soon—I think. It was still running when I came down to get you." And as he spoke there appeared in the sky ahead a machine that Mara remembered: it was a sky skimmer, an old machine, and as it settled on the road it was rattling and shaking and roaring as if it might collapse there and then. Out stepped the pilot, a person in bright blue clothes, not a tunic or a robe but close fitting trousers and top, a vision of cleanness and neatness. It was a woman, Mara decided after her eyes had cleared from the surprise and shock of seeing this being from another kind of world. Her yellow hair was smooth and glossy, her skin shone, and she smiled at them.

Dann walked straight up to her holding out the gold coin, as he did before, keeping an edge tight between his fingers. "How far?" he asked.

Before examining it she said, "I am Felice. Who are you?"

Dann did not reply, intent on the transaction; but Mara said, "Dann and Maro, from the Rock Village."

"You must be the last, then."

And then she bent, bit the coin, while Dann still held tight, straightened and said, "It's genuine, all right. I don't see one of these very often." She waited, but Dann said nothing, and she said, "Well, ask no questions and you'll hear no lies."

"I found it," said Dann.

"Of course you did." And she showed she was waiting for some tale by leaning there against her machine, all her very white teeth on show, and her eyes hard, but amused.

"I didn't kill anyone for it," said Dann, angry.

"I know he didn't," Mara came in, and this bright, shining creature transferred her attention to Mara. "He's my brother," she said.

"So I can see."

"That money was given to me by the woman who took us in when we were little and looked after us . . ." And Mara, not knowing she was

going to, began to cry. She was thinking of all that kindness, which she
had taken for granted. She was thinking, Oh I wish I could be little
again, and Daima could hold me. She could not stop crying. She turned
away and tried to wipe the tears from her face with the sleeve of her
dusty robe. This dirtied her face even more.

But Felice was kind, Mara knew, and without knowing she was going
to, held out her hands imploringly to her.

"Where do you want to go?"

"Chelops," said Dann.

Her face changed. She was incredulous. "Why Chelops?"

"We're going North."

"You are Mahondis," she stated. "And what makes you think you'll
get any farther north than Chelops?"

"But we do keep going north," said Dann.

"Have you been to Chelops?"

"Yes," said Dann, again surprising Mara.

"Are you sure? You mean to tell me you just walked through Chelops?"

"I . . . didn't just walk," said Dann. "I saw a lot of police, and so I hid . . .
and hid . . . and then made a run for it at night."

"You didn't notice the slaves?"

"I didn't see very much," said Dann. "But I liked what I saw."

Felice seemed too surprised to speak. She seemed to be thinking, or
even in doubt. Then she said, "Why don't you let me take you to
Majab? It's a nice town."

"Majab," said Dann, contemptuously. "Compared to Chelops it's just
nothing." As she still did not reply, and hesitated, and then began to
speak, but stopped, he said, "I know you go as far as Chelops."

"It's my base," she said. Then said, "I am employed by the Hadrons."

This meant nothing to either Dann or Mara.

Felice sighed. "I've warned you as much as I can," she said. "Very
well. But that coin: it would be enough to take the two of you to Majab.
What else can you pay me?"

At this Dann scrabbled around in the bottom of his sack, without
actually taking anything out so she could see it, and untied another gold
coin, and brought it forth.

"Well," she said. "If I were you I'd not let anyone know you'd got those."

Dann gave the sort of laugh that means, You think I'm a fool? She
was thinking they were foolish, but her face was soft and she smiled as
she helped Mara in.

This was a six-seater, but the seats were broken and they had to sit on the floor. The machine took off with a feeble, coughing roar. All the same, it got quite high, enough for them to have a good, wide view down. It was a brown landscape, with clumps of grey rocks and, very occasionally, a green blotch that was one of the trees that had deep roots. There were dead trees everywhere. The machine was following the road. Below were several columns of walkers, like the one the two had been part of till this morning. As the machine passed overhead all the people looked up to see this rare thing, a sky skimmer, and while it was not possible to see their faces, all of them were hating the machine and cursing it.

They crossed a wide river running west to east, but there was not much water in it. At the least the mud flats on either side were not white with bones. Now they were approaching some mountains, and the machine did not increase its height—could not, that was clear. At the last moment, when it seemed it would crash into a tall peak that had glittering streaks down it from past rains, it turned to slide through a pass to the other side, where the plain went on, and on, everything brown and dry. After about half an hour, in the middle of the plain, there appeared below them a town, rather like the one behind them that was full of spiders and scorpions, but here there seemed to be people in the streets and there was a market.

"Majab," whispered Dann. "That's where the old woman was—I told you, who hid me when I ran away."

"You were here a long time?"

"Two years. Then I went off with some people—East." He pointed.

"What's there—East?"

His face was so angry she was afraid of him. East was a town where he had seen monkeys, and people, in cages. He had seen the cages slung between work beasts, like the water cans on a carrying pole, people clinging to the bars and crying and begging, women and children as well as men, particularly children: they were to be sold in the towns along the coast.

"Dann," said Mara, touching his arm to bring him back out of his anger. After a few moments he did sigh, then nodded at her: All right. And then in the dust on the floor of the machine he drew Ifrik again, put a finger where she knew he meant the Rock Village, and then walked his fingers to a spot that he whispered was Majab, and then to the next, which was Chelops.

They had been flying for about two hours when the skimmer began to descend. It landed on a high ridge; beyond it they could see only sky. The sun was red and gold and violet, sending rays across the sky.

Felice got out of the pilot's seat and opened the door for them.

"But this isn't Chelops," said Dann. "You've cheated us."

"Chelops is over the ridge," she said. "Now listen to me. I am not supposed to say this. If they found out I'd said it . . . But don't go into Chelops. Make a detour."

"For one thing we haven't got any food and not much water left," said Mara.

"Well I don't know," she said. "I really don't know what to say. I like you two kids. Well, if it's possible, see if you can buy some food in the market up in the north-east. Don't go through the centre." And with that she was back in her machine, and they watched the machine labour into the sky and go over the ridge, just skimming it.

"It doesn't matter," said Dann. "I wanted to show you something up here anyway."

And he began walking on, to the top of the ridge, where they could look down on Chelops. It was enormous. She had not imagined there could be anything like it. The light was going, it was dusk down there, but she could see tall black towers clustered together, though all dark, and a town spreading away from them, a big spread of houses, a wide scattering of lights.

Dann seemed familiar with this place. He said he had come over this ridge when he was walking down Ifrik to get to her, that somewhere close there was an old city, ruins he had heard people talk about.

They found a higher place, like the other nights, with flat rocks on it. There was no moon, but the stars glittered and seemed to rustle and talk. They ate the last piece of their bread, drank almost the last of their water, and lay down on a rock and looked up. The heat stored in the rock would warm them through the night, and above was the cold shine of the stars. He slept while she watched. She did hear scuffling and clicking from quite near, but these were not the sounds the dragons or lizards made. Then she slept. He woke her to show her an enormous beetle, yellow, with black feelers, running off to some rocks.

Before the sun rose they moved off their rock with its store of warmth and walked along the ridge that marked the descent into Chelops. "And here it is," said Dann, "it is where they said . . ." He sounded perplexed. Ahead of them were buildings of all shapes, round or square or like bowls, but they had no roofs and were all of a piece, with round holes for windows. They were of a dull greenish or brown metal, sometimes two-storeyed with outside stairs, but were mostly one-storey. When the two stood a foot or so away from a wall they saw their reflections, brownish distorted pictures of themselves, deep in the dull metal. What was this metal that still reflected after so long? It was not rusted, or dulled, or dented or scratched. The smooth, dull walls enclosed spaces that were hot and airless, or, rather, the air seemed flat, like stale water: both of them were pleased to step outside into the heat. They went from one to another and found not a crack, not a hole, not a chip. Mara pulled out of her sack the tunic that could be worn for years and never show a mark, or a tear, never lose its dull sheen, and she said to Dann, "Look." She held the slippery glisten of the tunic near the wall of a house: they were the same; and she put the can for their water near a wall: the same. The same people made the houses, the tunics, the cans. The two walked about among the houses, the sun beating down on them, and the metal of the buildings did not absorb or throw out heat but kept a mild, indifferent tepidity, no matter where they laid their palms. This city extended along the edge of the ridge and back from it for a mile or so: lumps of buildings, dead, ugly things that could never change or decay.

Mara asked, "Did they tell you how old this place is?"

"They think it is three thousand years old."

"Do they know what kind of people they were?"

"They found bones. They used to throw their dead people down over the edge for the animals to eat. The bones were all broken up because they were so old, but those people were much taller than we are. They had bigger heads. They had long arms and their feet were big too."

The two were dispirited, dismayed, even angry. "How did they make this *thing*," said Mara, suddenly emotional, and she hit the wall of a house, first with her fist, then with a stone; but there was not a sound—nothing.

"No one knows," said Dann.

"No one?"

"Those old people were clever. They knew all kinds of things."

"Then I'm glad they're dead. I'm glad, I'm glad," said Mara, and began shouting, "I'm glad, I'm glad—" and she was shouting away into the hot air all her years of feeling the slippery deadness of the material sliding around her, on her body, her legs, her arms.

Dann was leaning with one hand on a wall, watching her. What he said was, "Mara, you're better, do you know that? When I saw you back there at the waterhole you couldn't have shouted, or made this kind of—fuss." And he was smiling at her, affectionate, and with those narrow, sharp eyes of his for once ordinary—kind. And then Mara began to laugh. It was with relief. She felt she had escaped for ever the nastiness of that dead, brown stuff, and the unpleasantness that had made these houses. He smiled, while she laughed. She knew this was a moment new for them, of trust and relaxation, after such effort and danger. Did he know how rare it was for him not to be on guard?

"The people who lived here," she said at last, summing up, ending their little moment, "they must have been monsters. How could they have borne it? To live all your life in houses that can't change, with things that never break, with clothes you can't tear, that never wear out?" And she kicked a house, hard, so that her long toenails scratched the metal—or would have, if this metal could be affected by anything. For three thousand years these *things* had been here. And she remembered the ruins of the cities near the Rock Village with affectionate respect for them, their generosity in giving up what made them to people who came after, so that the houses of the Rock People were made of the stones and pillars of those people who had lived there so much earlier.

She squatted in the dust, took up a little stick, and said, "Tell me about numbers, Dann. Tell me about three thousand." And she laid her two hands flat on the earth: ten; and stretched out her two feet: ten again. He knelt in the dust opposite her, and with a stick wrote 10, then 20, looking at her to see if she understood. Then he went on: 30, 40, 50, 60, 70, 80, 90, 100, saying the words as he wrote. And again he looked at her.

"Yes," she said. "One hundred." She had reached that point herself, though not to write it with these strange new marks. And now she could go on, with this little brother who knew so much more than she did.

He made ten marks side by side in the dust, at a little distance from each other; and under each, ten strokes; and under each of those, ten. "A thousand," he said, and sat back on his heels so she could have time to take it all in. How sweet it was, this being close here, alone, learning from him, while he taught her. Neither wanted it to end. They had not been alone with each other a moment all these past days. And now, in this deserted place, they were comfortable together, and not in danger, they were pretty sure—and then they saw the sweat running down each other's face and remembered they had only a mouthful of water each and that they were very thirsty.

They stood up.

"Where did you learn?" she asked.

"I was at school in Majab."

"At school?" she asked. "How?"

"I worked in the day and had lessons at night. But then I left and that was the end of school."

"What else do you know?"

"Not much, Mara."

They were standing not far from the rocky edge, and they went to it and looked down over the city, over Chelops. And now in the full daylight she could see clearly what had been impossible to see in the dusk. The whole city lay there, spread out, and they could understand its plan. The first thing you had to see was that roads ran in from north, south, east and west to the centre, which was an enormous, very tall, black building, dwarfing everything for miles around. The roads were like nothing Mara had even imagined. They were straight, wide, and were made of a smooth, dark stone—or so it looked from here. Nothing moved on those roads. Where they met at the central tower were four quarters, each filled with smaller but still important buildings, all exactly the same: six to a quarter, and each glum, threatening, solid, dark, with regular windows that the sun flashed off, like knives. There was no movement inside this central core of the city, which was defined by an encircling road, narrower, but the same as the quartering roads. A vastness of irregular, lively buildings of all sizes and shapes and colours began at the circling road, making courts and compounds and avenues where there were trees. The trees seemed to droop, but they were not dead. In the streets of this city a lot of people were moving, and vehicles too. There was a big market place that was not central, and there seemed to be others here and there.

"This city was built to be the first city of the country."

"Of Ifrik?"

"No, just of the country. It is a big country. It is from Majab in the south far up beyond Chelops in the north. We would need weeks to walk across it. It is the biggest country in this part of Ifrik."

She was for the first time in her life hearing of a country, rather than of towns, or villages. "What are the people like?"

"I don't know. I came through it so fast because of all the policemen, and it was at night."

6

Now they began walking down a steep slope of chalky sand, where long ago the people of the houses that looked like cooking pots had thrown their dead. There did not seem to be bones now—not on the surface, at least. The chalky white of the earth was old bones: she knew how bones became white dust. The white was rising all around them, and they were beginning to look like floury ghosts; and they laughed at each other, and slid down the slope, which became steeper and then so steep they had to step off to one side to a gentler slope, which was still made of white chalk; and then at the bottom there was green, and some living trees, and a little stream. It had once been a big river, but water was still bubbling up from somewhere, for it was not standing in holes but actually gently running. Clear water. Sweet water. And with a shout both flung off their dirty robes and were about to throw themselves in when they remembered their commonsense, and stood waiting at the edge, looking, for they did not know if there were water dragons or stingers or snakes. Dann took up his pole and began probing a pool. Here the bottom could not be reached. They moved to the next where the water spread and a sandy bottom showed. Dann pushed the pole into every bit of the pool, again and again. And then he flung down the pole and both of them jumped in. The cool water enclosed them, and they sank to the bottom, and lay on white sand, and then at the edge, their heads out; and their bodies felt as if they were drinking in the water, and Mara let the water run all over her dusty scalp with its little scruff of new hair. And then Dann produced from the bottom of his sack a little piece of hard soap, showing it in triumph, and they washed and soaped and scrubbed and then all over, again and again, till the soap vanished into the white bubbles that piled the pool.

They got out and stood looking at each other. Under all the dust and dirt had been Mara, had been Dann, and now they were there again. Their flesh was not firm and plump like the woman pilot's, but at least the skin lay healthily on their bones, even on Mara's, for she was no longer only bones and skin. And now at the same time they were shy and turned away. Dressed in dust they had not thought of covering themselves, but now they did. Mara averted her eyes from his thick tube and the two smooth balls in their little sac, and he glanced at her slit, with its fluff of hair, and looked away.

She could not bear to put on that filthy garment, so stiff with dust it was lying on the earth with her shape in it. Naked, she stepped back into the pool with her garment, and he too with his. And they rubbed and rubbed in the soap foam, the soap itself having dissolved away; and soon the water was brown and the white foam masses were pale brown too. Dann washed his robe with his back to her. It was a strong muscled back, and her body was as hard and strong. On her chest, above the knotted cord of coins, were hard round plates, like Dann's, but back at the waterhole in the Rock Village there had been no flesh there, only bones. When they had washed their robes, they laid them on a rock to dry. Their pool was no longer an invitation, being so dirty. Dann tested another, and they lolled in it and floated in it, while the sun sucked the water out of their two robes. And then it was midday, and they were hungry. Mara mixed the very last of their flour with water, and cooked it on the hot rock, and they ate, and drank a great deal of water, out of hunger, though Dann said that soon they would eat, he was sure of it.

Then they put on their almost dry robes. Mara's would never be white again, for it had been dyed by dust, and his was the same. But they were clean. They filled the water can from another pool and then, the carrying pole between them, the can hanging there, they set off to walk into Chelops, along the stream. In front of them soon was a barrier that they could not understand. It was several times their height, made of closely laced metal ribbons, covered with barbs like thorns, and rusty. There were holes in this fence where the metal had simply rotted away. There was a great gate, which they tried to push open, and then two men, big yellowish men with rolling, abundant flesh and cold yellow eyes, came running.

Dann shouted at Mara to run—but there was nowhere they could run, the fences went on and on. When a man grabbed Mara she fought, but her wrists were tied together with thin rope, which hurt. Dann too, though he kicked and twisted and several times got away and was caught, had his wrists tied.

Within half a day of entering Chelops, Mara and Dann were prisoners, charged with defiling the city's water source, and for being inside a forbidden area, and for resisting arrest. On that same afternoon they were put to stand in front of a magistrate. Mara had been expecting someone like the guards, whom she now knew were Hadrons. But the man sitting on a little platform, looking at them, Mara thought, with curiosity, was not a Hadron. He was more like a Mahondi, but could not be because he was large and even fat. This was Juba, who soon would become Mara's very good friend. Meanwhile he was seeing something that he expected to see several times a week: starved fugitives from the famine down south, whose first action was always to steal some food. These two had not, though they had no food at all. Juba never punished the thieves, merely sent them off to join the slave force. But in this case he had to find out what they were doing in the water pools. If they had come from the south then why not by the road everyone used? Why had they sneaked like criminals down over the escarpment?

Mara was doing the talking. Dann, from the moment the cord went around his wrists, had become listless and silent, and seemed to have given up hope. His stood beside his sister drooping, sometimes shivering a little, and would not look up.

"My brother is ill," said Mara. "He hasn't eaten enough."

"I can see that," said Juba. "You have committed a very serious crime. You don't seem to realise how bad. It is a death sentence for defiling the water supply. And then you resisted arrest too."

Mara said, "I didn't know about an arrest, or resisting."

"Where do you come from?"

"The Rock Village."

"But you aren't of the Rock People. You are a Mahondi."

"Yes," said Mara.

"Where were you born?"

"In Rustam."

"What is your name?" Here it was again, a small tugging at her memory.

"Maro."

"No, your family name."

"I don't know."

"You are going to have to tell me how you got down into our water supplies."

Mara had not wanted to mention Felice, but now she said, "Felice brought us to the top there."

This seemed to disturb him.

"Felice did? And how did you pay her?"

"She was—sorry for us," said Mara. And knew she had said something that Felice would be questioned about.

They were put in a little room near the court while someone went off to find Felice. They were given food, at Juba's order, and it was good, hot food, which made them feel better. Though Dann seemed not himself, and sat staring, and would not speak.

How was it possible? Mara thought. Could one night, one terrible night in a child's life, mark him for ever? So that he would never get free of it? Even though he couldn't—or wouldn't—remember it?

When the messenger came back, he said that Felice was asleep when he got there, but said that she had given a lift to the two boys, since she was coming back to Chelops anyway. They had asked to be set down on the ridge and would make their own way down into Chelops. She had not taken payment from them. This was a relief, because when the guards had gone through their sacks, not very thoroughly, because they had to do it so often, they had actually found Dann's cord of coins, but thought it was probably some sort of amulet or fetish, and had thrown it back into the bottom.

Juba sat there for quite a time, his head in his hand, thinking. He could understand why Felice—who had piloted him often enough on official business—had felt sorry for these two innocents. He knew quite well that he was not being told all the truth, but did not believe that truth for truth's sake had always to be insisted on.

In the end, he simply said to the guards, "Take the cords off." And, while Mara and Dann rubbed their wrists, "Take them to the slave quarters." These were buildings in a compound where Chelops' slaves were housed. Dann and Mara were slaves because they were Mahondis, who had "always" been the Hadrons' slaves. They were not at once put to work but fed double rations for a few days. They were sent out with the other slaves before either of them felt strong enough, but were given light tasks to begin with. Then they kept streets and public buildings clean, acted as bearers for the chairs on poles the Hadrons were carried about in, or pushed the old skimmers that were now ground vehicles, or did any other tasks that needed doing. The slaves were well fed, worked twelve hours a day, and one day a week wrestled and threw each other in a big hall used for that purpose. Male and female slaves slept in different buildings.

Dann and Mara had little opportunity to talk, for they were supervised by Hadron guards whose task it was to discourage any possible attempts at conspiracy.

Where they had come from was spoken of with contempt, which

masked a dread that what had happened—was happening—"down south" or "down there" in "the deadlands" or "the bad place" or "the dust country" or "the country without water," could happen here too. No one went south but officials, to Majab, when they had to.

The Mahondis were an inferior race and had always been servants and slaves.

The Hadrons had built this city, and many other cities in the country, called Hadron, which they had settled and had always administered.

Certain things were only whispered. No one lived in the administrative centre, those twenty-five grim buildings in the middle of the city, except criminals or runaway slaves or people passing through who did not want to attract the attention of the police. At some time in the past, when it was hard to find accommodation in the town, people lived there illegally; but Chelops had about a tenth of its earlier population, and many empty houses. Citizens were quietly leaving to go up North, fearing the spread of the drought. Water was not rationed, but the authorities punished those wasting it; there was food, but not as much as there had been. Both food and water supplies were in the hands of the Hadrons.

Moving about the streets on her cleaning duties, Mara recognised a good deal of what she saw. The trees, first. They were limp, some had dying branches, white stick-like limbs among the green, and there were many dead trees. The city had fountains, but there was no water in them, only rubbish, which Mara, with fellow slaves, was kept cleaning out.

The slaves were not all Mahondis, but all were fugitives from the famine and the drought. Some had already been here for years. Mara had believed that the Mahondis of Rustam had been all there were, but other Mahondi people had come from all over southern Ifrik, and some spoke of past comforts and pleasures—even high positions and riches.

Mara was tense, anxious, fearful, which climaxed every day when the tubs of water were brought in from where water was kept under guard and, when enough had been set aside for drinking, the slaves were expected to stand in groups around the tubs and wash themselves. Most stood naked, shedding the ubiquitous slaves' robes to wash, but not all stripped, and Mara washed her legs and body up to her hips, bunching up the robe, and then sliding it down a little, but never showing her chest. Her worry was the cord of coins, but her breasts were already a bit bigger. The Hadrons who guarded them were looking at her and wondering. Something told them she was not male, though she thought she still looked like a boy. Then what she dreaded happened. While she was washing, manipulating the folds of robe to keep herself covered, a guard lifted them with his stick and kept his stick there, so she was exposed to everyone—fellow slaves who first were surprised, but laughed, and the other guards, who laughed, and came to have a good look.

Within an hour she had been told to fetch her sack, and without being able to warn Dann, who was out portering a chair for some bigwig, she was led across the town to a large house, where she was taken in at once to see its mistress. She had expected to see a Hadron, but the guards had told her no, she was a Mahondi in charge of the female slaves. At first Mara thought, How can she be a Mahondi? We are tall, slim people, while this woman is fat, and sits in her chair with her little, plump feet on a stool. It occurred to Mara for the first time that she had believed her people to be thin by nature, because she had never known a time when food was not short, even when she was little. So Mahondis could be as fleshy and as large as Hadrons. Mara was not sure she liked this.

She was standing quietly before this woman, who was examining her, her head propped on a little hand with many rings on it. She wore a big, white, clean robe of fresh cotton, with black stripes around the sleeves, and ropes of coloured beads around her neck. Her long, black hair had a red flower in it. She smelled of a heavy, sleepy scent.

Her name was Ida, and on her depended Mara's fate.

Mara did not know what to think of her, but that pretty freshness, the clean white, the glossy hair, the sweet scent, was making her want to cry. She wanted so much to be like that, to be that, instead of ... She did not know she was going to say what she did: "Are you cruel?" she whispered, and saw Ida's eyes widen, then narrow, while her plump lips mocked her in a slow smile. All this was artificial, Mara knew, meant for her to see it and feel foolish. "That depends on ..." said Ida, laughing; but at once her face became serious, and she sighed, for Mara only stared.

Meanwhile what Ida was seeing was a tall, lanky youth with a brush of hair, a bony face and enormous, hungry eyes, a body all bone and hard muscle.

"Tell me about yourself," said Ida, flicking some dust or something off her skirt. There was a little dust in the room, but nothing like what Mara was used to.

Mara was dismayed. She wanted to sit down, because of the length of what she had to tell, but Ida only waited. Mara began from that moment when she and Dann were taken to be cross-examined by the man she still could not help thinking of as "the bad one." Almost at once Ida was alert and listening, her indolence gone. Mara told it all, leaving out nothing, went on to the flight, the stone room and Lord Gorda, went on to the rushing through the night, the two rescuers, the flood, and then to Daima, where Ida stopped her.

"What is your name? Maro?"

"No, Mara."

Ida looked hard at her, meaning her to see it. "You are going to have to tell us everything. We want to know everything that happened. We are related to the family at Rustam. You are probably some kind of cousin—we'll work it out. Meanwhile, I want you to do as I say. We have something called the sleep cure. I'm going to give you something to drink, and you are going to sleep. Every time you wake you'll have something to eat. Until we get some flesh on to you we aren't going to get anywhere."

Mara had thought she was doing well, with getting her bones covered, but she looked down and saw her long, spiky fingers and her long feet where all the bones showed. The thought of sleeping—oh it was wonderful. She had slept so little, in the barracks with the young male slaves. Apart from her fear of discovery—but being found out had turned out to be a good thing—it was Dann: she was worried sick about Dann. She knew he was going to do something foolish: run away again, start a fight, or a riot. She was sure he hadn't smiled or laughed since they had come down the hillside into Chelops. He was so angry she was even afraid of him herself.

"My brother," said Mara. "My brother, Dann . . ." but Ida broke in, "Don't worry about anything. I'll make enquiries about your brother. And when you wake up, believe me, we are all going to want to hear your story."

She clapped her hands; a young woman appeared, and stood waiting. "Kira, take Mara to the Health House, and tell Orphne to give her the sleep treatment, and feed her, and go on until it's enough. I'd say probably five days."

Kira led Mara through a courtyard where young women were sitting about, talking, laughing, with piles of flowers and plants in front of them, which they were picking over. There was a strong herbal smell. They all looked curiously at Mara, and Kira said, "Later. She's going to sleep now."

Kira walked with Mara fast through hot dusty lanes, where plants and trees stood drooping, to a big house, like Ida's, where she called to another young woman, Orphne, gave her the instructions, and went off.

Orphne was another large woman, full of health, pretty, with flowers in her hair, and she said to Mara, "Have you really come from down there? Is it as bad as they say?—well, I can see by looking at you that it is." She walked around Mara, examining her, touched her brush of hair, felt her arms and legs, and said, "Before anything else I'm going to clean you up a bit."

Mara had thought she was clean, but now she sat down, while Orphne cut her long claw nails and the hooks of nails on her toes, rubbed pads of callused skin from her soles with a rough stone, dug clogs of wax from her ears, lifted her lids to examine her eyes, and put in drops, shook her head over the loose teeth, and rubbed oil all over her arms and legs. Then she made Mara drink a long, warm, herb-smelling draught, and put her to bed in a room that had another bed in it, and said, "When you wake up you'll be all right again, you'll see."

Mara slept, sometimes deeply, sometimes shallowly, and whenever she woke there were heavily sugared cakes beside her, and fruit, and more of the herb drink. Once Kira was sitting by her head, watching. She said, "I'm going to give you a massage and then you can sleep again."

"I don't want a massage," said Mara, thinking of the coins under her chest.

"All right then. But I'm here to keep an eye on you. You're a restless one, aren't you?"

"I don't remember anything."

"You were crying out, 'Help me, help me'—and then calling for Dann. Who's he?"

"He's my little brother," said Mara, and began to cry, as if she had been waiting all her life to cry as she was now.

Kira waited a little, then called Orphne. Mara saw the two young women, with their young, fresh faces, their concerned smiles, their plump young bodies, and thought, And I'm so ugly, so ugly—and I've always been ugly. She went on crying, until Orphne lifted her and Kira held the herb drink to her lips, and she sank back into sleep again.

Another time when she woke it was night, a low flame burned in a dish of oil, and Orphne was asleep in the other bed.

And then she woke to find both Kira and Orphne there, and Orphne said, "Now that's enough of sleep. We don't want to make you ill. And soon Mother Ida will decide what to do with you."

Mara said, "If we are slaves, all the Mahondis, then why is everything so nice, how can you be so kind?"

At this Orphne embraced Mara as if she were a small girl and said, "Everything was much nicer, believe me. These are hard times." And Kira said, in the way she had, laughing, but with a little edge of petulance, "We are nice. We're lovely—aren't we, Orphne?" And Orphne patted and stroked Mara and said that now she must have a bath. "We're going to give you a bath," she said. At first Mara did not hear the "we," but then did, and was full of panic again. Orphne and Kira must not know about those coins hidden there. Then Mara thought, I'll confide in them, I'll ask them to keep it a secret—but knew this was nonsense. No, no, already Dann and I have been saved by the gold coins and they'll save us again—get us out of Chelops to the North, buy us our escape.

"What's the matter?" asked Orphne.

"I want to bath by myself."

"Goodness, what a shy little thing you are. Very well then."

In a room that had a stone floor stood a tub of water, not hot but warm, because the water had been in a tank in the sunlight. Orphne put clothes on a stool and went out. The door did not lock. Mara took off her slave's dress, so dirty and smelly, untied the lumpy rope from her chest, put it under her new clothes, and got into the water, which was up to her chin. In came Orphne again, with soap. "I'm just in and out," she said, humouring Mara; but what she wanted was really to take a good look at Mara's shoulders, which was all she could see of her.

"You're fattening up nicely," she said, and went out.

When the water was cold Mara put back the cord of coins and over it a loose, light, white dress, like Kira's and Orphne's. She went back into the other room and Orphne hugged and kissed her, saying she was pleased, and now Mara must go back to Mother Ida who was waiting for her.

Again Kira led Mara through dusty little lanes, and into Ida's house; and there was Ida, as before, sitting with her feet on a stool, and she was fanning herself slowly, using many turns of the wrist, with a fan made of feathers. This made Mara remember birds, and their variety and their songs and their beauty, and wonder if perhaps there were still some left in Chelops. She had not seen any birds.

Ida was looking closely at her with those clever eyes of hers, while she fanned and fanned, and then she said, "Good. I wouldn't have recognised you. You've got a face now." Then she lifted down her pretty feet and said, "I'm going to take you now and show you to the Hadrons. No, don't worry. You aren't pretty enough yet for it to be dangerous. But that's the point you see. They have to see you—it's the rule. And then they'll forget about you.

At least I hope they will." She draped a white scarf over Mara's brush of hair, and took her hand. She asked, "Are you feeling yourself again? Can you manage a little walk? It really is better if we do it now."

At this Mara had to remember for how long she had not felt herself, how she had forgotten what feeling yourself meant; and she stood smiling at Ida in gratitude, wanting to tell her everything, and she had begun, "You see, in the Rock Village, for all those years I don't think I was anywhere near what I really am—" when Ida laughed, gave her a little push to the door and said, "Save it for when we can all hear."

At the door stood one of the carrying chairs that so recently Mara had been portering, the shafts on her shoulders, and Ida got in, and pulled in Mara, who stood hesitating, knowing how her weight and Ida's would drag at the thin shoulders of the two slaves at the back and the front. One recognised her, and gave her a sullen look.

They were jogging through small lanes, then on a road, which had on either side of it red flowering shrubs; but the flowers seemed to Mara to be emitting a high, almost audible scream for help, because she was remembering, and identifying so strongly with a longing for rain. Then they turned into a big garden where there were shrubs and flowers that were watered and fresh. Beyond the big house they were approaching was a field full of very tall odoriferous plants, and their smell was unpleasant, rank and head-haunting.

"We used some of that for your sleep," said Ida, "but don't take it on your own, I'm warning you: we don't want you to become one of those—" and she pointed to a couple of slaves who lifted their faces as the carrying chair passed to show blank, drugged eyes.

Around this house were big, deep verandahs, and on them lounged half a dozen men with long stick-like weapons, which they pointed at the two women.

"Don't worry," said Ida, "they are as useful as the sky skimmers—they don't work. Or when they do, they give the poor fools such a fright they throw them down and run."

They stepped out of the chair. The two porters took it to the side of the garden, sat down by it and at once went to sleep.

They went past the guards, and into a big room that was half dark because the windows were shaded, with the glare showing through the blinds like a hot stare. In the room, on cushions all around the walls, sat very large men, very fat, with billows and pillows of yellow flesh, wearing robes of all colours that were loose to hide all that fat. Never had

Mara even imagined such ugliness, such disgustingness, such beasts of men. The bulging flesh reminded her of the big lizards and dragons.

These were Hadrons. But Mara was thinking, I've seen them before—surely I have? And then she understood: the Rock People were very similar in build and shape, and their hair was the same, a mass of pale, frizzy stuff. Each of these beast-men leaned his elbows on a cushion, and they all stared and dreamed, and the air was sickly sweet. There were all kinds of pipes and tubes set out, and some Hadrons used these, but others were chewing black lumps, slowly, the way Mishka and Mishkita had chewed their food—when there was any.

Ida walked to the middle of the floor, leading Mara by the hand. No one seemed to notice them. Ida made a very deep curtsy, clapped her hands gently at chest level, and then curtsied again. Some of the befogged faces turned to look.

"Your lordships," said Ida, "I've brought the new girl."

At this all the eyes turned towards Mara. It was the words "the new girl." But, clearly, what they saw did not attract them, and besides, it was at that moment, when questions might have been asked, that four slaves carried in two great trays of food, piled high, and the smells of spices and fat were added to the cloying smells of the drugs.

All faces turned to the food, and Ida and Mara were forgotten. Ida curtsied again, but the Hadrons were reaching out with fat hands, covered with jewels, to the food, and the two women went out, unnoticed.

"We have to do that," said Ida. "It's the rule. They must have a good look at every new arrival in the Women's Houses. And now we'll not have to do it again, when your hair is grown and you look nice."

Back they went in the carrying chair to Ida's house. There she told Mara to rest for a while, since she shouldn't overdo things after her sleep treatment, and showed her a room that had only one bed in it, and left her.

When Mara got up, she found Ida in her usual place, fanning herself, apparently contemplating her pretty feet. She looked so unhappy, Mara thought, in that moment before Ida saw her and smiled.

"Sit down," said Ida, and Mara sat.

"And now," said Ida, "what did you see?"

Mara smiled at Ida through tears: to hear these words again, after such a long time, it was like hearing Daima's voice, or her parents' voices.

"The Mahondis here are slaves of the Hadrons, but they decide everything and the Hadrons do not know it because they are lazy and stupid and take too much poppy."

"Very good," said Ida. "Well done. But don't you ever say it where they can hear you. But we don't decide everything. We can't stop them taking Mahondi girls as concubines. Or the boys, either." Then, because of Mara's surprised face, "You've never heard of what I'm saying?"

Mara shook her head. "Not men and men?" In her mind a warning was flaring: Dann, Dann, Dann. She thought, That's a danger for Dann, I am sure of it.

"Go on, Mara, what have you seen?"

"Chelops is emptying," she said. "And that is why you need so many slaves—there's no free labour to hire." And then, after a silence, while an old sadness dragged at her heart, "Chelops is coming to an end."

"The Hadrons say that Hadron will last for a thousand years," said Ida.

"That's silly."

"We have food growing out there. Our storehouses are full. We still have milk beasts. And we are still trading with the North: we sell them poppy and the ganja, they sell us food. It'll last our time."

Mara did not allow herself to say anything, and Ida went on, "So what have you seen?"

"There are hardly any children. I haven't seen any babies."

"The slaves in the Women's Houses are supposed to get pregnant, but for some reason it is hard for us to get pregnant."

"And the Hadrons?"

"There are very few Hadron children."

"Perhaps their stuff isn't any good?"

"And our stuff doesn't seem much good either."

Mara said, because it floated up into her mind from long ago, "Every woman has in her all the eggs she will ever have: she is born with them. And every man has in his stuff enough eggs to fertilise all of Chelops."

Ida's eyes widened, she sat up, she leaned forward. "Where did you hear that? Who told you?"

"Daima told me. She was from Rustam."

"Was she a Memory?"

"What's that?"

"A person who has to keep in her mind everything the family knows."

"I think she was."

"There is a lot we have forgotten—a lot we've lost. What else did she say?"

"That there is a time in the month when it is safe to—to—to . . ."

"For goodness' sake, Mara, speak out."

"I wish I could go to school," said Mara passionately.

"It seems to me that you know more about some things than we do. Meanwhile, something seems to have happened to our eggs; but whether it is the women's eggs or the men's eggs, there is no way of knowing."

"Surely it's a good thing, not to have babies when times are bad?"

"But they aren't bad here, they aren't," said Ida, distressed. Then she sighed, and she frowned, and shifted about, taking her feet down off the stool and putting them back up. "Mara, when you are yourself again, when you are strong, will you have a child for me?" Then she seemed to shrink away because of Mara's reaction. "Why not? I'll look after you, and the baby—always, I promise you."

Mara said, "I've been watching babies and small children and even big children die. You haven't seen babies die of hunger."

"I've told you, we've enough food and water to last." And Ida was stretching out her hands to Mara. "I long for a child. I cannot have children. I've been pregnant over and over but I always lose them." And she began to weep, bright little tears squeezing out from between thick painted lashes, and bouncing down off painted cheeks and landing on her white dress, making little smears. "You don't know what it is like," she whispered, "wanting a child, wanting, then conceiving—and then—they're gone."

"Meanwhile," said Mara, "I'm so ugly no one would look at me." She tried to make this sound like a joke but she was suffering, because of all these attractive smooth-fleshed women, and their bright, fresh clothes and their breasts, which they took for granted. Whereas Mara's breasts seemed to have disappeared for ever.

"Oh, Mara, just be patient. You don't know how you've changed in the last few days. And I'm not going to give up. I'm going to ask you again. Meanwhile Kira's trying for me, but so far she hasn't got pregnant."

Mara thought she had never seen anyone as unhappy. Desperate faces, anxious faces, fearful ones—that is what she had been seeing, but never anything like this fretful unhappiness. And she was fiercely thinking, She has plenty to eat, she has clean water, she can wash when she likes, and she is so pretty and fine . . .

"And now I'm going to take you to the other girls," said Ida. "Just so they can set eyes on you. They are all going mad with curiosity, because you come from down there. You don't have to tell them everything now, because you are going to have to tell us all everything tomorrow."

Mara was soon sitting among other young women, each one, she thought, as fresh as a flower, making her heart ache because she was so ugly, and she was given some curds to prepare. They asked her questions but did not understand what she told them. They had grown up in Chelops, and had never known hardship. When she said, "Sometimes we had only one cup of water to last for days," they did not believe her, thought she was making it up. When she said, "For years we ate roots and flour made into paste with water and cooked on the stones," they exchanged pretty glances and little grimaces of disbelief. She said, "We didn't wash at all, we couldn't, there wasn't any water," and they raised their eyebrows and shook their heads, and smiled at each other. They were being kind to her, as if she were a foolish child or a pet animal.

That night she asked Ida if she could use the room she had rested in, instead of sleeping in one of the big rooms that had in them several girls. All those kisses and cuddles, and pattings and strokings—she couldn't do all that, she wasn't used to it. Besides they would soon discover what she was wearing: the coins that would buy her freedom and Dann's. Ida said, "I can't understand anyone wanting to sleep by themselves," but said she could use that room. There was plenty of space. As for Ida, she always asked one of the girls to sleep on another bed in her room, preferably Kira.

Next day Mara was taken by Ida into a large room that had several people waiting for her. She knew Ida, Kira and Orphne, and then saw Juba, who had been the magistrate that day in court. He greeted her with a friendly, ironical little smile. A tall, lean, older woman, with a face that Mara seemed to remember was like her mother's, opened with the ritual, "And now, what have you seen, Mara?"

Mara knew they did not mean what had she seen here, in Chelops, and started, again, with the scene in Rustam where she and Dann were being interrogated. She began to feel embarrassed, because it was taking so long, and began to shorten the tale; but the woman like her mother, who was Candace, said, "No, we want to know it all—everything. We will go on tomorrow, and so there's no hurry at all."

And Mara talked, remembering more and more, details she had not known she had noticed: like the way water-starved skin shrinks into a rough, ridgy dryness, or how when they were hungry the milk beasts licked earth that had bits of old grass in it, or how very hot and thirsty people will sit panting with their mouths open, like birds when they are hot. And when she told about the old ruined cities on the hills above the Rock Village she saw in her mind's eye one of the painted people from a later layer of the cities: she had thought that she—or he, it was hard to tell—wore a headdress; but no, it was braided and woven hair— she knew because she was looking at a woman's head whose hair was the same, a marvel of inventive arrangement. This girl was Larissa. As she talked Mara was listening for names and trying to work out relationships. Next to Juba was a comfortable, greying lady, called Dromas; the two held hands. A young man with a fine, gentle, humorous face was Meryx, and he was their son. Two middle-aged men, Jan and John, were Candace's sons. The only young woman from that courtyard of merry and carefree females was Larissa—why she, and not the others? There were half a dozen people who sat silent and listened.

Mara was still talking about the ruined cities. She said, "I was lucky— wasn't I?—living with that story, those stories, so close to me. If I had been brought up near that horrible city up there on the ridge, I would have learned nothing about who lived there." A wave of the old longing gripped her and she said, "Please, please, can I go to school?"

Candace said, "Yes, you will—but first, your story. We need to know. It isn't often we have someone here who has seen all the changes down there in the south. You see, we make up a history of what has happened—as far as we can hear about it. And we have people who learn it all and they preserve it, and make sure it is handed on down to someone younger, and we teach it to the young people. We call these people Memories. So please, Mara, go on."

And Mara went on talking. It was quite late when Candace said, "That's enough for tonight."

Mara was in the room she had chosen, by herself. She had never in her life been alone to sleep, and she felt such a freedom, such an exultation in being alone. It was not a large room, and in it was only a low bed, and a jar for water and a cup, and a little glow of light from a wick floating in oil—but she was as happy as she had ever been.

Next day they asked her to go to the young women's courtyard, but she begged to be with Orphne, to learn what she could of herbs and healing; and besides, she felt, when with Orphne, as if she were being fed with cheerfulness, for that young woman's pleasure in everything she did, in her own competence, was truly infectious. Oh, if only I could be like her, Mara was thinking.

Next evening, again, the same people assembled. Mara went on with her tale until it ended with her and Dann's sliding down the chalky hillside, and bathing in the pools and washing their garments. Juba did raise his eyebrows, and allow himself a frown, but he then waved his hand as if to say, Enough, it's forgotten. The incident had certainly not been generally forgotten: the story of how two refugees had polluted the Chelops main water source and got away with it was being told to the extent that Juba had sent out warnings that the penalty for going anywhere near the water was still a death sentence.

"And now," said Candace, "what do you want to ask us?"

Mara said, "When you found out I am female, and brought me here, it was because all the female slaves are checked, for breeding purposes. Then you discovered I am Kin. But Dann is Kin, too, and you left him with the other slaves." She sounded reproachful, more than she had meant.

"He has run away," said Candace. "We can't find him."

"Oh no, no, no," said Mara, remembering how, with earlier disappearances of Dann, it had been as if half of her were torn away.

"We are looking for him," said Meryx. "But the other slaves say he was talking of going North."

Mara kept her counsel. She did not believe Dann had left without her. He was hiding somewhere. Probably somewhere in those Towers. And how was he doing? She had all this food and water and comfort and cleanness, she was being petted and favoured—but he?

She said, "The Mahondis control all the food-growing and supplies?"

"Yes." And Meryx made a little bow to her. "Here is the Controller of Food—in person."

"You control the guards, the police, the watchmen, and the army?"

"Yes," said Juba.

"But the Hadrons control the water?"

"Yes," said Candace.

"Or they believe they do?" asked Mara.

A pause. Some glances were exchanged. Then Juba leaned forward and said, "Exactly. And it is important they go on thinking they do."

"All right," said Mara.

Now Juba said, "Mara, we are going to ask you to do something important for all of us. We want you to work for a while with the poppy and the ganja." She felt so disappointed, she felt they were rejecting her; and, seeing her face, they leaned forward, with smiles and nods, to reassure her. "You must have seen how important it is, when you visited the Hadrons."

Mara still sat silent, but she was thinking.

"The difference between the Hadrons and us," said Meryx, "is that they use poppy and ganja and we don't."

Mara nodded.

The next moment was not for her, because Meryx looked hard at Ida and said, "Mahondis don't use these things."

Ida's smile became nervous and guilty; she shifted about, and her fan began fluttering and trembling. Everyone was looking at her.

"And you set a bad example," said Meryx; and now they were looking at Kira, who faced them with more self-command than Ida.

Kira said, "I only have a little puff sometimes." And she laughed her petulant, defiant laugh.

"Then don't," said Candace.

Ida was in tears. She went out, her fan loose in her hand, like a broken wing. Kira sat on, refusing to be guilty.

Next day Mara was in the courtyard with the young women, and she asked questions about the growing of poppy, and the supply of ganja, but realised they did not really think about it. Only Larissa understood, and Mara saw the answer to something that had been puzzling her: why were so few people there on the evenings when matters of importance were discussed? Larissa was there because she had come to certain conclusions by herself, and was promoted to the inner circle of the Kin. And that meant that those of the inner circle were always on the lookout for people who did ask questions, who understood, and could answer intelligently when asked, "And what did you see?"

Mara knew that she was about to be tested, and so it turned out. Juba, then Meryx, and Meryx again, took her to the fields where the poppies were growing, and then to the ganja, took her to the barns where the workers, male and female, were getting milky juice from the poppies, drying it, making big sticky balls, ready to smoke, or drying the ganja and crushing it and putting it into sacks. She was given poppy to smoke. She knew this was to make sure she could refuse it, having tried it. And indeed, while her head floated with imaginings, she thought she could not live without it; but when she was herself again, she was frightened by its seductive power, and swore never to touch it again. And she was offered it again, by the workers, and then by Ida, and finally by Meryx himself, who was openly apologetic. Then she smoked the ganja, but did not find that so enticing. She was

invited again, by Juba, by Candace, with whom she actually did share a little smile that said she knew she was being tested.

Then she was told, "There's no need for you to work with the ganja
and poppy again."

During this time most evenings she spent with Orphne, or with Larissa,
avoiding Ida who was always begging her to sit with her. But there were
other evenings when she was invited into the room for important occasions, and questioned. One evening was spent on what Mara had learned
about fertility from Daima. Everyone was present. The atmosphere was
tense. They were anxious. This was the heart of the Mahondi concern for
the future: that they were not reproducing. How had Daima told Mara
about the cycle?—"No, Mara, her exact words, please."

Mara said, using Daima's words, "Now listen, Mara. Once there was a
girl, rather like you, and she loved a young man—and one day you will
too. He begged her to lie with him, and she found it hard to refuse; and
then one night she gave in, but it was the wrong time in her cycle, and
she was at her most fertile. She was pregnant. He blamed her. He said it
was the woman's duty to know her blood cycle, and the safe days; and
when the case came to court, the judge agreed, and said it was the young
woman's first duty to herself and to her society to know her cycle."

Juba said, "That court must have been in Rustam. Do you know anything about how it worked? What the laws were?"

Dromas said, "Juba, she was seven years old when she left."

"But Daima might have told you, Mara—did she?"

But Mara sat silent. She was most bitterly regretting the opportunities
she had not taken. How had she seen Daima all those years? She had taken
her for granted: a kind old woman—but she was not really so old—who had
taken in two orphans, literally out of the dark, and loved them and looked
after them. She had lived like them on roots and bits of dried weed and
flour cakes; she had never complained about being thirsty and dirty and
very hungry. And yet she had been an important person in the court of
Mara's parents' predecessors, where she had lived cleanly and sweetly and
gently. And she had known so much that Mara had never asked her. How
much Mara would have given now to have Daima back for a week, a day,
even an hour, to ask her questions. Now Daima was dead, all that knowledge, all that information, was gone, for ever.

Mara said, "Once when I asked her how she knew about the old cities
up on the hills, she said the Mahondis had all kinds of bits of information from the past. She did not know where it all came from."

"Not these Mahondis," said Candace, grim.

"Why don't you have it too?"

"You forget, we have been slaves for a long time. But your family were never slaves."

And now Mara, who was forcing herself to ask this, said, "Do you know what happened to my parents?"

"They were killed the night you escaped."

"How do you know?"

"Gorda was here. He told us."

"What happened to him? Is he alive?"

"He made a rising against the Hadrons. A foolish uprising. He was killed with his followers."

"That means he did it without asking you; you didn't know about it—no, that's not possible, you must have known about it, but you didn't approve."

Meryx said, "You might have noticed that we do things more—quietly."

Mara was thinking of that night, the first time she had been in a rock house, and how he had been kind. "I'm sorry," she whispered. "We would have been killed without him."

"Yes," said Candace.

And now, when Mara was least expecting it, Candace asked her, "And what is your name?"

It seemed to her that her real name was about to appear on her tongue and she would say it here, among these friends, the Kin—her Kin—but at the last moment she remembered Lord Gorda's, "Your name is Mara. Remember that always. Mara."

"My name is Mara," she said. They all nodded and smiled, at each other and at her. "But what is my real name? Do you know it?"

"It would be better for you not to know it," said Candace. "Who knows what the Hadrons know?—what they got out of Gorda, before he died."

"Perhaps one day I'll know my real name again," she said.

"I hope you will," said Candace. "I for one think that we Mahondis have a good chance of ruling here one day. I know that not everyone agrees with me."

At this, the next reply Mara had planned to give when asked, "And what did you see?"—became impossible. She was thinking, I have seen the future, and they haven't. And they wouldn't believe me.

Instead she said, "I saw a beetle up there on the ridge. Do they ever come down into Chelops?"

"Yes, and we kill them," said Meryx. "But some people believe they are breeding in the tunnels—Gorda saw them: he was using the tunnels as a base for his uprising."

"How did he get water?" asked Mara.

"To the point, as always," said Meryx. "The water was cut off to the Towers long ago. But the people sympathetic to Gorda living near the Towers helped him with water."

Mara said, not knowing she was going to say it, surprising herself, "Is anyone living there now?—the Towers? Could Dann be there?"

"We don't think so," said Candace.

That meant Dann had been discussed when she was not there, and they knew things she did not.

"If he is there," said Juba, "then he can't last long."

"Do you ever send slaves to find out?"

"Listen, Mara," said Juba, leaning forward urgently, holding her eyes with his, making her listen, "we don't draw attention to ourselves. You seem to forget that we are slaves. There are penalties—death penalties—for being in the Towers. We Mahondis succeed because we are quiet, we make life easy for the Hadrons, and they don't need to think about us."

And Candace said, "Don't make trouble for us, Mara. You are thinking of going to the Towers, aren't you? Please don't."

That ended the session.

7

Now Mara spent her days in the fields with Meryx and went about with Juba, even to court sessions; she was with Candace when she organised provisions for the slaves, and was often with Orphne. One day Juba took her with him when he went to see the guards on the water supply—where she and Dann had come into the town, and been arrested. As she had thought, the officer in charge was a friend of the Mahondis; though nothing was said, or even hinted, she knew that when the two men talked, everything that was said carried other meanings.

She asked Juba, "The Hadrons that are our friends—what do they get out of it?"

"A good question. You see, they are ashamed—that is, the young ones are. They are bitter because the Hadrons in power are degenerate. They hope that when they take power themselves, they can restore Hadron to what it once was. Because once it was well governed, though it is hard to believe that now. We spend most of the time trying quietly to put right what the Hadrons have got wrong."

Meanwhile, a great excitement: Kira had become pregnant. The father was Jan, Candace's younger son. Mara could see, going about with Meryx and with Juba, how much the news affected them: a despondency had gone, a look of discouragement.

Kira summoned a session of the Kin to announce it formally, and they were all embracing and laughing. Jan was congratulated, but seemed uncomfortable with it.

And then Kira sent a message that she had miscarried. She stayed in her room and would not see anybody, not even Ida, who wept continuously, so that Orphne had to stay with her, day and night.

Kira summoned Mara, who found her sitting in her cool room, fanning herself with a pretty, pert little fan, not like Ida's great trailing fan, and not seeming particularly unhappy. The trouble was, Kira's style—her manner, her way of walking and laughing, everything about her—was pert and even impertinent; she was full of little stratagems and tricks. Kira did not like her life. She did not believe in a future for Chelops, and had agreed to have a baby for Ida because in return Ida had said that if there was ever a possibility, she would help Kira travel North, provided the baby was left with her. She wanted to find out from Mara how to prepare herself for travelling, but she had no idea at all of the hardships and dangers of travelling.

Ida sent for Mara, and begged her to have a baby, and Mara said, "If I did have a baby, what makes you think I'd want to give it up?"

"But I'd be so good to it, I have so much—oh Mara, do think about it. Look at yourself: you're better now, you could do it."

Mara certainly had breasts again, but her blood flow had not resumed. Candace had asked her to say when this happened.

"Are you going to make me have a child?" Mara asked Candace.

"You might have noticed that we don't *make* anyone do anything."

"But you want me to have a child?"

"You talk as if it would be easy. But yes, we'd like you to try."

Kira summoned a session. Everyone was there.

Jan spoke first. "Before you start, Kira—no, I'm not going to try again. Yours is not the first miscarriage. You forget Ida miscarried with my seed."

And his brother said, "And that goes for me. I'm not going through that again: all the expectations, and the hoping, and then—nothing. Three of the courtyard girls have lost my attempts at a child."

Kira said, "I wasn't thinking of either of you. I don't want another miscarriage—once is enough. I am invoking the old law. It has never been repealed, has it?"

This law was that a man could have two wives, a woman two husbands, if everyone agreed. This law had been made when it first became evident that fertility was lower, there were fewer children, and many miscarriages. So morality changed to suit a necessity. For a while it had worked: there had been more babies born, but then it was evident this was only a temporary improvement. The new law had caused a lot of unhappiness, and slowly fell out of use.

The fact was, Kira had fallen in love with Juba, and by now everyone knew it.

Juba sat quietly beside his wife, Dromas, and said, "I'm not going to pretend I'm not flattered, Kira . . ."—here he took Dromas's hand—"but why me? I'm old enough to be your grandfather."

Kira said, "You have a son, Juba. Your son doesn't have a son. Meryx is the only young man among the Kin."

Meryx had tried to father a child with one of the courtyard girls, but had failed.

Dromas had to agree with this mating, and she was composed, dignified, but did not hide her hurt. She said, "We have been married twenty years. But Kira, you know I am not going to say no. I couldn't, could I, if there's a chance of a child? I couldn't live with myself if I said no . . ."—and here she smiled, attempting humour in this very tense atmosphere—"I couldn't live with Juba either."

"Oh yes you could, always," said Juba, and kissed her hand.

At this Kira's eyes filled with tears, and she said, "So what are you going to lose? None of us young women will know what it is to say, 'I have been with my man for twenty years.'"

"I know," said Dromas. "And that is why I am saying yes. But I want to say something else. None of you will know what it is to be with a man all of your youth, and to have a child with him—you have no idea of what it is you are asking me to do and what it will cost me."

This was Kira's cue to withdraw, and perhaps say she would try with one of the field slaves. But she sat on, her face wet with tears, her eyes bright and defiant.

"Then you may start your month tomorrow," said Dromas, taking her hand away from Juba's.

The custom was that when a couple were trying for a child—that is when everyone had given their permission—they were given a room, well away from everyone else, and they were excused their ordinary duties for a month.

"Why a full month?" said Mara—and as she spoke, knew she was destroying Kira's dream of a month of love. "We know—don't we?—that the eggs can only reach each other for a week in the middle of the cycle."

"I'm prepared to let it be a week, Kira," said Juba, "and if it doesn't work the first time we can try another week later." To soften this, because Kira looked mortified, and angry, and miserable, all at once, "I'm so busy, Kira. For me to stop working for a month—it is a real difficulty."

"Bitch," said Kira to Mara, as they all went out, "bitch, bitch, bitch."

"But it's true," said Mara. "Someone would have said it, if I didn't."

"But it was you who said it," said Kira.

The week of love—as the women of the courtyard were calling it—began shortly after this discussion. They were all gossiping about this passion: falling in love belonged to the past, to stories and fables and history. They had liaisons with each other, sometimes with permanent partners—lovers was not a word much in use—or more often temporary ones. They did not break their hearts when someone wanted a change, and said, "I want a fling with . . . ."—whoever. In the courtyard they chattered and giggled and discussed each other's likes and dislikes, their bodies, their needs—for they varied very much. One might say, "When I've finished with you I'm going to try . . ."—whoever it might be; and the cool answer might be, "Oh suit yourself." It was as if deep feelings, or any feelings, had left these women, as if some silent agreement had been come to: We are not going to want, or yearn, or fret, or need, or suffer over that ridiculous thing, love. They all frankly said that choosing only women meant there would be no heartbreaks over miscarriages and infant deaths or not conceiving when they tried. "I don't want to know if I'm infertile," they said. "Who cares, anyway?"

Yet when one of the field slaves managed to have a baby, and brought it in to show the Kin, all the women in the courtyard wept over it, competed to hold it, and were pettish and cross and tended to burst into tears for a week afterwards.

During the week Juba was with Kira, Candace told Dromas to be with Mara. Dromas was a Memory, and she had learned every word of Mara's history, and now she was to tell Mara as much as she knew of the history of Ifrik, but beginning with Hadron. Dromas of course knew she was given this task so that she wouldn't be sitting by herself, thinking of her husband with a very pretty young woman; but as she talked, her voice kept fading into silence, and she would sit, looking down, her hand irritably and anxiously smoothing back her grey hair, over and over again, as if she were trying to soothe away painful thoughts.

And then Mara would say gently, "And what happened next?"

Plenty had happened. The history of Hadron was a long one: "Hundreds of years," said Dromas; and when Mara jested, "At least it's not thousands," Dromas did not see Mara's point. How strange, Mara thought, that an ignorant thing like me should think so easily of "thousands," of long stretches of time, while a real Memory doesn't seem to hear "thousands" when I say it.

The history of Hadron had begun with the conquest of this country, when the Mahondis who ruled it were defeated. In the middle of an empty plain, the cluster of twenty-five Towers had been built, with the four great, black, shining roads running in from the horizon; and this was where the rulers, the lawmakers, and the administrators were all supposed to live and govern. Soon they were making excuses, and would fly in by skimmer for a week or a day of meetings, and then go home to the regions. Then a law was passed that everyone, including the president, must live in the Towers. Meanwhile the twenty-five black, bleak, sullen buildings were being surrounded by little outcrops of shanty towns: every kind of shed, hut, lean-to, shack, made of every imaginable material, even cloth and mud and old bits of metal. The big roads remained mostly unused, except for visiting dignitaries. Alongside the roads ran dusty tracks, easier on the feet, and everywhere around the base of the Towers, and spreading farther out, were networks of paths, then simple dirt roads, from one little annexe town to another. Soon there were no spaces between the towns, and the mess of buildings stretched outwards from the Towers, but mostly to the east, where the good water was. The shanty towns were rebuilt in brick and wood, and beyond them new houses arose, some of them fine, in large gardens. The administrators, instead of living in the Towers, built themselves houses. Within fifty years of the building of the Towers, which had been meant to stand up straight and tall and alone on the plain, a self-contained city designed to strike awe into the whole country, they were deserted, except for criminals or fugitives or as temporary housing for families taking shelter on the lowest floors until they could find accommodation in the genial and human suburbs. The Towers had become a lesson in misguided town planning, and there had been a time when people came from other countries to take lessons in how not to do it.

And now Mara stood on the wide verandahs of this Mahondi house, which had once been the home of a rich Hadron, and looked across to that enormous, threatening central Tower, with the twenty-four smaller ones—small only in comparison: they were huge. Had she promised not to go there? Yes, she had, at least by implication. And how could she do anything to damage these people, her Kin, who had been so kind and who valued her? But suppose Dann was in those Towers, hiding? It must be as terrible for him as anything they had experienced together. No, more likely that he had gone North: if so, he would be back for her, she was sure of it.

Again Mara accompanied Juba to the water site. All the young men hated this duty, which was lonely and boring, and that was partly why Juba visited them. Six guards, who patrolled the rusty tangle of fencing, and their officer, who was the Mahondis' ally. These young Hadrons were not disgusting, like their elders. They were like the Rock People, and Juba said that the Hadrons had come from the south, and presumably some had decided to settle along the way. Poorly fed Rock People were still solid and big boned, but these, who fed well, were large, and smooth, and their yellowish skins shone. The glistening mass of pale hair, on soldiers, was shortened and looked like a silvery cap. They were proud of their military training and their weapons, which were mostly piles of sharpened sticks, and bows and arrows. Juba inspected them, solemnly. The officer had the weapon like a long stick, of metal, Mara had seen when she was taken to the Hadron house. Juba was careful to look at it, check it, hand it back with a stern nod, saying, "Very good." This was a gun: it came from somewhere in the North, it was very old, and the traders who brought them said they would terrorise any possible enemy. The trouble was, they had killed quite a few people, not enemies, by blowing up in the soldiers' faces.

Juba said to Mara, "Did you know that there were weapons once that could fire right around the world?"

"No." Mara was wrestling with the word, world. Her longing reached Juba, who patted her shoulder and said, "Don't worry, we will teach you everything we know. But as I am sure you are beginning to see, that isn't very much. And you must be prepared: it isn't easy, when you begin to learn just how little we know compared with those people—the ones who lived long ago. If they could see us they would think us savages."

They were standing looking past the great rusty fence up to the cliff where Mara and Dann had come. The scrub right at the top made Mara think of her short brush of hair—though if she used water she could plaster it down now. She was unhappy, and it was because of Kira, her week of being with this man, and of her being pregnant. All the women were restless, and sad, like Mara. Kira sat among them, with a softness about her, a sweetness, that none of them had. Because of Mara's own unhappiness she could feel Juba's. This strong man, of whom Mara had often thought, I am sure he is like my father was—a man with a grown-up son of whom Mara had caught herself thinking, If I did agree to have a baby then it would be with Meryx—this man who seemed so calm, so self-sufficient, was staring up at the cliff top but not seeing it, because his eyes were full of tears.

He said, "When Dromas was pregnant I was with her all the time, and I was part of it all. And now I spend a week with a woman who is going to have my child, but I am not supposed to want more. If I had not lived the way I have, with Dromas, then I would be the kind of man who could say to Kira, Thanks, that was very nice, goodbye. But how could I be?—after living with Dromas for twenty years."

Mara thought that "living with Dromas for twenty years" was like listening to a song, or a story, so far was it from her, or from anything she expected. She put her hand on his arm and said, "You know, Juba, there's a solution."

"What?" he said angrily. "There are things no one can change, nothing can make better—young people are like that, you think there must be a solution to everything, well there isn't. Dromas and I are—one person. And now I lie awake at night and I can't sleep because of that girl—and I don't even like her. I've never liked Kira. She's a sly, cold little piece. Dromas has taken her bed into another room because she can't bear it. I feel as if I've been cut in two."

For a while they stood silent, while in front of them the young men marched efficiently up and down, believing that Juba was watching them.

It was a hot day—but when was that not true? They were well into the dry season. Out on the plain the dust devils lazed by. Here, the stream that she and Dann had bathed in was lower and in places—Mara saw this with a feeling of foreboding—was not a stream, but had become a string of waterholes.

"So what is your solution, Mara?"

"You are fertile—you've proved it. If there were two, or three, or even more girls pregnant, then . . ."

"Oh, so you see me as a sort of breeding stud?"

"You asked."

And now he gave her a glance so wary, so circumspect, that she cried out, "No, you're wrong. I know I'm ugly, I wasn't thinking . . ." She felt that he had hit her, this kindly man. And she had been secretly thinking, I'm really not so thin and bony now, my hair is growing . . . Her eyes were full of tears. And he was remorseful and this was even worse for her. "Mara, give yourself time. You look so much better than you did. And don't imagine you aren't attractive. I wish you weren't—I don't want the Hadrons to notice you . . . Very well, what do you think I should do?"

"Some of the courtyard women are already saying they envy Kira. One or two have said they are going to ask you. Next time all the Kin are together, you should suggest it. And of course Ida is keen."

"Oh, Ida . . . "

"She wants me to get pregnant for her, when my flow begins." And then at his enquiring look, "Oh no, no, *no*. I'm afraid. There's nothing more terrible, children dying, the babies . . ."

And she thought, surprised at herself, It is true, back in the Rock Village, the children and the babies dying; but it was so terrible I wouldn't let myself feel it, and so when that child died on the journey here I felt nothing. I don't want to feel, I don't want that again—*never*. And she felt now the anguish of seeing the dying babies in the Rock Village, babies being born, then dying, or surviving for a while, so that everyone watched, hoping, and then another bad dry season—and they died. The mothers' stony faces, the fathers' angry faces as they dug little graves in the hard earth, or put the corpses out for the scavengers.

Juba put his arm around Mara, and she leaned against him and most bitterly sobbed, to make up for all the tears she had held back then. And he stood, full of sorrow, and thought that this girl could never understand his grief over Dromas.

Now Kira sent a message: she demanded a full meeting of the Kin, and when they were assembled she rushed into the room propelled by furious emotion, and was checked by Candace who said, "Sit down, there are still some others to come."

Kira was pouting and exclaiming, and did not sit.

"We have problems," said Candace, "serious ones."

"Oh, mine isn't serious, I see," said Kira.

Then Meryx came in, with Mara: they had been inspecting the food warehouses. Ida arrived, and sat and sighed, fanning herself, and at once everyone had to look. That fan of hers, made of the feathers of a bird Mara thought must be extinct, or gone North long ago, was like her sighs, her exclamations, her sorrow: the quick flutter near her face, the dramatic turn of the elegant, plump wrist, the click of the fan opening and shutting, the blur of colours as she fanned—she had not said a word, but everyone knew she felt betrayed because Kira was saying that she was going to keep the baby.

"Sit down," said Juba to Kira, who was still marching about, ironically watching Ida.

She did sit now, because it was he who had said so—she made this plain by her manner.

"I demand," she said, "to be allowed to marry Juba." She saw the shocked and astonished faces around her and burst into tears.

Candace said, "Don't be so absurd. Of course Juba isn't going to marry you."

Juba was sitting next to Dromas, who was looking strained, but she smiled.

Now Candace said to Kira, "You think only of yourself, Kira. Now listen." And she outlined a plan for Juba to try to impregnate the four girls from the courtyard who had agreed to it—not merely agreed, they were now desperate to try.

Kira began to wail and shout and fling herself about. Orphne supported her up out of her chair and said, "Don't worry, I'll calm you down." And Larissa joined the two, saying, "I think Kira should come and stay with me for a while. I'll look after you, Kira, you'll see."

Ida said, "Why does Kira hate me so much?" And Candace said, "Obviously, because you aren't Juba. Be quiet, Ida. We have serious problems." And almost as an afterthought added, "The women who want to try with Juba can arrange between themselves when and how."

Candace's tone was such that Ida was quiet, and even her fan lay still across her knees. And Mara thought that she had never suspected that behind Candace's gentleness and kindness lay this iron will.

Meanwhile Meryx was outlining the new difficulties. When he had finished he got up to leave and beckoned Mara to go with him. Normally Mara would have just left, but now looked to Candace for permission. Candace nodded, and Mara felt the shrewd—cold?—gaze on her back.

Meryx said, "I'm going to ask you something—don't be angry. But please will you wear my clothes—well, any of the men's clothes when you are out? And this?" It was a little cap like those worn by the slaves. Mara turned away so he could not see her face—her hair was just beginning to be nice to look at, and she loved the pretty frocks, pink and white and green, that she wore. Meryx caught her arm and turned her around. "Mara," he said, "I don't want . . . we don't want the Hadrons to notice you. Please. You are out and about all the time, everyone can see you . . ." She nodded, knowing he was right. He let his hand fall off her arm, took her hand and led her to his room. There he turned his back while she took off her pink dress and put on the brown top and loose trousers the men wore. Meryx turned, laughed and said, "Well, I would know you because—I know you." There was no doubt he liked what he saw. "And the next thing will be, you'll be sending a message to my father."

She wanted to say, Oh no, no, no, it would be you I'd ask . . . but the consciousness of her ugliness, which would not leave her, kept her silent. He said, with the little humorous smile that was characteristic, "How would you feel if you were me? It is my father who will be father to the new babies. Not me. No one expects anything of me."

And now she did go to him, put her hands on his upper arms, daring herself to do it, and said, stumbling over it, "Meryx, I haven't begun my flow yet."

"Sweet Mara," said Meryx. "Well, we'll see. Let's see how my father does."

And with that they went out to deal with the new difficulties.

Every dry season dust blew across the plain and the dry, dead bushes bounced and whirled about the air with the dust devils; but this season was worse than anybody remembered. The milk beasts had always stayed out during the dry months, led daily to water, and food was brought to them. But hardy as they were, used to eating unnourishing grass and thorny scrub, used to heat and dust, this year they stood together in their family groups with their backs to the blowing dust and bleated their protests. It had been decided to bring them into the big empty sheds until it rained. "There is one thing we aren't short of," said Meryx, "—empty buildings." But these animals had never been confined before. They were herded into the sheds, and complained at finding a roof over them, but then saw that the great doors stood open and they could go in and out. Soon it was evident they were pleased about the shade they could escape into any time they wanted. It was lucky these beasts were used to drinking so little, with the water so low in the streams and reservoirs.

But the milk beasts' plight was a small problem compared to what had happened the week before when traders from the River Towns came as usual with their dried fish, dried meat, river fruits and vegetables, bales of cotton cloth, to exchange for ganja and poppy. While a casual glance around the great storehouses showed everything was normal, when the slaves came to pull out last year's crops, leaving this year's to mature, most of them were gone. Now these storehouses, housing the most precious commodity of Chelops, were heavily guarded, day and night, by Juba's most trusted militia. They were all Mahondis, because Juba had to keep control of what controlled the Hadrons.

Not to tell the Hadrons would be foolish, and besides by now their spies would have informed them. They had to trust Juba: everything depended on that. Yet to confess the extent of the loss must be to throw doubt on his competence. The ruling Hadrons were suspicious anyway, jumpy and ready to see plots everywhere. They knew of course about the discontent among the younger Hadrons and feared above everything they would lay their hands on the country's main source of wealth.

Juba had thought, and thought again, and consulted Dromas and Meryx, and then Mara. It was she who suggested that Juba should see the chief Hadron, and ask that the guards on the storehouses should be half Mahondi, half Hadron. This meant that any future thefts must be the responsibility of both. Juba agreed, for he had come to the same conclusion, though the plan meant the easily suborned Hadron slaves might steal the drugs.

Juba said that the chief Hadron, an old man called Lord Karam, was intelligent, even if half the time he was drug-sodden. Juba went to see Karam, taking Meryx. Mara had hoped to go too, but the men said, You keep out of sight, Mara.

Karam was alone in his great throne room. He sat not on the throne but on the floor, on a cushion. He was not befuddled as he sometimes was when Juba came for a talk. That he was alone meant that he, like Juba, did not want the crisis to be generally known—yet. The first thing he said was that if Juba knew who the culprit was then he or she should be executed, as an example, according to law. Juba said that his spies believed a Hadron was responsible.

"Are you suggesting a Mahondi wouldn't steal?" asked the old man, smiling, dry—dangerous.

"No," said Juba. "But my guards are spied on, every minute they are on duty, and the spies are spied on. But we found a tunnel into one warehouse, the biggest, very cleverly constructed and concealed. And in another there was a place in the roof, very hard to see." And now Juba had to challenge Karam directly. "My spies tell me that your nephew Meson is selling poppy and ganja."

And now a long silence. Then Karam said, "To whom?"

"That we don't know." Juba did know, but knew that Karam must know too.

Karam thought for some time, his eyes hooded. Then he said, "It would be best if the extent of the losses were kept quiet."

"I agree."

"There will be no execution. My nephew will be given a warning."

Juba had to stop himself protesting: this was weakness, and he believed it was not the time for it. He dared to say, "Lord Karam, is a warning enough?" But what he was suggesting, not saying, was that Meson was the leader of the rebellious young Hadrons.

"It depends on the warning," said Karam.

Meryx told Mara that this was where the two men looked at each other, long and seriously. "I felt a lot was being said, but not in words. They respect each other—Karam and my father. Juba says that all of Hadron would have collapsed long ago if Karam had been stupid or weak."

The next thing that happened was that Karam's nephew Meson was arrested for brawling, with half a dozen of his friends, and they were given prison sentences, with hard labour. Short sentences, but it was as if they were not Hadrons at all, but common criminals.

Then the Hadrons announced that from now on all the milk, and the products of the milk, from all the milk beasts, would go to them and that included the beasts belonging to the Mahondis. Juba and Meryx went back to Lord Karam and said that there were pregnant women again, among the Mahondis, and it was in the interests of everybody, including Hadrons, that they should be well nourished. It was agreed that the pregnant women should have a ration of milk, but it wasn't very much.

There were four of the women pregnant—with Kira, five.

Mara was sent to the courtyard by Juba, who jested, though not with much conviction, that he was afraid of going himself, in case there would be other demands on him, and it had taken his recent experiences as a stud to make him feel old.

Kira was in her sixth month. She was not enjoying herself, was peevish, complaining and sat sighing and shifting her big body about. She and the four pregnant ones sat together, patronising the others, and demanding—and getting—special treats. Candace would come out to them, with a little dried fruit, or some broth, and Ida cooked them sweets, and this though there was talk of rationing because the crops had failed. The shade was less in the courtyard, and the women kept moving themselves out of the way of shafts of hot sun, for the leafy canopy was thinning. Candace arranged for a light cloth to be stretched across part of the courtyard.

Mara told them that Juba said they should offer to work with the milk beasts. As they began to complain and protest, she explained how little milk there was going to be. Then she waited for them to get the point. They did, but were wondering about this excessive caution. Usually there would be jokes: "Take a little swig when no one is looking"—that sort of thing. Mara said, "Do your best not to be noticed. And when the traders come from the River Towns we'll make sure we buy plenty of dried milk."

The young women looked at her with dislike, and not concealing it. Who was this Mara, who was always with Juba, with Meryx, with Orphne, who in such a short time had become so trusted a member of the Kin that she could give them orders? This cold, nervous, ugly woman, with her flat, bony body—well, yes, it did look better than it had, not that any of them had ever seen it, for she was always covered up . . . perhaps she had a scar or an infirmity she wanted to keep hidden? And her hair—it was growing out, she was less of a freak, but who did she think she was?

Mara knew how much she was disliked. And she thought with quiet bitterness, Why? I'm no threat to them. They're so soft and lovely and well fed and they have never felt that they have dust so deep in their skin it will never wash away.

Now the women competed to work with the milk beasts, and they milked them, and stole a little when they could, and often stood with their arms around the hairy, dusty necks whispering endearments, not minding that their bright, clean dresses had to be shaken free of dust. They took the beasts little treats of a wisp of hay or a bit of green stuff, or bread. Candace complained that they were all in a trance of dreams and imaginings, and she ordered them to attend some lessons she was arranging. And no, she said, the three new women who demanded Juba's attentions would have to wait until the five babies were born and everyone could see how these pregnancies turned out.

It was Larissa who gave the lessons, which were tales "from long ago, no one knows how long," and they were from a medical textbook found in ancient records.

The first tale was about a woman called Mam Bova, who hated her husband, tried to seduce a handsome youth, who rejected her, so she took poison and died.

The listening young women in their shaded courtyard, lolling about in their charming dresses, smiled sarcastically, for they knew why they had to listen: it was not only Kira who was sick with love, they were all falling subject to it as if a sweet poison were in the air.

The next tale was about a beautiful, powerful woman called Ankrena, who similarly hated her husband, left him for a handsome soldier, and committed suicide by throwing herself under a machine described in a note to the tale as "running on parallel rails, but this vehicle lacked freedom of movement and was soon superseded by ancient versions of the skimmer."

Then Larissa told a story about one Mam Bedfly, who was a young slave girl, in love with a sailor from across the sea (notes about sea, oceans, ships and so on were incomprehensible); but the point was, feeling abandoned, she killed herself.

Larissa then laughed at the sceptical, disapproving faces she saw all around her, stood up and said, "I'll give you another dose tomorrow."

Next morning the courtyard was crowded to hear Larissa's warnings.

The first was an old myth about a girl called Jull and a boy called Rom, from different clans, and they fell in love and killed themselves because the clans disapproved. This tale provoked much more discussion than yesterday's, for someone said, "Like Mahondis and Hadrons," and they shuddered at the idea of being in love with an ugly Hadron.

The second was about a young girl who wanted to marry a handsome young man instead of an old rich man her father had chosen; but instead of killing herself she was imprisoned for ever in a temple.

"What was a temple?"

"It was a place where they kept their God."

"What was God?"

"An invisible being who controlled their lives."

This caused a good deal of merriment.

The last tale was of a famous singer called Toski who befriended a young man escaping from the police because he was intriguing against an unjust king. In exchange for the promise of freedom for the young hero, Toski slept with the Chief of Police; but he betrayed her, and the famous singer killed herself.

This tale they took more seriously than the others. All knew about the young Hadrons who were waiting to rule this country, some of whom were currently in prison as a punishment, and that all the talk among the younger Hadrons not in prison was of assassinations, coups and uprisings.

The salutary tales did not seem to have much effect, for the three young women—by now four—who wanted babies, said they were going to insist on their rights. This time it was Juba himself who said, "Wait until the rains, and the other babies are born."

When Mara's flow began, she went to inform Candace, as she had been told to do, and found her in the big communal room where they all met, looking at a great map filling all of one wall. Mara had not known it was there: it was usually covered by a curtain. Mara quickly said what she had to, and then ran to the map, feeling she was being given food long denied. Candace had her hand on the cord that pulled the curtain across, and as Mara stood staring, said to her, "Aren't you supposed to be in the fields with Meryx?"

Mara said, "Candace, when may I begin my lessons?"

"What is it you want to know?"

"Everything." Then Mara managed a laugh, in response to Candace's dry little smile, and said, "Well, I could begin with numbers. Counting."

"But Mara, you know as much as any of us. You come here to report to us that there are so many sacks of grain or ganja or poppy."

"Is that really all any of you know?"

"We know all we need to know."

"But when I say ten thousand sacks of grain, it is because there are ten thousand. That is my limit, or the limit of the sacks, not the limit of numbers. Or we say, 'in the old times,' or 'ten thousand years ago,' or— yesterday I heard Meryx say, 'twenty thousand years ago.' But that's what we know, or imagine, but not how far back things really went. What do we know of *then*—and how do we know it?"

Candace sat down and nodded at Mara to sit. What Mara was seeing was Candace's hands: long, clever hands, but they were restless. Mara thought, She is impatient, but controlling it. She is trying to be patient with me.

"Long ago there were civilisations so far in advance of us that we cannot begin to imagine what they were."

"How do we know?"

"About five thousand years ago there was a terrible storm in a desert that everyone thought had always been a desert, just piles of sand, and the storm shifted the sand and exposed a city. It was very big. The city had been made to keep chronicles—records—books."

"We had books when we were children."

"Not of leather, not skins. Of paper. Quite like the stuff we make our shoes of . . . the indoor shoes. And on them printing."

"Our books had writing."

"Printing. Techniques we don't have. The city was a kind of Memory. Histories. Stories of all kinds, from every part of the world. The scholars of then—that was a time of peace—trained hundreds of young people to be Memories: not just to remember, but to write things down. They decided to preserve the histories of all the world . . ."

"The world," said Mara, desperate.

"The world. Some wrote it all down, but others were trained to remember. And that is where all our knowledge comes from—those old libraries. But it was just as well the Memories were trained, because when the books were exposed to the air they crumbled into dust and soon there weren't many left. But there are collections of them, or there used to be, in the stone graves where they used to bury people. The graves are cool and dry and the old books and records kept well."

"Why are we stupid compared with them?"

"We aren't," said Candace. "We are as clever as we need to be for our lives. For the level of living we have now."

"And we are the same as those old people that had all that knowledge?"

"Yes, we think so. One of the old records said that. Human beings are the same, but we become different according to how we have to live."

"I feel so stupid," said Mara.

"You aren't stupid. You came from a Rock Village and didn't know anything but how to keep alive, and now you know everything we know. Mara, if we said to you, 'Take charge of the food supplies,' or 'Run the militia,' or 'Manage the ganja and the poppy,' you could do it. You've learned what we know."

"Do we have Memories here with all that knowledge in their heads?"

Candace smiled. It was the smile that made Mara feel like a small child. "No. We are very unimportant people. What we know has filtered down from those old Memories who kept all the knowledge there was in their heads—but only a little has reached us. But because we know that it is important to preserve the past, we train people to be Memories, when we can."

"Are you training me to be a Memory?"

"Yes. But to understand what we have to tell you, you have to know first about practical things. It is no good telling you about different kinds of society or culture when you don't know what you are living in. And now you do. Besides, we need good people to help us run things— we are so short of them. You must see that."

"When are you going to start teaching me?"

"It seems to me you have made a start. You know the history of the Mahondis, right back to the beginning when we came down from the North, three thousand years ago."

"Are we the descendants of the old Memories?"

"Yes, we are."

"The world," said Mara. "Tell me about the world."

At this point Meryx came in and said, "Mara, I was looking for you."

Walking around the edge of a building that held the stores of poppy, Mara came face to face with Kulik. There was no doubt of it. She was wearing Meryx's clothes and the little cap into which she had bundled her hair. He stared at her: he was doubtful too. Last time he had seen her she had been a boy, half grown. She did not look much like she had in the Rock Village. But he did stare, and turned to stare again. He had got a job, pretending he was a Hadron, in their militia. They weren't going to ask too many questions, being as short of people as they were. And now Mara saw him every day, as she went about with Meryx or with Juba. She had been afraid of him as a child and she was afraid now. She told Meryx who he was, and said he was cruel and dangerous. Meryx said that fitted him perfectly to be a member of the Hadron militia.

It was time for the rainy season to start.

"I seem to have spent my life watching the skies for rain," said Mara, and Meryx said, "I know what you mean." But he didn't. Around Mara's heart lay a heaviness, a foreboding, for she could not keep the thought out of her mind, *It is not going to last.* She fought this with, They say there have been droughts before: I might be wrong. I'll say yes to Meryx and we'll have a child and then . . .

It did not rain. It was time to scatter the poppy seed and the ganja, but the earth was hard, and the wind blew away the seed. The ganja self-seeded and did better.

Kira gave birth, and it was at once clear that what she had wanted was not a baby, but Juba, for she took the infant to Ida and said, "I don't want it." Ida was transformed. She took into her house a woman from the fields who had wanted a child and failed, and the two women spent all their days watching over the infant.

The water was low in the reservoirs, and so it was rationed. Instead of tubs being taken every day to the male slaves, now it was once a week. No longer could the courtyard women spend hours in the basins that were kept filled in the bathhouse. The people of the town, used to the morning and evening watercarts, were told that there would be one delivery a day, and the penalty for wasting water would be death.

The townspeople were showing all kinds of initiative. In the dusty gardens were appearing food crops and—illegally—poppy. They began trading direct with the River Towns merchants. The Hadrons turned a blind eye, because that meant less food had to be found from the half-empty warehouses. Some old wells were discovered, and the owners sold water, and some even established bathhouses. The monopoly of water, which the Hadrons had used for so long to control the town, was weakened—not ended, for there were not many wells. But the Hadrons were losing power fast, and when Juba said that it would not be long before the ruling junta was ousted, no one disagreed.

Meryx said to Mara, "Please live with me, and let me try to give you a child."

Mara moved in with Meryx and found herself overthrown by love. She had not imagined there could be such happiness. Nor that there could be such fear. For her to get pregnant—what a catastrophe, she knew it. Only in a dream or a fever could she possibly have seen herself with a child, here, where the drought was creeping up from the south. For the first month she lied about her fertile time, she was so afraid. But Meryx knew it and she could not bear what he was feeling. And so she abandoned herself as she might have thrown herself into a fast flowing river, thinking that she might or might not find landfall. And yet she loved him—and it was terrible.

Meanwhile the rainy season trundled on. There was a brief, violent storm, enough to half fill the reservoirs. The river ran again from under the cliff. There was not another storm. The poppies sparsely sprang up, and died. They were replanted and there was patchy rain. The ganja was thick and odorous, but only half its usual height.

The four babies were born, all of them strong and well formed. The other waiting women reminded Juba of his promise, but then two of the babies died. It was the drought sickness. Mara knew it, but the others did not, because they had never seen it. Mara told the two mothers and Ida's nurse to sit by the babies and give them clean water, but the water was not really clean. The Kin commandeered water from one of the deep wells in a citizen's garden, and it was thought that this was keeping Kira's (or Ida's?) baby and the other two surviving babies alive. The babies were sheltered inside the house because of the dust blowing about, and it was touching, and wonderful, and frightening, to see how all the Kin made excuses to go into the rooms where they were, to touch them, beg to hold them, watch them sleeping—men as well as the women.

One day Kira was not there. She left a message for the Kin that she was going to try her chances up North.

Mara was hurt by Kira's leaving, as the Kin were. She thought, Why did I let myself love Meryx? It was better when I was hard and cold. Now I'm open to every feeling, and it hurts, loving Meryx.

Their rooms were in Juba and Dromas's house, and looked into a court where some cactuses were flowering. Mara and Meryx's bed was a low, soft pallet, heaped with cushions. Mara lay in Meryx's arms and thought how strange it was that this delight—lying with your love in a clean, soft, pretty place, and sometimes the scent from the cactus flowers blowing in—was something that could be taken for granted, as Meryx did. Mara let her palm slide down the smooth warmth of his arm, felt his hand close on her shoulder, and for her these were pleasures she felt newly with every breath she took: pleasures as fragile and sudden as the cactus flowers bursting impossibly out of dry brown skin. Meryx had lain with others before her, and he had always been with them in sweet-smelling beds, in rooms that were cool and kept the dust out. For him there was nothing extraordinary that two bodies with healthy flesh should lie wrapped around each other, while strong hearts beat their messages. Mara often did not sleep, not wanting to lose a moment of this delight, or she half-slept, or dreamed, and more than once she dreamed that it was Dann in her arms and this startled her awake and into grief. She knew that sometimes when she held Meryx she felt that he was part-child, and wondered if this was because of Dann; for Meryx was not childish at all. Except in this one thing: that he did not know life was so like a cactus flower, and could disappear in a breath. And this was really what separated them. Strange that no one, even the clever-est, could know anything except by direct experience. All his life Meryx had been sheltered in the Kin, been safe, and that was why he could not hear when she whispered, "Meryx, it is not going to last. Let's go now, while we can."

His hand often slid to her waist, and fingered the little ridge of skin the rope of coins had left there. She had had to trust him with her secret. She begged him not to tell the Kin, and he said he would not. She pushed the cord with its heavy knots into the middle of a big cush-ion that lived at the head of their bed. All the anxiety she carried with her, unable to subdue it, was concentrated on what was in that cushion. She insisted on cleaning this room herself, would not let anyone else do it. She sometimes came secretly to the room to put her hand down into the cushion and reassure herself. When Meryx saw her doing this he was unhappy, and said, "I believe that you care more for that little nest-egg of yours than you do for me." And she said, "Without that money we would not have reached here. We would have been killed on the road." She knew he did not understand, because he had never in his life been at that point where it could be life or death to own a root filled with juice, or a bit of dry bread, or a coin that could buy the right to be car-ried in a machine out of danger. He would let his fingers travel along the tiny, rough line of skin and say, "Mara, I sometimes wonder if you could have said no to me, to keep those coins a secret."

As that rainy season ended, with months of dry before even the possibility of skies that held the blessed water, there were rumours that bands of travellers were leaving Chelops for the North, and they were not passing through, from the south, but were from the Towers. More people had been living there than had been suspected. They were leaving because of water rationing. People living near the Towers sold water to anyone in them, whether fugitives, criminals or squatters. But now there was little water to sell.

And then this happened. Mara was with Juba, in the warehouses that held the sacks of precious poppy and ganja. When she had first seen them, the warehouses were crammed to their roofs, but now were half empty: so much had been stolen, and then there had been the poor rainy season. What were they going to trade with, when the River Towns traders came next, if they reserved enough to keep the Hadrons happy?

Mara was a little way from Juba, who was standing on a tall pile of sacks using a probe to make sure they held what they were supposed to, and not chalk or chaff. Kulik came to her and said loudly, "My replacement has not arrived, he is sick." Then he said, very low, "Your brother is on level two, Central Tower." And then aloud again, "I've been on duty twenty-four hours now." He winked at her, a slow closing of a fat, yellow eye, and there was such malevolence there, such hatred, that she literally went cold, and trembled. She told him loudly to go off and rest. As he turned, there was his smile, poisonous, a threat. She thought, How strange: all my childhood I was dodging out of the way of this man and now here I must be careful not to find myself in his hands again.

She did not tell Juba about Dann, and this made her feel treacherous. But surely he must have known about Dann? His spies and the Hadrons'—they knew everything. When she went back into her room she ran quickly to feel if the rope of coins was still there. They had gone. So Juba did know what Kulik had told her, and was making sure she would not bribe her way into the Towers? She was standing with her hand still deep inside the big cushion when Meryx came in, and what she saw on his face made her exclaim, "So you told the Kin about my coins? They knew all the time—"

"I had to, Mara. Surely you must see that?"

She asked for a full assembly of the Kin, at once. They were all there. Meryx did not sit by her, as he had been doing, but was with Juba and Dromas. She was alone again.

"You never trusted us," said Candace, saying in her tone, her manner, her cool, hard eyes, You aren't really one of us.

"And you don't trust me," said Mara. "You've known Dann was there. You knew all the time and you didn't tell me."

Juba said, "You see, Mara, we don't think as highly of Dann as you seem to."

"You don't know him."

"He's dealing in drugs," said Juba.

"And taking them," said Candace.

"He sent me a message," said Mara. "Why now?"

"We think it is because all the people from the Towers are leaving to go North," said Candace.

"And he is ill, apparently," added Juba.

Mara was silent, looking at the faces that seemed to press in on her: concerned faces, but calm, and at such a distance in experience, in feeling. And Meryx too: He could have sat by me, she thought.

"What do you want us to do, Mara?" asked Candace.

"What I would like is for you to give me some soldiers to go with me to the Towers—all right, I know that you won't. But you asked."

"And you know that everything depends on our keeping quiet, keeping out of sight, never making trouble."

"And all this," said Mara, "to preserve something that isn't going to last anyway." She spoke low, falteringly, hardly able to look at them, because she knew how strong their defences were. And what their faces were saying was, Poor child, there she goes again.

"We know that you are going to try to get to the Towers," said Juba, and his eyes were wet—yes, he was fond of her, Mara knew; they all were—and yet here she sat, and though she was wearing a green, flouncy dress, as pretty as anything there, and as fresh, and as clean, she felt as if she were still caked-with-dust Mara from the Rock Village.

"We aren't going to stop you," said Candace.

"Are you going to give me back my money?" she asked.

Candace took the cord of coins out of a little bag, and threw it across to her. Mara caught it and could not stop herself quickly counting them—and saw critical looks being exchanged. "Did you think we were going to steal them?" asked Candace gently.

"Can we see them?" asked Ida. "I've never seen a gold coin in my life." At this they all laughed. "Who has?" . . . "None of us" . . . "Only Mara" . . . were the comments.

Mara untied half a dozen of the coins and put them to lie on a dark blue cushion. Everyone craned forward, then Juba reached for one and soon they were being passed around.

"How lovely," sighed Ida. "You're richer than any of us, Mara." And she handed her coin back. Soon Mara had all knotted safe.

"If you take that to the Towers they'll kill you for it," said Juba.

"I can see you think I'm very stupid," said Mara. Then she said, deliberately, looking around, forcing them to look at her, "Dann came back for me to the Rock Village. He had got farther north than here. He didn't have to come back. I would have died if he hadn't. *I owe him my life.*" This last stopped them, impressed them: if someone saved your life, it was a debt of honour, and must be repaid, in one way or another. "I'm going to try tomorrow. And if I don't see you again—thank you," said Mara, through tears.

"Wait," said Candace, and threw her another little bag that had in it the small, light, flimsy coins everyone used.

In the room she had shared with Meryx she tied the cord tightly under her breasts, while he watched her. She took off the green dress, and put on the slave's robe from the bottom of her sack. She folded the green robe and laid it on the bed. Meryx was so hurt by this that he grabbed it and made her put it in her sack. "Why?" he accused her. "We haven't suddenly become enemies, have we?"

"I was wondering," said Mara. As he exclaimed, "*No,*" she put on the little cloth cap that she had been wearing as she went about her work with Juba and Meryx. Now she looked like a Mahondi slave: short, smooth hair, little cap, the rough woven robe that had once been white. She took off her house shoes, and Meryx snatched them up and put them in her sack. She pushed them right down, close to the wonderful clothes she had carried with her all the way from the Rock Village, and which all the Kin had marvelled over.

"I don't know what to say to you," she said to him. "I know I'll never lose my sadness that I didn't give you the chance to show you are as fertile as your father. But surely it's just as well—if I had been pregnant, or had a small baby, what would I be doing now?"

"Staying with me," said Meryx.

8

Mara set off for the centre of Chelops watched by many pairs of eyes, as she knew. The Kin were watching from the windows, and who else? She had not directed herself westwards since the Kin had taken her in. The fields, the pastures for the milk beasts, the warehouses, the suburbs where the Hadrons lived, the reservoirs and the streams—all these spread to the east of the Mahondi quarter, and that is where she had walked and worked every day. Now, her back to the east, she strode out, fast, towards the great Towers, at first through the pleasant houses of the Mahondis, in their gardens, which were mostly neglected, since so many houses were empty. For the year of her stay in Chelops she had been inside the protection of the Kin, and had become accustomed to the feeling of being enclosed, like a child looking out at the world from safe arms. Now she was on her own again. She was walking through smaller houses, in a mesh of little crooked lanes, where a big tree stood at a cor-ner, its leaves drooping, the shade under it no longer inviting passers-by to linger. Dust filmed it. Dust hung in the air, though the rainy season had only just finished. In a small, fenced garden a milk beast stood glar-ing, its tongue lolling: it had been fed and watered and perhaps petted, but its owner had fled, leaving it. Mara opened the gate, and saw how the beast had scarcely the vitality left to step out into the lane. Perhaps someone will help it, she thought. Now she was cautious, her eyes on the alert, because she knew that any person she encountered would probably be a Mahondi or Hadron spy. How empty the place was; had everyone left Chelops? This had been a big, populous city. The Towers were still a long way off. It was early afternoon now, and it would take her to mid-afternoon to reach them, and then she had to find Dann. The black of the Towers was dull, did not flash or gleam, but the great sullen buildings seemed to pulse out the stored heat of the drought. As the little lane she was following reached a big street, a running chair stood waiting for custom. This was the first of the spies, probably Juba's. She asked the Mahondi slave between the shafts, how much. She could have sworn that he was on the point of shaking his head, Not for you.

But he reflected and said, "Ten." She paid over ten of the ugly little flakes of coins and was soon being jogged along street after street, the Towers always coming nearer. Dann had done this work: both on these chairs, with one porter, and on the others, like boxes, that had two. She imagined his hard, muscular, thin back, his sprinting legs, between these shafts. This youth was tough, but perhaps too thin. Rations had been cut to the slaves, but surely not to hunger point? He had not asked where she was going, so he must have been told. She stopped him where the decent order of the streets gave way to the jumble of the crowded lanes and houses that had so long ago marked the first citizens' revulsion from the Towers. And here, at last, were people. When she got out, she saw that he set down his shafts and leaned on the chair, watching her. She quickly moved out of his sight, and into an eating house that was only a room with a few tables and chairs, and a long trestle where stood plates of rough slices of bread and jugs of water. The place was quite full yet everyone turned to stare at her. Did slaves not come in here? She was thirsty, drank a glass of brownish water, and almost forgot to pay the woman proprietor, so used was she to not paying for anything. She sat in a corner, pretending indifference to her surroundings, and listened. They soon forgot her. They were poor people, wearing clothes that had come from Mahondi warehouses. These faces were sharp and dissatisfied. She was not shocked by what they were saying, nor even surprised, for already, having left behind the comparative riches and comfort of eastern Chelops, she was seeing it as they did. They did not distinguish between Hadron lords and Mahondi slaves, but saw them as one: ruthless, grabbing, cruel masters who stole everything good for themselves and doled out what was spare to them, the poor people. But above all, Mara was seeing those gentle, favoured suburbs as a narrow fringe on the edge of this hungry town, clinging on there at the edge of the real town—the town that had been real, because from the talk it was evident how fast people were leaving. The Mahondis and the Hadrons, for all their spies and their webs of information gatherers, had no idea of how they were hated, how happy any one of these people would be to cut their throats. And Mara could hear Candace's indifferent, "Oh, there'll always be some malcontents."

Mara sat on, turning her mug of brown water between her long, pretty, well-kept fingers, making herself eat the coarse bread, remembering how only a year ago it would have seemed a feast; and saw in her mind's eye clever Candace, sighing Ida, Juba, whom she thought of secretly as a father, Meryx, with his kind, humorous face, Dromas, who loved her husband in a way that seemed to Mara like an old song or a story, Orphne, who knew everything about plants and healing, Candace's elderly sons, Larissa, whom you could hear laughing from one end of the house to the other, the women of the courtyard—all these people, Mara's friends, her family—and could not fit this picture together with knowing how they were hated, seen as wicked people.

Yet she, Mara, sitting quietly here, was left alone, with only the occasional curious or hostile glance. The woman who was serving watched her: she knew who she was. How much had she been paid? More importantly, by whom? Mara went to her, asked if rooms were let, and asked how much. The woman nodded, not looking at her, keeping her face neutral, and said, "For how long?" "I don't know," said Mara. "For tonight, anyway?" At this a spasm of something—amusement?—crossed the woman's face and she said, "Is that so?" And added, almost laughing, "There's a room."

Mara went out, looking out for the next person who had been paid to keep an eye on her, but she could not see anyone. The Towers were now close. They were very high, oppressive, and she was all at once filled with anger against the people who had built them: she knew that this feeling, a rebellious hate, united her with the people she had left behind her in the eating house.

It was afternoon, and the sky a hot glare. The Towers flung back shadows across the little houses. Ahead was the ring road around the Towers, and now she could see the tall fence, of the same kind as barred the stream running from the cliff in the east of the city: a jangle of rusty metal, as intricate and tangled as the lace the courtyard women made to edge their dresses. But there were gaps in this fence. Mara set her face to the north, to walk right around this inner town, with its twenty-five Towers, and she thought that it would be dark before she found Dann. Then ahead, opportunely, was the same running chair, and the same lad who had brought her here. She gave him ten bits of the metal money, without asking him, and told him to take her around the edge of the Towers, saying she wanted to see the entrance to the tunnels. He did not seem surprised, but she could see he was setting himself to be wary: she knew that set of the face, the shoulders, from Dann. He looked for a gap in the rusty wall of the fence, went in, and they were on the ring road. The entrances to the six Towers of this, the south-eastern quadrant, were all blocked by heaps of the same rusty, interlaced metal; but almost at once there was the opening of an earth tunnel, and nailed to its entrance was the crude picture scrawled on a square of wood of one of the yellow beetles she had seen on the escarpment high above the city. The young man jogged faster past this entrance, peering fearfully in. A foul smell came from it.

Two other attempts at tunnels had been made and abandoned. One had gone in about twenty paces, but had met with a reef: the stones were embedded in the red sandy earth like white teeth. A little farther on a tunnel had caved in. Now they had to cross the big road that ran east, which was easy, because it was hard and wide and smooth. Looking to the east there was nothing and nobody to be seen on this road. If Mara directed this youth to turn right now, on the road, in less than an hour she would be back at the beginnings of the Mahondi quarter, and for a moment she was desperately tempted to do just that. But they went on around the ring road, which was equally empty. There was one large earth tunnel here and it was well used. There were even two women sitting in the entrance, their legs stretched out. At first they seemed the picture of ease, but then discontented faces told a different story. A group of men came out of this tunnel, not taking any notice of the women, nor of Mara in her chair: not seeing anything much—their empty, staring eyes said why. They walked back along the ring road, presumably to the eating house. Now Mara and the youth were at the big road going north, the north-eastern quadrant behind them. When travellers went North, was this the road they used? She leaned forward to shout the question at her porter, but he shook his head and shouted back, "Too dangerous." In the north-western quadrant were several earth tunnels, and at the entrances of all of them were the warning pictures of the beetles. Could creatures the size of a five-year-old child still be called a beetle? Mara's flesh seemed to shrink and tremble at the thought of them, but Mara said to herself, How soft you've got! You lived with scorpions and lizards and dragons and outwitted them.

Now they crossed the big road running west, and here was the south-western quadrant, and again there was a large, well used tunnel, and at its entrance a group of youths seemed to be waiting: they lounged there, with sticks in their hands, and she saw a glint of their knives in the belts that held their tunics. They watched Mara go past, curiously. And she knew from their faces and postures that they could as easily attack her as stand there, apparently indifferent. They were drugged too, probably ganja. Which of the two used tunnels was she to choose? It had taken her longer to make the circuit of the Towers than she had expected. It was past mid-afternoon. She would spend the night in the eating house, and start again in the morning. She would use the south-western quadrant's tunnel, which was nearer than the others. Now they traversed the highway running south. She had seen it from the skimmer: a dark and shining straight line cutting the brown landscape. Soon they were in sight of the eating house and she asked to be set down. The youth stopped, let the chair tilt forward—and as she stepped to the ground Kulik came fast towards her from a lane, with two Hadrons behind him. He hustled her back into the chair and got in beside her. The chair porter was not surprised, merely lifted the shafts, while the other two waited till the chair was in motion, and went off to the eating house.

"Where are you taking me?" she asked, and he did not reply. He was sitting gripping the side rail with one hand, his eyes always on the move, and the other hand held a knife with which he was threatening any possible assailant as much as he was her. The two scars on his face were staring at her, promising cruelty. They had healed, but the flesh on either side of the scars did not fit, and there was a puckering, and that mouth, usually in a threatening grin, was permanently lifted in one corner to show yellow teeth.

"Did a dragon do that?" she asked. She thought he wasn't going to answer, but he said, "A water dragon. And there's poison in those claws. I thought I was dead." This last was said in the jocular, jeering way that she had been hearing from him since she was a small girl setting eyes on him for the first time. "And it's left poison in me, because I can sometimes feel it in my bones."

They were going back to the eastern suburbs. They passed the lane where earlier she had seen the milk beast. It was down on its knees, but sitting in the dust near it was a Mahondi field woman, and she was holding a dish of water to its mouth. They went through the Mahondi quarter. Now she was thinking, with horror, that he was taking her to the Hadrons: those foul, obese, drug-cruel old men, with their flesh lapping around them under their robes, their little, cold eyes. She thought, I won't, I'll kill myself—imagining being touched by those hands like pads of cold tallow. But the porter was jogging past the great house with its still-fresh gardens where the senior Hadrons lived. "Where are you taking me?" she asked again, but Kulik was here even more alert and on guard—well, yes, at any moment they might see Juba, or Meryx, or

Orphne, who would stop the chair or at least set up an alarm. The chair turned into a garden surrounding another big house that she knew was used by the young Hadrons.

The porter stopped, lowered the shafts, stood up, stretched, shook the sweat out of his eyes. Kulik took a grip on Mara's upper arm, which hurt—and his bared-teeth grin at her said he knew it did—and pushed her down in front of him out of the chair, then propelled her up some steps and on to a verandah where a Hadron guard lolled against the wall, asleep. Kulik knocked at the side of an open door and a young Hadron male came out, whom Mara recognised. And he knew her, and said, "Let her go." At which Kulik did as he was told, transformed from the bully into obedience.

This Hadron was Olec, and she knew him as a leader among the Hadron youth. He was one of those who had been given a suspended prison sentence. He was leading her by the hand into a large room full of young Hadrons, whose faces she knew. They sat about on cushions and pallets, indolent, and infinitely at their ease, just like their elders, she thought. These were not sick with drugs, they were not fat and disgusting, their flesh was not running to yellow grease, but they shared with their seniors a look of innate, taken-for-granted power. Every movement they made, the set of their heads, the way they lounged there, their confident faces—everything—said, We are rulers and shall continue to be. And Mara thought, sickened, But that is how we Mahondis were, back in our palace in Rustam, and the Mahondis here, slaves or not, seem like that to the townspeople.

"Sit down, Mara," said Olec, and let himself fall gracefully on to a cushion. "So, you were running away?" And this was not unkind, or an accusation, but that easy amusement at others which is a sign of confidence in power.

"A runaway slave," said another, laughing.

Mara sat on a low stool, from which she looked down on these, the golden youth, as they were called, and she thought, When they get into power they'll be just the same as their parents. They think they won't but they will.

"What do you want of me?" she asked, using the same almost easy camaraderie, which was because they were all young, and at least equals in that.

"I wonder if you are going to be surprised when we tell you?" said Olec.

"Try me."

"You are going to be my concubine," said Olec. "And you are going to produce children. For me. For us."

Now, the Hadrons had been a little more successful than the Mahondis with their breeding, but not much. "Hadron babies have been dying and we want to be sure of slaves."

Mara sat thinking, making herself smile, seeming cool and even amused. Then she said, "Are you planning a harem of Mahondis? Are you going to capture others? Juba won't like that."

"Juba will do as he is told," said Olec. "And you had run away. We didn't capture you from your family."

"Why didn't you take Kira?—she ran away."

"True," said Olec. "But we knew about Kira. More trouble than she was worth, we decided."

Here there was a loud, general and genial laugh. This was an all-male gathering. It was with this laugh that they discussed the qualities of the Mahondi women. What were the Hadron women thinking of this scheme?

"Well, Mara," said Olec, "do you have anything against me? If you don't fancy me, then take your pick." And she saw how these complacent young men's faces waited, smiling, for her to choose one—they were just like, she thought, a tray of Ida's sweets.

"There is just one thing," she said. "I am pregnant already."

At this there was an exchange of looks: first disbelief, then disappointment. And then, discontent. A couple of Hadrons actually got up and went out: this is a waste of time, said the set of their bodies.

Olec said, "But Mara, Meryx has never yet made anyone pregnant."

"No," said Mara. "But Juba has, several times."

And now she had to force herself to sit still, smiling, while Olec's eyes seemed to bore into her, travelled all over her, searching her body, her face, her eyes. Then he sat back and sighed, then nodded and even laughed.

"All right," he said. "Then why are you running away?"

"Who said I was running away? The Kin know all about it. I'm looking for my brother."

"What makes you think you'll like what you find?"

"How do you know what I'll find?"

"Your Kulik seems well informed."

"Why my Kulik?"

"He told us you were his sex friend when you were with the Rock People."

At this Mara was so angry that for the first time she was out of control. She could feel herself going white and cold with anger. She jumped up, stood staring, and it was hard to breathe.

At last she said, "It's not true." She was thinking, If he were here I'd kill him. Then she said, trying to make herself sound crisp and cool, though she was still breathless, "You should be careful who you use to do your dirty work for you."

"We know he's dealing in drugs," said Olec. "But provided we know when, why and to whom, that's quite useful."

"So you think he'll be loyal to you and you can trust him?"

"If we pay him enough, yes."

"If I were you I'd find out who else he is keeping informed," she said. She meant, the senior Hadrons. She was in command of herself again, and smiled, and said, "Are you going to let me go?"

"What can I say? Of course. Better luck with this baby than some of your others."

"We still have three alive and well," said Mara.

"Not enough."

"Don't trouble to come with me—I do know my way."

"But I shall come with you," said Olec, and he walked with her to where they could see the Mahondi quarters. This was to make sure she was going there. Then he said, "See you around," and she said, "I expect so."

In the courtyard the women sat about in their pretty dresses and sang, and played little games to amuse the babies. Mara thought, They are like cactus flowers, blossoming for a day, and her heart ached.

She changed into a clean robe, a pink one, thinking that she wanted to please Meryx, and then went to Ida to ask if she could visit the looking-wall—that is what it was called. A long time ago some craftsman had covered a whole wall in flakes of bright substance, which was mined in the eastern mountains, so cleverly that they fitted together in a single sheet, and the joins were like a fine net over a surface that reflected what was in front of it. The wall was like still water with a spider's web over it, and here all the women would come to look at themselves. Mara stood there, saw her smooth, shining hair, her smooth, healthy skin, her new breasts, and she thought, No one could say I am ugly now. She tried smiling at herself. The trouble was, her eyes, for she was cursed with seriousness. Big,

deep, serious eyes . . . She sighed, left the looking-wall and found Meryx
in their bedroom. They fell into each other's arms.

Then she asked that all the Kin should assemble that night to hear
her. And so, that evening, when the lamps were lit and set about the big
room, Mara, with Meryx beside her and holding her hand (like Juba and
Dromas; oh I wish it were the same), began to talk.

She could see from Juba's face that he knew what had happened in
the young Hadrons' house, and so she began with that. She said she had
been kidnapped "for breeding purposes" but that she had told a lie: she
had said she was pregnant, by Juba. At this Meryx's hand fell away from
hers; she knew what a dreadful blow she was dealing him. "It's not true,
Meryx. I had to get away. I had to say something that would make them
let me go."

"It's not true," said Juba to Dromas.

"It's not true," said Mara to Dromas, and then again to Meryx, "But
it's not true."

Dromas looked closely at her Juba, who nodded at her, smiling, and
took her hands and said, "Believe me, Dromas."

But Meryx sat beside Mara, silent and not looking at her, and his
face—it hurt Mara to look at it.

Candace said, "Begin at the beginning."

And Mara said humorously, "But surely you already know everything?"

"Not everything. Tell it so everybody knows."

There were more people than usual that night, twenty or so, all
curious.

Mara began with leaving this house, the walk through empty streets,
the dying milk beast—which was rescued, she assured them—the waiting chair and its porter, the eating house and the woman proprietor who
was obviously expecting her.

"Not my doing," said Juba.

"No, it was the junior Hadrons," said Mara. "They organised it all."
And went on to describe, and now in slow and careful detail, the journey around the perimeter of the Towers, the tunnels, the notices warning of the beetles, the mass of wire that had holes torn in it, the way the
chair runner had been appointed to be available for her all day. She
dared to take a look at Meryx, but he sat with his face turned away and
Mara could see how concerned Dromas was for him, for she watched
him, sighing.

Every detail, every moment; until she was kidnapped by Kulik, and taken to the young Hadrons. There, she told what had been said, but left out that Kulik had lied about her.

When she said that she had told Olec she was pregnant by Juba she could feel how Meryx took the blow as if he had not heard it before.

"Meryx," she said, direct to him, "it was a lie. I had to. Please believe me."

He simply sat on, listless, and shook his head as if to say, But it's all too much.

Now people were getting up, about to drift off, and she said, "Please don't go. I must say something, I must." And they sat down again.

And now she began an impassioned plea that they must leave, leave Chelops, while they still could. "You can take a lot of food and clothes; it won't be a hardship, as it was for us. Please leave—I don't know why I can't make you see it." They were looking at each other, doubtful, serious, but she was afraid they were already deciding not to listen.

"What is happening here is exactly the same as I remember from Rustam."

"You were a small child," said Candace. "How can you remember?"

"I do remember. And this is the same. People leaving. Criminals. The gardens dying. The water going. Less food." But she thought, But up here it is not so bad. And they don't know how bad things are down there, in the town. They live in this soft little place on the edge of the city . . .

Juba said, "We have had a bad rainy season."

"You told me yourself you have had several poor seasons recently," said Mara. "Majab's emptying now, so the travellers are saying. I heard it in the eating house. There's almost no one left. When we flew over it a year ago there were still people and things seemed not too bad. Then it was like what Chelops is like now. It happens so fast. In the Rock Village we heard that Rustam was empty and filling with sand. The Rock Village must be, by now. The sand is blowing into Majab, so they say."

A silence now, a worried silence, but restless, people fiddling with their clothes, their hair, not looking at each other then looking, and smiling, wanting to smile it all away.

"You should make preparations now," said Mara. "Pack everything up. Hire every kind of transport there is left."

Now Candace leaned forward, and insisted, "Mara, it is quite understandable, with your history, that you should be nervous. But it only needs one good season for everything to go back to normal . . ."

"No," said Mara, and Juba backed her up. "It will take more than one."

"And," went on Candace, "you don't understand something. It doesn't matter to us if everyone in the town leaves. We won't have to feed them—it will be a good thing. We are quite self-sufficient here."

"The Hadrons wouldn't let us leave," said Juba.

"Then fight them," said Mara. "The militia will obey you, not the Hadrons."

But she could see from their faces that it was the enormity of the effort they would need that was dismaying them. She thought, All this gentle, lovely living has made them soft. They aren't fit for such an effort. But they have to be, they must be . . .

And she went on persuading, pleading, begging. Then she had an inspiration, and said to Candace, "Draw back the curtain off that map you have there."

And Candace got up and said, "No, Mara. I won't. It's enough for one evening." Then, to the others, "Let's say goodnight, and let's thank Mara for all the information she has given us."

The company dispersed, and the note of their talk was a subdued grumbling and complaint.

Mara went with Meryx to their room, and she had to persuade him, again and again, that no, she had never mated with Juba, nor ever thought of it, "You must believe me!"—and she supposed he did, in the end. But he wept, and she wept, they clung to each other, and they made love again and again. It was the middle of her fertile period. And Meryx said, "If you get pregnant tonight, I'll never know if it is mine or Juba's." And then he said, "You make love with me as if you love me, but you are leaving me."

And she was making love most hungrily: because of the long, frightening day; because of how exposed she had felt, away from the protection of the Kin; because of the dying milk beast, which haunted her, for she knew there must be others; because she was going away from Chelops, and she knew she would leave her heart behind in this place, with these people, with him.

In the morning Juba summoned them all to tell them that a messenger had arrived from Karam, saying two things. First, that the young women working with the milk beasts must stop stealing the milk. If they did it again, they would be beaten. This reminded them that they were slaves. The second part of the message was that four Mahondi girls must be sent to the young Hadrons. There would be no coercion as to choice. The girls could choose from among the young men. When they were proved pregnant, they could return to the Kin, if they wanted. There was much anger, outrage, protests of "But I won't go." But Karam had said which girls must go, by name, and these choices proved how well the Hadrons knew all their characteristics. The four were the youngest, good natured, and eager to please.

Meanwhile Mara was going to the Towers. Juba had said he would allow her to go only if he sent guards with her. She said, "But you didn't insist on guards yesterday." He said, "I didn't know the Hadrons planned to kidnap you." "The Hadrons said Dann was ill. I might have to stay in the Towers to look after him." Meaning: I know you don't want him here. Juba said, "Bring him here." Which meant Dann had been discussed, and the Kin had decided to indulge her.

Four running chairs arrived. In three were two militia, and there was one in the chair for Mara. He held a knife, and a big club lay beside him.

Now she knew exactly where to go, and they arrived at the tunnel in the south-western quadrant before midday. Six militiamen had been ordered to wait for her, with the chairs, the porters, and their weapons. She wanted to go into the Towers alone, but the man with her in the chair insisted on coming too: Juba's orders, he said.

The two stood hesitating at the entrance to the tunnel. They were afraid, and did not hide it. They did not know how long the tunnel was: a little, round eye of light meant its end. The air coming from it was bad. They were afraid of who they would meet inside it. Mara lit a big torch of brushwood soaked with tallow, and the militiaman took it from her and held it high. Now she was glad he was there. The earth of the tunnel was hard: it had been in use a long time. They passed the yellow carapace of a beetle, killed some time ago, for shards of black and yellow lay about. The torchlight illuminated rough earth walls and a low earth ceiling. There were felted spiders' webs on the ceiling, but these were not the monsters Mara had seen before, just ordinary working spiders, watching from their stations. About fifteen minutes of slow, cautious progress took them out into the air, from where they could look back and see the rusting tangles of the fence, which no longer could keep anyone out. They were right under the six black Towers of the south-western quadrant.

"Central Tower, second level," she told the man, and they walked through the six, noting how the dust was heaping around their bases, and that it looked untouched, like sand piling around an impeding stone or dead tree. They were right under the Central Tower, and ahead was an entrance, with black steps going up to it. The steps had sand filling the back of the treads. The doorway into the Tower had had a door, but it was slanting half off its hinges, and they walked straight into the long passage, as big as a hall, that bisected the building. Near the entrance were the machines that had once, on a system of weights and pulleys, carried people to the top of the building, but they were disused now. Stairs went up. Feet had recently used those stairs: dusty footprints were on every step. The first level showed a corridor running high and wide to where a light came in through a broken window. The guard was walking just behind Mara, his knife in one hand, his club in the other. He said, "If someone is in front, then get behind me. If someone attacks from behind, then run up the stairs but keep me in sight." The stairs to the second level were steep and there were many of them. They arrived safely, having seen no one. Again there was the long, empty corridor, doors opening off it, as many as thirty or forty doors.

"I shall go in first," said the man. "No, I have my orders."

And they began on a systematic inspection of the rooms. Some had had recent occupants. There were discarded containers, a roll of stained and torn bedding, old clothes like rags left on the floor. Everything was dusty. No people. Where had they gone? "North," said the guard. "They've all gone up North." There was the heavy, sickly smell of poppy, and there were whiffs of ganja, but not as strong.

Then, at the eleventh or twelfth attempt—they were losing count— the guard opened a door, stepped smartly back because of what he saw and stood to one side to let her in, with his knife held out in front of him. "Be careful now," he said.

Mara saw three bodies, lying with their heads to the opposite wall, very still. Asleep . . . or dead? The smell was horrible: a concentration of fumes and sickness. The guard briefly retched, but stopped himself, holding the back of the hand with the knife in it to his mouth. His eyes, staring at the bodies, were appalled, shocked, afraid. Mara would have liked to run away, but she made herself walk in. She bent over the body nearest to her, whose face was hidden by an arm, probably to keep off light falling painfully into his eyes, and saw that this man was so ill, he was nearly dead. His breathing was feeble, coming at long, irregular intervals, and his eyes were half open. He could die on any one of these light, gasping breaths. A Mahondi. The second body was indisputably a corpse. Again, a Mahondi, and there was a gash across his throat, and a pool of glazing blood.

Now Mara knew, because of the shape of the head, what she would see. She knelt beside Dann, who was prone. She turned him over. He was drugged senseless. His face was covered in sores. On his arms and legs were sores and scabs on dry, flaky skin. His eyes were glued with pus. His whole body was festering, and sick, thin flesh clinging to bones.

"Dann," she said, "it's Mara."

He did not open his eyes but he groaned. He tried to speak between gummed lips. "Mara," he said, and muttered and groaned, until at last she understood what he was saying: "I killed the bad one."

And now, at least partially enlightened, Mara looked again at the face of the dead man and the face of the nearly dead one and saw they were alike. Brothers, perhaps—or could have been. Dann was here because he had been a prisoner, certainly of these two men, but most of all because of his own ancient and terrible obsession.

"He was bad," said Dann, in a child's voice. "Mara, he was the bad man."

In a corner stood the can Dann had carried so far, when they travelled here, and in it slopped a little sound of water when she shook it. She poured water into that sick, foul-smelling mouth, and his lips reached up towards it as if they were creatures on their own account, desperate for water.

"Can you get up?" she asked.

Of course he could not get up, but Mara had said it because she could not connect this poor, sick thing with the lithe and light Dann she knew. The guard gave her the knife and the club and, his face screwed with disgust, easily lifted the starved body into his arms. Around the clear space where Dann had been was a litter of lumps of black, sticky, poppy stuff, pipes, matches, and bags of bright green, dried leaf. Mara quickly took the matches and hid them. The guard looked at her strangely: he had never known that you could lack matches.

She looked at the dying man and the guard said, "That one won't be alive tonight." And in fact it looked as if he had died already: he was very still.

And so Mara and the guard, with Dann in his arms, went back down the corridor to the stairs, down the stairs to the first level, and down

more stairs to the ground level. All the way Dann lay limp, but now his
eyes were open. At the foot of the stairs the guard laid him down to take
a rest, and Dann muttered, "Water, water," and Mara gave him all that
was left in the can—which she had not been able to leave behind. Outside the Tower, Dann put up his arm to shield his face, and this encouraged Mara, that he had that much strength. And then they went back
through the tunnel, Mara holding up the torch. Near the entrance a
couple of girls came towards them.

"Where are all the people?" asked Mara.

They were rigid with terror—of her, or of the club and the knife she
held, and pressed past, backs to the earth wall.

"Isn't there anyone left?" Mara persisted.

"Why should we stay? What for? We're off this afternoon." And they
began to run as fast as they could. Mara heard, "Mahondi spies."
"They're spies."

Mara had Dann beside her in the chair, the guard who had carried
him on the other side. Dann groaned and his eyes rolled. The movement of the chair was making him sick. The four chairs jogged their way
back to the Mahondi quarter, slowly, because the runner in Mara's chair
was finding it hard to pull three of them. Mara stopped them at
Orphne's house. Dann would end up there anyway. She did not want
the Kin to see him in this state. When the guard lifted out Dann the
four runners came to stare at him, recognising him. Their faces, and
those of the guards, staring down at Dann, had that look that puts the
observer at a distance, like a judge pronouncing sentence. Dann was
going to die, those faces said. And the young men thankfully turned
away, the porters back to their chairs, the guards to their barracks, away
from the ill luck of death.

Mara told the guard to lay Dann on a bed, and thanked him and
saw him, too, hasten away. Mara found Orphne stirring cordials in her
dispensary, and showed her Dann. Orphne lifted Dann's hand, saw
how it fell, apparently lifeless. "So this is the famous Dann," she said;
and as she stood there, in a white, floaty dress, a red flower in her
hair, she seemed to have walked into that room out of another life, or
truth.

"I thought you were as bad as I was likely to see," she said, and then,
"Let's start." She went into her medicine room and came back with a
strong-smelling drink. Between them, the two women got most of it
into Dann, because he did swallow at last when choking became immi-

nent, and went on swallowing, slowly, mechanically. "Good," said Orphne.

And now she took off her white dress and stood there in her long, flouncy, white knickers, her big breasts loose, and said, "If you don't want that outfit to be filthy, take it off." Mara removed her clothes—Meryx's. She could not stop herself looking enviously at Orphne's breasts, when hers were still mere plumpnesses on her chest. Orphne saw her looking and said, "You had nothing at all there when I first saw you. Now, lift."

They lifted the unconscious boy and took him next door, and laid him in a shallow bath. Over him Orphne poured sun-warmed water, full of herby substances. Dann was dirty, but nothing like as grimed as he had been a year ago, when the two of them came down the cliff into Chelops. The water was soon dark with dirt and blood and full of crusts from the scratches and ulcers. Then, as his body became visible, they saw around his waist a chain of scars that looked like knife cuts, as if he had decided to make a belt of scars for decoration or for ritual. They were red and sore-looking. The round, flat shapes under the skin told Mara what she was looking at, and she cried out to Orphne, who was manipulating the flesh there, "No, don't squeeze." Dann had cut himself and slid in coins for safe keeping, and let the flesh heal over them. Orphne's eyebrows were demanding explanation and Mara, close to tears, said, "I'll tell you . . . I'll explain."

That water was flung out into the hot sun where its filth could be burned harmless, and more medicinal water was poured around Dann, who lay quite still, eyes closed, and did not move when Orphne wiped his face and his eyes, and then held his head to wash his hair. They dried him and laid him back on the bed. Orphne cut Dann's nails, which were not far off claws, rubbed oil into dry skin, and examined his teeth, which were loose in inflamed gums, as Mara's had been so recently. But now they were white, and tight in her head, and she was proud of them: so would Dann's be, quite soon.

"So," said Orphne again, "this is the famous Dann. He looks like you, or will when he's better." The big, strong woman, with her big breasts, which shone with health, and which seemed to shine, too, with kindness, stood looking down at her patient; and then, evidently pleased, because he was already less inert, slipped on her pretty, white dress, replaced the cactus flower in her hair, and said, "Now Mara, you aren't going to like what's going to happen next, so I suggest you leave."

"No, I'll stay."

Orphne tied Dann to the bed with cords, interposing soft pads of cloth between them and his skin, laid a single piece of cloth over him, because of the heat, and sat down next to the bed. "Have you ever seen someone while the poppy is leaving them? No? Well, I'm warning you."

Mara replaced her tunic and trousers, and sat down. She thought, It doesn't seem as if he knows I am here, but perhaps he does.

For some time Dann slept, or was unconscious, or both, but then he began to moan and shiver, and to fight against his bonds; great spasms shook his body, while his teeth clenched and his eyes rolled, and yet all the time he seemed insensible, so that it was like watching someone fighting in his sleep with an assailant, or a drowning person struggling just under the water. It was sickening, and Mara wanted to untie him, and hold him as she had the small child, to lift that body of his, as light as bones picked up from beside a road, and run away with him, shelter him, hide him—but she knew that this Orphne with her skills was right, was curing him, and that she must sit quiet and watch.

Juba came, and Dromas, and then Candace and Meryx, and one after another all the Kin came and stood gazing down; and their faces were like the guards' and the runners', and—Mara thought—probably like hers when she looked at the dying milk beast. Which was not going to die, because a woman had given it water, and Dann was not going to die either.

Late that night Meryx came, found Orphne alert by Dann, and Mara sitting dozing in her chair. He tried to lift Mara up, to take her to bed, but her hand tightened around Dann's. Orphne shook her head at Meryx, who stood beside Mara for a while, stroking her hair, and Orphne watched, smiling drily. Then Meryx kissed Mara, and went off to bed; and Orphne said, meaning the way Mara envied her big body and her breasts, "But you have the lover, and I don't."

Through that night Orphne poured her soporific drinks and potions into Dann; but as she said, what goes in must come out, and she had a shallow pan by her, which she slid under Dann, watching for the moment. Then she had to clean him, and he screamed at the first touch. Orphne pulled apart his legs. The two women bent, shocked, to see how the area around the anus was bruised black and green and blue, and the anus itself was loose and bleeding. Mara had not seen anything like this, nor even thought about it; but Orphne knew and said, "They enjoy it when they are young but they don't think that when they are old they won't be able to hold their shit."

"Old," said Mara, for this was one of the moments when she felt as if she lived a different life from these gentle people. "Which of us do you imagine will live to be old?"

"I will," said Orphne, smearing ointment on Dann. "I shall be a wise old woman. I shall be a famous healer. Even the Hadrons will honour me and use my cures."

"They do now," said Mara.

"And my little hospital will be twice as big, and I shall train people to be famous healers."

And Orphne sat smiling at Mara, calm, confident, and with only a hint of the pugnacity that means doubt.

"You know," said Mara, after a long pause of not knowing what to say, "I have learned something important here. Do you want to know what it is?"

"I suppose so," said Orphne, her smile meaning now: There she goes again.

"You can tell someone something true, but if they haven't experienced anything like it they won't understand. Orphne, if I say to you, 'You can't buy something if you haven't got the money,' you'll say, 'Well, of course.'"

"Of course," said Orphne, laughing.

"But you don't understand what it means to have a cache of gold coins, each one enough to buy a house, or three hours in a sky skimmer that means saving many days of walking—but if you don't have a little coin, you can't buy a piece of bread or some matches."

"Then change a gold one," said Orphne. "What's the problem?"

"That's the problem," said Mara.

All the next day Dann shook and screamed and begged for poppy, and Orphne kept him bound and cared for him; and that night he was so exhausted she gave him the same strong sleeping draught she had given Mara. It had in it ganja, and a little poppy; and when Mara said, "But surely that is only prolonging the agony," Orphne said, "There is only very little poppy, but it will be enough to calm him. To take someone off the stuff suddenly—you can, but it is dangerous when he is as weak as Dann."

And so Dann was put soundly to sleep, and Mara went to Meryx, and he held her as if he had recovered a treasure he had thought lost for ever.

And so the days passed, Mara and Orphne fighting to bring Dann back, and slowly succeeding. At night Meryx claimed Mara.

Then Dann was himself, though still weak, and Mara asked him what had held him so long in the Tower.

He seemed to be speaking of events long in the past. His eyes searched the ceiling as he spoke, as if what he remembered was pictured there, and he did not look at Mara or at Orphne, who held his hands, one on each side.

He said he had run away from the barracks for the male slaves when he heard the Towers were occupied. There he joined a gang of runaway slaves, mostly Mahondis, but there were some Hadrons and others. They were all men. There were women in the Towers but they kept to their own groups, afraid of rape. No woman by herself could survive. Dann's gang lived by stealing food from the fields, and then poppy from the warehouses, through intermediaries. He mentioned Kulik. At first Dann had sold the stuff to get food, but then he began taking it: now his words became halting, and he said, "There was a bad man." And now this was little Dann's voice: "A very bad man," piped little Dann. "He hurt Dann."

He had done it again: his memory had refused to accept a truth too painful to be borne. "Weren't there two men?" asked Mara.

"Two? Two?" muttered Dann, his eyes darting this way and that, frantic, evading some memory.

Mara said steadily, taking a risk, "When I came into the Tower and found you, there were two men with you. One was very ill, near dead. One was dead. His throat had been cut."

"No, no," screamed Dann, and struggled terribly inside his bonds. Orphne shook her head at Mara, and brought another soothing drink.

Mara sat on while Dann sank back into sleep, and she thought how he had always refused to remember that first time, when two men became one, "the bad one," and now again there's one man. Dann killed him but he's not going to remember.

This, the returning of his mind to his time in the Tower, made Dann relapse. He became childish and spoke in a child's voice; but soon that left him and he lay for hours, conscious, but sombre, apparently a long way from either woman; and when he did look at them, he was surprised by what he saw. And Mara thought, We sit here beside him, kind and smiling, in our clean, pretty dresses, and now even I have a flower in my hair. And we must seem to him like some kind of a dream.

Soon Orphne had another patient. Ida was brought in, raving that her baby had died of drought sickness, though in fact the infant was well and had become the pet—with the other two babies—of the whole Kin, so starved were they for the pleasantness of babies and small children.

Ida was in the room next to Dann's, and Orphne tended her while Mara sat through long days with Dann, watching as he was returning to normal. He was nearly himself again.

But perhaps that was painful, like swimming up out of dark dreams, for his eyes were always haunted and sad. And Mara caught him sitting up, leaning forward to look at his own backside over his balls and prick, where the bruises had faded, the flesh no longer ragged. But it was still ugly, and Dann's face twisted up in disgust, and he lay for a long time with his arm over his face, not wanting to see Mara.

It was soon more than a month since the four girls had gone to the young Hadrons, and three of them had conceived. Juba went to visit them and found they were well and happy. They no longer thought the Hadrons were disgusting, and two decided to stay with their lovers. Soon another four girls went to the Hadrons, and there were six Mahondis there. The courtyard seemed sad and empty, with half the women gone, though one was pregnant. Pregnant by a Hadron, though. There were not enough hands for all the work, and Mara went to join the slaves making food, since it was dangerous for her to be out in the fields, where the Hadrons might capture her again. She had not conceived. Meryx said, dry and sad, for this was how most of what he said sounded these days, "And so you didn't sleep with Juba." "But I told you I didn't," said Mara.

Dann got out of his bed and went to the courtyard where the girls were, for company; but there was something about this sad, restless-eyed, silent young man that subdued them, though they did not know the full story of his experiences. So Dann sat in the big general sitting room. Something new had happened. Candace no longer kept the curtain over the wall map. Mara had gone to her, and begged to be taught, and asked for the wall map to be exposed. She was there so much that soon the curtain was left pulled back. Dann sat there looking, thinking, sometimes for hours, and when she could Mara was with him.

Ida got better, and was full of accusations and discontent. She hated Kira; she complained the Hadrons had not asked for her to go and be made pregnant. She said that Dann was a thief—and that was on the day he found that the gold coins he had hidden in the bottom of his sack, those that were not around his waist, were gone. He complained to Juba. Juba said he was not to worry, the coins would be returned. And meanwhile Ida sat playing with the softly shining, enticing things. Eleven of them. She let her fingers move among them, while she smiled, and seemed to feel that from them she was receiving something delightful that was feeding happiness into her.

Mara asked Dann if those coins in the flesh around his waist were uncomfortable, and he said they were, when he thought about it.

"Perhaps I should ask Orphne to do the same for me," said Mara.

Orphne was present and said, "Then you'll ask in vain."

Dann said to Mara, "You were quite right when you decided we should never put things up our backsides or your cunt. That's where they always look first."

Orphne was upset, really distressed, and looked pleadingly at them both. "My dear Dann," she said, "my *dear* Mara!"

When she was out of the room Mara said, "We have to soften things up for them. They don't understand."

Orphne brought Mara a necklace of seed cases: big, brown, flat ones into which the coins would fit. But the contraption would slide heavily around Mara's neck, making any observer curious. "Besides," said Mara, "when you are travelling you don't wear necklaces."

"Are you going to keep all yours in one place?" asked Dann, meaning Mara's cord of coins, again in its place under her breasts.

"Well, where can we put them? My hair is too short."

"How about in our shoes? These heavy Mahondi working shoes—we could slip a few into the soles?"

"It is easy to lose a shoe. Or someone might steal them."

"I think the best place is with my knife, at the bottom of the knife pocket."

"Yes. Eleven coins won't show."

"First I have to get them back from Ida."

"She's gone crazy," said Orphne, "just a little. Humour her."

Dann said, "I'm going to get you a knife—you must have a good knife, Mara."

Dann wanted to leave now; Mara, Orphne backing her up, said he wasn't strong enough yet.

Soon they were into the second dry season since the two had come to Chelops. The milk beasts were happy to stay in their sheds and let the dust blow past outside.

"There'll be riots in the town," said Larissa: "we've cut the rations again." For although they knew that the townspeople were going, and going, and mostly gone, none of the Mahondis seemed able to take the fact in.

Of the twelve young women who had been chosen by the Hadrons, ten had conceived, and six had chosen to stay with the men they had once thought of as enemies.

Mara wore a robe too big for her and kept it unbelted, for she had told the Hadrons she was pregnant and that was four months ago.

Again Dann said they should leave, before the dry season sucked all the life out of Chelops. Mara knew they should, but her heart hurt and ached at the thought of leaving Meryx. Yet she had to go. Yet she could not bear it.

Juba was summoned to Lord Karam and asked about the health of the new Mahondi babies. And by the way, how was Mara? Was she carrying well? Was she healthy?

"Very healthy," said Juba, putting on a look of self-congratulation.

And now that was it: they must leave.

On the evening before Mara and Dann left, all the Kin together with the new babies and their nurses were in the communal room. Mara and Meryx had put on the wonderful robes that Mara had carried with her at the bottom of her sack, and appeared, as the others said, as if they were going to their wedding. Again everyone exclaimed over the workmanship, the material—which no one there had ever seen, or dreamed of, and they fingered a sleeve, caressed a bit of embroidery, wondered over the dyes.

"Give it to me, I want it," said Ida, tugging at Mara's robe.

"You can't have it," said Dann. And then, "I want my gold coins. Give them to me."

Ida pouted and sighed and ogled Dann, and said, "Ida wants them. I want them. I won't give them to you."

Dann stood over Ida and said, "Give them back. Now." Then, as Ida writhed her shoulders about and lisped, "No, no, no," Dann whipped out his knife and was holding it at her throat. "Give them back or I'll . . ."

She wailed, and took the little bag of gold coins from her bosom, and he snatched them from her.

Everyone was shocked—Mara too. Angry—but Mara knew the dreadful anxiety that had been gnawing Dann. She went to stand by him.

"It was only a game, Dann," said Dromas. "Ida was only playing."

"Then it's our lives she was playing with," said Dann.

The good humour, the charm, of the occasion had gone. In a moment everyone would have left. Mara said to Candace, "I want you to show everyone that wall of yours. I want to say something."

On this evening the curtain was hiding the map, and Candace was unwilling to show it. But as Mara stood confronting her, Candace at last got up, went to the wall, and pulled back the curtain. Most people had seen what was there, but had not really understood, as Mara had found out. It was just some old thing that had nothing to do with them, that old map, which for some reason Candace valued. Now all the Kin turned so they could see the wall. Candace moved lamps so that it was illuminated. Mara would remember that scene, hold it in her mind, and come back to it when she thought of Chelops. There were about twenty people in the room. The women sat in their soft tinted gowns, their black hair loose on their shoulders; the men were in their yellow house robes; and all the alert and apprehensive faces seemed to float above bubbles of soft colour, the whole scene glowing in the light from the lamps.

At first it seemed that the picture they were looking at had been blanked out with white: the top half was white from one edge of the frame to the other. Beneath this nullity of white hung, or projected, fringes or edges of colour, on a background of blue. Blue filled the bottom half of the picture, and in it were bigger coloured shapes, and two very large shapes, one of which had scrawled across it, IFRIK. This map was no delicate creation: it did not come from the same world of accomplishments as the robes Mara and Meryx had on. It was painted crudely on white leather: the joins of the hides that had gone to make this great map had to be identified and discounted in the general picture.

The other big shape, which resembled Ifrik, was South Imrik. Both were merely outlines on the white, crudely coloured, with dots for towns and their names, and black lines for their rivers.

Mara, who had sat in this room with Candace and with Dann, sometimes for hours, knew that what it said could not be grasped without explanation. And now Candace began, in a heavy, reluctant voice, and with many pauses.

"This white represents ice," she said. "None of us has ever seen ice. It is what water becomes when it is very cold. Water becomes solid white, like rock. All of this . . ."—she walked slowly along the wall, pointing—"is ice or snow." She pointed to the bottom half: "And this part of the world is free of ice. It is where we live. Ifrik." And she pointed to a black dot somewhere in the middle of Ifrik: "This is where we are. This is Chelops." At this there were sighs, almost groans, because of the little-ness of their world. "When we say the world, we should not see it flat, like that map. It is round. Like this." And here she said, "Wait a minute." And she reached into a niche in the wall under the map and brought out a very big, round shape, and set it on a table. It was one of the gourds grown for the milk beasts to eat. The surface had been rubbed smooth and white chalk rubbed in, and the information on the wall map was done here in black for the outlines and blue dyes for back-ground. But on this globe there was no white mass covering the top half.

Candace pointed to the very top of the globe. "Look," she said, and they saw a small cap of white. "Ice," said Candace. "Just a little, at the top of the world. And at the bottom, too, this small shape of ice. That is how the world was once—they say about twenty thousand years ago, but perhaps it was more—there was no ice or snow here." And she swept her hand over the white expanse on the map. "It was warm. All of this . . ."—and she walked again, from one edge of the wall map to the other, pointing at the white—"it was all free of ice, and there were cities and very large numbers of people. They think that for fifteen thousand years all this area was free of ice, and during that time there were civilisations. They were much more advanced than anything we know. And then the climate changed, and the ice came down and covered all this space . . ." And she walked, pointing. "The cities and civilisations disappeared under sheets of ice. The 'world' for us is this . . ." And she swept her hand over the fringes and projections from the ice, and the two big shapes, Ifrik and South Imrik. "But once the world was this . . ." And she pointed to the globe.

Mara knew, because she had gone through the process herself, that all present were wrestling in their minds with immensities. Yet, at the same time, with smallness. They looked at Ifrik, and knew with their minds that it was vast because they could see the dot called Chelops; looked at a little triangular projection beneath the white that Candace said was Ind, a large country, full of people—so it was believed, or it had been in the past—and then at Chelops again, which was their world, and the centre of Hadron, which Candace outlined with her finger: just a little shape there in the middle of that immensity, Ifrik.

"These have never had ice," said Candace, pointing. "Ifrik has never known ice. South Imrik has never known ice. The climate has changed

for us, many times, but never ice. Or so we believe. Nor Ind. Nor . . ."
And she pointed to the east of Ind where thick fringes of colour hung
below the white, and dots and splodges of colour spread out. "Islands,"
said Candace. "None of us has seen the sea, and probably won't ever see
it. I know some of you have not heard of it. It is water. Salt water. Most
of the surface of the world is water." And she turned the big gourd so
that they could see how much blue there was.

"How do you know all this?" asked one of the girls, and could not
conceal her resentment. Mara knew this resentment well: it was what
people feel when being asked to take in too much that threatens their
idea of themselves, or their world.

"It was all in the sand libraries," said Candace. "Our Memories knew
it." And now she said to Mara, "You want to say something, I think."

Mara went to the wall and from there looked back at the faces which,
every one, showed something like anger, or reluctance. They did not
want to know all this. She said, "All this happened quickly—so Candace told me. This . . . "—and she indicated the globe, with its tiny caps
of ice top and bottom—"was how things were for fifteen thousand years.
And then the ice came down, quite fast, in a hundred years."

"Fast?" jeered one of the girls. She was seventeen. To her the hundreds, and the thousands, and the tens of thousands, meant no more
than the kind of talk children overhear: grown-ups conversing above
their heads using words they do not know.

"It began," said Mara, "when these lands here . . . "—and she pointed
to the north of the globe—"which had people and towns and plenty to
eat, had to empty because it got so cold, and they knew the ice was
coming. And that took . . . "—she looked at the girl who had spoken—
"not much more than twice seventeen years."

The girl burst into tears.

"These things can happen quickly," Mara pleaded, imploring them,
begging them. "Just imagine: all of this, all . . . "—and she made the
globe spin slowly—"all of it here, the top half, beautiful and good to live
in, and then the ice came down over it."

The people were restless, their eyes evasive and gloomy, and they
sighed, and wanted to leave.

Juba said, "Mara is concerned for us all. She wants us to leave Chelops."

"Where to?" . . . "When?" . . . . "How, move?"—came from various
people.

"North. Move North now before you have to. Up there they say there is water and plenty of food."

But it was too much for them, even those who knew what Mara thought, and had heard her pleas before, and they were leaving the room, not looking at her, exchanging little smiles.

Dann said to Mara, as if they were alone and all the others irrelevant, that she must be awake very early, and he would come to pack with her. He apparently did not notice that the Kin ignored him as they left. Only Orphne embraced him, told him to be careful and remember that poppy did not suit him.

Meryx and Mara did not sleep.

While Mara and Dann packed their sacks, Meryx watched. He was pale and seemed ill.

Into the very bottom of Mara's sack went the ancient robes she and Meryx had worn last night: "wedding robes"—she said she would remember them like that. Then the one brown garment they had left. A green house dress and a blue one: Meryx would not let her leave them behind. Light shoes. Trousers and tunic—Meryx's—that she had been wearing outside. A clean slave's robe. Matches. Soap. A comb. Salt. Flaps of flat bread. Dried fruit. A small skin of water, in case she and Dann were separated.

In Dann's sack was a spare slave's robe. Loin cloths. The same provisions. The top of his sack was filled with the old can, which held clean water from a good well. The robe he wore was the one he had arrived in, and he said it was a good thing it was stained and old. He had his eleven gold coins pushed well down into the bottom of his knife pocket. Mara too had on the robe she had come in. Orphne had sewn into it a new knife pocket: she had wept doing it. In that was a knife in a leather sheath. Mara had on her head a little woollen cap.

Meryx said angrily that if he had met her like this in the fields, he would have ordered her never to wear that disgraceful old rag again. His voice was thick with tears.

A message came from Candace that she wanted to see Mara before she left.

Mara found her staring at the map whose upper parts were all white—the Ice.

Candace said, "Mara, you are an obstinate woman. And you don't seem to realise you have put me in a position where I must either keep you here by force or let you go off into such terrible dangers."

Mara was silent. She saw, to her surprise, that Candace was not far off tears. She was thinking, Then I suppose she does care for me.

"And you are unfeeling. You don't mind that Meryx will be unhappy and that we shall miss you."

"I know that I shall be thinking of you all."

Candace's laugh was a sad little sound. "You may think of us, because you know us and how we live. But we will not be able to think about you—where will you be? And how will you be?"

And now she was weeping. Mara dared to approach her, and take her in her arms. A frail thing, she was, this formidable old woman, who ruled her tribe with such authority.

"It is a terrible thing," whispered Candace, "you can't imagine how terrible, watching your family get less, slowly disappear." She recovered herself, pushed Mara away and said, very bitter, very angry, "People risked their lives for you. Gorda—the others. The two precious children . . . And you don't care about that." And on her face was clear to see how her words, her thoughts, were betrayed by what she was seeing: Mara in her travelling clothes, and Dann, as she thought of him.

"Well," said Mara, "no one has yet explained why we are so precious. And who thinks so?—you do." She knew this was brutal: Candace's face showed it. "You are the Hadrons' slaves. And whatever Dann and I were once—then all that is under the sand in Rustam. And if we are so precious, then the important thing is that we survive. And we are not going to agree about that, Candace, are we?"

Candace sat silent. The distance between them was very great. Mara thought wildly that she should again put her arms around the old woman, to make up for what she had said; but what she saw on Candace's face was too bad to be softened by hugs, kisses—even tears.

Candace reached out for a leather bag that lay near on a table. She gave it to Mara. It had in it some light coins, easy to change. Candace said, "And now go. And if you know of someone coming our way, send news of yourself, tell us how you are."

Mara said, "Candace, no one travels south, no one. Don't you understand?"

On the verandah Meryx and Mara stood in each other's arms, feeling how the wet of their tears tried to glue their cheeks together, and not knowing if the trembling was their own or the other's. Dann leaned against a pillar and looked out into the early light: the sun was rising behind the house and throwing great shadows westwards.

Yesterday Dann had gone to find the depot where Felice, who had brought them to the cliff above Chelops, was to be found—or they hoped she was, for there were rumours she was leaving Chelops to go North. Mara let Dann go alone: she did not dare to be seen by the Hadrons, who must know by now that she had told them a lie, and would be looking out for her, to take her for their harem.

Dann had found Felice working on her machine. "It's you," she said. "So you don't like being a slave. And the other one, your sister?" Because of his surprise she said, "Not many secrets now in Chelops—not enough people left to absorb secrets. But I must confess it took me some time to connect that poor little lad with the new boss woman in the Mahondi quarter."

"We want to go North. How much?"

"How far?"

"The River Towns."

"If you stop there you'll have to move on again. They aren't doing too well either. You'll see for yourself, because I have to make a landing to refuel. If you give me two gold coins for each of you I'll take you to where you can get on to the big river. You can go a good long way on that. But you'll have to be here just after sunrise tomorrow."

Dann agreed.

"This is my last trip. There's nothing for me here, and Majab is finished."

When he returned to tell Mara, she said, "When Felice picked us up—when she landed on the road because she saw us down there—it was because her orders were to collect any stray travellers, by themselves, and tell them some lie, and then take them to the Hadrons. Why do you think she won't cheat us now?"

"Four gold coins," said Dann. "Besides, she didn't cheat us last time."

"She might take the four and sell us to somebody else."

"But she didn't bring us right into Chelops, did she? And she told us to avoid it. She warned us."

"We don't have any choice, I suppose."

9

In the running chair, Mara held her sack, Dann his, and each clutched two coins. Their knives lay beside them on the seat.

They reached the depot as the sun did. Felice was standing in a pose that surprised them, because she was rigid, staring at something on the ground, as if she had seen a snake and was afraid a movement might provoke it to strike. Mara was thinking, When I first saw Felice she seemed to me a wonder in her blue working suit, with her clean face and nice hair. But now compared with the Mahondi women she seems shabby and tired. Then she saw what Felice was staring at but could not at first understand.

Under the skimmer and around it were a dozen or so yellow balls, the size of sour fruits, or Mara's fist, and they glistened and were fresh and with-out dust, because they were inside a webbing or net of thick slime, like saliva. They were vital and alive, these balls: they seemed to pulse, and as the three watched, one cracked open and out crawled a pincer beetle, and it sat in the mess of its egg and slime resting from the effort of getting out. These were eggs, the eggs of a pincer beetle. And then they saw the beetle itself, half concealed by a wheel of the skimmer, its yellow body, the colour of its eggs, vibrating as out of its back end emerged slowly, one by one, more of its eggs. The great black pincers, the size of its body, stretched in front of it, and its black eyes stared at the three. The newly hatched beetle was crawling up a wheel; other eggs were cracking open, and a swarm of baby beetles were struggling free of the slime. Another reached a wheel.

"Quick," said Felice and, straddling the mess of eggs and new beetles, pulled herself up into the machine, and then hauled first Mara and then Dann in by the other door. Felice started the engine and the machine rolled away from the beetle and her progeny. The creature was still lay-ing eggs and, unable to attack this machine, was clacking her pincers like knives, in warning.

Half a dozen soldiers came in sight, and when they saw the machine, began to run towards it.

"They don't want to let you go," said Felice, shouting over her shoulder at them. The machine rose out of reach of the soldiers, who went to the beetle, to attack it with clubs and knives. One slipped in the slime, and vomited, with disgust. Meanwhile the beetle, with incredible speed, had scuttled off and disappeared behind houses. And then the machine had risen too high for the three to see more than that there were soldiers standing gazing up after them. Felice slid back a shutter in the floor of the machine and peered down at the wheels: where were the beetles that had climbed up? Two were there, obstinately clinging to a wheel with their six clawlike legs. "They'll be blown off," said Felice, and slid back the shutter.

They were flying low along the big road north, which shone below them like water. It was empty, but beside it on a parallel dust track were groups of travellers, hundreds of them. From up here it was easy to see that Chelops was dying. Over in the east were little dots in the fields and streets that meant people were about, but the central areas seemed deserted. The reservoirs were low, and did not shine, because there was dust on the water. And now there was the Kin's central house, just visible, a tiny thing, and in the courtyard they were assembling for the early meal, and perhaps missing her. It seemed to Mara that her heart was all a bruise, a painfulness, that was making it hard for her to breathe. She sighed, she suffered, and yet her eyes were dry. She thought that quite soon the Kin, and Meryx, and all the loving and the kindness, all that would seem a dream and her heart would become cold again.

Soon Chelops' Towers were a little black hand of sticking up fingers, and then they, and the town, and the eastern fields—the Kin, Meryx—had gone; and not long after that they were leaving Hadron the country, because the big road was ending, and now they were flying over scrubby bushland.

Dann opened the floor shutter, and exclaimed that the beetles had fallen off: they could see a tiny speck falling into the scrub. Mara was wondering how the Kin, and the Hadrons, would deal with an invasion of these creatures, whose pincers could sever a limb or cut a child in half . . . But she felt she couldn't bear it, those monstrous beasts anywhere near the Kin: it was as if those giant pincers threatened her own heart, but it was all too bad to think about. She knew her feelings were becoming numbed, and she was glad.

An hour of flying over scrub and semi-desert, and scrub again, and the yellowish brown became infused with green, and below was a little, thin river, edged with bright green. There was a town ahead, and Felice said she must stop here for the sugar-oil fuel, and they must stay in the machine and remain calm. This town had people in it who all looked alike, and the first time you saw them it was a shock, and sometimes there were hysterics and even panic. "But it won't be the first time for us," shouted Mara, remembering how that band of people, all alike, had come to the Rock Village, and how Dann had scared them away because of his fascinated, horrified staring.

"Do you remember?" she urgently shouted at Dann. "Their faces—exactly the same."

Dann smiled, and took her hands, and said, "Mara, you worry about me too much. Thank you, but it's all right. I've seen these people when I was travelling, when I was away from you. I saw a whole town of them, in the East."

This was certainly not little Dann speaking, and Mara felt her heart ease and the worry lift.

The machine landed in a big square. At once a heavy, warm air enveloped them, and they felt the sweat start all over their bodies. Felice took cans from beside her, and said again, "*Don't* get out." She walked quickly off, ignoring the people who were crowding in to see the machine.

They were the same as Mara remembered: large, solid, heavy . . . But no, their eyes were different, not pale but brownish. Their skins were not greyish but dull brown. Their hair was not a mass of light frizz but a mass of brownish frizz. Their faces were all the same, with lumpy noses and low foreheads made lower because of the frizzy bush above. Their clothes were all of the same colour: it seemed that these creatures had been dipped into the same dye tub, fully dressed, so that everything was an ugly, lightless brown.

Dann took her hand. "They are stupid," he whispered. "Don't do anything to surprise them. I think they have only one mind between them. They are like animals."

It was like being surrounded by animals that were being drawn into a centre by curiosity: wary, ready to take fright and break away in a run. Those staring faces, those eyes!—and how did they tell each other apart? What could it be like, being one of a people exactly alike, every tiny detail the same, so that you turned your gaze from one face to the next, but it was as if you were still staring at the first? They were coming in slowly from everywhere, all the surrounding streets and lanes, a big crowd of them, and the skimmer seemed a frail thing in the middle of that crush and press. What big, solid people they were, and their hands so big, and their bare feet splayed out into the dust on great pads of flesh, and their toes continually curling and moving like an insect's antennae sensing the air. One lifted an enormous hand and felt Mara's hair. "Careful," she heard from Dann. "Don't move." Another poked her cheek. Was this one a man? Were they male, all of them? They seemed so. On the other side of the machine one was peering into the empty seat beside the pilot's, and was trying the handle, but the door was locked. The machine began to rock. Feeling it rock, they all put their hands to it and pushed; both sides pushed. They were not co-ordinating, and so for a moment the machine shook and seemed to jump about, but was not in danger of falling over. And then Dann let out a shout of alarm, which caused the creatures to jump back and glare, mouthing and muttering. One of the pincer beetles had survived the flight, and was trying to scuttle away from the machine between the big feet towards the houses. Dann shouted, "Kill it, kill it," but they were slow in turning, and then in seeing it; and then they turned to stare at him, not understanding; and then, at last understanding, went after it, all jostling together like a herd of beasts. Then, having lost it, because it scuttled away somewhere, they were slow in turning and resuming their slow pressure in on the machine. Felice appeared, running, with a can in each hand, shouting to scare them away so she could pass, and when a gap appeared as they turned to stare, she jumped in and at once started the machine, and it began to rise. As it did, the enormous hands were reaching up to bring it down, and could have done, had they been a moment sooner. The skimmer flew off, and the three looked down at those upturned dull faces, a multitudinous unity, a nightmare.

Beyond the town, the skimmer dropped among the dry grasses of the savannah. Felice got out and fed the machine with the sugar-oil in her cans. Then she said, "Get out, you two."

The brother and sister stood side by side while the young woman walked all around them, stood examining them. Meanwhile she talked. The town just behind them had only males in it. There was a town near by that had females. They all met at stated times, to mate: at the equinoxes and solstices. You could hardly tell the males and females apart.

Now, having thoroughly inspected the two, she pronounced judgement.

"You are altogether too appetising, both of you. You've got to disguise yourselves a bit."

Mara knew she was in danger: she felt her aptitude for fertility strong in her body, and had seen that her black shining hair and her new soft breasts had invited stares. And Dann was a handsome youth and, with all his scars and weals well hidden, looked like a sleek and well fed member of the Kin.

"Runaway slaves," said Felice. "That's what you are and that's what you look like. You're an invitation to any slave trader. And don't imagine that all slavers are sweet and kind like me."

"Tell me," said Mara, "if you had sold me and Dann to the Hadrons, what would you have got for us?"

"Not much. You were in such a terrible state. In good condition, the equivalent of one of your gold coins. Yes, you are right—it was easy to let you go because I wouldn't have got anything for you anyway."

Mara smiled: this exchange was without ill-feeling.

"So I can see I'm not going to make you believe in my kind heart."

"Have you got a lot saved?" asked Dann.

"I'm glad to say, yes. A profitable business, buying and selling people."

Now she went to her machine, and took from it one of her working uniforms, faded blue, top and trousers and belt, and said, "I'll charge you as little as I can." Dann counted small coins into her hand till she said it was enough. "You wear it," she said to him. "You are in even worse danger than your sister is."

"I know I am," said Dann, and this acknowledgement eased Mara's anxiety, for she had seen how he had been looked at recently, in Chelops. He stripped off his robe, put it into his sack and for a moment stood almost naked. He had on a small loin cloth. Felice laughed and said that she could fancy him herself, but unfortunately fate would soon separate them. Dann responded to Felice's flirting, and that cheered Mara too. For she secretly feared Dann's returning to drugs, and being used by men again.

He put on the tunic and trousers, slipped his knife into a pocket, and again the two stood side by side.

"Better," said Felice. "You could pass for a workman and his slave." She fetched water and bread from the skimmer, and the three sat on the earth and ate and drank. Around them stretched the yellow, beaten-down grasses of the dry season, and under them was the soft detritus of last year's wet season, for there had been rain here, if not enough. The sky was tall, and so blue, and there was only a little dust in the air.

"We have a long flight," said Felice. "And when we get to the next town you must go straight to the river and make sure of your places in tomorrow's boat. Then go for the night to an address I will give you. Pretend you are a couple, it will be safer. Don't go into the town, they don't like travellers. If I can refuel I'll leave straight away for the East. I'm going to sell the skimmer. It's too hard to get sugar-oil and spare parts."

"And then?" asked Dann.

"Then I'll take what turns up." They could see that the idea of throwing herself on the chances of luck invigorated her. "I might buy a boat with the skimmer money and run a river service instead."

"And I suppose I won't see you again," said Mara.

"Well, that's how we live now: we meet people, we become friends, and then that's it. Perhaps we'll run across each other somewhere or other."

Dann was drawing a shape in the dust. It was Ifrik. He put a bit of straw down for Rustam, a little stone for the Rock Village, a leaf for Chelops, and then handed Felice a pebble and said, "Where will we be tonight?"

Felice put down the stone half a hand's span from Chelops. Now it took the span of Dann's hand, his long fingers at full stretch, to reach between Rustam and where they were going. He said to Mara, "See how far we've gone already?"

Felice watched this, not smiling: Mara could see she did not believe they would get much farther.

Mara said, "We did well in Chelops, and you didn't think we would."

"True," said Felice. "And, anyway, good luck. I don't know why I like you two, but I do."

"Luck?" said Dann. "It's knowing that matters." He pointed to the place where Felice had said they were going, and said, "On the globe this area was all green, and it was full of rivers."

"What globe?" said Felice.

"Of how the world was long ago."

Felice shrugged. "I don't know anything about that."

"On the map that has the Ice all over the north of the world, the north part of Ifrik is not brown, the way it is on the globe, because before the Ice it was all desert—all the north of Ifrik was a desert. But it isn't now. And on the globe the only part that is green is where we are going: rivers and a lot of green."

"Rivers, yes," said Felice. "But not much green, you'll find." Then, "But I don't know what you are talking about, not really." She was offended. "And let me give you a word of advice. Not all the tall tales you hear in the Mahondi quarter are true. They go in for a lot of mystification, you know, to impress people."

And they were off, the sun standing above them, and beneath them the scrubby plain; and then the sun was on their left, shining hot and clear, not dulled by dust; and then it was low; and below them was a river and a small town that as they came down seemed full of people. They landed. The people were what Mara was now used to: a mix of every kind of person, with every shade of skin, and hair sometimes straight and sometimes frizzed, and of every colour. There were no Mahondis, no Hadrons, and none of the kind who looked all the same.

Already there was a small crowd around the machine. Felice told Mara and Dann an address, pointed where they should go, said, "See you some time, somewhere," and flew off, this time to the East.

Mara and Dann were surrounded by staring, curious eyes. Not hostile, or at least not yet. They walked quickly to where they had been directed, followed by stares. It was hot, the wet heat, and they could feel the sweat trickling, and the air going into their lungs was like steam.

The houses were of wood, a few of mud bricks. The roofs were of grass. It looked a prosperous enough place, certainly not threatened with emptying, as Felice had said these River Towns were.

They found a little house in a lane. They walked into a room where a big, homely woman was cutting up roots. She looked them up and down, heard that Felice had recommended them, nodded, and said, "Sit down." They sat at a big, wooden table, laid with bowls and spoons for supper. She put questions to them, which they answered guardedly, saying that they had come from Chelops. She nodded and said, "Yes, refugees from Chelops have become rather more than we can manage."

Dann asked where the landing stage was, and she said that she would send her son to book them places. Her advice was to stay indoors until they had to go to the boat. "A lot of refugees have been robbed," she said. "You don't look as if you've got much to steal, but one never knows. And there have been a couple of slavers around, too." Here she examined Mara's slave dress, but said nothing.

She fed them the kind of supper that Mara had not eaten for a long time, of stewed roots, and bread: this was hardly the fare that the Mahondis were used to.

She did not ask what their relationship was, but showed them a room at the back, with barred windows. The room had several beds in it. Mara lay where she could watch the window, and Dann squatted on a bed, and counted out the small money Candace had given them, then dividing it and putting it into little leather bags. He gave her half. He counted the nine gold coins he had left, and tried various places to put them, an inner pocket, his shoes, but ended by choosing one of the little leather bags, where they could seem only another purse of cheap coins. They checked their store of bread, and decided they should try to buy more from their landlady.

All this went on for a good hour or more, the contriving and planning.

Mara thought, And this is the difference between having enough, as in Chelops, when all this business of keeping alive takes care of itself, just one of the things you do, and being on the edge, when you think of nothing else.

They slept, and in the night woke to see the dark outlines of two people trying to get in at the window, but the bars held. They slept again, and Mara dreamed of Meryx and woke thinking she was in his arms. But it was not the dream that had woken her. Dann was thrashing about and fighting in his sleep, and was muttering threats, "I'll kill you," with names Mara could not catch, but she thought she heard him say Kulik.

In the morning she told him he had been dreaming. He said he knew that: he had terrible nightmares most nights. She asked about Kulik, but Dann said that he was only one of the suppliers. Clearly he did not want to talk about it, and they went down, and were given hot tea made from some plant the woman said grew on the river bank, and some bread. They paid what she asked for, enquired if they could buy some bread, were given a few pieces, for a couple of little coins, and went as fast as they could to the river.

A big boat, about thirty paces in length, and half as much wide, was tied up to a stump, and people were already going aboard. Mara and Dann took their places on a bench under a little roof of reeds, and felt the wet river heat soak them and their clothes. There were tiny biting insects, in clouds. The passengers were making fans from anything they had, bits of clothing, their hands, even a flap of bread. Then a boy came running and jumped on to the boat just as it moved. He was selling fans made of river grass. Mara and Dann bought two and sat fanning away the insects, while the boy made a prodigious leap from the boat to the bank, earning applause, and the town they had scarcely seen moved away from them into the past.

And so Mara and Dann, who had known in their lives only drought and dust, thirst and anxiety over water, were floating on a river that seemed to them enormous; but it had been wider, they could see, for the water had, though not recently, filled the banks to the brim. Now the level was a good ten feet lower, and grass was growing over the part of the banks that had once known only lapping water and river weeds. And there were water dragons, who were lying on the banks, half in and half out of the water, some of them half as long as the boat. Two men propelled the boat, standing at the prow and at the stern, using long poles. That meant the water could not be very deep: when the river was full, poles would not have found the bottom to propel the boat from. The boatmen wore loose, baggy trousers tucked into their shoes, and tops that tied at the neck, and cloth tied tight over heads and necks to keep the midges off, but their faces were red and lumpy from bites. Their hands were inside bags of material tied at the wrists.

There were twenty passengers: men and women, and two children. Mara's eyes kept going to the children, to reassure her that they were healthy and well fed.

Mara believed that she might be pregnant. Or was it that she hoped she was? It seemed that her body yearned, craved, a child—or was it Meryx she was longing for? And if she was pregnant, what would Dann say, when everything was so difficult already?

North: he wanted to go north, north to water, leaving the drought behind. But were they going to stop at the first place not threatened with dryness? How far was North? What was North? From the map on Candace's wall North was only a whiteness, was ice and snow, covering half the world. She thought, Perhaps that is where all the water is, held in ice and snow, that can't move and flow? Is that what people from the South mean when they say that the water is up North?

It was very hot and the water dazzled. Mara drowsed and was woken by the plop and splash of the water dragons sliding into the water off the banks. These dragons had been in the rivers for thousands of years: the pictures on the walls of the Rock Village said so. And they were just the same, great clumsy monsters with long jaws full of irregular, ugly teeth and bulging with meat and confidence. Perhaps they planned to overturn this boat? If they all got together they were strong enough to do it. She asked Dann to ask the boatman in front, who said that sometimes when the boat was overloaded and low in the water the dragons might try to leap up and take a passenger. And did they succeed? "Oh sometimes," said the boatman, bad-tempered because of the midges. "Sit down and keep still, or they'll have a bite off you."

The day went on, so hot, so damp, a torment of midges, and the boatmen let down containers into the stream and brought up water which all the passengers drank and poured over themselves, and then they asked for more. Was there disease in the water? If so they were all too hot to care. They wanted only to drink. And then had to pee it out, over the edge of the boat, no one attempting much modesty or concealment, because of the languors of the heat. That day they stopped at sunset at a small town that was used to the boat travellers and took no notice of them. They all went together, for protection, to an inn that fed them root stew and bread and sour fruit, stewed. They all slept in a very big room, on reed mats, stretching out arms and legs, as naked as they could manage, trying to believe that it was cooler because it was night. But Mara kept herself covered. Her pallet was next to Dann's, so she could wake him if he had bad dreams.

In the morning they were off again. The river did not change, rolling along, glossy green and clear, because it was the dry season, with some green trees along it where there were birds, actually birds, most of which Mara and Dann had never seen. On either side the country was dry and yellowish, and tall dry grasses fringed the banks. This was the country that had once been the green part of Ifrik, long, long ago, with great forests, and innumerable feeder streams—so Candace had said—and those streams had baby streams running into them. Now no forests, only savannah, and water running slow and low between dry banks. For seven days they travelled up the river, stopping every night in little towns where the inns that served the river trade seemed all the same; and at the end of that time they had gone up Ifrik the breadth of Dann's forefinger laid in the dust of the map he drew to show Mara. And now there was a choice: to get off this boat and rest a little in the town that filled the fork between this tributary and the larger river, or to transfer to another boat, and go on, for this boat was returning to where it had started, which was where they had got on. Mara would have liked to stop, but Dann did not want to. He was driven by his need to go north, always north. Most of the passengers transferred to the new boat, a bigger one. None seemed to know where they were going, only that it must be better than where they had come from. Not all were from Chelops: some were from Majab. Mara and Dann had come farther than any of them, but were discreet about their origins. Bad enough that the passengers from Chelops knew that they were Mahondis, and hated them for it. Mara would see how Dann looked from face to face of these people, the close, intent look she knew so well: was he recognising faces, friends or enemies, from his time in the Tower? If so, he gave no sign. At night Mara always lay within touching distance, because she was afraid of what he might say in his sleep, or shout out if she did not wake him fast enough from his nightmares.

This river they were on now was a very different affair. It was wider, and though the top part of its banks showed that it had shrunk in its bed, it was still much deeper than the river they had been on, which now seemed a mere stream in comparison. To use poles here was not possible; there were two oarsmen on each side, and a man to steer. This boat was lower in the water, and kept to the middle of the river, well away from the dragons that crowded its banks. On the tributary, towns and villages had appeared infrequently, but here they seemed almost continuous. All were of baked mud bricks, with reed thatched roofs— clearly there were no forests near this river: on either side spread the thorny scrub of semi-desert, and even, in patches, the hot yellow glare of real desert. Thick reeds grew along the banks, and clumps of bamboo. The trees were all varieties of palm. This landscape was new to all the passengers, and the boatmen had to keep explaining what they were travelling through.

On the first stop at a town much larger and finer that any on the other river, they all walked close together, looking out for possible assailants, though the boatmen said these were peaceful people who welcomed travellers for the money they brought in. In this inn they could choose to sleep in a big communal room or in smaller rooms, and Mara and Dann managed to get one of these for themselves. They had not been alone for days, and now they were able to count what coins they had left and talk freely. In fact their supply of small coins was running low, and to change a gold one in inns such as these was out of the question: very likely these people would never have heard of such a thing outside of some tale, or legend. Now there was a bit of luck. One of the boatmen fell ill and had to be left behind. Dann offered to replace him, and so could travel free. He was in the middle of the boat, at the side, and Mara sat just behind him and watched him row. The blue outfit Felice had given him was much too hot, and he only wore a loincloth, like all the male passengers. Mara was watching the muscles work in that strong muscled back: a fine back, yes, but much too thin. All the travellers were losing flesh fast, they sweated so much, and it was too hot to eat. Mara held out her arm free of her sleeve and knew that if Orphne could see her and Dann she would be ordering them special food and rest. Meanwhile Dann was pulling his oar from sunrise to sunset. He was so strong, and so quick in learning everything, always ready to haul water out of the river for everyone to drink, helping people on and off the boat, making himself the best of the oarsmen, so that he could keep his job. At least, in the very middle of the river, the midges were absent. Mara watched the banks with their reeds and tufty palms glide past, and averted her eyes, and then shut them. She was feeling sick, longed to get off the boat and lie down. The dazzle on the water, even the regular splash of water dripping off the oars, made her queasy, and she more than once vomited over the side. On the bench beside her was a woman, who had not said much till then, but now she spoke very low, "You had better not let anyone know what you are carrying, if you know what's good for you." Then it was that Mara realised she was pregnant and thought that she after all had not had much confidence in Meryx's fertility, if she had to be told she was pregnant by this stranger. "There's plenty of people who'll make a grab for you if they know what you've got," this woman went on, and she took from her bag a fistful of dried leaves and said, "Chew these, they settle the stomach." Mara chewed, and they were bitter and dry, but her sickness stopped. This new friend, one of the last people to leave Majab, was Sasha, and she stayed in the seat near Mara, just behind Dann, and kept an eye on her, making her chew dry bread, and drink water, always more water.

When they landed that night she gave Mara a supply of the dried leaf and repeated that she should tell no one she was pregnant. There was no opportunity to tell Dann, because they were in a room with others. Next day Mara asked Sasha if she had a medicine for someone who slept badly, and offered a coin. Sasha took the coin, and gave Mara bark to put in water. She said, "Plenty of people sleep badly these days." As she watched Mara give Dann the water the bark had been soaked in to drink, her eyes were sad. Mara thought, If I asked her she might tell me a story worse than mine. Perhaps that's why we are frightened to talk to each other: we are afraid of what we might hear.

Next morning, as they were walking down to the boat, apart from the others, Mara told Dann she was pregnant, and asked if they might get off this boat so she could rest for a few days. He said, so low she could hardly hear it, that there was someone after him. "He was in the town where we changed boats. I saw him." Mara held him back, because he was already hastening to join the others, and said, "Dann, sometimes you imagine things. Are you sure?" He seemed to shrink and become little in her grip and he said in little Dann's voice, "He was the bad one, Mara." But she held fast, gripping his two arms and said, "Dann, don't do that." And, amazingly, he heard, straightened, shed little Dann, and looked straight at her, and said, "Mara, there were a lot of things that happened in the Towers you don't know about." And now he tried to smile, trusting her. "I'll tell you—some time. I hate thinking about that time."

"You do think about it, when you are asleep."

"I know," he said, and pulled himself away and went ahead of her to the boat. If he heard her saying she was pregnant, he hadn't taken it in.

Mara suffered through the long, hot, damp days, the dazzle in her eyes being the worst torment; but Sasha supported her with herbs to chew, and bits of dry bread, and encouragement. "This is the worst part of being pregnant," she said. "Soon you'll feel well—you'll see." Mara could not be more than six weeks pregnant: a period had been scant, had started and stopped and started; another had been late, but she did not expect them to be regular—how could they be, when she had scarcely been a female at all, until a year ago? She wished she could let Meryx know, and kept seeing his bitter, miserable face on the night he had believed she had slept with Juba. If he knew—well, she could imagine how he would look: he would stand differently, taller; and a shrinking and diffidence, almost an apology, that was always in his face, his smile—all that would go. She imagined standing beside him, pregnant, her hand in his, telling the Kin this news, and how he would smile as they all rushed to congratulate him. How far away he seemed—and was; how out of reach—and he was; and yet her thoughts flew to him a hundred times a day and to all of them, in their illusory safe place.

Day after day she sat at touching distance behind Dann, watched his lean muscled arms pulling the oar, saw how his cheeks lost the fullness they had got from the Kin's good food. All day, with the sickness beating up in waves, with Sasha beside her, whispering, "Don't be sick. Don't let them see." How she hated this endless, gliding journey up the middle of the river that reflected blue sky, and sometimes slow, white clouds, and along its edges the reeds and bamboos and palm trees, while among the reflections often appeared the dark shape of a dragon, or the white grin as it propped its jaws open so that the little birds could clean its mouth. How she longed to stop, simply to stop moving; and then on the twentieth morning of this journey Dann woke feverish, and had to agree to stay behind when the boat went on. Now the faces of the people they had been with day and night for what seemed now to be a long time were those of friends, and Mara thought that without Sasha she could not go on. Without Sasha—well, she would have been reported to the authorities by now, and kept to wait for the arrival of the next slaver. She and Dann took a room in a little town, and both of them slept, and slept, he sleeping away his fever, she the nausea of movement. But she had to get up often to sponge off Dann's sweats, and hold water to his lips, making him drink, though it was bitter with Sasha's herbs.

In his sleep he muttered, "We must go on, Mara. He'll catch up with me." "Who, Dann, who?" Once he replied, "Kulik," but there were other names she did not know.

Mara became well quicker than Dann did, and trusting that it was true that the people in this town were friendly, as the innkeeper said, she went out into streets—rather, lanes—of mud-brick houses, and wandered through the town ignoring the people she met, and being ignored. She had seen from the room windows large buildings some distance from this town, and now she walked there, watching the low grass for snakes, and gratefully smelling the aromatic bushes that brushed against her. The clean, medicinal smell so appealed to her that she chewed some of the little leaves, not able to believe they were poisonous, and their effect was to make her hungry. The buildings were tall, six or seven levels, and of stone. There was no surface stone anywhere near, so there must be a quarry somewhere. When she reached the buildings she saw they were old, and it had been a long time since they had had roofs. No sign of a roof, or rafters, no fallen beams, just walls. There were signs of old fires, old scorch marks that had eaten into the stone so one might think the stones were black, and new fires, the ghosts of aromatic bushes that had burned where they stood inside the walls, each a little cloud of pale twigs and stems.

This had been a big town, laid out in a regular way, streets intersecting each other in squares. They had been paved with big blocks of stone, and there were grooves in the stone made by wheels. The buildings were full of birds that had their nests anywhere there was a ledge or a hole. Creepers had reached high up the walls, thin green fingers clutching the stone. When had people lived here? She asked at the inn and they said that no one knew: before the trees went, they said. Once there had been great forests here, but that was so long ago you could hardly find an old tree trunk or a bit of dry wood, not for several days' walking distance. A rain forest it had been—so it was said. Well there was not enough rain these days even to keep the palms happy. Along this river in the dry season the trees were watered by teams of townspeople who made themselves responsible for them. The trees provided all kinds of food, and fibre for weaving, and a kind of milk, which was welcome now that it was getting difficult to keep the domesticated animals alive. Mara went to see these animals. There was a small version of the milk beasts down south, no higher than Mara's waist, and she thought of Mishka and Mishkita and wondered what they would have thought of these small copies of their kind. There were animals with horns and great udders, that stood to Mara's shoulders. They were fed on palm leaves. There were very tall animals, with great feet like floats and long necks called Khamels, which had been imported from the north at a time when North had been all sand and stone, because they needed so little to live on. And when was that? Oh, hundreds of years, perhaps thousands, no one knew now. Mara asked if skimmers were known here and the reply was that there used to be plenty, at least once a week, but now hardly ever. It was the river that everyone relied on, and that was not likely to disappear. This river led into a larger one, believed to be the main one, and there had always been rivers here, though it was known they had sometimes changed course.

Rain forest, thought Mara, going to stand in the deserted town, gazing at ancient wheelmarks in streets that had been empty for hundreds—or thousands?—of years. A rain forest . . . what could that mean? She shut her eyes to imagine it, and heard the sounds of water running and splashing off oars. What could it have been like, to wander in a forest that held rain in its branches, was always wet, and little streams ran everywhere?

She went to the river, saw the rolling glitter, and felt her stomach turn over, for it remembered the movement of the boat. Soon she would have to get on a boat again and face days—how long?—of that heat, the movement, the glitter in her eyes . . . She heard Sasha's whisper, Don't let anyone know you are pregnant, and she closed her eyes to conquer the nausea. When she opened them in front of her stood a vision, a beautiful young woman in a pink dress, with her hair braided and shining, and she was smiling at her. It was Kira, who said, "I'm not surprised to see you: anyone sensible would leave."

And she took Mara by the hand and led her to a mud house larger than the others, of two storeys, and into a large, cool room full of coloured things—cushions, hangings, embroideries, bright pots and jars. Mara sank into a reed chair, thankful to be able to keep still, and Kira clapped her hands and a servant came in, who was told to bring drinks. She was a black girl, and her hair was as intricately done as Kira's.

"And now tell me everything," Kira said, fanning herself, clicking and turning and displaying the fan, of scarlet birds' feathers, just as Ida did. Her pink dress billowed about her to the floor.

When Mara had finished her tale, she asked Kira, "If you had known what the journey was going to be like, would you have left?"

Now, this directness was not at all Kira's style, for she evaded it, pouting, and laughing, and flirting her fan—as she had always done; but at last, faced by Mara's seriousness, she sighed and said, "No. I would not. That boat nearly killed me."

"And are you sorry you left your baby?"

"Ida's baby."

"I want to know."

Another sigh, not petulant or staged. "Mara, if I had brought that baby with me it would have died on the boat. What baby could survive that?—so hot, the insects, not enough to eat . . ."

Here the servant brought milk from the palm trees and fruit.

"Is there enough food here?"

"Plenty. And my husband is a trader."

"Your husband! I didn't think husbands were your style."

"They aren't. But there are different kinds of marriage here. He wants a full marriage, he thinks I am a marvel." And she laughed, all her lovely teeth on show. Then she leaned forward and whispered, "If he knew I had been a slave in Chelops . . . I wouldn't let him touch me until I had a legal security here." Aloud she said, "I love him and he's good to me." On this a big black man came in. He had heard what she said and was pleased. He shone with pleasure in his handsome blackness. His hair was a great black bush. He stood with his hand on Kira's shoulder and looked at Mara, and he did not think she was a marvel, as Mara could see.

"Who's your friend?"

"She's my cousin. From Chelops. She was married to the son of the chief man."

This man nodded, smiled politely, squeezed Kira's shoulder and went out.

"He's jealous," said Mara.

"Of men and of women. But I don't get up to any of that here, he'd kill me. Of course I never went in for it much—girls. That was just to pass the time." On she chattered, and did not ask Mara another question, because she had created her vision of the life in Chelops and had no intention of letting it be challenged.

One thing was clear. She was lonely and desperate to talk. Not to exchange talk, but to talk. Mara tried to stop the flow, several times, and then the servant came in to say that the innkeeper wanted her.

She thought, Oh *no*, it's Dann, he must have said something—what has he said?—and she apologised to Kira, who said, "I'll come and visit you and Dann," and she ran through the heavy yellow sunlight to the inn where the innkeeper was waiting, with a man he introduced as Chombi. She found him frightening. He was very tall, thin and his skin was of an ugly white colour she had never seen before. His hair was like Mahondi hair, but there was this unhealthy white skin—repulsive.

"Your brother is making a noise," he said.

"He's my husband, not my brother," said Mara.

The trouble was, Dann might or might not remember to lie. She ran into their room and found Dann crouched by the head of the bed, panting. He had dreamed, that was clear. She made him lie down, gave him more medicine, and said, "Dann, I've told them we're married. Will you remember that?" She repeated it until he said yes, he would, and dropped off back to sleep.

Mara sat at the low window and watched the river glide past a hundred yards away, and saw the moon paths swaying on the water. Even that little movement made her feel sick.

Chombi came to enquire after Dann. She said he had the river sickness, the one insects give you, but he was getting better. Chombi was full of suspicion and hostility. He enquired after her health too. He had heard she was sick, when she arrived. Mara said she had the river sickness, but not badly, and was better now.

While Kira had talked, and talked, Mara had been able to make a picture of this place.

The region of the River Towns was governed by the Goidel people, who had their headquarters in the next town up the river, called Goidel. Each river town had its local representative, and this town's government man—Kira called him The Spy—was the tall, white, thin man, Chombi.

Kira had seen Mara's nausea—but only when she actually asked to be shown a place where she could be sick—and said that Mara must not be ill. If Dann was ill, and she was too, that would be seen as the possible beginnings of an epidemic and both would be taken to Goidel into an isolation hospital. More than anything, this region feared epidemics, for there had been several recently, and many had died, mostly children. Mara had been afraid to tell Kira she was pregnant, but when she had to be sick again Kira said, "And you'd better not tell them you are pregnant either, because they'll take you for breeding. But if you can make them believe that Dann is your husband, it will be all right. They don't take women away from husbands."

Mara, then, could be neither ill nor pregnant, and what was she to do? It seemed to her she had no choice, except to go on with the journey and hope for the best. Choice: were there people who had choices? Kira, for instance. If she stayed in Chelops, probably the Kin themselves would have been delighted to lose her to the Hadrons, because she was such a nuisance. If she had kept the baby then Ida would have made her life a misery. If she had brought the baby with her it would almost certainly have died on the river.

Mara could decide to make the slow, difficult—and sickening—journey back to Chelops, and tell Meryx, Look, I'm pregnant, you are like your father, a maker of children. But the Hadrons would take her the moment the baby was born. And she would still be in that situation which both she and Kira knew: Chelops could not last for long.

Why was Kira so clear-headed about this, unlike the rest of the Kin? She was an orphan, had been taken into the Kin as a child, from an inferior branch of the Mahondis. She had never felt part of the Kin, had always seen herself as an outsider; and was able to see the Kin from an outsider's view, had never been lulled into complacency.

There was a hard end to this run of thoughts: Kira would probably survive, having run away and left her child, when the Kin, and the Hadrons—and Kira's baby—might easily not survive.

And what was Mara to do now?

She listened to Dann muttering or shouting in his sleep, hushed him, told him, Dann, be quiet—and he woke apparently himself, demanding to leave at once.

"Have you remembered I am pregnant?" she whispered. "And that I am your wife?"

"Up North it will be better," he said, and slipped back into fever, shaking and sweating again. Kira came to sit with him while Mara slept. Mara knew that Dann was good-looking, but she had not thought of him as someone immediately attractive—in spite of Felice—but it seemed Kira liked Dann very much, and she helped Mara change the slave's robe for a clean one, and she exclaimed over his scars, and the weals around his middle, and sighed and said that perhaps she would come with them when they left. This was such a boring little place. After all, this was only a minor river. It would join the main river about ten days' from here, and on that one you could travel right up to the edge of the country that the Khamels came from. But up there they spoke a different language and Kira didn't think she could be bothered with that.

"I thought the same language was spoken everywhere," said Mara, and Kira laughed at her and said that Mara's trouble was—and it had been Kira's—that she had believed Hadron to be most of Ifrik, instead of just a little place, and that since all of southern Ifrik spoke one language, they had thought it must be the same everywhere.

It seemed that Kira's presence was calming the suspicions of the tall, white spy, for he kept away until she left, and then said he had noticed Mara was not in health, and he had a duty to tell his superiors so. "I am perfectly well," said Mara. This man, whom she thought was like a worm or the white belly of a lizard, and who she hated touching her, then took her wrist and felt her pulse, put a thin, bony thumb on her neck pulse, bent to look into her mouth and check her teeth, and lifted an eyelid. Mara knew that he was checking on more than her present health. He would report on her physical condition to the superiors in Goidel.

"If you are pregnant," he said, "you have nothing to fear, if that man is your husband."

"He is."

"You look very much alike."

"Mahondis do look alike. We are inbred," she said, not knowing that in fact she thought this.

"Then that is a fault easily cured," he said.

Dann was awake and listening, and on his face was a look that told Mara he was fighting inner demons.

"And do you claim this child?" Chombi asked him.

"Yes, I do," said Dann, forgetting that Mara had told him not to say she was pregnant.

Mara asked Kira how long it took to get a message to Goidel. Two days there. Then a couple of days of deliberations and a decision, and two days on the return boat. Altogether, allow a week.

Mara told Dann that she might be taken as a concubine for the Goidels. He said, "Oh no, they won't." As always now there was a pause after her speaking, before he heard, and responded. She believed that this bout of fever had done him real harm—not physically, for he was recovering, but by bringing his nightmares nearer. She wondered if Dann was perhaps a little mad. Sometimes, yes. On certain subjects.

That week she spent feeding Dann and herself, and making him strong by walking with him around the mud lanes, and to the old deserted city in the savannah. She knew they were being observed. They sat with Kira, and Mara watched to see if Dann was attracted to Kira, for she longed to be reassured: there was a death sentence in the River Towns for men finding men attractive. And Dann did respond to Kira, but she made such a joke of everything it was hard to say what she felt.

At the end of ten days two uniformed men came off the river boat from Goidel to the inn and demanded to see Mara and Dann. They were in the communal room, eating. At the sight of the two men Dann gave a shout and darted out of the door and disappeared into the maze of lanes and little houses. Yes, the two men were quite alike, Mara thought. Like most people around here they were very black, well-built, with lean faces, but their hair was long and black, like the Mahondis'.

"I see your husband has run away," said one man, genially. "Well, that makes things easier. Get your things. You are coming with us to Goidel." Mara said nothing. She knew Dann had run away because of the two similar men, who later would become, in his mind, one man. Perhaps he would ask Kira for help. And he had not committed a crime, was not sick—or pregnant.

"Better for you that you are pregnant than ill," said the other gaoler. "It would be isolation for you and that's no joke."

They watched her pay the bill. She had none of the small coins left after that. She watched them conferring with Chombi, while he reported the events of the little town, and was given orders.

The upriver boat came. Mara got on with her sack, and sat where she had before, but this time she had two men behind her, watching. What did they think she might do? Jump into this big, dangerous river, full of water dragons? Swim through them to a bank that edged empty savannah and ancient, deserted towns?

That night in the inn they made her sleep between them. The next day on the boat was the same. She did not dislike these men, who were only doing a job. They were kind, in their way, making sure she ate and drank. That evening they arrived in Goidel and she was taken to a gaol and put in the charge of two women who fed her, washed her, were jocular and tried to make her laugh.

Next morning she went in front of an elderly magistrate who reminded her, by his manner at least, of Juba.

"So you claim you are married?"

"Yes."

"What degree of marriage?"

Kira had told her to say, second degree. That meant, here, either man or woman could have other partners, but the man must assume responsibility for any child, since there was no way of establishing paternity. This was one of the laws introduced when it was becoming clear that fertility was dropping.

"Second degree," said Mara.

"Whatever the degree, when the husband is not present, it is irrelevant—wouldn't you agree?"

"Yes," said Mara.

"Well, you must go back to prison. If your husband does not claim you within a week, then you will go to the breeding programme."

Mara had walked between the two gaolers to the court, and now back again. Going she had been too anxious to notice much; returning, her mind easier, since she believed Dann would come, she was able to see the streets she was walking through. Goidel was very different from the little mud towns down the river, several times larger, and while the buildings were of mud or mud-brick, the façades of most were covered with the same fine plaster she had seen in the old ruined cities above the Rock Village. So, instead of looking like an extension of the river bank mud, the buildings were white, or a pale earth colour, or yellow, or even pink. None of these façades was new or clean; some were chipped, or areas of plaster had fallen and not been replaced. The roofs, of reed, needed replacing. In some, birds had nested. Many buildings were empty. But there were hundreds of people in the streets and they wore garments striped with bright colours, or plain, of the same very fine material as the robes she carried rolled at the bottom of her sack. Delicate, almost transparent material, with embroidery around necks and sleeves when the garment was plain. These were well fed people. Above all, there was an air of general confidence and calm. People stood about in groups talking, and laughing. In a little garden families were sitting on the grass eating and drinking. Her gaolers were not marching like soldiers, but strolling along and stopping to explain things when she asked.

The two women gaolers took her in, making jokes with the two soldiers. These were, Mara knew, clever, surviving women, and she wanted to trust them. She decided she would: after all, she had no alternative.

She asked them if they knew any medicine for aborting a baby. She was whispering, so even the walls could not have heard. They were not surprised. Whispering, one said that if they were found out it would be the death sentence for both of them, and the other that they must be well paid.

Mara put her hands up under her robe, to untie a gold coin, then saw she was ridiculous: with one movement they could fling up her robe and see the cord of coins. She untied the cord and brought it forth. Twenty-two. She offered them one. First one, then the other tested it. Then they asked for another. She gave them another. All three knowing that they could have taken everything, there was a moment when Mara despaired and she believed that they were being tempted. But they said, "All right, put it back." And she tied the cord again, where it had been.

It was lucky, they said, that she was the only woman in the gaol, because otherwise it would have been too much of a risk. Then they joked that it was more usual for them to be asked for drugs to increase fertility, and this was their reputation, which made it easier for them to help Mara.

They gave her bitter drinks, which she had to get down her as hot as she could bear. This was for three days. Then, on the fourth, very late at night, they put her on a pallet on the floor, and got to work on manipulating her stomach. She felt those long knowledgeable fingers probe deep, through her flesh, seeking out her womb, looking for the child—finding it. The pain was intense and she fainted, and came to, and the fingers still probed and pushed. Both women kept their gaze on her face, and when they saw that she really could not bear any more, gave her another potion.

Towards morning she felt the warm rush between her legs.

"Do you want to see it?" one asked, and Mara caught a glimpse of a tiny creature in its bloody mess. She felt the most terrible pang in her heart—a knife would have been kinder—and shook her head for them to take it away. She was sorry she had said she would look.

"Three months," said one, and the other, "Could be even a few days more?"

So Meryx's child was alive when Mara saw it. When it was dead one of the women crept out into the savannah—for the prison was on the edge of the town—and when she returned she said briskly, "That's done."

Mara was thinking, I've chosen between Meryx's baby and Dann. And then, No, that's foolish. No baby could survive a boat journey in this heat. That was no choice.

The two women made her sleep, and woke her to say that Dann had arrived at the magistrate's court in good time to claim her. But there was a problem. He seemed ill. Mara knew he was not ill; it was his terror that made him ill. She knew what it had cost him to go and confront the soldiers that stood guarding the court. She could feel little Dann's fear in her own nerves, see his face, for that moment little Dann's face.

"He has been told that you have miscarried," said the soldier who brought the message.

Before Mara was released she again drew the two women into the very centre of a large room, and whispered that she needed to change a gold coin, or if they could, two. And they said, "Two. One each. But we shall not be giving you the full value. It's dangerous for us." She gave them two coins, leaving nineteen in the cord, and she got back a mass of the light, trashy-looking coins in exchange. About half the value, she judged, but did not blame them. This change she put into her sack, and thanked them both, and said she would always remember them, which was true. And they embraced her and wished her well.

Dann was in a guest house, waiting for her. He was not ill, but he was frightened still, and haunted, and when Mara thanked him for coming to rescue her he burst into a terrible sobbing, and clung to her—almost little Dann, but not quite, for there was a hardness and obstinacy there, adult, responsible, and his voice, "Mara, if I'd lost you . . ." was far from little Dann's.

"Or if I'd lost you," she said.

These two were not in the habit of physical affection, but now they sat close together on the bed, arms around each other, resting and quiet.

At peace, that's what they were; and Mara felt the tension go out of his body, and her own.

A brave thing that was, what he had done. She knew that soldiers, guards, the police, turned him to water. To have made himself walk into that courtroom—what was it she could do that was anything like as brave? But then she did not fear standing in a court, to be judged: that is what tormented him. She knew it, but did he? And then, the two men, two men . . .

She dared, "The two men who came to arrest us back in that other town . . ." And waited for him to say, "No, not two, one man." But he only searched and searched her face with his eyes.

"Mara, I know you don't believe me, but there is somebody after me. I've seen him."

"Who, Dann, who is it?"

He only let his head fall on her shoulder, with a groan.

She said, "If you hadn't come to claim me they would have taken me for their breeding programme."

"I know, they told me." And then he said quietly, almost humbly, and smiling, "Mara, I think it would be better if you didn't let yourself get pregnant again."

They had two days to rest in. She was still a little weak, but was herself: she had not felt anything like herself yet on this journey. He ate a lot, and they walked together around and about this most pleasant river town. They were watched by agents from the magistrate's court, and when they caught the upriver boat the agents went with them. This was to make sure, even now, that they were neither of them ill. Mara had been told by the women gaolers, and Dann had been told, for everyone talked of it, how much epidemics were feared. Terrible diseases arrived in the River Towns, for no reason, made people ill or killed them and then disappeared, for no reason. The river sickness everyone understood, and they did not fear it. Its symptoms were always the same: the sufferers shook and shivered and ran high fevers, and then a lull, and then another attack: lulls and fevers, and sometimes people died, and sometimes not. In every house were medicines for the river sickness, but there was none for these new diseases, if they were new. There was talk among the old people that this was not the first time illnesses had swept along the river, and disappeared.

When two days later the boat went in to the shore for the night, where this river joined the main one, which was called Cong, it was already dusk and so they did not see until morning that if the river they were leaving had made the first one they embarked on seem like a creek, so now that river, which had been so large and powerful, seemed a mere preparation for what they gazed at. They walked down from the inn, still watched by Goidel agents, since this was where Goidel sovereignty ended, to yet another boat, a much larger one, waiting at a pier where boats of all sizes were tied. The river was so wide that the birds in the trees on the other bank were white dots and the trees were a little, low fringe. From this bank it could be seen that on this river were still many kinds of palm, but there were big, green trees, and some like green hands pointing up, covered with thorns. Along the sides of the boat were oars, but they were at rest, lodged in their supports, because this boat was propelled by a device that used sunlight, concentrated and focused on to a slanting square of material that had a dull shine. The secret of this use of the sun had been lost long ago, and so precious was the device—very few were left now— that guards protected it, day and night. Dann, to find a way of travelling free, offered himself as a guard. The owner of this boat, and the navigator, was Han, an elderly woman as lean and dry and brown as a tree trunk, and as wrinkled. She looked long at him, and finally nodded. Dann inspired confidence. He did not have that ease and openness that people have who have never experienced treachery, so it must be, thought Mara, that his many skills and aptitudes were evident in his expectation that he would be accepted. He also offered to cook the midday meal, or to serve it. And he would travel free. The voyage would take a month. They were going on this stage farther than all their travelling from the Rock Village. Mara paid out three of her gold coins, from the nineteen she had left. Now she had sixteen. There were about a hundred people on this boat, some of them from as far as Chelops, some from the first River Towns they had passed. She felt she must know these faces, that they were familiar, and saw how Dann's eyes went from one face to another, slow, concentrated, memorising each one.

10

This wide river did not have the force of its tributaries. It was much shallower. It was running low in its bed, but here there were no grassy verges because of a fallen water level, only the eroded gullies and collapsed banks of rivers that flood, with the detritus of flood high above the water and even leaving wisps of straw and dead weeds in the trees. The water dragons were not on these banks, but deep in the water, or floating like logs: the blunt wedge heads could be seen just under the water, the nostrils exposed, or long, dark shapes steered beside or behind the boat, for the beasts were hoping that something or someone might fall in; and the deck was too high to attempt a leap. The sky was hot and blue and empty—not a cloud. Through the palms and thorn trees on the bank could be glimpsed the little dance and whirl of the dust devils sucking up dirt from between the grass clumps. It was sultry, the air clinging to the skin. But Mara was not sick now. She looked back on the days of nausea on the other boats and wondered how she had borne them. Well, she had because she had to. Now she sat at ease and wondered about the city of Shari, where they were going. They would be on this river, Cong, going upstream, for half their journey, and then, after a brief, tight squeeze through a canal, would join another river that flowed into a lake called Charad. On that river they would travel downstream, and the precious machine that gathered sunlight would be switched off, to save it. That is when the oars would come into use. All this she was told by Dann, during the intervals he was stood down from his post as guard, with three others, and came to sit with her. He said to her, "Mara, all the time it gets better, doesn't it?" And he glanced anxiously into her face to see if she did feel what he felt: a relief, a reassurance, a kind of awe perhaps, that things were going well for them, after being so very bad.

Mara sat neither asleep nor awake, but in a reverie where everywhere her eyes rested seemed sharp and clear, but far from her; and she was in a dream, a dream, and the silent boat that clove its way up the river, the gliding banks, the cloudless sky where occasionally appeared a visiting cloud—all this floated through her mind as if she were transparent, or two people, for always she remembered the Mara whose skin had forgotten water, and who had often woken from sleep, her mouth dry and cracked and longing for water. When the pails of water dipped from the river went about among the passengers, and it was her turn, she felt that every gulp of the coolness going down her was like a whisper: Mara, you are safe now; and when she dipped her hands in and splashed her face her skin remembered old hungers.

Sometimes sandbanks appeared ahead, and on them the water dragons lay, and slid into the water when the boat appeared. The banks were too far on either side to see the details of nests and birds' lives; nor did they see animals standing to drink, because they ran away when they saw the boat. And so, day after day, they went along. Every night they tied up, sometimes in a town or village, sometimes at an inn that stood by itself on the bank, waiting for the river travellers. All these inns and guest houses were simple, and clean, and pleasant. They supplied evening and morning meals of bread, and sometimes cheese, and vegetable stew, and a drink made from palm tree juice. The travellers were given big communal rooms to sleep in, or were four, five, six in a room. Dann and Mara were never out of each other's sight. The towns were like Goidel, each one with its own individuality, expressing itself in the eyes and faces and ways of moving and talking of the inhabitants, which Mara found invigorating, a challenge, because she had not till recently known living, busy towns full of confidence, each one needing to be understood, like a person. When the boat was tied up in the evenings, sometimes she and Dann wandered about the streets, looking—always—into faces, perhaps risking the purchase of a fruit, or sweets, or a small cake, for its taste of this place, so different from other places. Sometimes Dann would stare so long and hard at someone that he, or she, would be annoyed, and disturbed, and stare back: What do you want?

"Who is this person you are waiting to see, Dann? Please, tell me."

But he did not answer. Sometimes she thought he did not hear, so deep was he in this inner pursuit. Sometimes, trying to keep contact with him, staying close, she might talk, commenting on what they saw, for minutes, half an hour, with no reply from him at all. Yet later he might say something that meant he had heard her, had stored up what she said. These evening strolls through the towns they visited were delightful to her but, she thought, not to him. How could they be, when he was so fearful and on guard? Yet he said unexpectedly, "I like these walks with you, Mara. I look forward to them all day, on the boat."

Day after day. Sometimes Dann came back to crouch by her and measure on the wood of the boat's deck a little distance with his fingers:

how far they had come on this boat. And then, how far since Chelops. Then, the Rock Village. When he drew a capacious shape of Ifrik, on the planks, other people saw, and joined in, showing with their hands the distances they had come—but none as far as Dann and Mara. Some of them knew the shape of Ifrik. Others stared, and puzzled, and could not take in what Mara and Dann explained.

Most of the time Dann was up in the front of the boat watching the sun device. There were six guards, always changing. At night Han left two guards when she went ashore to eat or sleep, but usually stayed on the boat, with the guards. More than once one was Dann, but Mara hated that, afraid she would not see him again, and could not sleep. Han used Dann more and more. This dried-up woman, like a tall, clever old monkey, so quick and alert, watched the men guards all the time, seeing if they drifted into a day dream or turned their faces away too long from the sun trap. Dann seemed able to stay alert all the time. He stood in the prow, balancing on his set-apart feet, sideways on to the sun trap, so that he could see all the boat (and, Mara knew, anyone who might be creeping up on him), and his eyes moved slowly and steadily around the faces of the travellers, to the trap, and then around again. He saw at once if someone went too close to the trap, or was careless in settling their bags and sacks. People begged Han to let them see the sun trap, and sometimes she agreed, but stood near it, and them, watching every movement. And they would stand staring at the square of metal, which was unknown now, something invented in the distant past and forgotten, this square which seemed like a blank, dully shining surface. But then, if you stared into it, there were changes and shifts of light in its depths, and colours too, strengthening and fading, like the colours of water or sky at sunset and sunrise, so it was as if you stared into water, deep water; and it was always with surprise and unease that the travellers saw—returning to themselves out of the illusory depths of the metal—that it was after all only a piece of something not far off the tin they had used all their lives made into cups and plates and containers, and which came from manufactories that some of them had seen. Just a square of metal, flat and thin, nothing to it, which you might kick aside or throw on to a rubbish heap; and yet it was something to make you feel awe or even terror, because this bit of nothing much, that looked as if it had come off a scrap heap, could make this boat move upstream day after day, pushing aside the waters of this great river.

Soon there were many shoals and sandbanks and Han navigated her-

self, not leaving the task to one of the guards who, when the river was
deep enough, had only to stand at the tiller and keep the boat moving
straight. Now Han swung the boat from this side of the river to the
other, or between sandbanks, and two guards stood on one side and two
on the other to ward off a shoal or push the boat off a shallow bank.
There were no rocks on this river, only sand, that shifted as the currents
flowed. Day after day . . . Mara felt she had been on this boat all her life,
and would never leave it, each night sleeping in an inn so like all the
others she sometimes felt she had not left the last one, each morning
embarking and settling on the same bench; and feeling, as the boat
swung out into the stream, that the walk around this particular town,
and the restless sleep in the inn, had not happened, for the reality was
the river, the shoals, the sandbanks, the shores that slid backwards with
their trees and birds; and sometimes, deep in the water, fish or the stubbornly following water dragons. It seemed that the dragons had divided
up the river, for as the boat entered a stretch of water they saw nosing
towards them four or five from the sandbanks; and these would follow
for a while, and then propel themselves away to where there was a flat
beach or a bank. And then another population of the creatures would
take over. Day after day . . . and then there was a change, and it was in
the air. Instead of the smell of river water, and sometimes a blast of hot
sand smell, there was a bad taint coming to them from ahead of the
boat, and then it went, to be forgotten, but came again, stronger; and
soon there were foul blasts of air in their faces, and before long the smell
was continuous. People were being sick over the side of the boat, or sat
holding cloth to their faces. That night Han went ashore to the proprietor of the guest house and conferred with him for a long time, while
she eyed the travellers eating their frugal meal. Or deciding they could
not eat, for it was not possible to avoid the smell here, no matter where
they sat or how they shut the doors and windows.

Han called them together and said that there had been a war, probably
still going on, in the territory they were going to pass through, and there
were great numbers of people fleeing from the war, living how they could
on either side of the river. They had no food. They often had only the
clothes they wore. They were dying. All they had was water. If the passengers wanted to go on, they would have to pass between banks crowded with
these desperate people. The alternative was to return, going back down-
river. She took it that no one wanted to do that. Then, tomorrow would be
a difficult day. Everyone must be ready to fend off possible attempts by

boarders, and above all, to defend the sun trap. She was going to position ten of the strongest men by the sun trap. She wanted contributions from everyone to buy a big sack of bread to throw to the refugees: she waited while people gave a few small coins each. She told everyone to find a stick, and sharpen it. Before they left for the boat in the morning, there would be a tub of water by the door of the inn, full of strong smelling herbs, and they should soak cloths or even bits of clothing in it, and tie these around their faces, because then the smell would be less.

Next morning this crowd of people, who by now knew each other very well, went down to the boat in a wary company, and each held a long stick or a knife. On the boat Han positioned ten guards all together around the sun trap, Dann in charge of them, and made the rest of the men line the sides of the boat, with the women around the back, all with their weapons. She stood at the prow steering, watching everything and everybody. The smell was by now almost unendurable. For a couple of hours the boat went steadily up the middle of the river, in and out of the sandbanks, while corpses floated past and the water dragons fought over them. Then they turned into a new reach of the river, and there they were, the desperate people, massed on the banks, staring at the boat. Then a shout went up and from both shores they crowded into the water which was shallow almost to the middle. Nowhere was the river deep. In a moment they were splashing, wading, swimming to the boat. The dragons snatched and snapped at this fresh meat. Several of the attackers were dragged down out of sight, or struggled in the shallows with the beasts, but on they all came, hundreds, cursing, wailing, screaming, pleading. In a moment the guards at the front were beating off people trying to climb up the front of the boat. Someone reached up to cling on to the sun trap but Dann knocked him off into the water. All along both sides of the boat the passengers were using sticks, poles, oars—anything—to push the refugees back. A woman drowned: she could not swim. Some children reached a sandbank and began leaping up at the boat as it passed, and were beaten down. Mara, who was at the back with the women, saw how the people who had been shoved off the sides tried to swim after the boat. Han took the big bag of bread and threw bread into the water; soon all the attackers were fighting over the bread, snatching it from each other, eating it as they swam or waded. Then that stretch of river with its crowds was past, but the danger was not over, because there was another bend, and more swarms of refugees.

Again the guards were beating off people trying to reach up for a hold on the projecting sun trap. Again the water dragons dragged people under. Again the screams and cries and pleas filled the travellers with a frenzy of fear themselves, and they were crueller than with the earlier attackers. This was a bigger crowd, and they seemed to be well established on both banks, in a hundred different varieties of shack, shelter, hut, and lean-to. The smell here was worse, too, because of these refugee camps. Because they had been longer on the banks, they had attacked boats before, as could be seen by the way they were planning the assault. For ten minutes or so there was a real battle, and both Mara and Dann were in the thick of it, Dann at the front of the boat, Mara at the back. And then, another bend, and the din was gone. One minute it seemed the whole world was shrieks, yells, the sound of wood hitting flesh—and they were again on a peaceful river where trees and reeds stood along the banks. There were no water dragons: they had all gone downstream to the feast. The wind blowing into their faces meant that the smell had gone. And the travellers sank down into their places, took the cloths off their faces, and sat exhausted, while the fear and anger left them.

What would happen to those refugees? What had happened to the inhabitants of Rustam and the Rock Village, of Chelops and many other towns which had emptied because of the long drought? What did happen to people who lost their little place and had to flee? And if those refugees they had left behind did go back to their homes, what would they find, who would they find?

The boat was again moving slowly ahead. It had been two weeks since they had left Goidel. Now Han made them all listen, and said that because of the lowness of the water and the necessity of dodging the banks and shoals, and the nastiness of the attacks, she wanted more money from them. They realised that she did this on all these trips—this ugly, yellow, monkey woman with her little greedy eyes; they hated her, but they all paid out what she asked, because they were dependent on her knowledge of the river. More than once there had been mutters and grumbles, that they should throw her overboard and take the boat on themselves. But without her they would be aground on a sandbank within a few minutes, and they knew it. Mara gave her a bag of small coins. So much had been paid out for food and lodging at the inns for her and Dann that she now had only a few little coins left. And there was so much of this journey still to come before they got—where? North. Everyone talked all the time about "up there" and "up north" where things were so much better. How did they know? Who did know? When Han was asked if she knew she said, with her short, ugly little laugh, which despised the world, "It depends where you end up, doesn't it?"

Now the travellers had to brace themselves for another trial. In a couple of days, Han said, they would reach the canal where there would be a whole day of propelling the boat between banks so close that from them even a child could jump on to the deck. She had been up this way six months before, with no danger at this one place where it could be almost expected—the canal; but the war that had made refugees of so many people had spread this way from the East, and bands of soldiers were roaming the country. Han was keeping a closer watch than usual. Her eyes were always on the move, first one bank, and beyond it to the savannah, then the other bank, then ahead, as the river turned a bend, and behind, from where they had come.

Next day, they heard shouts, gruff commands, the thudding of feet on hard earth, and the boat was running level with a band of soldiers. When they turned their heads—all at the same moment—to stare at the boat, their faces were all alike: these were another version of the people who seemed, every one, to be cut from the same mould. They were heavy, ugly people. Their hair was a pale frizz. They were as alike as insects. They were Hennes soldiers, said Han: the Hennes were rulers in these parts. It was easy to imagine those robustly planted legs, stamp, stamp, stamp, as the legs of a single organism, perhaps one of those long, shiny, brown insects like worms, the length of a forearm, and their legs moving all together, like a rippling fringe. And the brown uniforms made a blur, like a long, brown crawler which, if crushed, shows it is filled with a whitish ooze. Easy to believe, too, that the Hennes were filled with it, and not with the healthy red blood of real people.

For a short time the boat and the soldiers were going along at the same pace. Another order was barked out, and the travellers understood that they were hearing a new language. For the first time in their lives, all of them, their ears did not understand words. Mara felt dismayed, lost, a support gone. They were leaving behind that Ifrik where everyone spoke Mahondi, and soon she would understand nothing. This seemed to her worse than anything that had happened until now. There was another barked order, and the soldiers turned sharply right and ran off to the east. During this time Han had stood still, watching, apprehensive. They were approaching the canal.

Mara sat waiting, watching Han, thinking that she looked like one of those long, lean, furry animals that stand on their hind legs peering everywhere with sharp eyes, when they sense danger, their little paws tucked up in front of them, like Han's, clutching her money bags. Mara was trying to take it all in, everything, every sound, the anxious faces around her, Han's every change of expression. *What did you see, Mara? What did you see?* That early lesson had been so thoroughly fixed in her that it was as if she still expected someone to say to her at the end of the day, "Mara, what did you see?" And today she would have said, before anything else, "I saw Han staring at something a long way off beyond the west bank. And when I looked I saw it too. Two people, but they were so far off you couldn't tell what they were."

But Han knew, for she said sharply to her passengers, "Spies. Men. Soldiers. Keep a good lookout."

But time passed, it lulled past like the sounds of water, and in Mara's mind was not only this river scene but in her inner eye the map on Candace's wall, and the big gourd globe. That globe, from "thousands of years ago"—or at least the information on it—showed where they were now a dense green, the rain forests, and big rivers everywhere; and they all flowed westwards towards the sea, which in Mara's mind was a flat blueness. Beyond the net on the globe that meant rivers, were the beginnings of other rivers, running north, and then west, a whole different net, separated on the globe by a distance the size of Mara's little fingernail. North—were they now approaching North? How would they know when North began? Ahead was nearly half the length of Ifrik, and she and Dann had travelled more than a third. On that old gourd globe that showed the big stain of green, the thick, wet rain forests, was now the savannah she could see, where rivers ran between dry banks. Beyond, on the globe, a yellow colour stretched almost from West to East, right across Ifrik: a desert of sand, covering most of North. But that was not desert now, for on the wall map that came from fewer of those "thousands of years ago"—how they enticed, and sang, those thousands, thousands of years ago—that North was a forest, not rain forest, but the kind of forest that had surrounded Rustam once. And through those forests that grew where once had been sand had run big rivers where on the globe no rivers had been. But the map, after all, was thousands of years ago too, and so who knew what was there now? Sand again? Sands shifted about, forests came and went, and this river she and Dann were on now might in a dry season simply disappear into its sandy bed. But it was the dry season. In the inns along its banks the inn keepers complained of hard times and shortages. This season of drought was not as bad as could be, for sometimes on the banks or sticking up out of the water could be seen skeletons of all kinds of animals from a previous drought. They had died from lack of water where water now was running between banks that had trees and rushes.

Han did not have to announce, "Soon we will have to enter the canal," because they could see the entrance; but before that was something that shocked and frightened them all. Squatting on a sandbank was a boat like this one, with a couple of dragons sunning themselves beside it, and on the boat, nobody. Han steered her boat near to it, and told the guards to use the oars to slow it. Han took an oar and banged it on the hull of the deserted boat. Nothing happened. No smell came from it. No one appeared from a hiding place. The little square of the sun trap had gone—no, it had been wrenched off its swivelling stalk and lay on the sand near one of the dragons. Han began hitting the dragons with an oar, and they slowly waddled into the water, which was shallow here, so they did not disappear but lay half-submerged, watching. Dann leaped from the side of their boat into the water, with a big splash, and had snatched up the sun trap, had splashed back, and had reached the trap up to Han, and grabbed at the hands reaching down to him, as one of the dragons whipped up out of the water—but he was already on the deck.

Han said, "They were taken to be soldiers. Or slaves." She threw the sun trap down, and went back to the prow. The canal banks were not much wider than the boat, and the water was low. It would be necessary to push the boat in, with oars, from the river that here spread into a shallow lake. Slowly the boat was pushed on to the water of the canal that stretched ahead out of sight, so low that the deck of the boat was well below the banks. Usually a day would be needed to get through the canal but conditions were so bad that this time it would take two days. And again Han demanded another fee from them all. She moved about among them, holding out a little bag, and their hatred of her seemed to feed her, because her face was screwed into a triumphant grin, and her eyes were full of malice. Mara thought, Isn't she afraid we will kill her?— and was surprised how easily the idea lodged in her brain, how pleasant was the picture of Han lying dead. Her heart had gone to sleep again, and she tested it by thinking of Meryx, which she tried hard not to do, and while her body was suddenly wrenched with need, her heart remained calm. A long time ago that seemed, and yet it was only a few weeks, and back in Chelops the Kin were still living through the difficulties of the dry season, which would not end there for a month. And now she did think of the new babes, and from there had to think of what was lying hidden in the dry dust outside Goidel, and it seemed her heart was not dead after all, for it began to ache. Would she ever hold her own child? In normal times—but Mara was beginning to wonder if there had ever been normal times—by now the older women would be admonishing her, Be quick, you are losing your best time for breeding. She was twenty. In normal times she would have had three or four children by now. The slaves in Chelops—that is, the slaves that served the Kin, slaves of slaves—had their first babies when they were fifteen or sixteen. Even the Hadron women began at about that age. As the slave of slaves, in Chelops, she would have had her own little house, with three or four children, and a man who might or might not live with her, but who would give her another child at the right time. In normal times . . . instead she was standing at the side of a boat, pushing with an oar at the side of a canal. Above her was a hot, blue sky. There was a smell from the slow canal water of steamy heat. As the oars and poles dug into the canal sides, the earth crumbled and fell in showers of dust and little stones on to the deck. Han was standing on her tiptoes to see as far over the edges of the canal as she could—and then again came the sound of thudding feet, this time not marching, but running, and shouts in that foreign language that dismayed and frightened all the travellers. On the western shore of the canal, opposite to the side where yesterday had appeared soldiers, there were about twenty soldiers, different ones. These were, Mara first thought, Mahondis, but then was doubtful: yes, they are—no, they can't be . . . yes, but they don't look . . .

There was nothing to be done. The soldiers stood immediately above the boat and barked orders at Han, in their language, which Han translated. "They are going to take the young women and the young men." Meanwhile, the six guards, strong men, three of them young, not much more than boys, like Dann, stood just behind Han, and for a moment did not know what to do. Then Dann hurled himself forward as the soldiers jumped down to grab the nearest young woman. The other guards joined him, while Han shouted, "No, don't, stupid idiots . . ." But there was already a noisy fight on that side of the boat, and other passengers were joining in. Han was knocked down, and disappeared among scuffling, kicking, stamping feet. Her money bags scattered. Mara did not know she was going to do it, but she dived forward, snatched one up, and had returned to her place, so fast, so skilfully, it was as if she had been in a different time, for just a moment—only a second, two, and yet she had time to plan her move, which bag to choose, and how to slide back unnoticed while the bag went into her sack. She was amazed at herself. Now knives were flashing and she heard again the sickening sound of wood hitting bones, hitting flesh. There appeared on the bank a man, a soldier, who was clearly in command, for he shouted orders in that alien language, and then in Mahondi, "Stop it, at once." The soldiers at once stood back, and then so did the guards. Han, bruised, hurt, crawled on hands and knees to the front of the boat and crouched there, her head in her arms. This new man was a Mahondi. At the first sight of him Mara knew that he was, and the others were not. He was very like the men she remembered from her childhood, and like the Mahondis of Chelops. He was tall. He was strong and broad, because he was a soldier. His face—but at the moment he was angry, and frightening. An order. The soldiers went to the young women, tied their wrists, and lifted them up over the edge of the boat on to the bank. Four young women. When they came to Mara she said, in Mahondi, looking at the commander, "There is no need to tie me." And she went to the edge and jumped up herself. The three youngest of the guards, including Dann, and four other young men were tied and put up on the bank. Han was still crouching against the side, her arms over her head. The other passengers began poling the boat along, not looking at the soldiers on the bank. Then Mara said to the commander, "Quick, take that,"—pointing to the broken sun trap from the other boat that Dann had rescued. An order. A soldier jumped down and back, with the sun trap. A dull square of tin, on a broken stem, no more than something to be kicked on to the nearest rubbish heap. The commander looked enquiringly at Mara, and she said, "It could be valuable."

An order. And the soldier who had rescued it put it on his shoulder, holding it by the stalk. He gave a cry, and dropped the trap. Mara took it up and put it in her sack.

"If you say so," said the commander and his look at Mara was—but she could not read it. He was not angry now. She thought him sympathetic.

The company of soldiers and captives stood waiting, while the commander looked them over. The young men were sullen, the girls softly crying. They were standing with the canal behind them, where the boat was creeping slowly along between the banks, and from where now came angry voices, laments, and people wailing the names of the young people who had been kidnapped. Around them was the same savannah they had been travelling through, day after day: the dry, dull grasses of the end of the rainy season, low aromatic bushes, the occasional thorny tree.

An order. The soldiers divided into two groups, one with the men, one with the women captives. Mara was watching, when the commander said to her, "You too." And Mara fell in with the women.

They were walking westwards. Soon some ruins appeared, of stone. Then, later, more ruins, recent ones, of wooden houses where fire had left blackened beams and posts. They walked for about two hours, at an easy pace, the commander coming along behind. When Mara turned to look, she caught him looking at her. They came to a group of low brick buildings, and beyond, more ruins. On a great expanse of red dust some soldiers were marching. The commander gave an order. The soldiers with the young men went off, with Dann, who turned to give Mara such a wild, despairing look that she took a step forward, on her way to joining him, but the soldiers restrained her. Another order. Mara was pushed out of the group of young women, who were marched off by their escort. She was left standing by herself, still staring after Dann.

"Don't worry about him," said the Commander. "Now, come with me." He led the way into one of the brick houses, if it was a house. She was in a room that had brick walls, a brick floor, a low ceiling, of reeds. There was a trestle table, and some wooden chairs.

"Sit down," he said, and sat down himself behind the trestle. "I am General Shabis. What is your name?" He was looking intently at her, and she said carefully, "My name is Mara."

"Good. Now. I know a good deal about you, but not enough. You are from the family in Rustam. You were with the Kin in Chelops. You were in trouble with the Goidels, but they let you go. I shall need to hear about Chelops."

"How do you know I was there?"

"I have an efficient spy service." Then, at her look, "But you would be amazed at the different versions I've heard of you in Chelops."

"No, perhaps I wouldn't be."

"No. I am going to have to hear your whole story."

"That will take some time."

"We have plenty of time. Meanwhile, you would probably like to ask a few questions yourself?"

"Yes. Were you expecting me and Dann to come on that boat?"

"We were expecting you round about now, yes. We always keep an eye on the boats. Well, there aren't many of them, only one every week or so."

"And you always kidnap the girls for breeding and the boys for soldiers?"

"Both for soldiers. And believe me, they are better off with us than they would be with the Hennes. At least we educate ours."

At this she leaned forward and said, breathless, "And me? You'll teach me?"

At this he smiled, and then he laughed, and said, "Well Mara, you'd think I'd promised you a fine marriage."

"I want to learn," she said.

"What do you want to learn?"

"Everything," she said, and he laughed again.

"Very well. But meanwhile, I'm going to tell you about what you'll find here. You do know, I suppose, that you are in Charad—the country of Charad—and that there are two people here, different from each other—very different: one the Hennes, and the other, the Agre—us. We fight each other. The war has been going on for years. It is a stalemate. I and my opposite number, General Izrak, are trying to make a truce. But they are very difficult people. When you think you've agreed on something then—nothing."

"They've probably forgotten," said Mara.

"Ah, I see you know them. But first of all—what was that thing you were making such a fuss about on the boat?"

Mara told him. Then she said, "Don't all the boats have them?"

"No. It's the first I've seen."

"That boat that is stuck on the sandbank. The one that was attacked. It had one. It's the one we've got."

"The Hennes did that. And you don't know how it works?"

"The old woman knew—Han. At least she knew how to make it work. But it looked to me as if she is going to die. She said it was very old. There are hardly any left. One less, now." And her eyes filled with tears because she was thinking of the senselessness of it. If Han died then there was a bit of knowledge—gone.

"These things happen," he said.

"Yes, they do. And then something is gone for ever."

He was affected by her reproach to the extent that he got up, walked about, then made himself sit down.

"I'm sorry. But my soldiers weren't expecting resistance. There never is. I don't remember anyone being hurt—badly hurt—before. And it was Dann who began it."

"Yes."

"You mustn't worry about him."

"I know enough about people who fight—the soldiers will punish Dann because he fought them."

"No they won't, because I've given orders. And now, begin your story."

Mara began at the beginning, with what she remembered of her child-hood, her father and mother, her lessons, told him what she knew of the feuds and changes of power, and then how she and Dann were saved. Shabis sat listening, watching her face. She had reached how Dann had come back for her to the Rock Village, when her voice seemed to her to be floating away, and Shabis said, "Enough. You must eat."

A servant brought food. It was good food. Shabis watched her, while pretending not to, working at something on the trestle—what was it? He was writing, on pieces of fine, soft, white leather. She had not seen anything like that since she was a little girl—and she could not stop looking.

"What's the matter, don't you like the food?"

"Oh yes, I'm not used to eating so well." For this was better and finer than even the Chelops food.

"In the army we get the best of everything."

She was thinking that he did not like what he was saying. And did not mind her knowing it. This captor of hers, was he going to be a friend? Was she safe? She did like him. He was what she had been hap-piest with in her life. He was a fine man, and now that it was not angry, his face was kind and, she was pretty sure, to be trusted. Probably Dann would look something like Shabis, when he was older.

When she had eaten, the servant took her into a room where she washed and used a lavatory unlike any she had seen. It had a lever which sent water rushing through channels below. She thought, Well, first of all you have to have water.

On an impulse she took off the old slave's robe she had been wearing day after day for weeks, and put on the top and trousers Meryx had given her. It smelled of him, and she had to fight down homesickness. When she went back Shabis said, "You look like a soldier."

She told him this is what the men of Chelops wore.

"Do you have a dress?"

"It didn't seem the right thing, a dress."

"No. You're right."

He studied her. "Do you always wear your hair like that?"

Her hair was now long enough to be held behind her head in a leather clasp. Like his: his hair was the length of hers and in a clasp. And like poor Dann's. Black, straight, shining hair, all three of them. Long-fingered hands. Long, quick feet. And the deep, dark Mahondi eyes.

She began her tale again. When she reached the Kin in Chelops he kept stopping her, wanting more detail, about how they lived; how they managed to keep some kind of independence, although slaves, about the Hadrons, and then, the drought. She knew he had got the essential point when he asked, "And you think they can't see their situation because they've lived too comfortably for too long?"

"Perhaps not everyone who lives comfortably is so blind?"

"I can hardly remember what peace was like. I was very young when the war began—fifteen. Then I was in the army. But before the war it was a good life. Perhaps we too were blind? I don't know."

She went on. There was another break, when the servant brought in a drink made of milk, and bread, about the time the sun went down. She was thinking about Dann, afraid he would try to run away—or fight, or despair.

She dared to plead, "I am so worried about Dann."

"Don't be. He's going to have special training. He would make a good officer."

"How do you know?"

"It's my job to know."

"Because he is a Mahondi?"

"Partly. But you do know there are very few of us left now? The real Mahondis?"

"How should I know? I know nothing. I have been taught nothing. I don't know how to read or write."

"Tomorrow we'll decide what you are to learn. And I've already ordered someone to come and teach you Charad. It is spoken all over northern Ifrik. It is the one language everyone speaks."

"Until today I never thought about people speaking different languages. I've always heard Mahondi . . . but I never had to think about it."

"Once everyone did speak Mahondi, all over Ifrik. That was when we ruled Ifrik. It was the only language. But then Charad came into the North. Now everyone speaks Charad and a few still speak Mahondi."

"I'll never forget how frightened I was when I heard people talking but I didn't understand what they said."

"You'll understand it soon. Now go on with your story."

But she did not finish that night, because he wanted to know about everyone she had met in the River Towns: the inns and the innkeepers; how people looked, how they talked, what they ate; about Goidel and the easy style of that government. She hesitated before telling him about the gaol, the two women, and what they did for her, but suspected that he knew something already. And so she did tell him, and even how hurt she felt because Meryx did not know. She could see from his face that he was sorry for her and, which she liked as much, that he was sorry for Meryx.

"That's very hard," he said. "It really is. Poor man." Then he hesitated, but said, "You didn't know there had been an uprising in Chelops?"

"No." And her heart sank, thinking first of Meryx, then of the new babies.

"There was a boat through here a week ago. The stories of travellers are not necessarily reliable, but it is clear that there was an uprising. And that is about it."

"Who rose up?"

"They said, slaves."

"Well it can't be the Kin, so it must have been the ordinary slaves."

"Can you remember the names of the people you met in the River Towns?"

But it was no good, she was thinking of Chelops. And so he told her to go to bed and they would start again in the morning.

She stumbled into bed and was asleep without seeing the room she was shown; and when she opened her eyes in the morning she thought she was back on the hill near the Rock Village, looking at the pictures cut into the walls, or painted on the plaster. Then she thought, But these are different people, very different. They are tall and thin and built light, not at all like the ones she had been studying all her childhood. And the animals—yes, here were the water dragons again, and the lizards, but also all kinds of animals she had never seen. The carving was fine and precise, though the stone was so old all the edges of the carving had blunted. Once the rock carver must have used knives so delicate and fine that nothing like that was known now, and he—she?—had held in their minds images of what they carved as bright and clear as life; and those lines and shapes had travelled down into long, thin, agile fingers—here those hands and fingers were, on the rock face—on to the rock face. You could see the muscles on a leg, long clever eyes, the nails on hands and feet. Once these pictures had been tinted. There were tiny smears of pigment, red, green, yellow . . . There was a sound in the room behind her and she had whirled around, was across the room, and standing over the servant from last night, who was just about to slide the bag of coins she had snatched yesterday into his pocket. Mara brought down the side of her hand hard on his wrist and he dropped the bag and howled. He began to plead and gibber in Charad, while he smiled and fawned. In her own language, he knew only the words "sorry," "please" and "princess." "Get out," she said, in Mahondi.

He ran out holding his wrist and whimpering.

She sat on the edge of the narrow board bed she had slept on, under a single thin cover. It was hot, but not the wet heat of the River Towns. This was a large room. The lower parts of the wall were very old, with the incised pictures on them; and above these, though irregularly, for ruins do not make for evenness, the walls continued up to a roof of reeds. The upper walls were of mud mixed with straw. The floor, from the past, was of coloured, shining, tiny stones, set in patterns. Between the lower walls and the floor, and what rose up above them—how many years? Thousands? Those old people, what would they have said to these lumpy, crude, upper walls where tiny shreds of straw glinted? Ruined cities. Cities of all kinds. What was it, why was it, this law that beautiful cities had to fall into ruins? Well, she knew one answer, because she had seen what had happened to the Rock Village: drought. But was it always drought? On the walls of old ruins, on the beams of the fallen buildings she had seen coming here were marks of fire. But fires swept across a country year after year, and the people protected their homes. If they did not keep a watch day and night through the dry season, then fire could consume everything in the time it took for a strong wind to change direction. But people did keep watch. So fires could be too strong, or people too lazy? Drought. Fires. Water? That was not something easy to imagine.

Mara went to her sack, and took out the blue and green cotton robes from Chelops. They were crumpled but they were wrong for this place, she knew, like the delicate older robes rolled at the very bottom of her sack. She brought out the brown, slippery tunic from the squashed depths, and there was not a crease in it. She put on the garments she had worn yesterday, and combed her hair, and tied it back. She checked that the rope of coins under her breasts was still in place. She went into the room next door with the bag of coins the servant had tried to steal, and the brown tunic. Shabis was eating breakfast. He nodded at her to sit down. She did and he pushed bread and fruit towards her. Then he saw the brown garment and stared.

"What is that stuff?"

She told him. "I wore this day and night for years. It never tears, or gets dirty. You shake out the dust. It never wears out."

He felt the material and could not prevent a grimace.

"It could be useful for the army," he said.

"Like the sun traps, no one knows how to make it now. But I was thinking, Shabis. You should send someone after the boat. If Han is alive you could make her tell you how the sun traps work."

He was silent. She realised it was because of how she had spoken. Then he said, "I can see that you are not likely to conduct yourself towards me in the proper manner."

"And what is that?" She spoke smiling. She was not afraid of him. He was treating her like—well, like one of his family.

"Never mind. But I agree with you. I sent a platoon to the boat. It hadn't gone far. The woman you call Han was dead. They were using oars, so it seems that no one knew how to keep the boat going with the sun trap. Our soldiers were just leaving when some Hennes came along. I didn't know they were so close."

"We saw them running along the bank yesterday."

"You didn't say so." He spoke sharply. She knew this was partly because she had spoken incorrectly towards him. "That was the most important thing you could have told me."

"But we hadn't reached that part of my story."

"I suppose you couldn't know how important it was. And now, shall we go on?"

"First, will you keep this safe for me?"

He looked at the leather bag, tipped out a few coins, and said, "This isn't the currency used here."

"Not at all?"

"Perhaps farther North. I hear they are more lax about what coins they use."

"We're going North."

"No, Mara, you are not going anywhere."

He was not humorous, or gentle now, but severe. His mouth was tight, his eyes—no, not unfriendly—serious.

And she was in a panic, knowing she was a prisoner again. She wanted to get up from this table and her good breakfast and run and run, and find Dann . . . And then?

"Mara, between here and Shari there are Hennes, there is the Hennes army. Do you really want to be a Hennes soldier? Believe me, it's not like being an Agre soldier." He pushed over her bag of coins. "No one is going to steal these. By the way, did you know you broke that boy's wrist?"

"Good. He is a thief." And at his look, which was a reproof, "I haven't done all the things I've done to let some little thief take what was so hard to get. When I grabbed this bag up yesterday from among all those feet I could have been killed. Like Han." And, as he sat silent, "Without the money we carried we wouldn't have got far from the Rock Village."

"Don't worry, no one is going to touch anything of yours, seeing what you can do."

"Good. And why did he call me 'princess'?"

"It's a way of flattery. When they want to soften me up they call me 'prince.'"

Here they sat seriously, eyeing each other, because of things that were not being said.

"Are you going to start talking about precious children and mysterious plans?"

"I could, but I've got more urgent things on my mind."

"But there is a plan that involves Dann and me?"

"Not a plan. Possibilities. And I think you'd better know I am not interested." He amended this. "I am not the one who is interested." A pause. He added, "And I don't see much point in your being interested yet, because you are so very far away from any place where it matters. Far in time," he emphasised. "And far in travelling—hundreds of miles."

"Well," said Mara, having taken all this in, "it seems to me that being Prince and Princess, all that kind of thing, isn't much use—not living like this."

"I agree. And I want you to know that in my opinion the time has long gone past when it could be of any use, or of any interest. And now, can you go on with your story?"

She went on. When she got to the bit where the Hennes soldiers appeared he asked question after question. What had they worn? In what condition were their uniforms? What were the colours of the shoulder straps? What was on their feet? Did they look well fed? Were they dusty and dirty? How many were there?

She was able to answer in detail. "And they carried weapons I know aren't of any use." She described them. "The Hadrons have them."

"Why do you say they aren't of any use?" She told him. "They aren't obsolete. They are copies of something very old. Very old. Some Hennes soldier with a talent for that kind of thing saw a weapon from an ancient museum. He thought out how to replicate it. Not exactly of course. We don't have that technology. But they do work. Most of the time. At first the Hennes army had the advantage, but then we got the thing too. So we are exactly balanced again. All that has happened is that many more people get killed and wounded."

"How do they work?"

"They shoot out bullets. We make bullets. You put the stuff we make matches from into a hole and light it and the bullet is shot out." He was silent, and grim. "I was taught at school that only five centuries after the ancients discovered how to make this kind of gun the whole world was in the grip of a technology that made them slaves. Luckily we don't have the resources or the people. Not yet, anyway."

There was so much information here, and she only understood part of it. She cried out, "Last night you promised I will have lessons."

"Language lessons first."

"There's always something else first." And then, seeing his grave, uneasy look, she cried out passionately, "You don't know what it's like, knowing you're so ignorant, not knowing anything."

"I thought you said that in Chelops you found out you knew more than they do—about certain things, anyhow."

"That's not saying much. And I did know more—but what I really knew more about was not the kind of thing I want to learn. I know about how to stay alive. And they don't. When I look back now they seem to me like children . . ." And now she was weeping. She put her head down in her arms and wept. She felt Shabis's hand on her shoulder. It was a kind hand, but it was also a warning.

"That's enough, Mara. Now, stop."

Slowly, she stopped. The warm pressure on her shoulder stopped too. She lifted her head.

"You will begin the language lessons tomorrow. Today I want you to do something for us. You will tell the officers your story."

"How can I? I don't speak Charad."

"Most of them know some Mahondi. I would like them to know more. You will have to speak slowly, and don't use any long words."

"I don't know any long words."

"Now don't start crying again."

"Why only the officers?"

"Do you want an audience of ten thousand?"

"You have ten thousand soldiers?"

"In this part of the country, ten thousand. Over in the West, under General Chad, ten thousand. In the North, twenty thousand—that is, centred on Shari. To the East, keeping the Hennes in their place, ten thousand."

"How many people live in all of Charad?"

"Most people are in the army."

"Everyone, in the army?"

"As you know wars are hard on the ordinary people of a country. We found that all the young men were coming to us, begging to be taken into the army. Then the women. We make most of them soldiers or they work for the army in some capacity. You see, with us they get clothed and fed. Soon we found there were parts of Charad that had no ordinary citizens left. The war had been going on for twenty years. Their fields were destroyed, and their animals taken. Soon Agre was all army. Many of them have never seen a fight, or even a raid, or seen a Hennes."

"What you are saying is that the whole country is a kind of—tyranny."

"That's about it."

"Who is the ruler? You?"

"There are four of us generals. We rule. And we rule well."

"And are the people protesting?"

"Indeed they do."

"So what happens then?"

"What did you do to the poor lad who was going to steal your money?"

"What do they want? If they want a change, what is it?"

"Sometimes we wonder—we four. They call us The Four. They are fed. They are well fed. They are safe."

"And soon you will have your truce with the Hennes. Are they also in the army?"

"No. They have a large, discontented civilian population. Mara, you will get lessons, I promise you. And now we are going to the parade ground. There will be a thousand officers there."

"You expect me to address a thousand people?"

"Why not? You'll manage all right. If you begin now, you should be finished with your story by midday. Don't dwell on the personal aspect. I want you to tell them about the changes in the climate, about how the animals are changing, the scorpions and so on. Describe the setup in

Chelops. Tell them about the River Towns. Some of the soldiers came from there, as refugees. Tell them about the shortages of food—all that kind of thing." He was smiling, and pleased with himself—or her. "My soldiers are the best educated in Charad."

How much she liked and admired him then! And she felt so very much at home with him. And yet he was not like the easygoing, friendly, smiling people that she was sure had been all that she had known in her early childhood. And he was not like Juba, and certainly not Meryx, whom she was seeing now in her mind's eye smiling at her, his gentle, charming smile, which faded as she looked, Goodbye Mara, goodbye—as he turned and went. This man had been a soldier for twenty years, and he never made a gesture, or a turn of the head, or of the body, he never took a step that did not fit exactly into some pattern he had been taught. And yet this discipline of his was nothing like the horrible sameness of the Hennes.

They walked through the flat, low army buildings to where they could see the officers marching on to the parade ground, all the same in their brown, baggy uniforms. The dust spurted up under their stamping feet and drifted about among their legs and began to settle as they came to a stop and stood at ease. She looked for Dann and at last saw him, unfamiliar to her as one of this mass of men, standing in a bloc of ten. She smiled at him, and he nodded, slightly, keeping his face soldierly severe.

Now she could see so many together, she felt uneasy again: they were Mahondis, most of them, and yet not. She thought that if you took any one of these men in front of her by himself, then you would think, Yes, a Mahondi, but perhaps not the best-built or most good-looking one I've seen. But take fifty of these, and put them beside fifty of the real Mahondis, then the difference would be seen at once. But what difference? It was not easy to see.

Shabis signalled and she began talking. She was on a little wooden platform, looking down at them. It was quiet, and she could make herself heard. What was hard for her was, because they were soldiers, their faces kept immobile, she did not know how interested she was keeping them. But from time to time Shabis nodded at her to go on, when she hesitated. Then, after about an hour, she ended with a minute description of the Hennes soldiers on the river bank, and when Shabis asked them if they would like to put questions, one after another raised his hand and it was the Hennes they wanted to know more about. Only later were the questions about drought and the River Towns.

Walking back with Shabis she asked him if there had ever been a famine here, and if so, was this why the Agre people seemed like poor copies of the Mahondis. He said that he believed there had been, but a good long time ago, and then answered her real question with, "But when their children are born, they are not like us. Not really. At first you think that this is a Mahondi baby, and then you take another look."

"So what happened? Why?"

"Nobody knows. Why are those scorpions you told me about, and the spiders and lizards, changing?"

They sat on opposite sides of the trestle table and were served the midday meal. There were cooked vegetables, and meat. She told him she had hardly ever eaten meat, even in Chelops. She would get used to it, she said, but a slab of muscle from some beast, brown on the outside and still red in the middle, made her think of Mishka and Mishkita and the milk beasts of Chelops.

He said that in these parts it was easier to feed people with meat than it was to grow enough vegetables. There were large herds of meat animals, and a good part of the women's army were appointed to look after them. These were hardy animals who thrived even when fodder was short, and they only needed to drink once a week. Now, the Hennes grew vegetables well, but were not much good with animals. If only the Agres and the Hennes could agree on a truce, there could be much beneficial trading.

Then he said that he was going to leave her, because he was going on reconnaissance.

And she said, "But first, I have something really important to ask. Do you know what my name is?"

"Didn't you say it was Mara?"

"Why was it so important for me and Dann to forget our real names?"

"Surely you know that there were people out looking for you, to kill you?"

"Is that all it was?"

"Wasn't that enough? You do know that all your family were murdered?"

"Yes."

"As it turned out, the other side are all dead too. So you and Dann are the only ones left of the Mahondis of Rustam."

"It's so sad, not knowing your real name."

He was silent for a while. "Sad but safe. What's wrong with Mara? It's a very pretty name." And now he got up, seemed ready to leave. "Shall I take your brother Dann with me on reconnaissance? He seems quick off the mark—as you are. Perhaps you'd like to be a female soldier? They are very good." But seeing her face, he laughed and said, "No, but you would be a good soldier. Don't worry. I'm going to train you to be my aide. I need one. And you get the point so quickly."

She said, and it was with difficulty, being stubborn, when he sounded so light-hearted and friendly: "We are going North, Dann and I. When we can."

"And what are you going to find there?"

"Aren't things better there? Is that all just a dream?"

And, exactly like Han, he said, "It depends where you find yourself."

Then, seeing her face, he said, "Mara, what are you expecting? What are you dreaming?"

In Mara's mind were visions of water and trees and beautiful cities—but these were rather misty, for she had never seen a city that was not threatened—and gentle, friendly people.

"Have you been North?"

"You mean really North? North north?"

"Yes."

"I was brought up in Shari and then for a time at school north from there in Karas. But I've only heard about real North."

"Is it true that there is a place up there that has . . . where you can find out about . . . I mean, about those old people, those people who knew everything?"

"Something like that. So they say. I have friends who have been there. But you know, Mara, my life is here. I must confess I have moments when I wish I lived somewhere easier. And now I'm off."

And Mara sat on alone for a while in this room, his room, and then went into the one she slept in, and walked around it and looked carefully at the rock pictures. Those had been a more handsome and a finer people than she had ever been able to imagine. Shabis was good-looking, and his face was intelligent and good—but these people . . . She thought, If one of them walked in here now I'd feel even more of a clod and a lump than I usually do. Everything about them was fine. The clothes they wore were not just pieces of cloth sewn together with holes for arms and head, for that after all was the basic pattern of every garment she had ever seen. Even trousers were two lengths of cloth slit and sewn for legs, and tied at waist and ankle. These clothes the ancient

people on the wall had worn were cunningly cut, with pleats and gath-
ers and folds, and sleeves set in so cleverly she found herself smiling as
she looked. And the ornaments in their ears—long, narrow ears—were
so intricately made . . . But the dulling of paint made it impossible now
to see the details. And the rings on the long, thin fingers, and the neck-
laces . . . What a brilliant show they must have made, a crowd of
these—what had they been called? What did they call each other? They
were a brown people; a warm, light brown, with long eyes made longer
by paint, and smiling mouths, and thin noses, and short brown hair,
held with circlets of—it looked like gold. And they had lived in this
city—for now Mara knew that these army buildings had simply been put
down in a space between miles of ruins—a city of houses that had had
many layers, eight, or ten, and . . . But who knew now how long they
had lived here? How had they lived? Scene after scene showed them
dancing, or sitting around low tables eating, showed them with their
familiar animals, dogs, like the ones she remembered, and others like
her little pet Shera, whose gentle licks on her cheeks she could feel
even now, and birds, brightly coloured, flitting about. There had been a
river, perhaps the same one she had travelled on, and there were boats
so large that each had on its deck something like a small house, where
people sat and amused themselves. Servants—slaves?—brought food on
platters, and drinks in coloured cups. There was nothing here of what
she had seen in the Rock Village ruins: lines of people tied to each other
by the waist, or by chains around their necks.

It occurred to her that when people had said "up North"—perhaps
for hundreds of years, in the cities and towns farther south—what they
meant was this city here. Perhaps even for thousands of years they had
talked everywhere in Ifrik about this wonderful place. No, not thousands: for some reason cities did not live so long. Cities were like people:
they were born and lived and died.

Later, when the light went, the servant came in with a jug of milk and
some little cakes. His wrist was bandaged. He never took his eyes off her,
and sidled out of the room, terrified. He said something under his breath
and it was not friendly. Well, tomorrow she would begin to learn this language and then no one would say things she could not understand.

Before she slept she went out to see the glitter of the stars . . . And
lingered there until she saw that a soldier was watching her: he was on
guard. She went in and to bed thinking about Dann and how soon she
could see him.

Next morning, at breakfast, Shabis asked about the scars around Dann's waist, and she said that had happened when he was very ill in Chelops. Shabis said that there were parts of Ifrik where slaves wore chains around their waists with blunt barbs on them, making scars rather like Dann's. She said she had never heard of anything like that. He nodded, after a while; she supposed he believed her, but did not mind much. She thought, I'm not going to care about him; we'll be going North.

The Charad lessons were with an old woman, a good teacher, and Mara learned fast. Every morning lessons in Charad and every afternoon, for at least an hour, or longer, if he had time, Shabis taught her, by a simple means. She asked questions and he answered them. Only occasionally he said, "I don't know." She protested she was so ignorant and she did not know what questions to ask, but he said that when she ran out of questions then it would be time to worry.

She asked to see Dann. He said that he was in that stage of training when it would be disadvantageous to interrupt it, and Dann was doing so well, that would be a pity.

11

Most evenings Shabis was not there; on reconnaissance, he said, or instructing his soldiers. Then she learned he had a wife. Since he did not mention her, she did not. Would she like it if he wanted to sleep with her? At the thought, her body woke and wailed that it missed Meryx and did not want anyone else. And indeed the thought of him was so painful that she refused to let herself think of him. That time when she had lain every night in Meryx's arms, as if that was the normal thing to do, instead of being cold or hungry or exhausted, or on the run, now seemed like some other life and in another time. To wake in the dark to feel the breathing wonder of a body you loved passionately, tenderly . . . No, she did not want to think of it, or even remember.

Now she was glad Shabis had a wife and was not there in the evenings, for she was able to sit quietly and think of what she had learned in the day, from Shabis, and in her study of Charad.

Another boat arrived on the canal, from down South, and it was stopped long enough to get news. The drought had not broken in the South, and there had been no rain at all. Things were very bad. And Chelops? Nothing definite, only that there had been fighting. She wondered if, when the next boat came, the Chelops Mahondis would be on it, or perhaps even Hadrons? And what was happening in the River Towns? The ones farthest south were emptying, but Goidel was not too bad.

The days passed and then it was weeks. Dann came to see her. They had been sending each other messages, "I am fine. How are you?"—that kind of thing.

Mara watched him walk towards her. The army had fed him and he had lost his lean, knobbly look, like a gnawed bone at his worst. He had grown taller. He was good-looking, very, in his uniform and he moved with confidence. Once, every movement he made was of a hunted thing. They did not embrace but sat looking at each other. They were in her room, where she slept. Dann glanced at the wall pictures, then again, then was caught by them, and only with difficulty left them to sit and talk. It was a shock to see the uniformed man in this room, adding to it yet another layer of time. For she had joked with Shabis that from her shoulders down, in this room, she lived in an ancient civilisation more wonderful than anything people now could imagine, but from the shoulders up, she was a mud-hut dweller. But Dann belonged in a modern barracks.

"Mara, when are we going to leave?"

She had known he was going to say this. "How can we? How far would we get?"

"We've managed before."

"Not in a country where everybody's movements are known. And if you left the army that would be treason, and the punishment for that is death."

He began moving restlessly in his chair, the old Dann, a barely controlled rebelliousness.

Mara got up to look into the next room to see if anyone was listening. The young boy whose wrist she had broken was tidying near the door. He ran out when he saw her. Now she knew enough Charad to understand what he said: he was calling her witch, bag, hag, snake. She called after him in Charad similar epithets and saw him panic.

"What is this Shabis like?" asked Dann.

"You should know. You go out with him often enough on reconnaissance."

"All right—yes, he's brave. He never asks us to do what he won't do himself. But that isn't what I meant."

"He is married."

"I know." His smile, worldly wise and cynical, was something the army had taught him.

"And I haven't forgotten Meryx."

Dann hesitated, then said gently, "Mara, Meryx is probably dead."

"Why? How do you know?"

"There's been more fighting in Chelops. The people from the town went up into the eastern suburbs and massacred Hadrons and quite a few Mahondis."

"Who said so?"

"Kira. She came up on the last boat. She had heard about it from some refugees. She agreed to be a soldier here, but she's not much good at doing what she's told, and so she's looking after animals."

"Do you see Kira?"

He answered only the surface of her question with, "We meet in the eating house. We are friends."

She had learned what she needed to know and she was pleased. So he had a friend. She said, "Dann, I'm learning to read and write in Charad, as well as talking. And I'm learning a lot of things. It's what I've always wanted."

"It'll be useful when we go North."

"Dann, have you every wondered why we say North, North?"

"Of course I have. And it is because everyone has said that things are better."

"They are better here."

"But this isn't what I was hoping for."

"No," she said softly, "it isn't."

"They say that North—really North—there are all kinds of things and people and we've never seen anything like them."

"Dann, you and I—we haven't seen very much, have we? Only everything drying up and fighting and . . ."

"And poppy and murder," he said.

"And poppy and murder. Dann, are you still afraid of him—the one you said was following you?"

Up he leaped from his chair, away from the question, and stood looking out into the glare of mid-morning. "He did try to kill me. He got away."

"Where was this? Here?"

"I'll tell you another time. But I want you to know—if you hear I've gone, then I'll be in Shari waiting for you. Or in Karas."

"Both are inside the Charad spy system. Dann, did you know that you're in line for a tisitch?"

Almost from the start Dann had been a platoon leader: ten men. His basic training over, he was made a cent; that is, he had a hundred men under him. If he became a tisitch, then he would be responsible for a thousand men. He would be one of fifty officers immediately under the general—Shabis. And he would become part of the administration of south Charad.

He had turned himself around, and stood looking closely into her face, in his old way. "Did General Shabis say so?"

"Yes. They think very highly of you. He said you are the youngest cent they've had. And all the tisitches will be much older than you."

"I don't want to be an Agre. I don't want to stay in Charad." But she could see he was pleased. Then he said, "Everything is stagnant here, isn't it?"

"It won't go on being. They are trying to make a truce. Then all of Charad will change."

"And when is this truce going to happen?"

"Shabis is trying to get a meeting with General Izrak."

"Well, good luck. You can't trust them—the Hennes."

She knew that this was more than a professional soldier talking about an enemy—the automatic thing. "Trust? Who cares about trust? If there's a truce there will have to be safeguards, which means that both sides will lose if they break it."

"Clever Mara. But you've forgotten, the Hennes are stupid. And, I've noticed, clever people often don't understand stupid ones."

This talk was sweet to them, after such a long time, almost six months. They could have gone on, but he had to return to his duties. Shabis came in and Dann saluted and stood at ease. Shabis asked Dann about some army problem, and Dann answered well and carefully, but not at too great a length. Mara could see that Shabis was testing him. Then he nodded and said, "Right. Dismiss. You can come and see your sister again soon." Dann saluted and went out, with a look at Mara that claimed her for their plans of escape.

Shabis sat himself where Dann had been and said, "Mara, how do you like the idea of becoming a spy?" And he laughed at her dismay. "I want you to come with me when we negotiate the truce, and then stay behind to work on the details—and report to me everything you see. It wouldn't be for long."

"I should be alone? Among the Hennes?" She was really horrified. "I can't tell one from another. I wonder that they can."

"Sometimes they can't. They all wear some sort of badge or mark."

"What is wrong with them? There is something . . ."

"I think it is that the life—you know, the stuff of life—of one person is diluted with them so that ten—or who knows, fifty?—of them are the same as one of us."

She said,

The inward spark,
The vital flame,
Can go as quickly as it came."

"What is that?"

"I don't know. My mind is full of—things, bits of words, ideas, and I don't know where they come from. Perhaps my childhood."

"Well, that's it. Their vital spark. Perhaps they don't have it. But they are clever enough at some things. After all, one of them copied that gun and made it work."

"I don't think that makes me like them any better."

"Well, are you refusing to do it?"

"I thought I was your prisoner and had to do as I'm told?"

"Is that what you are?"

"I'll think about it. The trouble is, they make my flesh creep. I don't think I ever understood that saying until I saw the Hennes."

And she did think, hard and long when she was alone in her room. In *her* room—alone. What a happiness it was for her, this room, and being alone when she wanted.

Shabis wanted to change the whole country into something freer, easier, and to use money now spent on fighting and raids for improvement. And yet was there so much spent on war? There were battles, but not often. There were skirmishes. Dann had been right when he said Charad—or at least this part of it—was stagnant. The armies had farms and manufactories, they built towns over old ruins that were everywhere in Charad, they educated the men and the women in the armies, and it was a pretty easy life.

Shabis wanted to dismiss half the army back into civilian life and, as war receded into the past, keep only enough soldiers for an unexpected attack. But if you took away the army, the generals would have on their hands many thousands of people who were used to discipline and order, looking for work. What work? Everyone was fed and clothed as it was. Shabis said the former soldiers would be useful rebuilding towns and digging out silted rivers. Very well. For a while the invisible bonds of old disciplines would confine them, and then there would come a time when people would have to be forced by needs now satisfied so automatically no one need think about it, to compete for work. There would have to be money and systems of exchange, and if they refused to work or earn then they would not be fed. How simple it all sounded, how easily Shabis talked about it. But there would be a great turbulence and dissatisfaction and as Mara knew, though it seemed Shabis did not, there would follow the threat of poppy. When she said this to him he replied, "There would be punishments for that." For Shabis, the soldier, had to rely on punishments and rebukes. There would follow courts and prisons and police.

And there were the Hennes, a people within the mass of the Agre, a country within a country. Mara had said, "Why not let the Hennes split off and have their own country? Why do you want them?"

"They want us," was the reply. "They want what we have. They know we are quicker and cleverer than they are. I believe they think that if they capture our part of Charad—Agre territory—then they will become like us."

"But if you have a truce, then they must agree to stop trying to take Agre land, and be content with what they have."

"Exactly. We will trade and be at peace."

A likely story, Mara thought. Shabis's life, spent since he was sixteen in the army, had narrowed his mind away from—well, the kind of experience she and Dann had at their fingertips. He did not understand anarchy, disorder, and the rages of frightened people.

The best part of Mara's life was now the afternoon talks, the "lessons," with Shabis. She was still taking language lessons every morning, though she was speaking pretty well by now, and understood everything that was said. She could write, just a little. Shabis owned an ancient book of tales from the distant past, made of tree bark. It was in

Mahondi. But her writing lessons were in Charad. She tried to use what she had in her brain—the Mahondi—to puzzle out the written words. Shabis helped her. He was spending more time with her, sometimes three or four hours every afternoon. They set aside one of these hours to say what they had to in Charad, to give her practice.

What she liked best was to talk about "those long ago people from thousands of years in the past." He said that he didn't have much to tell her, but as they went on, it turned out he did know a good deal, picked up here and there. They were piecing together what they knew, from her memories of her old home, from Daima, from the Mahondis of Chelops. Shabis said that if it had ever been possible to get all the different Mahondi families into one place then a pretty good record of the filtered down knowledge would result. "The trouble is," he said, "that we all know a little but not how it fits together." For instance he had not seen anything like Candace's wall map and the gourd globe, which came from such different times, separated by—well, probably, by hundreds of years. Or thousands. He asked Mara to draw him the map that had the white blanking out the top of it, and brought her a newly prepared white animal skin, as soft as cloth, and sticks of charcoal, and some vegetable dyes. Then he wanted another, of the time before that, when there was no white covering up so much of the picture.

Sometimes it was by accident that they found out what the other knew. For instance, Shabis remarked that in those long ago times there was a period when people lived to be quite old, even a hundred years or more, while, nowadays, if someone lived to be fifty that was pretty good. "I am an old man, Mara—thirty-five. Then a thirty-five-year-old man was still a young man. And there was a time when women had one child after another and sometimes died young because of it, or were old at forty, but then they discovered some medicine or herb that stopped them having children . . ."

"*What?*" said Mara. "What are you saying?"

She was staring, she was breathless.

"What's wrong, Mara?"

"I can't . . . I don't think I can take that in . . . do you mean to say . . . you're saying that those ancient women, if they took some drug, then they didn't have children?"

"Yes. It's in the Sand Records."

"That meant, those women then didn't have to be afraid of men."

Shabis said, drily, "I haven't noticed your being afraid."

"You don't understand. Daima used to tell me and tell me until I sometimes got angry with her, Remember when you meet a man, he could make you pregnant. Think if you're in your fertile period and if you are, then be on your guard."

"My dear Mara, it sounds as if you are accusing me."

"You just don't know what it means, always to be thinking, Be careful, they are stronger than you are, they could make you pregnant."

"No, I suppose I don't."

"I cannot even begin to imagine what it could be like, being at ease when you meet a man. And then, when it suits you, at the time you want it, you have a baby. They must have been quite different from us, those women in ancient times. So different . . ." She was silent, thinking. "They were free. We could never be free, in that way." Now she was remembering Kulik, how she had dodged and evaded and run away, and even had nightmares. Dreams of helplessness. That was the point. Being helpless.

She told him about Kulik, and how glad she had been when the drought stopped her flow. She said that when she had her fertile times she sometimes did not go out of the rock house, she was so afraid of him.

Her voice was tense and tight and angry when she spoke of Kulik, and Shabis was so affected by it, he at first got up and walked about the room, then came back, and sat down and took her hands. "Mara, please don't. You're safe here. I promise you, no one would dare . . ." And then, as her hands lay limp in his, he withdrew them and said, "It's strange, sitting here talking about fear of pregnancy, when most talk now is about the opposite. Did you know that if one of our women soldiers gets pregnant, then there is a feast, and everyone makes a fuss of her? She has a special nurse assigned to her."

There was something in his face and his voice; she said suddenly, "You haven't had children?

"No."

"And you wanted them."

"Yes."

"I'm so sorry, Shabis."

She was thinking wildly, I could give him a child—and was shocked at herself. She had wanted to have a child with Meryx, to console him, to prove . . .

"No, I'm not like your Meryx. I'm not infertile. I had a child with a woman I met when I was on a campaign. But she was married and the child is now part of her family."

She was thinking, We go around in circles—women do. I could give
Shabis a child, and then I would be stuck here in Charad, and I'd never
be able to leave and go North.

Not long after that afternoon, Shabis said that his wife wanted to
meet her, and invited her to supper.

12

Mara had not seen much more than what immediately surrounded what
she lived in—Shabis's H.Q.—partly because the sentry stopped her if she
showed signs of walking off and, too, because she felt Shabis did not want
her to be noticed. Now, on the evening of the supper, she walked with
Shabis through ruins, of the kind she knew so well, and then into an area
that had been rebuilt to resemble what that long ago city might have
looked like. Here were fine houses, streets of them. Here were stone figures
in little, dusty gardens. The house they stopped at had a lantern hanging
outside the door, made of coloured stone sliced so thin that the flame inside
it showed the pink and white veining. A big vestibule was decorated with
more lamps, of all kinds, and with hangings, and a door of a wood Mara had
never seen, which sent out a spicy smell, opened into a large room that
reminded Mara of the family meeting room in Chelops. The furniture,
though, was much finer, and there were rugs on the floor so beautiful she
longed to kneel down beside each one, and examine it at her leisure. A
woman had come in, and at first glance Mara distrusted her. She was a
large, handsome woman, with her hair piled up on her head and held there
with a silvery clasp, and she was smiling—so Mara thought—as if her face
would soon split. She was all smiles and exclamations, "So this is Mara, at
last," and she pressed Mara's hands inside hers, and narrowed her eyes and
smiled and stared into her face. "How wonderful to see you here in my
house . . . I've been trying to get Shabis to bring you . . . but my husband is
so busy—but you know that better than I do . . ." So she went on, smiling,
and poisonous, and Mara let that flow by her, while she was thinking, vastly
dismayed, that here in this fine house with this woman was Shabis's real

life; it was where he spent his evenings, when he left her, Mara, in his office, and where he spent his nights, no doubt in a room as fine as this one—with this woman.

Mara was wearing the brown snake-tunic, over Meryx's trousers, because this woman, Shabis's wife, had said she wanted to see this material her husband had told her about. Now began a whole business of her feeling the stuff, shuddering *Ugh*, saying how she admired Mara for being prepared to wear the horrible thing—for years? Shabis had told her. How brave Mara was. And when Mara left here, as she, Panis, believed Mara intended to do, she, Panis, was asking a big favour: Please leave this garment behind so that Shabis and I may have a memento of you.

Shabis was uncomfortable, but smiling. Mara could see that this evening was something that had to be got through. Meanwhile, through a good, but fortunately short meal, the eyes of this woman who owned Shabis were suspicious, cold, moved from her to Shabis, and when one answered the other, or a joke was attempted, the black eyes in that cold face glittered with hate. How stupid this was, thought Mara, how very far she was from it all, for that life of loving or jealous looks seemed buried somewhere south in Chelops where—so reports were now coming in from the travellers—fire had raged through all the eastern suburbs.

As soon as the meal was over, Shabis said that he was sure Mara was tired, after studying so hard all day, and that he would walk back with her. Panis was so angry at this it was clear Shabis could not possibly walk back with Mara, who said it was only a short way, a few streets, and she would walk by herself. Mara could see Shabis hated this: he was pale with anxiety for her, and with anger, too. He was actually about to defy his wife and set off with Mara when Panis gripped his arm with two hands and said, "I am sure a few minutes' walk in the dark will be nothing to Mara, after all she's done and seen."

Shabis said, "The password for tonight is 'Duty,' if the sentry tries to stop you."

It was a night when the sky was black, and occluded, the clouds of the rainy season still being with them. Mara walked quietly along the centre of the restored street, where lamps hung outside every house, so that she could see everything, and then into the streets of the ruined area. She went carefully, for it was very dark. And then a shadow moved forward from a deep shadow, and she was just about to say the password, "Duty," when a hand came over her mouth and she was carried off, one Hennes holding her feet and one her shoulders, and keeping her mouth

tightly covered by an enormous, sour-smelling hand. She was carried in
this way through the ruins, always in the shadows that edged the already
dark streets; and then a group of shadows stole forward when they were
in a street in the eastern verges of the ruined town, and she was carried
in a litter made by interlaced arms as solid as tree trunks until she was
set down near a company of fifty Hennes soldiers. Her mouth was bound
with cloth, and she was marched into Hennes territory, keeping up a
steady pace all night, until the light came, and then she was in a camp
made of mud-brick, and tents of thick, dark cloth. This was an army
camp, unlike the towns the Agre army lived in. It was a very big camp.
They took the cloth off her mouth and pushed her into a hut, set a candle down in a corner, said that there was bread and water there, in that
corner, and that she would be summoned to General Izrak.

Her first thought was that now she and Dann were in two armies that
were enemies. Her second was that she was separated from her sack,
from which she was never apart, for she felt her life depended on it. All
her possessions were in it. The two ancient Mahondi robes. Two pretty
dresses from Chelops. Meryx's clothes, a whole outfit and a tunic, for
she was wearing the trousers of another with this brown tunic. And a
comb, a brush, soap, toothbrush. A bag of the coins she had snatched up
from that boat when Han fell among those deadly feet. Not very much,
but her own, and without them she possessed nothing but the trousers
and tunic she wore and the light bark shoes the Agre wore. Well, what
of it? She was still here wasn't she?—standing healthy and strong and
not at all afraid, because she knew she was a match for the Hennes.
There was a low bed, and she fell on it and slept and did not wake until
late afternoon. Now she saw that the window was barred and the door
did not open from inside. This prison was no more than the merest
shed: she could probably be through these rough mud walls in an hour
or two. There was a door into a room with a lavatory and a basin with
water. She used them. More or less clean, she stood by the window to
see what she could, which was only expanses of reddish earth and some
more sheds and tents; and then in came a Hennes and said that the
General would see her tomorrow, and meanwhile she must exercise. He
did not look at her in any way she was used to: his gaze was directed
towards her but did not seem to take her in. His way of speaking,
monotonous, but at the same time jerky, disturbed her, as everything
Hennes did, but she knew she must not give way to this.

Outside the hut an earth road went through the camp, eastward, and she was able to get an impression of the place. Hennes guards stood outside a big building, holding guns, which she knew now were not just for show, and they were outside other buildings, probably stores. The Hennes who was guarding her began a steady loping run, and she jogged along beside him. He made no effort to speak to her. She was tired, having walked all night, and wondered why it was considered necessary that she should exercise. But she understood that these were creatures of habit: prisoners must exercise every day. Having left the camp behind, and finding herself in open scrubland, she said to him, breathless, that she was tired, and he stopped, turned and began jogging back. It was as if she had reached out and turned him around by the shoulder. Late afternoon: the sun seemed to flatten the huts, sheds and tents of the camp down into the long black shadows. On a parade ground outside the camp soldiers were drilling while officers barked orders. This was the same kind of drill, the same orders, as she had been hearing in the other army. If she had not learned Charad she would be feeling very frightened now, and lost: in her mind she thanked Shabis for her mornings of language lessons.

As they passed the large building with the guards, a group of Hennes emerged and stood watching her. She thought that probably one was the General—certainly they all had the look of authority. What could they be making of her, this Mahondi female jogging slowly past them, so unlike them and unlike, too, most of the Agre they were used to? At that moment she saw, emerging from a tent, two of the race of people from the walls of Shabis's headquarters, and the room she had been sleeping in. Tall, light, with elegant long limbs, and narrow heads, creatures as far from the ugly thick Hennes as could possibly be—but they seemed to be servants of some kind, carrying food plates.

In her hut she was brought a meal by the same Hennes warder, and then, ready to sleep again, lay down; but instead was awake for a long time, thinking. What did they want her for? What had the spies told them? Breeding? *Again?* Well, what else did she expect? A female was for breeding, and with the fertility falling, falling—here, too, and everywhere in Charad—of course a woman with all her eggs in her . . . But the Hennes would not know about all that: even Shabis hadn't, until she told him. There was one thing she was sure of, and it was that rather lie with a Hennes she would kill herself. So, that solved that . . . No, it didn't. She would not kill herself. To have survived everything she had and then . . . No. But she would not breed. She would make sure there would not be sex during her fertile period: she lay thinking about the ways she could use to avoid penetration. And then, she would escape. She would run away and find Dann and . . . She slept, and woke thinking she was back in the Rock Village, because of the way this old slippery tunic slid about her.

She was ready when the guard came to take her to the General. He was in the large building she had seen yesterday: walls of mud and grass mix, roof of reeds, floor of stamped mud. Around a long table sat twenty or so Hennes, each in their uniform, similar to the army she had come from, of dull brown cloth. Each had exactly the same face, staring at her. She was sitting immediately opposite the General, distinguished from the others by a red tab on his shoulder. Each Hennes wore a coloured tab, or button or a badge. The large, flattish, yellowish face—it had a greasy look; the pale eyes; the large mat or bush of hair that looked greasy too. Did they put oil on their hair? Fat of some kind? All the exposed flesh and hair seemed wet, but it was grease or oil.

She had armed herself to tell her tale yet again, making it as short as possible, but this man, the General, said, "When do you expect your child?"

This was so much what she did not expect!—and she sat silent, collecting herself, and then said, "I'm not having a child."

At this, the large, flat faces turned towards each other, then back, and the General said, "You are having General Shabis's child."

"No, I am not."

"You are General Shabis's woman."

"No, I am not. I never have been."

And again the faces turned towards each other to share—presumably—astonishment.

"You never have been."

This was not a question, but a statement; their statements were questions in a context, but their voices did not change—were flat, toneless, heavy.

"You have been misinformed," said Mara.

"We have been misinformed. You are not General Shabis's woman. You are not pregnant by him. You are not pregnant."

This last was a question, and Mara said, "No." Then, but realising as she spoke that to joke with these creatures was a waste of time, said, "If you have captured me because of wrong information, then why not just send me back again?"

"We shall not send you back. You will be of use. We will have work for you."

At least, she thought, it had not occurred to them to use her as a sex woman. "May I ask a question?"

They looked at each other—the slow turn of the faces, then back at her.

"You may ask a question."

"If I had been pregnant by General Shabis, what use would that have been to you?"

"He is a good general. He is very successful. We would rear the child to be a general. We plan to capture the children of the other three generals."

"What are you going to use me for?"

"That is a question. You had not asked for permission."

"I am sorry."

"But I shall answer it. You have learned to speak Charad, and you know Mahondi."

Here she expected him to ask for her history, but he was not curious. Nor had any of them leaned forward to look at the tunic she wore, of that astonishing indestructible material. Yet none of them could have seen it before.

"I would like to ask another question."

"You may ask another question."

"General Shabis wants a truce with you. He thinks a truce will benefit all of Charad."

"But I have not yet come to that part of the examination," reproved the General. "Before that I must tell you that you will be informed of the tasks that will be given you. It is possible you will be put in the army. Knowing Mahondi will be of use."

"In the meanwhile I have no clothes, not even a comb or a toothbrush. Perhaps you could arrange for another raid so you could fetch me my things?" As if she had not learned that to make jokes would only upset them.

"We would not be prepared to make a raid solely for the purpose of getting your possessions. It is very foolish of you to think that."

Mara now knew that whatever else she might suffer with the Hennes, boredom was likely to be the worst.

"What is the real reason behind General Shabis's demand for a truce?"

"He believes it would benefit the whole country."

"I am asking you for the real reason."

"That is the reason. He would like the war to end. He says you have been at war for twenty years and neither side has gained anything."

"But we often win our battles with them."

"But the Four Generals administer the territory of the Agres, as they have done for years, and you hold this territory—nothing changes.".

"It is not correct to say that," said General Izrak, apparently agitated, for his eyes seemed to twitch a little in their sockets. "We won a considerable tract of their territory a month ago. It was in the trenches that mark the division between our armies, on our western front and their eastern front. A year ago they won about as much territory as is occupied by this camp. A month ago we won it back. We lost only five hundred soldiers and they lost four hundred."

"General Shabis would consider that an unnecessary loss of life of soldiers who could be better occupied."

"Occupied doing what?" said the General, getting more and more upset. And all around the table the large, glistening Hennes faces turned this way and that, and their eyes flickered.

"Building towns. Improving farms. Clearing rivers. Making children. Growing food."

Down came the General's great fist on the table and then all the Hennes banged their fists, exactly like him, one after the other.

"We all get all the food we need. We raid them and get food, and besides our civilian populations grow food and we take what we need from them."

It was clear that Shabis's demand for a truce was not going to succeed. She wished she could tell him so. It occurred to her that he had wanted a spy in the Hennes camp and here she was. But the Hennes had a spy from the other camp—herself, for she could tell them everything she knew. And she was ready to do so. If they knew just how well organised, how satisfactory, how stable, was the rule of the Four Generals, would they then—the Hennes—be prepared to change their ideas? Did they ever change? Could they?

In came two of the tall, beautiful wall-people, carrying trays. Their elegance made these gross, ugly people even more repulsive. Did they know that long, long ago—thousands of years?—their ancestors had lived in a wonderful city that was only a night's walk away, and their civilisation had, probably, influenced all of Ifrik?

Each Hennes had in front of him a plate of food. It was nothing like as good as the food in the other camp. They began to eat. Then Mara saw that these were not all men: some were female, with flattened bulges in front. There was no other sign of their being women. They all ate slowly and methodically, while the two elegant slaves stood waiting.

"You will get your food in your own quarters," said the General.

"May I ask a question?"

They all appeared to be surprised. "We do not talk and eat at the same time. This discussion is at an end. There might be things we want to ask tomorrow."

And Mara was taken to her prison hut by the guard. She tried to get him to talk to her, but he answered, "You will be informed."

She was brought food. How could she escape? If she were made a soldier, then perhaps . . . She was taken for the routine run that afternoon, and again saw the General and his staff on the way back. With normal people, their faces could be read as saying they had never seen or heard of her, but with the Hennes, who knew?

In the morning she was brought two uniforms, of the kind they all wore: brownish top and trousers, and a brown woollen cap, with a flap in front that could be buttoned back. Two pairs of light bark shoes, clearly not meant for marching in. Some brushwood sticks for her teeth. Soap. A small bag or pouch to be attached at the shoulders to hang at the back. This was the equipment, evidently, for a female soldier, for as well came a bag of rags and a cord to tie them on with. Also, a message from the General, that when she knew she was not pregnant, she must send him the evidence.

Her guard informed her, "You are no longer a prisoner. We shall not be locking this door."

She thought of joking, "If I am not a prisoner, would it be in order for me to walk out of this camp and go back to the Agres?" But she knew this poor man's mental apparatus would be so discommoded he would have to run to the General for instructions.

In four days she would have some blood to show the General, and meanwhile she would use the time to get what information she could by using her eyes. No one took any notice of her as she wandered about—or so it seemed. She was surprised at the apparent confusion of this camp. Then she saw there were blocks of order, unconnected with the others. A block of tents was neatly set out, with tidy paths between, but this was set at an angle to some rows of sheds, equally well arranged, and both were unrelated to an adjacent little suburb which itself was composed of rows of little boxes. To get from one part to another of this camp—but it was a town, really, since it had been here, clearly, so long—was difficult, for she found herself following the neatest of paths, hoping to achieve the next settlement, but it ended perhaps against the wall of a house, or simply stopped. Storehouses, water tanks, stood here and there, and there was a watchtower in the very centre of the camp, or town, when surely it should have been at its edge?

Finding herself looking westwards, on a well-used road—the one she had been brought on—she simply began walking, thinking she might not be noticed; but she had not reached the camp's outskirts before she heard a soft thudding of feet on dust and turned to see a graceful creature, a Neanthes, flying rather than walking, long delicate hands outstretched. "You must come back. You are not allowed."

They walked back together. Mara said that she wished she could have a writing stick and some writing leaves, to learn more Charad, but the girl replied that learning was not encouraged among the soldiers. "And particularly not the Neanthes. They are afraid of us, you see." And having reached Mara's hut, this Neanthes went off, seeming to dance rather than walk, sending Mara a delightful conspiratorial smile.

On the proper day, Mara sent the General a message that there was blood, and therefore no pregnancy; but back came the Neanthes to say she had been instructed to see the blood with her own eyes. "But I could have pricked my finger," Mara whispered, and the whisper came back, "You see? they're stupid." She ran off to the General with the evidence and brought back the message, "You have blood. You are therefore not pregnant. You will begin training tomorrow."

The next day she found the new recruits were not all Hennes. On the drill ground were a hundred recruits, males and females, mostly Hennes, with a few Neanthes, but about a third were people Mara had not seen before. They were small, stocky, strong, yellowish, with the knobbly look that Dann had had when he was underfed—and presumably Mara herself. These were Thores, and they had come voluntarily to the camp to join the army where they would be fed: their home province was impoverished because the Hennes had raided it for food recently. It was immediately evident that the tall, long-legged Neanthes could not drill together with the small, short-legged Thores, since the stride of one was twice that of the other, and the new recruits were sorted out into six platoons of Hennes, ten each, three of Thores, and one of Neanthes. Mara was with the Neanthes. She was not as tall, as lithe, or as slender, but she was not very different from their shortest.

Marching about on the dusty drill ground, while a Hennes instructor shouted at them, was boring rather than arduous, but he kept them at it, hour after hour, in the hot sun, while the dust rose up in clouds and they grew thirsty and tired. He was trying to bring them to an extreme of physical exhaustion, but again there was the problem of their differences. The platoons of solid, stolid Hennes showed few signs of fatigue, while the Thores, in any case undernourished, were in a bad way, and the Neanthes were falling and fainting. They could not all do the same drill. It appeared that this problem arose every time with the new recruits, but apparently the Hennes always thought that this time things would be different, and were taken by surprise that what was happening was exactly what always happened.

From now on the Hennes would begin two hours before the Thores, and then there would be an hour before the Neanthes joined in. And that set the pattern for the month of drilling that was needed to turn Mara and the others into soldiers. She neither liked it nor disliked it. Soldiers had to be trained, and a soldier was what she was now—though not for long, if she could help it.

Suddenly everything changed. There was a raid to the east one night, and there were prisoners. Mara's hut was needed and she was ousted from it, and watched while four Thores were hustled in to take her place.

She was ordered to march north with a company that was to replace watch-guards on the northern frontier. She was expecting to hear something from General Izrak before she left, but there was nothing: she had only been of interest to them for one reason.

13

At first they marched through grasslands broken by clumps of thorn trees; but when they camped on the first night they were on the edge of a great plain broken by hills which next day, as they marched down on to it, they could see was no longer the sandy or reddish soil around the Hennes camp, but a dark earth, fibrous, growing sparse, low plants. A wind blew straight from the north into their faces, carrying showers of this earth with it, and soon all the soldiers had tied cloths around their lower faces to breathe through. All that day they marched through low,

lumpy hills with an occasional Thores village, and that night they had
come up from the plain and were again on a rise, and ahead was a deso-
lation of rough hills and broken ground. This was the last day's marching. That evening, ahead, stood a line of watchtowers, each on a rise;
and around each was a camp, more of a village, since there were huts,
not tents, and a great blaze of sunset lit most luridly a flatness between
the towers, where earth moved and blew about, seeming to heave, like a
creature, and little hills whose tops were briefly lit with a ruddy glow
before the sun plunged down and there was an absolute dark; and then
into the black overhead the stars came, not glittery and clear, but dim,
because of the dusty air.

The company separated, moving off to different watchtowers. Mara
went to the farthest, and to the very top from where the watchfires could
be seen burning here and there in the darkness. This was the extreme
northern frontier. Ahead was the territory of the Agre Northern
General, which stretched as far as Shari, about ten days' march away. Far
away was a line of answering fires, the enemy's. For all Mara knew, Dann
was there—her enemy. Well, it would not be for long—and why did she
think that? she questioned herself, most uncomfortably. It was because
she had never stayed anywhere for long, had always been moved on by
some pressure or danger; but everyone knew that the soldiers sent to the
frontiers were sometimes there for years.

There were two platoons, or twenty soldiers, at this outpost. They
were Neanthes and Thores, mixed—the Hennes did not like frontier-
watching—and under the command of a Thores woman, Roz, who had
been captured as a child and had never known anything but the army.
This outpost was well ordered, efficient, clean, and Mara knew she had
been in very much worse situations than this one. Soon, she was in a
hut by herself, and was able to be on watch-duty, usually with people
she liked. Commander Roz put people together who got on, and she saw
to it that her soldiers on the whole did the duties that appealed to them.
Mara liked being on watch, so that was what she did. Others collected
firewood, fetched water, repaired huts, or cooked. Not that there was
much to cook: once a month runners came from the Hennes camp with
supplies, but they lived mostly on bread, dried fruit, and vegetables.
Sometimes the commander ordered a couple of soldiers to go out and
see if they could snare a deer or a couple of birds, but there wasn't much
wildlife now, in the dry season. This was the third dry season since Mara
had left the Rock Village.

She was often on duty alone on the tower. Regulations said there must always be two on watch; but even when there were, one would usually be asleep. Along this front there had been no fighting, no raid, not even an "incident" for years. A spy was the worst they had to fear. When Mara was on duty the Commander often came up. She was fascinated by Mara, as Mara was with her. She remembered little of her life before her capture, aged eleven, had always been a soldier, had always known where her next meal was coming from, and what she was to wear and do. She was not "in" the army, she *was* army. She listened to Mara's tales of her vicissitudes with her hand pressed to her mouth and her eyes wide above it, and she giggled nervously when Mara laughed and said, "You don't believe a word I am saying." Whether she did or not, she would say, "Tell me about the house with the spiders," or how the sky skimmer crashed, or how people lived in the River Towns. She had not been out of the Hennes camp, ever, except on watch-duty, had never heard of sky skimmers. Particularly she wanted to know about the flash floods, and it was pleasant to talk about flowing waters while the dust storms blew from the north.

Mara stood alone on her tower and listened to the dry whine of the wind around the corners and struts of the old, shaky building, and heard the thud, thud, thud of soil hitting the base of the tower, where it piled on a bad night as high as the shoulders of the Thores soldiers—who cleared it away in the morning—or to the waists of the Neanthes. All around this tower was a thick layer of the blown, dark earth, and as soon as the rains began vegetables would be planted, which would race into maturity, because this was fertile soil. Mara stood with her back to the south lands, or "down there," and saw the dim lights of the watchfires, that went on for miles east and west and, across a hollow of dark, the answering Agre fires. She listened to the soldiers singing below: the delicate, keening songs of the Neanthes, the Thores songs, whose words, when you listened carefully, were the double-tongued complaints of a subject people afraid to speak openly. On some nights, when the winds were not blowing, these songs seemed to rise like a many-voiced plea along miles of the frontier; and on a still night, threads and shreds of song came from the enemy lines.

One night, coming off watch-duty, she saw a movement among the heaps of dirt around the base of the tower and, then, a gleam of eyes. She leaped forward and hauled out a terrified wretch who wept and begged as she held her knife at his throat. "Be quiet," she said. "Tell me, what news of the Agre Southern Army? Do you know anything about General Shabis?" "No, I don't know anything." "Do you know about Tisitch Dann?" "No, I told you, I don't know anything." "Then what is the news along your sector?" "Nothing, only that your army is going to attack Shari." "Is that what you're spying down here to find out? Well, you can go back and tell them that it's nonsense." And she let him go to creep back to his lines.

She told Commander Roz, who wondered if she should report this back to the base when the food runners came next. She decided not to, but said she would organise a reconnaissance. Mara asked if she could go by herself. She showed Roz her old robe, which changed with the light, sometimes becoming colourless, or even invisible and said she would put it on one night when the dust was blowing, and try to overhear what was said at the watch-post opposite. When the Commander saw the garment she felt it—and made a face, as everyone did.

Mara put it on over the thick underclothes they had, for cold, and ran into the dark. It was a cold night and a noisy one, for the wind buffeted and gusted. She could feel the dust rising about her legs. She crawled the last few yards and lay flat, just outside a circle of firelight. The soldiers around the fire were speaking Charad and Mahondi too, and eating and throwing bones and scraps into the fire, and talking about the boredom of this watching life, and how they longed for their replacements so they could return to Shari. The only thing of interest they said was that General Shabis was coming to take command of the Northern Army and of Shari, and that would be a fine thing. "He's the best of the lot, General Shabis, he won't let us rot out here." Then the talk turned to women.

Mara had been thinking that she would rise up from her concealment behind some low bushes, and say she was General Shabis's aide—they would welcome her as one of them, of their army and take her to . . . She must have been mad to think it. She was a female, alone, and fair game. These were men who had been without women for months. No, if she was going to desert then she must choose a time when she could steal some provisions and some water, and steal through the dark evading their own line of watchfires, then the enemy watchfires and forts, and run like a rabbit to . . . She did not believe Shabis was anywhere near Shari.

She lay quite still, and the only bad moment was when a soldier stepped out into the dark a few paces away to pee. She heard the liquid hiss in the dry soil, and saw his face—full of longing as he stared out into the dark, thinking of his home—while the firelight flickered over it. Then he returned to his comrades around the fire. Some wrapped themselves and lay down to sleep. Two kept watch. Behind them on their watchtower others were staring over their heads into the night—to the tower where Mara spent so much of her time. She wriggled back and away and ran home. For her home now was this outpost. She told Commander Roz that General Shabis might or might not be coming to Shari, but she believed it was only hopeful thinking on the soldiers' part, because Shabis was the kindest of the generals.

The dry season passed. The lightning danced around the horizons, and the thunder came crashing as the rain fell in rivers out of the sky. In the morning all the land between them and the opposing front was covered in silvery, meandering rivulets, for the soil was so dry that at first it repelled water but then, as the nets of water thickened and glistered, the wet sank in and the soil was a dark, springy sponge. There were flowers jumping up everywhere, bright, frail flowers, and birds running about among them.

Out went the Commander to plant vegetables, with her soldiers. The sun dragged up clouds of steam. The clear air transmitted the singing from the opposite lines, so that the soldiers along this front answered enemy songs with their own; and for the whole of the first week of the rains it was as if the two armies were serenading each other.

All the soldiers ran out at night into the rain naked and held up their arms into it and exulted as the streams ran down their bodies. All but Mara. She was afraid to take off her cord of coins, and could not be seen with it. When they teased her about her shyness she said she had been brought up never to show her body to anyone but a husband. This made them laugh at her even more.

Commander Roz came creeping to Mara's bed and begged to come in, like a little animal, and when Mara was unwelcoming, she said, "Don't you like me, Mara?" Mara did like her. She would have liked very much to open her arms to this companion, but she did not dare. If it were known what she wore under her uniform . . .

Roz was kneeling by the bed and Mara was holding her hands, and she began talking about her husband, Meryx, whom she was afraid was dead, and how she could not bear anyone to touch her, only him.

This made Roz love Mara even more, this romantic woman with a dead love, who was so faithful to him and so pure.

She went back to the soldiers and told them that Mara was not to be persuaded. The women soldiers, who of course dreamed of a love of their own—and some had found love here on the frontier—and the men soldiers, who might have wives and lovers at home, all admired Mara. She became even more of a lonely and romantic figure, and people envied her.

What she had told Roz was not far off the truth. While she would not allow herself to think at all of Chelops and his possible—no, probable—death, she often felt Meryx close to her. She had only to summon up his image, when she was alone, or in bed, to feel that he was there. So it could be said that she never thought of Meryx, refused to, and yet he was with her, like a friendly shadow.

Mara stood on the tower and looked north and thought that she had been here now six months. The soldiers sent out to the watchtowers were supposed to be relieved after six months. The ration-runners came and said nothing had been said about a relieving company. Asked, What's new?—they replied that there were rumours of a putsch north. But there were always rumours of a putsch somewhere. Mara asked if there was news of General Shabis, but they said "everyone" was saying he and the other generals had quarrelled. Who was everyone? Some spies had said so. Had they heard anything about a tisitch called Dann? One said that he thought there was a General Dann. "A general?" A deputy-general: you know, each general has a little general attached, and he trains him up the way he should go.

Life at the watch-post became pleasanter as the rainy season went on. Farmers brought in food, and asked outrageous prices, and were bargained down. Commander Roz was always present at these encounters, for often spies were with them. Mara did manage to extract from a particularly suspect farmer, who asked too many questions, that General Shabis was in Shari. He was there to counter the expected Hennes putsch.

The rainy season went on but it was patchy. The flowers of the first rain had disappeared but there was a green film over the brown. Rabbits and deer ventured from the hills and made meals for the soldiers. As always in a land where the rains mean life, there was in everyone's mind a calendar or record of the rainy seasons, thus: last season had been a good one and filled the dams; the one before that had been poor, and the dams were low; before that had been two goodish seasons, but before them a run of bad ones. This one they were in was not really good but could be worse. Now next year—everyone would be waiting to see how that one would turn out.

Mara stood on her tower and looked north. She had been here

nearly a year. Then it was a year. She had been forgotten. The dry season was here again and the black earth lightened to dark grey, though it would take some time for the soil really to dry out, so the winds could begin their work of lifting and shifting and reshaping the land.

14

Then, unexpectedly, since no one had believed the rumours, a runner came to say the army would be marching north past here, and they, the watchers on the frontier, would be absorbed into it, and must have their equipment and weapons ready. There were guns stacked in the fort. No one used them, because they were afraid the things would blow up in their faces, as they so often did. Now they were brought forth and cleaned, and every soldier checked a little stock of explosive powder. They did this because they had to but, by now experienced old soldiers, they stuffed their satchels and bags with food and warm clothing, and sharpened their knives.

Then they waited, staring south, until the horizon began to move towards them, and then there was the Hennes army, which engulfed them. The great army—it was ten thousand strong—marched for six hours, and rested for two, marched for six and rested, and so on, day and night, for ten days. The moon was high and bright and its light filled the sky but the clouds of dust raised by all those marching feet obscured the view around them. All the way Roz the platoon commander was beside Mara, chattering about how fine it would be when they occupied Shari, and that she had never before been with an army when it took a city. Mara was wondering how to escape. When the whole great company stopped on the rise outside Shari and looked down and saw the turrets and towers shining white above trees and populous streets, there was a silence and then a spontaneous cheer. Loot and good times were in every mind. But Mara was wondering, Why is there no opposing army to stop us? Already the truth was in her mind and she was wondering why General Izrak could not see it. If there was no defence, and this army was going to be allowed to march unopposed into the city, then a trap had been set. Mara knew that in the low hills on either side of Shari, General Shabis's troops must be waiting. She knew that she herself would be an animal in a trap if she could not think of a way to escape— but she could not, and she marched with the army, positioned about a third of the way along the column, into the streets of Shari, which were finer and grander than anything she had imagined. And still all that could be seen were the desperate inhabitants—running, taking cover in buildings, shops, even up trees. The army was halted, its head in the main square. Probably General Izrak only now understood that he was trapped, and he was wondering whether to retreat or fight. The soldiers had understood by now. And this army, which had not fought a real battle for years, was in a panic. Then Mara's chance came. The ranks broke, soldiers went off into side streets and alleys, into garden squares and houses, half in a frenzy of fear, but lured by loot. Mara dived into a shop, by herself, and had her Hennes uniform off, or rather the top part of it, and pulled on the old, brown, skin-like garment she kept at the bottom of her army satchel. Then she was out of the shop and into the crowd of fleeing inhabitants, no different from them, except that she had left the army issue kitbag with her trousers in the shop. Also all her food and clothing. She now possessed nothing at all, apart from the Hennes trousers and that old indestructible tunic. The refugees were crowding north out of Shari. Shabis's army, drawn up outside the town, stood on either side of the main road to let them through. The officers were shouting, "Go to Karas—we'll have this scum out of Shari before the solstice." "You'll be back home before you know it." "You'll find food on the road." And so on. But the refugees seemed not to hear, they were haunted and hunted and were determined on one thing: to get as far away from the Hennes troops as they could. Already they all had tales of horrors: rapes, murders, muggings.

And if Mara wasn't careful she would find herself out of Shari and on the road to Karas. She stepped out of the flood of people and there, under a big thorn tree, just where the town ended, a group of Agre officers stood watching the refugees. Mara reminded herself that she was not a soldier now, she did not have the protection of a uniform, she was a young woman. She swiftly unknotted a coin from her cord of them, using an empty booth to hide her for that moment, and went up to them, saying, "I want to speak to General Shabis."

She had expected what she got: astonishment, then incredulity, and then the ritual jeer the occasion demanded.

"He knows me," she said.

"So he knows you, does he?"

Now she took a big chance: "General Dann, is he here?"

"I suppose you know him too?"

"Yes, I do."

And now their faces were those of soldiers whose mental apparatus had been overloaded. It was her assurance, her self-command that confused them. And, too, that she was a Mahondi, who looked like generals Shabis and Dann.

It was touch and go; the group could have gone on with another question, but instead there was a cacophony of leers, and then one of them came forward, took her by the wrist and, to the accompaniment of laughter, pulled her into an empty place that was usually a tea house. Before he could whip off her garment and show her what he could do, she held out the gold coin, on her palm, hoping he was not one of those who did not know what gold was, and said, "You can have this if you take me to either General Shabis or General Dann. And I won't tell them you tried to rape me."

It was her manner that stopped him, her calm. He rearranged his clothing and said, "I'm on duty."

"So I can see."

His eyes swivelled about, expressions chased themselves across his face—for a moment he was tempted to rape her after all; then he reached out for the coin, and she closed her fist over it.

"Wait," he said. He ran back to the group of his comrades. She saw their expressions change as he talked. He came to her, running. "Quick," he said. And, running, the two went off, avoiding the columns of fleeing people, through increasingly grand streets to a big building that had guards outside it. "General Shabis is on the other side of the town," said the officer. "General Dann is in there." She held out the coin; he took it, and said, "If you're on the level, tell General Dann I brought you here." And he ran off.

She walked up the steps and said to the guards that she wanted to see General Dann.

"He's busy," said one, contemptuous of a civilian.

"I think you'll find he'll see me. Tell him his sister is here."

At once the guards' faces changed. One went into the building, the other stood eyeing her, frowning, trying to match what he was seeing, this dusty female in her odd-looking clothes, and the great General Dann.

She was taken in, along a central hall full of officers trying to look busy, and into a side room. There at the window, looking down at the chaotic scene, stood a young officer so handsome, so appealing to her that she experienced him as an assault to all her senses; and she had begun to say, "Where is General Dann?" when she saw it was Dann, and at the same moment he turned and said accusingly, "Mara, where have you been?"

At which she sank into a chair and laughed, but then began to cry, and she dropped her head on her arms sobbing, while her brother stood over her scolding, "Mara, we thought you were dead." And his voice, impatient, loving, *Dann's*—made her feel that she had come home. "Now you are here we can leave," he said. "We can go North."

At this she began laughing again and said, "Oh Dann, how I have missed you."

And now, as she lifted her head to look at Dann, she noticed sitting opposite her a young man, a boy, and his face was bitter as he smiled, *Wouldn't you know it!* And he was very jealous. Mara realised, as Dann did, at the same moment, they had been talking in Charad; and now they switched into their own tongue, and that for her—she had not spoken Mahondi for so long—was a coming home, a return to herself.

She stood up and the two embraced, and now Dann's eyes were full of tears too. "Oh Mara," he said, "you don't know what it has been like without you."

At this the young man got up from his place and began to exit, intending this to be seen. Dann quickly went to him, laid his hand on his shoulder, and said, "This is my sister." But with a disdainful movement the youth shook off Dann's hand and went out, shutting the door with exaggerated care.

Brother and sister sat, close, and he held her hand and looked into her face and this—his way of looking—told her how much he had changed, for it was far from the hunted, haunted, close look she knew so well, but a frank, friendly, open examination.

"Shabis sent out spies to find out where you were, but they came back and said you were dead."

She told him where she had been, while he listened.

Then he said, "Let's go, Mara. I didn't believe you were dead. I was only hanging around in case you'd turn up."

"But you're a general, how can you just go?"

He got up, laughing, and paced about because he was so full of elation and happiness, he could not keep still. "I'm just a trainee general. And anyway Mara, I don't care about that—do you care about that? No, of course you don't. Shabis likes me—that's the point. He said he thinks of me as his family. But this war—it's stupid. I don't want to be part of it."

He explained the plan—the Agre plan. General Shabis's troops were closing in around the southern suburbs, and General Izrak was trapped. When Shabis had cleaned up in Shari, then his army would make forced marches to the Hennes H.Q. and then take all the south part of Hennes occupied territory. Soon the whole country would be in the hands of the Four Generals. And the war would be over. As Dann outlined these plans, he spoke mockingly, and Mara agreed.

Dann ended, "A trapped boar can inflict nasty wounds."

"Cleaning up," said Mara. "That means a massacre."

"Who is going to weep for the Hennes? Or any of their kind anywhere?"

"The army isn't just Hennes. There are a lot of Neanthes and Thores people too." He was silent. "Why don't you announce an amnesty for the Neanthes and Thores? They were all taken prisoner and made into soldiers."

"Mara, this isn't our problem."

"I don't understand why Shabis agreed to this plan. It's silly. He could have stopped the Hennes getting to Shari."

"He didn't agree. You forget, there are four generals. He was outvoted. He wanted to make a stand well south of Shari. The other three wanted a trap."

"And a massacre."

"And a massacre."

"I wish I could see Shabis. He was so good to me, Dann. He taught me so much."

"And me too. But Mara, are you forgetting we were captured? We are formally Agre prisoners. Well you are, anyway. Do you imagine Shabis would just say, 'Oh, you're off are you? Bless you my children.'"

"Why shouldn't he? He might."

"They've put a lot of work into me. They intend me to take Shabis's position when he takes over General Command. They're not going to waste all that."

"What are we going to do?"

"Get to Karas, first."

"And then?"

"The frontier with the North Lands. It is a day's march from Karas. Once we're there, we're free."

"First we have to get to Karas."

"And that is the most difficult part."

In the street outside there was a sudden tumult of shouting and running feet. The refugees were running past this building too. Dann closed the big windows, so they could hear each other. Mara had never seen windows like those: tall, from floor to ceiling, and of thick glass. She knew about glass, had seen it a little—in the windows of Shabis's house, she believed, but it had been too dark to see well—and here were sheets of glass; and she was thinking that a town with glass in its windows knows it is a safe town, because a single thrown stone can shatter glass. Well, Shari today was learning something very different.

Now Dann and she discussed difficulties. As always it was a question of details, for both knew—how well they knew—that getting one small thing wrong could mean calamity.

First of all Dann was a senior officer and could not be seen just walking off on the road north: that would be desertion. He must have the right clothes on. Then, both he and Mara were conspicuous. Here Dann took her to a wall where there was, she thought, a window beyond which was a tree; but she saw it was a glass that showed a tree which was behind them, outside the windows in the garden. She was longing to examine it, find out—but Dann said, "Quick, we must be quick." They stood in front of this glass, which reflected, and saw how alike they were: tall—Dann must have grown six inches since she saw him last—strongly built but finely made, with shining black hair and great, dark eyes. He was handsome, as she had seen in that first moment of shock; but already she was feeling him as something like an extension of herself, and she needed this little distance put by the glass that showed them to themselves, even if in a confusion of leaves and branches, so it seemed they were standing in a tree, to see just how good-looking he was. And he was smiling at her reflection. "Look how you've turned out," he said. "You're a beauty. You're going to get yourself raped if you aren't careful."

"I nearly was." And she told him what had happened. "But I bought myself off. Do you ever think that we nearly left the gold behind?"

"Yes. Often. And how many have you left?"

"Fifteen."

"And I have six hidden. Apart from . . ." He touched his waist. "When I can get these out safely, I must. They itch sometimes. Meanwhile I'm glad to have them there."

What were they going to wear on that dangerous road?

Now he went to a cupboard and produced Mara's old sack. "I've always taken it with me. Just in case. I didn't really believe you were dead. That wouldn't be like you. And now it's going to save us."

She pulled out the two slaves' robes.

He said, "You've got to get those Hennes uniform trousers off."

She pulled them off and stood in the brown tunic, reaching now to her knees.

"You've got to get that off too. People would be curious."

She was shy of him; he saw it, turned around, and she slipped on the old robe that would never be white because of the dust that had dyed it.

There was a knock. Dann went to the door, and opened it a little. A lot of noise came from the hall. He said, "Right, I'll deal with it. Meanwhile, don't disturb me until I say."

"And now we really do have to be quick." He whipped off his uniform and, as he did, said, "Goodbye, General Dann." Was he regretting it? At this last moment was he hesitating? If so, Mara could not see that he did. She caught just a glimpse of naked Dann, not ugly or starved or all ribs and bones or knobbly, but beautiful, he really was so beautiful—and then he had on the slave's robe, and she said, "What a pair of freaks we look."

"Not freaks enough. Get your hair covered." She bundled it into a piece of cloth and tied it tight. He pulled on the woollen cap Mara had kept in her sack. Into this sack he emptied some fruit and bread that had been brought in for General Dann's consumption.

"Water," she said.

"We are supplying water on the route to Karas," he said. "Water and soup, for the refugees."

"Which we are now."

"Yes. Quick." This room was on the ground floor, and the windows looked into a little garden, beyond which the refugees were streaming past. Dann took his knife from the discarded uniform, put it into his

knife pocket, slid in a little bag which held the coins. She took up her
sack, but she had left her knife in the army satchel she had jettisoned.
Dann flung open the window, admitting the sounds of shouting and
anger, and leaped out, and she followed. In a moment they were across
the garden and among the refugees. A sentry who had been idly watching the fleeing crowds saw the two too late, perhaps thought they were
refugees who had strayed into the garden, or decided, to save trouble,
that he had not seen them.

15

Mara and Dann, each with a sack over a shoulder, were among people who were half running, ten or twelve abreast, along the road to
Karas. On each face was a stunned, disbelieving anger. All knew that
when they returned to Shari their homes might not be there, would at
least be looted and despoiled. Children were crying. Already people
were falling out of the stream to rest a little by the side of the road,
unable to keep up.

Outside the town the crowds turned for a last look: smoke was rising
here and there. The trapped soldiers, careless, or drunk, or perhaps
deliberately, were causing fires. There was a clamour from the besieged
town, shouting and screaming but also singing.

The refugees passed through the troops that were on either side of the
road, and Dann was trying to make himself inconspicuous, and held his
arm across his face, as if shielding it from the sun.

Immediately beyond the town was the first feeding station set up by
Shabis for the refugees, serving soup and bread and water.

Mara and Dann waited in line for some water—they had no con-
tainer—drank as much as they could, and ran on. They were attracting
attention because of this vigorous youthful running, and so they slowed
to a fast walk. It grew dark, and some people settled for the night near
the next feeding station, but most went on. The moon was now at half,
but still yellow, and bright, and it illuminated the road. It was easy to

walk. In the middle of the night, near a feeding station, the two ate soup and drank from the great jars that stood by the road, each guarded by a soldier. They slept a couple of hours, with a crowd of others, and felt they were reliving old times when they lay down back to back, each facing out, to be alert for thieves.

No thieves, only the restlessness, the weeping, the mourning, of the people, and the crying of the children. It was so noisy that soon Dann and Mara went on. That day's march was easy, because it was a huge, jostling crowd, though more than once someone did look closely at Dann, as if he were recognised. The feeding stations were well placed, and frequent. Now Shari was a good way behind, and whenever they reached a high point on the road, everyone turned to see what they could—but there were only columns of dark smoke, which sight brought forth more tears, imprecations, curses, impotent rage. That night was the same as the last, lit dimly by the shrinking moon, and Mara and Dann slept, but not much, for they could not lose the habit of being on guard at all times. There was one difference. Beside the road had stood a little inn, and Mara had darted in, found a knife in the deserted kitchen, and it was now safe in her robe.

Next day, at mid-morning, they saw Karas ahead, a town smaller than Shari, but pleasant enough. It was where Shabis had been educated, Mara reminded Dann, and said that here somewhere must be the school he had been at.

And now it was necessary to think carefully about what they would buy. It had been easy to feed themselves on the road here, because of the feeding stations, but now every eating place and inn would be crammed with people. They went to a public square and sat down under a tree on the paving. This was made of differently coloured stones, very attractive, arranged to make patterns and pictures. Some of the pictures were of people not unlike the Neanthes. And there were animals they had not seen, too. People were already lining up to drink from a fountain.

What were they going to wear? Dann said that in the North Lands men and women both wore long cotton robes, white or striped, cut loose with long, straight, loose sleeves. This design was to allow air to flow easily about the body, for where they were going it would be hot.

"And it hasn't been hot until now?" protested Mara.

She took out from her sack the blue and green loose dresses from Chelops that had never seemed appropriate at any place since, and which she had to associate with the easy life in the deep shade of the courtyard. They did not seem appropriate now either. Then they looked at the exquisite robes she could not bear to part with—but she replaced them at the bottom of the sack. Then the snake dress, which in this strong sunlight seemed to have lost its colour when she held it up, and looked milky and transparent. The two slave tunics were too short and skimpy. They would have to buy robes for the North Lands, so they could be inconspicuous.

They found a large clothing shop, selling what they wanted. They were called Sahar robes, and they chose two striped ones, in brown and white. The shopkeeper, when he saw the bag of coins that Mara pulled out of her sack, the ones she had snatched from Han on the boat, said he wouldn't accept them.

"But they are still currency," said Dann, with more than a touch of the young General.

The shopkeeper, an old man peevish with age, grumbled and said that he would make a loss when he changed the coins. Eventually they paid twice what the robes were worth. They bought some pieces of cloth. They bought some leather bottles, for water. Then they asked for a place to change.

"Are you running from the police?" asked the old man, but he didn't care.

"No, the army," said Mara.

"What have we done to have all these refugees landed on us?" he grumbled.

"You'll make a lot of money out of us," said Mara.

"I'd rather have peace and quiet. My wife's dead. If they turn up here expecting me to take them in, who'll be feeding them and looking after them? This old fool, that's who."

"It won't be for long," said Dann, "General Shabis has got them surrounded and everyone can go back home soon."

"And suppose they don't want to go back home, but want to stay here, in Karas? That'll be a fine state of affairs."

"They won't want to do that," said Dann, "because Shari is much nicer than Karas."

"Oh, is that so? And what's wrong with Karas, tell me that."

They changed, made sure their two knives were safely in the new robes, and went to look for an inn to rest in. They already knew what their problem was going to be: everyone, despite their miseries and worries, turned to look at them. This was a most striking young couple, and both knew they would earn trouble because of it.

In the inn they ordered a meal, and while they waited Dann, smiling, elated, triumphant, drew as large a map of Ifrik as would fit on to the table top, put a mark for Rustam, one for the Rock Village, one for Majab and one for Chelops. He made thick branchy lines for the rivers, little dots for the River Towns and for Goidel, marked Shari and Karas, and sat with the span of his long fingers stretched wide to cover the distance they had come. The two sat smiling at each other, pleased with themselves.

Dann said, "On that old gourd globe, from here to the Middle Sea was desert. Sand. Sahar. Only one river, Nilus. On the wall map, thousands of years later, no desert, but a lot of different kinds of country. But two big rivers. Nilus and Adrar. Both flow north. Both have lots of little rivers running into them. We are a long way from both of them. Nilus is away to the east and Adrar the same distance to the west. To reach either would be a major effort in itself. There are no rivers ahead of us, I think. The next town north of here is Bilma. Then Kanaz. Bilma is some days' walk from here. I know there are Thores people ahead. A spy told me. And Neanthes."

"And Mahondis? The Kin said that Mahondis were the predominant people all over Ifrik?"

"So where are they all?"

It was pleasant sitting together in this inn, pleasant in Karas, an old trading town, full of travellers from everywhere even when it was, as now, filling with refugees. So crowded and clamorous became this room that they decided to go. They filled their water bottles, bought bread and dry fruit for the road, and Mara took two of the coins off the cord, and hid them in her pocket under her knife: she did not want unfriendly eyes to watch her fumbling for the cord under her gown.

It was a long day's fast walk to the frontier. Inns and resting places close to a frontier are of particular interest to the authorities in every country, and, as the two approached the Inn at the Edge, a large building reddened by the flaring sunset, every sense was alert and they were ready to take to their heels. They had debated whether to sleep outside, under the stars, but they were tired and needed a rest. They believed that they were the first of the overflow from Karas to arrive here. As they walked through a room crowded with travellers, a sharp-eyed woman who was evidently the proprietor watched them, and they knew that not a detail escaped her.

Mara asked for a room, preferably on the ground floor, and at the back, and when she added the excuse "because we sleep badly and need quiet," the shrewd little smile on the woman's face said she heard this request often. Then she remarked that runners from Shari and from Karas were expected. They told her that Shari was under siege, but she knew that already. They saw that she was probably as well equipped with informers as any warlord or city official. "They often have interesting news," said she. "I don't always tell them what they want to know. It depends."

Now was the moment for a coin to appear. The trouble was, Mara believed that a whole coin was too much for what they wanted, which was only a warning if the runners knew about them.

"Can you change this?" said Mara.

The woman's eyes narrowed and glinted: she was certainly not one who did not know what a gold coin was. She took the coin from Mara as if she had been given it, and, resting her two hands on the counter, the coin lying between them, she looked full at Mara and then at Dann.

"Interesting news about the young General," she said. "You'd not think that General Shabis's favourite would run off, in the middle of a war." But she smiled, at Dann and then at Mara. "They are saying it was for love."

She took up the coin, deliberately, and put it deep between her breasts. Then she said, "There are ways across the frontier that avoid the roads and the guards."

Mara fetched the other coin from her pocket, and the woman took it from her.

"You rest. I'll call you if you have to run for it."

In the room she gave them, at the back, with a low window, there were two beds and they looked comfortable, but it seemed too dangerous to sleep. They lay down with their belongings close to them.

Mara thought how sweet it had been, the sharing of the time before sleep, with Meryx, the lazy chat about this and that, the intimacy, and how sweet this would be now with Dann, if their ears were not straining.

"If Shabis caught up with you—would he punish you?"

"He would have to. Death sentence. Discipline."

"Yet he loves you."

"It's not me he loves." He sounded tired and irritated. "Mara, didn't you ever think it was a bit odd, your being in his house?"

"That wasn't his home. It was where he worked."

"And did you ever wonder why the Hennes abducted you?"

"Of course. But it was all because they thought I was pregnant by Shabis. Another breeding programme."

"And how would they know you were pregnant? Shabis's wife sent a message to Izrak that you were pregnant by Shabis. She wanted to get rid of you." She was silent with the shock of it. "She was jealous. Surely you aren't surprised?"

"I didn't even know he had a wife, at first."

"And when you did?"

"I suppose I thought that if . . . I thought it must be all right."

"You are a funny woman. You didn't even notice he was in love with you?"

"No. All I cared about was—he was teaching me. That's all. I've never been so happy in all my life, Dann."

He laughed. She did not like the laugh. The male soldiers at the watchtower laughed like that, talking about women.

"And if I'm so strange, what about you? That boy of yours in the headquarters in Shari . . . You left him just like that, you didn't care."

"Mara, I told him every day, sometimes several times a day, that I was going to leave. One day I'd just walk off and leave and he had to be pre-pared for that."

"All the same, he was jealous; if looks could kill, then . . ."

"He came to H.Q. and begged me to take him as an army servant. He had run away from the Hennes. He wanted to work for me. And so he did." Again, she did not like his laugh. "He was in rags and he was starv-ing when he came. He was fed. He was given a uniform. He'll find another officer to take him on. He's probably done that already."

"And you don't care."

"I care more about Kira, as it happens." She saw him lift his head up off the pillow, to see how she reacted. She was astonished. "Kira and I were together. I wanted her to come with me when I was posted to the Northern Army, but she likes her comforts, Kira does. She preferred her nice little house and her nice little life. And her nice poppy." He mim-icked Kira's, "But I only smoke a little bit, Dann, just a teeny little bit sometimes, Dann . . . She's probably got someone else already too."

"And you had that boy and Kira going at the same time."

"You know what, Mara? Because you were living with Meryx all that time, all cosy and nice, you talk like an old woman."

"All that time," said Mara, fierce. "It was less than a year."

"A long time, for people like us." He yawned. "We do get about Mara, don't we?"

From the big communal room came a commotion. Voices raised sharply. Commands.

"We'd better leave," said Dann.

At this the door opened and in came the proprietor. "Time to go," she said. "They're after you, all right. Go out through the window. There's a girl there. She'll show you the way." And then, turning back to say it, "Good luck. You'll be safe when you're across." She went out.

"People like us," said Dann.

"Or very much don't like us."

"But they always like the gold. Quick." He was out of the window, and gone; and she followed him. A young girl was crouching in the bushes, her eyes glinting in the light that fell from the window. She went fast out of the garden, looking back to see if they followed. The moon was a tiny yellow slice, and the stars were brighter; the stars glittered and crowded and the starlight was strong enough to make faint shadows. In a moment the three were running through trees and a pursuer would find it hard to see them at all: birds or ghosts flying through the forest.

16

It was past midnight when the girl gasped, "Here it is," meaning the frontier; but there was nothing to be seen, only a line of hills where they jumped and scrambled through rocks. Then the forest continued: great, old trees with a soft litter beneath that absorbed the sounds of their running feet. Mara and Dann expected her to go back, but she ran on with them until they stopped on the crest of a rise, and pointed forward. The sky was lightening. The town they were looking down on spread widely, and as far as they could see north. The lights of the town were low and little, netting the darkness in a dim twinkling. Here the girl said, "I'm going back," and was already off when both Dann and Mara caught hold of her. They needed to know certain things. First, what language was spoken here? Charad, she said, surprised that there could be even the possibility of another language, for the foreign talk she heard at the inn was as strange to her as the night cries of the birds they had been hearing. What money did they use? Money, she said. Mara fetched out from the bottom of her sack a little handful of old coins, and the girl shook her head when she saw them, putting out her hand to touch them, disbelieving. Did things go well here? Was Bilma prosperous? Was it suffering drought? What were the people who ruled this country like? But the two saw that she was a girl whose longings had been satisfied when she got employment at that grand dynamic centre, the Inn at the Edge, the last in Charad on the road north, where travellers passed through with tales of lands she had scarcely heard of. And one day a handsome young man would come to the inn and . . . All this they knew about the skinny little girl whose meagre flesh was not because she had lacked food, but because she was still a child. Mara offered her some of old Han's coins, but she giggled, and said that she was only doing as she had been ordered. And off she ran, disappearing into the trees.

Which here, close to the town, stood sparse and often with a branch or two lopped off. And between the edge of the forest and the beginning of the town stretched soiled and beaten grass, where an occasional shack or hut stood.

Under the last of the great, untouched forest trees—new to both of them, for neither had seen a forest like this, where trees were two or three times the height of the savannah trees—they sat down to rest, and to talk. Decisions had to be made. First they pooled what they knew, or had been told, about Bilma.

It was large and powerful, but not the main city of the North Lands. It was a trading town: several trade routes passed through it or ended here. Like all the towns of the North Lands it was governed by a military junta that had got power in a rebellion, and the central government to which they paid tribute was weak, or at least lax, and each town in its district or province was virtually self-governing. The climate was not the same as in the south, which was sharply defined rainy seasons with long periods of dryness between. Here the forests of the North Lands were watered by mild rains in the summer, but the winters were severe. Farther north still, so Dann had heard, the winters might last months

They needed now to sleep and to eat, but they were afraid to sleep. They had some bread left. They had not seen fruit as they ran but, in the dark, fruits and the big leaves of some trees had been indistinguishable. There was a small stream. They drank. The stream had thick bushes along it, and they hid in them, and did sleep a little but were startled awake thinking there were voices; but what had wakened them were birds. They lay and saw birds, so many, of all sizes and kinds, listened to their talk in so many different voices—but meanwhile it was midday and they did not know what to do next.

Mara said, "You realise that our problem has always been how to change money?"

"Our main problem might have been that we had no money."

And now Mara took the cord of coins out from under her robe, laid it down and said, "Thirteen left."

Dann laid on the earth four coins, and said, touching his waist, "Ten left here." And then, "We shouldn't use any more of yours. We might be separated again." He slid out of his long, new robe, and sat before her naked except for the little loin cloth, suddenly a slim boy, really not more than that, all the weight and importance of General Dann gone. He was so beautiful, this lithe, elegant youth, and yet Mara had to look at the savage scar around his waist . . . He had his knife out and the point was in his flesh just above the scar and he levered out a coin, which fell on the earth between them, shining and clean and new, though with a bit of blood on it. He was pale and his lips set, but he levered out another. Then two on the other end of the scar.

"I used two to buy presents for Kira," he said. "So I know how to do it. And it's not too bad." But he was looking sick.

"Enough," she said.

"No." And he went on until there were six on the earth. "Six still inside and safe," he said. The scar was bleeding. Dann took a bit of cloth from the sack, and wetted it in the stream, and dabbed and dabbed at the blood, but it kept coming.

"I wish we had Orphne here to tell us what plants to use."

"Or Kira. She picked up a lot from Orphne. But the plants are different here."

"Perhaps not so different." Mara began searching along the banks of the stream, pulling at the plants and smelling them; and then she found one, a greyish plant with spiky leaves, whose smell was not unlike one that Orphne used to stop bleeding. She offered this to Dann. He sniffed at it, vigorously chewed a bit, then smeared the juice from his mouth on to the raw places. The bleeding stopped, but it was a real wound and looked ugly.

"Well, at least we have enough money to keep going. You, thirteen. Me, ten."

Mara put back the cord with its thirteen knots under her breasts, and wondered what it could be like to live inside a body you did not have to be conscious of, as a source of danger, never letting herself be seen undressed, always afraid the cloth of her robe might blow up or be lifted.

Dann lay among the soft grasses by the stream, his eyes shut. It was quiet: only birds and the sounds of water. And she could not resist and lay down too, and slept. When they woke it was late afternoon. He said the wound at his waist was painful. Mara said she hoped the knife had been clean. He joked that that was hardly likely, living the life it did. It was his best friend, he said, that knife.

It was time they left the forest. They walked along the paths past the shacks and huts where the very poor people lived, into the edges of the town, then nearer the centre, and found an inn, a large one, where they hoped they would not be much noticed. And it was full of every kind of person, of every colour, including some new to both of them, very pale of skin or reddish, with light eyes of blue or green. But there was such a mix of people, and most wearing the long Sahar robes, that Mara and Dann believed they were enough like them not to be noticed. They ate quickly at a general table, a vegetable stew, and some roast meat, and fruit. They asked for a room. This time the proprietor did not have the look of a spy. A lazy, indifferent man, he asked where they had come from and when they said, "From the south," he only remarked, "I hear things aren't too good down there."

The room was on the third floor, large and comfortable, and there were two beds in it. There was a great bolt on the door. They slept, and for the first time they could remember, were happy to pull over them a thick cover.

Mara woke in the night to hear Dann groan, and in the morning they inspected his waist and knew they must find some sort of medical help. But they didn't want anyone to see those concealed coins. She went down to the big general room where the owner stood, as if he had not moved since she saw him last, by a table from where he surveyed his guests. So many, such a noisy lot, so animated, so confident: Mara had not seen anything like this. Over these people was no cloud of apprehension, of threat. She said she wanted the name and address of a doctor and at once saw in his eyes the alertness that had not been there till now: he was afraid of an infectious disease. So she at once said that there was a flesh wound that would not heal but was not dangerous.

She walked, following directions, through crowded, lively streets, and heard a dozen different languages, but more than the others, Charad. Not once, Mahondi. In the doctor's house was an old woman, bent and nearly blind, who peered at her, seemed hardly to see her; and when Mara asked for a lotion to heal infected flesh, she reached down a jar off a shelf. And now it was a question of paying. Mara had with her the bag of coins she had got off Han, and put some down on the table the old woman stood behind. And now the blind old eyes peered and blinked and the old fingers fumbled, and then, "What's this? Haven't seen this money for a while."

"It's legal tender," Mara said.

"I don't know about that." And she shouted in Charad into a back room and out came a young man whom Mara disliked and distrusted at first sight. He was wiping his mouth on the back of his hand. He had been eating. There was a smell of spicy food. Everything about him was sharp and sly, with a conceit in each movement and look.

"Are you the doctor?" asked Mara.

He did not answer, but took up the coins and then looked at her, suspicious, curious, and said, "We don't often see these." He took a few of them, and pushed back the others. He was doing everything slowly so that he could go on examining her. She was afraid. "Who is the medicine for?" he asked, and she said, "My brother."

"Is it bad?"

"Bad enough."

"If it's not better by tomorrow, come back." But he did not turn away and nor did Mara.

"I want to change some money," she said, knowing as she spoke that she was making a mistake. It was as if the words had been pulled out of her by those cold eyes of his.

"What money?"

She had a gold coin ready in her pocket, and she laid it down, and again those clever fingers went to work, testing and assessing.

"I haven't seen one of these for a long time either. Where have you come from?"

"A long way."

"I can see that." He pushed the coin back at her and said, "If you come to the Transit Eating House any night, you'll change your money."

He stood watching her leave. She knew that everything that had happened with him was wrong and dangerous.

She bathed Dann's wound with the lotion, and then went down to negotiate about payment. At last she persuaded the innkeeper to accept the old coins, but knew that yet again she was paying twice what she should. And now she sat with Dann. He drank but would not eat, slept but kept waking. He was feverish and the wound was worse.

Next day she went back to the doctor's house. There the old woman at once summoned the young man, to whom she said she wanted medicine for a fever.

"I'll tell my father to come and see your brother."

"No, no, the medicine will be enough." And she knew her tone was wrong, and that he knew she was hiding something. She wondered why with this man she seemed unable to behave in any way but guiltily, nervously.

"He'd better come and see him," said the young man.

Mara walked back to the inn with an elderly man, the doctor, whom she did not much like either, but he was not as instantly unlikeable as his son. Dann was hot and the wound was nasty. The doctor did not touch it, to Mara's relief, so he did not feel the coins that were still there; but he looked at Dann's tongue, turned up his eyelids, listened to his chest and—this Mara found unpleasant—examined Dann's genitals. She knew that probably this was what doctors had to do; but it was what slavers did. And besides, the sight of that hand pushing and probing there made her flustered and uneasy. She wanted to knock the hand away. Then the doctor made Dann turn over and laid his ear to Dann's upper back, first on one side and then the other. He straightened up and said, "That's an old wound. A slave chain, I suppose? Why is it open now? Was your brother trying to scrape off the roughness of the scar?"

Mara had never heard of, or even imagined such a thing, and said so. The doctor said, "Well, that's a bit of a mystery then." He left three kinds of medicine: one for applying to the wound, the others to drink. He accepted payment in the old coins without bargaining. He then said that when her brother was better they might find the Transit Eating House an entertaining place. Mara felt that she was in a trap, but could not see what it was; and when he said, "When the wound is better I'll take a proper look at that scar. There might be an internal infection for some reason," she was saying to herself, Oh no you won't, we won't let you.

And now for several days and nights Mara nursed Dann, who at first did not seem to get better. He was delirious and shouted threats and warnings, which Mara knew were because in his mind he was back in the Tower. And he gave orders, like an army officer, and then might try to salute, as he lay, accepting orders, muttering, "Yes, sir." In the long hours of his fever Dann seemed to be reliving several different times in his past, and Mara could recognise from what he said, or moaned, or shouted, that he went back and back again to the Tower, and his suffering at these moments was terrible. Again little Dann clung to his big sister, gripped her, cried out that she mustn't let them take him ... And then at last he slept and was better. With every dose of the medicine he improved, until about a week after arriving at the inn he seemed himself. And now she was able to start feeding him. The food here was nourishing and various; but there were tastes and spices new to them because, after all, through this town had for centuries passed traders and travellers from all over the North Lands and from the east where the Middle Lands were. But all they knew of these was that they were very far away.

Mara stood at the window and looked down into a quiet back street. This was a suburb. All the houses were of brick and wood and set in gardens. Over to the east rose, pale and gaunt, tall buildings, like the Towers of Chelops, clusters of them; but here they were not the haunts of criminals but were where the rich lived, the rulers of Bilma. Mara looked and wondered and wished she could go out, and felt Dann's gaze on her back, and heard, "Mara, do go out. I feel all right now." There was a peevishness here, which she was hearing often. Too often. She turned, careful to be seen smiling. She knew her anxiety annoyed him. And indeed she was saddened and worried, and much more than he knew. This was not the bright, confident, high-spirited young soldier of such a very short time ago, but a man who was tormented. Was he remembering those terrible nightmares and how he had clung and pleaded for her protection?

"Very well, I will," she said, and knew that as she went her steps quickened with pleasure and anticipation. She had been longing to see this city. She stopped herself saying, Be careful Dann. Don't do too much, too soon.

And now she was out of the quiet suburban streets and in central Bilma, where she walked, and stopped, and looked and thought, This is the first time I've seen streets like this. Bilma was busy, confident, noisy, fast, full of traders and buyers and bargainers, of shops and stalls and booths, and there were several markets, where she went for the pleasure of sharing in the energetic animation. In every other town she had been in the people seemed to be listening always for news of the dryness that crept northwards; but here they talked of "down there," "down south," "the war in the south," "the southern drought," as if they were immune from all that. And probably they were, for this was a very different country, with its capacious forests and the old rivers that had not stopped running in anybody's memory. So occupied was Mara in her enjoyment of this successful place and its polyglot people that she forgot herself and her caution until she noticed that she was getting more attention than she wanted. Then she saw that her robe, the Sahar, the long, striped garment she had bought to be like everybody else in the North Lands, was in fact worn by men. They were all in plain white, or white striped black or dark brown or blue or green, while the women were in light, clear colours, yellow and rose and blue, or patterned in ways Mara had never seen, so that she wanted to stare, and marvel over a skirt, or a sleeve, because of its wondrously subtle weave. Light, gauzy dresses. The nearest to them were the bright dresses worn by the Kin, but she knew she could not find anonymity in those, because they were full and flounced, whereas these robes were straight, so that the patterns on them could be better seen. She went to a market stall and bought a robe that was a happy miracle of delightful patternings, and she knew that in it she would be like everybody else. When she had paid for it—and she had to persuade the stallholder to accept the coins—she knew that it was essential to change a gold one, for she had so few of the others left.

Back she went to the inn, where the proprietor stopped her and said he had to warn her: he knew that customs were probably different down south, but a woman too much on her own in the streets was asking for trouble. She thanked him, went up to the room, and there Dann sat where she had left him, listless and sombre. He turned his head to watch her slip off the striped gown and put on this new one. "Beautiful," he said, meaning her as well as the dress. "Beautiful Mara." She told him about the busy streets and the markets, and he did listen, but she knew that when he looked at her he was seeing more than her. She said, not expecting that she was going to say anything of the kind, "Are you missing Kira?"

"Yes," he said. "Very much."

Daring a great deal, for he was always on the edge of irritability, she said, "And the boy?"

He said angrily, "You don't understand. He was there, that's all."

She ordered food for them both, and watched him eat until he said, "Stop it, Mara. I'm eating all I can. I don't have an appetite."

And then she was restless again, and he saw it, and he said, "Go out if you want. I'll sleep."

She descended to where the proprietor stood, a fixture, it seemed, watching his customers, and stood before him in her new robe which made her—surely?—one of the local people. "Now I'm wearing this, is it all right to go out?"

"It's all right," he said, but reluctantly. "But be careful." And added a warning, and a stern one: "You are an attractive female."

"I've seen attractive females in every street."

"Yes, but are they alone?"

Mara went out, thinking how surprising it was that police, police spies, the watchful, suspicious eyes she knew so well, were not in evidence here. *What did you see, Mara? What did you see?* On this morning's excursion she had been too dazzled by what she saw to see it well. Now that she was alert, her wary self again, she saw that while every street held as many women as men, they were in groups, or walked two or three together, and usually with children, or they were with a man or men. If you saw a woman by herself she was old, or a servant with children, taking them somewhere, or a servant going to market, with her baskets. In these streets women did not saunter or dawdle or stand staring. And now that she was noticing everything, there was no doubt the proprietor of the inn was right. When people saw her, they looked again, and their faces were fixed in the immobility of interested surprise. So what was it about her? That she was good-looking she knew, but there was not exactly a shortage of handsome women. She was a Mahondi—was that it? She had not seen any in her wanderings here in Bilma. But there was such a variety here: people as tall and slight as the Neanthes, stubby and sturdy as the Thores, and everything in between. No Hennes, not one. And no Hadrons. And certainly no Rock People. Just imagine, she could have lived her life out in that Rock Village and never known that there could be lively, clever, laughing crowds so various that she was for ever seeing a new kind of body, or hair, or skin. But her ease in exploring these streets was gone, and she felt danger everywhere. She went back to the inn, and the proprietor said, first, that she had visitors, and then that it was time he was given more payment.

She asked if he would change a gold coin. She had seen the money-changers in the markets, but, watching the transactions, knew she would not get a fair exchange. Those men, and women, sitting behind their little tables piled with coins, each with a guard standing beside them who was well armed with knives and cudgels, they all minutely observed every approaching trader or traveller; and Mara had taken good note of the greedy faces and looks of self-congratulation when the fleeced ones went off with less money than they should have.

"You can change money in the Transit Eating House."

She found Dann with the doctor, and the son, the young man she disliked so much. And Dann was sitting up, animated and laughing. When Mara came in, he stopped laughing.

"Your patient is doing very well," said the doctor.

"Your medicine did very well," she said.

"My father is a famous doctor," said the young man.

The two were rising from where they had been sitting, on her bed: her coming had ended the pleasantness of the visit. Dann was obviously sorry this new friend was leaving. And now Mara looked again at the youth to see if she had been unjust in disliking him, but could see only a sharp face—she thought a cunning face—with eyes that were impudent and shameless. And, too, there was a subdued anger, and she believed she knew why, remembering the tone of "My father is a famous doctor." For if his father was famous, then he was not, and if he turned out to be famous then it would not be for the kind of wholesome knowledge that gave this doctor his self-possession and his consciousness of worth.

But Dann liked Bergos, the son of the good doctor.

The two men went off. Dann said he was thinking of going out that evening, and Mara knew it would be the Transit Eating House. Oh yes, she was in a trap all right, but she did not know what it was, only that there was nothing she could do about it until it was sprung. Dann was not well enough to leave this town and move on. As he lay down on the bed again to rest, he said, "We could stay here, Mara. It's a nice town. You seem to think so . . ."

And Mara watched him fall asleep, and thought that going North, the dangerous difficulties of always going North, could end in this town, because it was agreeable and apparently welcoming. What had going North meant if not finding something like this, which was better than anything she had imagined? Water, first of all: water that you did not have to measure by the drop or even the cup; water that stood in great barrels on street corners for people to drink out of generous wooden ladles that hung ready; water that ran in reed pipes into the houses; water splashing in the many fountains; water close by in beneficent rivers; water in the public baths that stood in every street; water that fell ungrudgingly from the skies—water that you took for granted, like air. And, because of the water, healthy people, and children everywhere, and children's voices—she could hear them playing in a garden nearby.

It was mid-afternoon, the rest hour just coming to an end. Here everyone lay in their rooms through the warm hours, or sat lazing in the shade of tea houses. In this darkened room, where the slats of the shutters made stripes over the floor and across the bed where Dann slept, so that she thought fearfully that it was as if he lay trapped in a cage, Mara sat and thought; she thought hard and carefully, and knew that she did not want to give up here in Bilma. This was not what she had been journeying to find. Well, what was she looking for? Not this: she knew that much.

That evening they went downstairs to eat, Dann for the first time, the proprietor congratulating him on his recovery; and Dann said, "Let's go to the Transit. I need a change."

17

In the street a couple of men strode fast towards them and then turned around to look at Mara, and Dann said, "What a lucky fellow I am, to be with such a beautiful woman."

His tone was affected, even coquettish, as if he were observing himself with a congratulating eye; and she thought, her heart heavy, its beat repeating *A trap, A trap*, that she would never have believed him capable of that dandyish drawl. When he had said he was not himself, that was the truth: a Dann she did not know strolled along at her side, and she could almost see in his hand a flower, holding it to his lips, teasing them with it, as some of the men—but what kind of men?—were doing as they walked, casting glances over the flowers at the women, and the men too. And in a moment Dann had reached out to a hedge and torn off a bright red flower. She was silently begging him, Don't raise it to your lips, as if his not doing it would be proof of his safety—and he did not, only twirled it between his fingers. This was not a pleasant area, the route to the Transit Eating House. Mara, who had been so captivated by this town that she had refused to see anything unpleasant, now made herself look at the ugliness of these poor streets, at a woman with her brows drawn tight and her mouth set, a child whose flesh was tight on his bones, a man with defeat written on his face.

The Transit was a large building, spilling out lights, and its customers coming and going populated the street outside. Their faces were restless and excited—like Dann's now. The room they went into was very large, brightly lit, and crammed full. Here were mostly men, and Mara saw at once that she was the only woman there wearing an ordinary garment. All the rest were young, some not much more than children, and they wore flimsy, transparent skirts, with breasts just covered or not at all. Dann and she sat down and were at once brought beakers of strong-smelling drink. It was a grain drink, of the kind she had helped make in Chelops. The place was very noisy. No point in Dann's or her even try-ing to speak, unless they wanted to shout. Again this was a mix of peo-ples, some of kinds they had not seen before, and the languages they were overhearing were strange to them. This was a place, then, not for Bilma's inhabitants, but for the traders and travellers and visitors.

A tap on Mara's shoulder. "You want to change money?" she heard, and a waiter pointed across the room to a door that was shut, unlike most doors in this place. She told Dann she would not be long, and across the room she went.

It was a small room, for transactions and business, and in it was wait-ing for her a fat old woman who scarcely came up to her shoulder. She was very black, so she did not come from this region. She wore a hand-some, scarlet, shiny dress whose skirts seemed to bounce around her as she walked back to a chair behind a plain plank table. She sat, and pointed Mara to an empty chair.

Her examination of Mara was brisk, frank and impartial: she might have been assessing a bale of new cloth.

"How much do you want to change?"

Mara took out one gold coin from her pocket, where she had it ready, and then took out another. She was remembering the recurrent anxi-eties about changing money.

"I shall give you more than the market-place value."

Mara smiled, meaning this old woman to see that she, Mara, did not think this was saying much. And in fact this crone—she was really old, in spite of her scarlet flounces and the glitter of earrings and neck-laces—was ready to smile too, sharing Mara's criticism: it was the way of the world, her smile said.

"My name is Dalide," she said. "I have been changing money for as many years as you have lived."

"I am twenty-two."

"You are in the best of your beauty."

Mara could have sworn that Dalide could easily have leaned forward and opened her mouth to examine her teeth, and then pinch her flesh here and there between fingers that had many times assessed the exact degree of a young woman's toothsomeness.

Mara put down the two gold coins. Dalide picked one up, while the other hand fondled the second coin. "I have never seen these," Dalide said. "Who is this person?"—pointing at the faint outline of a face, probably male, on the coin.

"I have no idea."

"Gold is gold," said Dalide. "But gold as old as this is even better." She pulled out bags of coins from a bigger bag, and began laying out in front of Mara piles of coins of differing values, meanwhile giving emphatic glances at Mara as each new pile was completed. These were not the flimsy coins she had been carrying about, making a light mass of money that you had to pay out in handfuls. Dalide was giving her coins that would be easy to handle and be changed, yet each worth a good bit. Mara counted them. She knew roughly what she should expect, and this was not far off. She swept the coins into a cloth bag she had with her, and Dalide exclaimed, "You aren't going to walk through the streets at night with that on you?"

"Do I have an alternative?"

"If you didn't have your brother I'd send my bodyguard with you."

"People are very well informed about us."

"You are an interesting couple."

"And why is that?"

Dalide did not answer, but said, "Would you like me to find you a good husband?"

And now Mara laughed, because of the incongruity.

Dalide did not laugh. "A good husband," she insisted.

"Well," said Mara, still laughing, "what would it cost me? Could I buy a husband with this?" And she shook her bag of coins so they clinked.

"Not quite," said Dalide, and waited for Mara to say how much money she had.

Mara said, "I do not have enough money to buy a husband." And added, laughing, "Not a good one."

Dalide nodded, allowing herself a brief smile, as a little concession to Mara. "I can change money for you—as you know. And I can find you a husband for a price."

"I'm not flattered that you think I would have to buy myself a husband.

Not so long ago I had a husband without money ever being mentioned."
And she could not prevent her eyes from filling.

Dalide nodded, seeing her tears. "Hard times," she said briskly.

"Surely not in this town. If these are hard times, then I don't know
what you'd say if I told you what I've seen."

"What have you seen?" asked Dalide softly.

Mara saw no reason to be secretive and said, "I've watched Ifrik drying up since I was a tiny child. I've seen things you'd not believe."

"I was a child in the River Towns. In Goidel. I was playing with my sisters when a slaver snatched me—I was for some years a slave in Kharab. I
escaped. I was beautiful. I used men and became independent. Now I'm a
rich woman. But there isn't much you could tell me about hardship."

Mara looked at this ugly old thing and thought that she had been
beautiful. She said, "If I need you, I'll come back." She got up, and so
did Dalide. As Mara went to the door, Dalide came too, and they left
the business room behind. "Are you coming with me?" asked Mara, seeing how everyone in the big room turned to look at this grotesque old
woman in her scarlet and her fine jewels.

"I don't work here," said Dalide. "I only came to meet you. I wanted
to have a good look at you."

"And you've done that."

"I've done that. So, goodbye—for now."

Dalide made her way out of the crowded room and Mara looked for
Dann, but he had disappeared. Then the same waiter, seeing her standing here, pointed at another door, this time an open one. She went in.
And saw a smaller room full of tables where mostly men were gambling.
Dann stood by one, with Bergos, and watched the fast movement of the
hands throwing dice. She went to Dann, who when he saw her said,
"Let's go home." He sounded irritated. If she had not come then, he
would soon have been seated among the gamblers. Dann exchanged a
few low words with Bergos. Mara and he went out into the street, which
was not crowded now. Mara was conscious of the heavy bag of coins
which she was trying to conceal, and said, "Dann, let's go quickly." And
he said, "How much did you get?"

And now for the first time in her life Mara lied to him and said she
had changed one gold coin and not two.

When they got safely back to the room, Mara fiddled with the coins,
so that they would not seem as many as there were, sitting half turned
from Dann. She gave him half of the worth of one coin, and told him

that their gold coins were not known here and probably were much
more valuable than they knew.

Dann lay on his bed looking up out of the window at the moon that
was coming up again to the full. His face—oh, how afraid she felt, seeing it; and then he was asleep, and she could look directly at him, and
wonder, Is that the new Dann, who seemed to be her enemy, or was it
the real Dann, her friend? How was it possible that a person can turn
into somebody not himself, just like that . . . But perhaps this new person, whom she disliked and feared, was the real person, not the one she
thought of as real. After all, when he had been General Dann, with that
boy, what was he then?

She slept with the little bag of money under her arm, and in the
morning Dann was not there. The proprietor said he had gone out for a
walk with Bergos. Mara paid him what was owed, and he said, "So, how
did you find Mother Dalide?" Mara merely smiled at him, meaning,
Mind your own business, while feeling it was probably his business too,
and felt herself go quite cold when she heard him whisper, "Be careful.
You must be careful." And then, as he glanced about for possible eaves-
droppers, "Leave. You must leave this town."

And now there was a lot she wanted to ask, but had to stand back as
some people came to ask for rooms. She and Dann had said that there
were people who liked them very much and helped them: was this man
one? More people wanted to pay their bills and leave. So Mara thought,
I'll ask him later, when I can get him alone, and she went out. She
wanted to walk up a little hill that overlooked the town, so as to get a
good view of it, spread out; but she was feeling so uneasy she sat down at
a table outside an inn in the central part, where customers ate and drank
under a canopy of green leaves and red flowers. They also watched people passing on the pavement, and commented on them and their clothes.
And the passers seemed to know they were being discussed and did not
mind, but on the contrary were self-conscious, like performers.

Mara knew that she was being observed. In this town surveillance
was discreet, invisible; she did not believe it was the police who were
watching her now. Who, then?

A girl passing with a tray of some kind of yellow drink, put a mug of
it down in front of Mara, who was suddenly sure that this mug had been
apart from the others, put there for a purpose. She put back the mug on
the tray and took another. The girl gave her an offended look. Mara
thought, Well, it might have been poisoned, anything is possible. I

should go away from here—meaning both this place and Bilma. But having got up, she sat down again, for she had seen Dann coming along the street with Bergos and a new man, a Mahondi—a real one? Yes, he was, like herself and Dann. She liked the look of him as much as she disliked Bergos. The three men sat down at a table well away from her, but she knew Dann had seen her, and was pretending not to. They sat chatting, out of earshot.

Mara could scarcely breathe, the oppression on her heart was so great. Never could she have believed that Dann and she could be in the same place, and he pretend he had not seen her. This cheerful, noisy scene—people drinking and eating, talking and lazing, all under a little ceiling of greenery and flowers—lost its charm, and all she could see were vulgar or foolish faces, and Dann, as he talked with Bergos, seemed no better.

Her heart was hurting, her eyes hurt. Why was she trying so hard to run, always running and fighting so hard for her life and for Dann's life? What for? Now she seemed absurd to herself, this little, frightened fugitive, always glancing over her shoulder, always alert for thieves, guarding Dann or, when he was not there, worrying about him. Mara looked back down her life, from the moment when she had stood up to "the bad one" in her parents' house, and seemed to herself like a scurrying little beetle.

And now the thought arrived in her mind, as she watched Bergos, that the person who had been organising her surveillance—had been Bergos. It was he whom she had to fear. And those who employed him. Who? Dalide? But what could she be hoping to get out of her, apart from a fee as a marriage broker?

Mara thought she would get up, deliberately and slowly, to be noticed, go to where the men sat, smile prettily at all three, talk a little, then refuse their invitation that she should sit down. Then leave. But suppose they did not invite her to sit down? She quietly rose, slipped away through a side door in the leafy screen, and walked as fast as she could to the hill, not looking now to see who observed her. She did not care what happened to her. There were footsteps behind her. From their speed she understood how fast she was walking. Dann caught up with her, and took her arm. She shook him off and walked on. He was beside her. He did not speak until they were at the top of the low hill, where there was a big garden, or park, which on its north side had a tall fence, with guards along it.

"Stop, Mara, let us sit down."

There was a bench. A glance told her that here was "her" Dann, not *the other one*, as she now called the impostor. He was grave, affable, composed and was smiling at her. He put his hand over hers.

"Mara. Don't go on being angry, please."

The angry, protesting thoughts that were filling her mind faded away. "Who is that Mahondi?"

"His name is Darian. He has just come from Shabis. He has news. But first . . ." He took from an inner pocket a coil of heavy, dull metal, beaten silver, and held it out to her. It was a bangle, but for the upper arm, not the wrist, meant to fit close. It was a serpent, and the head end was slightly raised, to strike. Mara slid it up on to her upper arm, easing it over the elbow joint, and saw how well it looked. Then she let the sleeve fall over it, the lovely sleeve with its delicate, shadowy patterns. "Take it off again." Mara did so. He pressed the tail of the serpent where there was a little indentation, and a knife shot out of its mouth, a mere sliver of glittering metal. Dann pressed again and the knife slid back. "It's poisoned. Immediate death." Then, because of her unease: "Shabis sent it to you."

"A loving present."

"Yes, Mara, it is. He said to Darian that if you had had this when the Hennes patrol captured you, you could have killed them all and escaped."

Mara slid it back up her arm, and let the sleeve fall.

"It's so pretty," said Dann, stroking the sleeve, and through it, her. "And now, there's news, but it isn't good. After we ran away, half of the Hennes army escaped. This is what Shabis told the other three generals would happen. Our army chased their army back to the line of the watchtowers, where the Hennes made a stand. There was a terrible battle. They held their territory. Our army retreated back to our lines. So all that happened was that thousands of people got killed, soldiers and civilians too. Neanthes, Hennes and Thores civilians."

"So everything is exactly as it was?"

"Yes. Stalemate."

"Oh no," she said, rebellious, "no, nothing stays the same."

"But it has all been like that for years. What can change it?"

"Drought, for one."

"Drought, drought . . . that's how we see everything, because of what we've seen. But here there isn't going to be drought. Floods are more in Bilma's line."

And now both of them, brother and sister, he still holding her forearm, turned to look down at Bilma spread out there, gardens and houses, parks and houses, fountains everywhere. She heard his sigh. She saw his face change, and instinctively drew her arm away. He did not notice, he was looking over to where the big, pleasant houses spread on the slopes there.

"Mara, why don't we stay here?" She shook her head, and again felt the nets of danger closing around her. "I want to show you something." He pulled her up from the bench, and they walked with their backs to the town to where the tall fence dipped down the other side of the hill. The guards watched them. "Darian showed me this, early this morning. We came here." Where the fence began to descend the hill, they could see through it down to where, at the foot of the hill, was a long, low building, with platforms on either side. Running north from the building were two parallel lines, close together, shining gently in the sunlight. From a platform, something that looked like a long, covered box was in the process of being pushed along the lines by a group of young men. The lines ran north, at first through light forest and then through grassland. The two stood silent, watching how the young men pushing the box laboured, their backs bent. Twenty of them, and then half ran past the box and picked up some ropes, or lines, invisible to them where they stood on the hill, and went ahead, pulling, as the ten behind pushed.

"That is the way out of Bilma," said Dann.

"And who is in that—conveyance?"

"Who do you suppose? Can't you see the guards? The rich use it. Those lines run north to the next town, Kanaz. Once there were machines that ran on their own power on lines like those."

"Once? Oh I suppose the usual thousands of years ago?"

"No. Two or three hundred, they are not sure. But now slaves do the work."

"I didn't know there were slaves in Bilma."

"They aren't called slaves. Mara, Darian wants me to join him as a labourer pushing the coaches—that is what they are called. And when we get to the next town, or the one after—run away." And, before he said it, she knew what she would hear. "I'd rather die, Mara. I've done that, pushing dead machines up and down hills."

"And not long ago you were General Dann." She smiled at him, meaning to tease him a little, but saw his face was dark and angry. Her Dann was not there. This Dann would not take my hand, hold my arm, so simply and nicely, out of affection for me.

"There's something else. Kira came north with Darian. He replaced me in her affections, when I left. Well, he's been after her a long time. Darian is a deserter. So Shabis would have death squads ready for more than one of his officers."

"Dann, I'm sure that Shabis wouldn't . . ."

"Oh, you can be so stupid, Mara. An army has rules. If they caught me I'd be for it. And so would Darian. That means, if people knew here they could get a ransom for us . . . That is why Darian wants to go North. There is going to be trouble between the Four Generals. Now the three are blaming Shabis for the mess in Shari. There is a lot of disaffection in the army. If the Generals could have little General Dann and Major Darian publicly executed, it would buck up discipline no end."

He was staring down again. Another of the coaches was being pushed out of it along the lines. "Perhaps Kira is down there. She left Darian as soon as they got here. He was just a means of getting away. I hear she has already got another protector. So she has been here in the same town with me, but I didn't know it. Perhaps I am looking at her now."

"Oh, you do love her," said Mara, but shrank, seeing his face still dark and angry.

"That is how you would have to travel North, Mara. A protector. That's the way it's done, and I would push your coach." He turned, and took her hands, gently. This was not *the other one.* "I love her, yes. And you shouldn't mind that, Mara, because my heart was as small as a dried bean, before Kira. Like yours is now." Here tears flooded Mara's eyes, thinking of her cold, aching heart. "But when I loved Kira so much, I knew how much I love you. I didn't know it till then. I began to remember . . . I know how you looked after me and defended me, Mara. And you sang to me, kept Kulik away from me . . . Kulik is here, I saw him." And then, seeing her face, said, "I tell you, I saw him. You never believe me, do you?" And now, right in front of her was *the other one.* She felt afraid.

"I was just little Dann. And you were a big girl. We're equal now, though. I want to stay here in Bilma. I want to buy one of those houses . . ." he turned himself around, pulling her with him. The great, white houses stood shining in their gardens. "I want to live here in a house like that."

"Dann, we don't have the money."

He pressed her robe close in to her so that he could feel the cord of coins nestling there.

"Give me your coins, Mara."

He was gently shaking her, and then not so gently. "Give them to me."

"No. You could take them by force."

His face was puckering and twitching, little convulsive tics near the eyes and mouth. It was as if the face of the other one was fighting to hold off the Dann she knew. His eyes were staring, and sombre, his mouth half open—the dreadful little convulsions of the flesh went on.

"I have ten gold coins. Did you know we could buy a house with that? We could settle down—a little house, not one of those . . . But I know how to get more money, I know I can. And I want yours . . ."

His face was convulsed, briefly, and then it was over. "Right, I can manage without you, Mara. That's it. Now I know where we stand."

"There's just one thing," she attempted feebly. "If you're afraid people here would take you back to Charad to be executed, then you shouldn't stay here."

"I told you, I'm not little Dann any more. I can look after myself." And he was off, running, back into the town. He called back, "Perhaps I shall cut myself open again. That would be another six."

"Don't Dann, don't," she called after him, and heard his derisive call back, "Don't Dann, don't."

She went back to the inn, and asked for food in her room. She could not bear the pressure of hostile inspection, even if she was imagining it. The proprietor only nodded, but his eyes were concerned. Yes, he was one of the ones who liked them—or at least her. She knew Dann would not be in the room, and did not expect him back. He had taken all his things. And he had taken his share of the money Dalide had changed. She lay through the hot hours looking out of the window where the sky blazed hot, and then paled, and then flared into sunset. She did not sleep. She knew something bad was brewing. When there was a knock at the door and the proprietor called to her, she knew what she would hear. "You must go to the Transit Eating House," he said. "Your brother is there." And then, "I'll send a boy with you."

She looked around the room, thinking, What should I take? Suppose I don't come back here? But why should I think that . . . it's silly. All the same . . . And she filled her faithful sack with everything she owned.

The proprietor saw the sack, and said, "Pay me what you owe."

"I'm not leaving," she said.

"Pay me."

She paid, and he called for the boy to go with her. She was pleased to

have him there, though he was an urchin of ten or so and could not
defend her, and she knew his function was to report back to the proprietor what he had seen.

The big room of the Transit was jammed with people, and the noise
was like a shout in her ears. She walked through to the gambling room,
and there was Dann. He was flushed and wild and laughing. The room
was crammed except for the area immediately around the table. Beside
the man who handled the dice and the chips, stood the owner of the
Transit, a usually genial host, but now he was pale and agitated—as well
he might be, for in front of Dann were stacked coins in every possible
denomination. A fortune. Dann called to her over the piles of money,
"And now who is stupid, Mara? Look at what I've won."

"Now stop," she shouted. "Stop while you've got it." For she could see
he meant to go on.

Dann did hesitate. For a few moments time slowed. Dann stood, his
face stretched in a triumphant grin. The onlookers' faces were full of
warnings and dismay. The big lamp hanging over the table swung gently,
making the shadows move. And then Dann put his hands down on his
piles of winnings and said to the owner, "I'll go on."

"Don't, please don't," said Mara and he echoed her as he did earlier,
"Don't Dann, please don't."

He shook the dice, threw, shook, threw, shook—and let out an exul-
tant yell, and began to dance where he stood. A long pause, while the
owner, who was looking ill now, wrote the amount on a piece of wood.
And then his name.

Dann held it up, showing it around and then thrust it forwards to
Mara.

Now Mara saw Bergos, standing with his back to a wall among a press
of people. Well, he would have to be here. Near him was the newcomer,
Darian. Bergos was grinning, full of spiteful pleasure, but Darian was
sober and concerned. Mara looked beseechingly at him. He shrugged.
But then he did squeeze his way through and laid his hand on Dann's
shoulder. He said something to him in a low voice. While this man
whom he regarded as a friend spoke to him, Dann's face twitched and
grimaced because of the conflict in him, but he shook Darian off. He
stood with his hands held just above the great heap of wealth in front of
him. There was so much there that people's mouths fell and they stared,
looking at it. Dann's face was now a medley of emotion: he was scared,

but intended to be defiant, and he nodded for the dice. He stood with his hand poised over the shaker, and at that last moment he could have stopped, and been safe, but he was driven and, his lips held tight to contain their twitching, he threw . . . And lost, as he was bound to.

The owner went swiftly forward and scooped all Dann's late winnings into a bag. One moment the table was piled, the next empty.

Dann stood smiling foolishly. It was absolutely silent in that room.

"I haven't finished," he said.

Mara knew that he meant the six gold pieces under his scar, but at that moment Bergos said softly, "You could stake your sister."

There was a groan, or a moan, around the room.

Dann said, "I'll stake Mara. I'll stake my sister." Darian again put his hand on Dann's shoulder and it was shaken off. "Don't worry, Mara," called Dann, but now his grin was foolish and weak, and his hand shook. "This is my winning night."

Again Darian attempted to stop him, but Bergos had come forward and stood beside Dann. Dann reached for the shaker and the dice—threw, and lost.

And now Dann howled; he howled like a dog, and pulled his hair with both hands, and moaned, "Mara, Mara, Mara."

But already Mara felt a hand on either of her arms, and she was being turned around, and then pushed out through the people, and then into the big room, where they had heard of the drama being played out in the gambling room, and were standing to watch her being pushed through, but fell back, away from the touch of this unfortunate one. In the street she was not surprised to see on one side of her the grinning face of Bergos. The other man she did not know.

She was thinking of Dann as she was hustled through the streets. Dann had gambled away all his money, including the six gold coins. What is he going to do? Is he going to cut out the others? Without anyone to help him?

It was not far to where they were going. She asked, "What is this house?" And Bergos said, "Dalide's house."

She thought, If she wanted me why didn't she just kidnap me? She said to Bergos, "Wouldn't it have been easier to just capture me?"

"Against the law," he said.

They were in a large, dimly lit hall. Ahead hung a voluminous dark red curtain.

"Not against the law to gamble a woman away," she said, and found herself being pulled through the curtain's large folds; and she was in a large, brightly lit room full of women, and girls, most fancifully dressed and some half naked. They stared at Mara. Their faces, their eyes, were some curious, some resentful. There was the smell of poppy. At this point the man she did not know dropped her arm, and went off to where a big, ugly man lounged near a wall, guarding the women. The two conferred, watching as Bergos pushed her through a door into a sober and dark corridor, where stairs went up. These she ascended, while Bergos held tight to her arm. At the top was another corridor, and Bergos pushed her into a room, and she heard the door lock as he shut it.

It was a large room, well furnished, with pleasant colours, not like the room where the women were downstairs. There was a wide, low bed in a recess, a round table, and chairs that were carved and cushioned. She had not seen furniture like this, nor ornamental lamps, nor a floor covered with soft rugs, since she was in Shabis's house. But she felt that the room was closing around her and she ran to the window and pushed back heavy curtains. Outside was the sky, a glitter of stars, and beneath her a shadowy garden; and there was a small fire and around it men crouched. She could hear them talking, in low voices, but she did not know what language they used.

Her heart was pounding. Perhaps it was her beating heart that was suffocating her. She began a fast, frantic walk up and down, up and down, her hand pressing her heart, trying to silence it; and then a sound alerted her and Dalide stood in the doorway, a fantastic sight: a white flounced dress, with ribbons and bows of scarlet, and then the old, brown wrinkled face with its withered mouth, and small black eyes in webs of wrinkles. This apparition swayed over the carpet on black heels, and sat itself at the table. Dalide signalled Mara to sit. Mara sat. Dalide clapped her hands. The same big, ugly man Mara had seen downstairs came in with a jug and two beakers. He also carried Mara's sack, which he set down. He did not look at Mara. He went out.

Dalide said, "You forgot your sack in the Transit."

Mara said, "I'll kill the first man who touches me."

Dalide cackled with laughter, and reached out a claw of a hand, pointed at the snake visible under Mara's thin sleeve and said, "Yes, I've seen these toys before. And very useful they can be." And then, seeing that Mara's hand was held protectively over the coil of metal, "I'm not going to take away your little snake."

She poured yellow, frothy liquid into two beakers, and began at once to sip from hers, so Mara felt safe to drink.

"And I'm not going to poison you."

"Or drug me?"

"Well, who knows?" said Dalide.

"What do you want then? What did you do with my brother?"

"Why should I do anything with him?"

"He has gambled away everything. He has nothing."

"I don't deal in men, I deal in women."

Mara felt that her body, her face, her heart, were quietening. She trusted Dalide, she decided. Or perhaps it was relief because of this silent room, the comfort, the soft colours.

"I shall come to the point," said Dalide. "I'm going to sell you for a very good price—a very good price indeed—to a man who will know how to value you. But he's not here at the moment. He's up in Kanaz. When he comes back he'll want to have a good look and then I know what he'll decide."

"What makes you think I won't kill him? I'm not going to be anyone's property."

"Why don't you wait and see?"

"Who is this man?"

"He is one of the Council—a leading member."

"And they run Bilma?"

"And all this country."

"Why should such an important man be interested in—a runaway slave?"

"You forget, I was a runaway slave myself. The condition makes for cleverness. And I have a hunch—it is my business to know men and the women who will suit them."

She got herself up, with difficulty, from her chair. "You'll be sleepy soon. I have shared my sleeping draught with you. In the morning we can talk—if you want. But it doesn't matter. You don't like me, but you need me. You may go anywhere in this house and the garden. Don't try to run away. You will be watched. And if you use that little snake of yours on any of my people, I'll hand you over to the police. I never break the law, nor do I connive at lawbreaking." And she tottered out, the ridiculous white dress swaying over little black shoes like hooves.

Mara was assaulted by the need to sleep. She pulled off her dress and, as she was about to throw herself on the bed, was arrested by the feeling that someone was watching her. She saw, among a confusion of shadows and deeper shadows, and gleams and rays of light from the lamp, a tall figure standing by a wall, spying on her. She shrieked. The door at once opened and her gaoler was there, the big brutal-looking man.

"What's wrong?" he asked in clumsy Charad.

She pointed at the watcher, who pointed at her. The truth of the situation rushed into her mind, but she was so shocked, she was trembling. The man looked where she was pointing, then disbelievingly at her, shook his head meaning, She's mad . . . And went out, laughing.

Mara, half asleep, managed a few steps to the wall, and watched Mara come towards her. Menacing, silent, an enemy . . . But she was about to slide to the floor. She reached the bed and collapsed on it.

She woke late. The room was full of light. Mara had dreamed of a journey where at each turn she was confronted by different Maras: Mara the little child; Mara crouching over a drying waterhole and peering to see her small monkey face in the dust-filmed water; Mara with the Kin—with Juba, with Meryx, her arms around his neck, laughing; Mara in her slave's dress, running, always running.

She got out of bed and stood naked in front of the part of the wall that reflected what was in front of it. This was a very different affair from Ida's wall, where she had seen herself dimly through what seemed to be a net of little cracks, or the window glass in Shari, where she had hardly been able to see herself for leaves and branches. She put out a hand and saw hand touching hand—a cool, hard surface like solidified water. Hard to tell which was the image and which was the one that breathed and could move away. Mara saw a tall, slim woman, with full breasts that half concealed what she hid under them. A peering, staring woman, and behind her the bed and a good part of the room. Moving a little, this magical water-wall included a window sill and sky where clouds sailed by. She could not make what she saw fit with her sense of herself. She thought, All the time people see *that*, but they don't see *this*—meaning what she felt as Mara, her sense of herself. And she went close to the water-wall and peered into her eyes, dark eyes in her serious face. They look into my face and then eyes, as I look into faces and eyes, hoping I will see who is there; they hope they will reach me, Mara, Mara inside here. But Mara is not my real name. For years I waited to hear my real name, but now I know it wouldn't matter. When I hear it at last, I'll think, Is that my real name, after all? Mara is my name. Yet Mara is not the name of what I feel myself to be, inside here; it is the name of that person looking back at me. They say she is beautiful. She is not beautiful now, she is so nervous and staring. And Mara tried to smile and let herself be beautiful, but she seemed to herself more like a snake about to strike. And she nearly took off the metal coil from her upper arm with its raised snake's head, ready to strike, for that is how she seemed to herself. And then, as she turned from the water-wall, she caught a glimpse of someone different, smiling, because of her thoughts about herself, the runaway slave.

Her mouth was dry. She felt a little sick. She found a room next to this one where there were toilet arrangements and she washed, and slowly, because the sleeping drug had made her shaky, brushed her hair and put on the dress that looked as if it had butterflies woven into it. Back she went to the water-wall, to see herself, dressed. Well, that was better. As she stood there, the door opened and in came the man from last night, with a tray. He grinned as he saw her there and made a gesture: You see, you were foolish.

She saw he did not mean her harm, was merely stupid. She looked carefully at him, so as to know him later, in an ambush, or a fight. He was tall and powerfully built, all muscles and strong flesh. The neck was thick. A large, ugly face. Yellow: he was a yellow man. He went to her sack and started taking out her clothes and she went forward to stop him. He made the motions of washing.

"What's your name?" she asked, in Mahondi. He shook his head. "What's your name?" in Charad.

"Senghor."

"Where are you from?"

"Kharab. Mother Dalide's servants are Kharabian. She was a slave there, and now we are her slaves." He smiled, offering this is as a jest. She could see that this was a general joke in the household, among the servants. He called himself a slave, though. "It is good for us that no one knows our language. We can say what we like." And he began roaring with laughter and thumping himself on the chest. Then he went out with her dresses over his arm.

She stood at the window. Down there in the big garden was the low pile of ash where last night the watchmen had crouched and gossiped—in Kharabian, which no one else understood. Except Dalide, of course. Then she looked at the tall, slim, white towers where the rich lived, and around them great mansions in their gardens. For a few moments last night Dann had the money to buy one of those houses, and to live there as a rich man.

Dann would have gone back to the inn, where everybody already knew what had happened, and where they would shrink away from him—from the bearer of so much ill luck. The proprietor would have said that his sister had paid the bill until now, but how did Dann propose to pay the next bill? Dann would have stood there, silent, still stunned by the shock. What would he have said? Did he bluff? He might still have had a few bits of money in his pockets, but not enough for more than a night or two, and a little food.

Food—again food, the need to eat. For the time she had been here, she had not been anxious about eating—food was arriving in front of her when she wanted it. But food would not be there for Dann, quite soon.

She went to the tray waiting on the table. This was better than anything she had eaten: soft, light cakes, and honey, and the drink was frothy and brown and fragrant. Presumably, as long as she was in this brothel she would not be worrying about what she was going to eat next.

Would Dann be tempted to cut out another gold coin or two? He wouldn't dare. If it went bad he would have to call the doctor again. And how long would Dann live, if they knew of what lay hidden under that scar? It was so astonishing a thing that they would not easily believe it. And she, now, sitting over that breakfast tray, eating the delicate food, thought that what was simply good sense in one condition was lunacy in another. Dann, with the criminals in the Tower, who would have killed him for even one of those coins, hid them in his own flesh, crouching somewhere in a corner by himself, cutting, pushing in the coins, tying cloth around to stop the bleeding. And all that was the merest good sense and it had kept him alive. But now, in this pleasant town, this safe town—well, not for everybody—it was simply mad. How could she get a coin to him, unobserved? She couldn't. She was being observed every minute.

Oh, she was so tired, so sleepy. She lay on her bed and slept again and when she woke her midday meal was on the table untouched, and it was evening. She went to the door, which was unlocked, and saw Senghor squatting just outside, his back against the wall, and if he had been asleep he woke quickly enough to spring up and put out a hand to stop her.

"Tell Dalide not to give me any more sleeping potion. It makes me ill. I'm not used to it. And tell her if I find myself drugged again I shall starve myself."

Senghor nodded. He motioned her back inside the room, locked it from outside so that she stood angry and trembling, just inside it, and then in a few minutes she heard it being unlocked. He said that Mother Dalide had given her the sleeping potion because she could see Mara was so tired that she probably would not sleep without it. But Mara could be sure that Dalide would give her no more potions of any kind.

"When can I see Dalide?"

"Mother Dalide is leaving tonight to visit her other house in Kanaz."

"When will she be back?"

"I don't know. Sometimes she goes for seven days, perhaps thirty."

And now Mara was tempted to fall into despair. Dalide was in no hurry with her plans to sell Mara profitably. "Did she send me a message?"

"Yes. No more medicines."

"No, about her going away?"

He stared, and sneered. "Why tell you? You are only one of the house women. She feed you well because she sell you well."

So that comfortable room, which she already felt as a home, a refuge, often had in it a woman whom Mother Dalide would sell well.

"I'm going to look at the garden."

"You will stay in the house."

"Dalide said I could go where I liked, in the house and the garden."

"She did not tell me so."

"If she has not left, go and ask her."

Again she was pushed into the room, and the door locked. She waited, and he came back.

"You may be in the house and the garden."

Mara went down the stairs and through the curtain into the room the girls used. They were sitting about, in their half nakedness and their finery. As she went through, a little, fat, pretty girl caught at her hand and said, "Stay with us. Talk to us."

They were bored, so bored. She could feel their boredom in the air of that sad room. Twenty girls, waiting. Clearly this house was well patronised.

Mara went to the front of the house, and opened the door, Senghor immediately behind her. When she reached it he sprang in front of her and held his thick arm across. Over it she saw Dalide, not in frills and flounces now, but in a brown leather costume that made her look like a stout parcel tied in the middle, sitting in a flimsy carriage. Between the shafts were two horses. She waited for the old woman to recognise her, and send a signal of some kind, but Dalide pretended not to see her. The carriage was already moving off.

Mara looked into the rooms on either side of the hall. They were all furnished with couches and sofas as well as tables and chairs. In one a servant was moving soiled linen from a great sofa like a bed, and putting on clean.

Mara went back through the big room, smiling all around, to show friendliness, and evading the reaching hands of the little plump girl, who was sitting in the embrace of a woman who gave Mara something of a fright. She was so pale she was almost green, with straight, pale hair and green eyes. Mara had never seen anything like her, and was repulsed. She opened a door and saw that in this room was a bed, and chairs, and on a small table were set jugs of the yellow drink, and cakes. Another room had in it only a bed, and another water-wall, like the one in her room. She did know now that these reflecting surfaces were called mirrors, but could only think, when she saw one, of clear, deep water.

She went to the back of the house and there were rooms she supposed must be Dalide's, solidly furnished, comfortable, with the pretty lamps standing about and sending out their soft light, which seemed to beckon you towards them. Then she stood on the back steps, looking into the garden, which was already shadowy with evening. The watchmen were making their fire. One was putting meat and vegetables into a pot. Others squatted, waiting, singing a sad, homesick song. Big yellow men, like Senghor. She took a step down into the garden, and as Senghor did the same, lost interest. His presence there, so close, that big, ugly body, the smell of him, an acrid, dry, powerful smell, made her feel encompassed, imprisoned, even without the immediate fact of her imprisonment.

When she returned to the great room where the women waited, men had already come in, and were talking to the girls they had chosen. These girls were all flirtatious looks and pretty little laughs, and animation. The others sat watching. The men were traders, visitors to the town, and seemed elated because of the generosity of the hospitality, the drinks and the food and the willing servants. Well, Mara would have seen this room as splendid, once. One of the men saw her and pointed, but Senghor shook his head and hurried her through. But she had time to see another group come in. These she recognised as the same as the Hadrons, not physically, because they were a mix, like most of the people to be seen in the streets, but because she recognised the self-satisfied conceit of the consciousness of power: gross, indulged men, and certainly brutal. They saw her as she was going out, and let out cries like hunting cries, and were about to come after her; but Senghor put his arm across to bar them, and when they were through the curtain, and the door, locked it. Now she was glad to have him there. Those men— how well she knew them. So, Bilma's danger was not that it was drying up, or likely to, but that it was corruptly governed. But if these were the rulers of Bilma, as Senghor's demeanour said they were—he had shown none of the cringing humility at the sight of the traders—then was it the same here as in Chelops, which had a layer of apparent subordinates who in fact ran the place? *Those faces*—Dalide had said that the man she planned to sell Mara to was one of them. She reached her room trembling with fear at her probable future.

As Senghor was about to shut the door on her, she said, "I want some information."

"What?"

"Do you know anything about my brother, Dann?"

"Your brother? Why should I know?"

"I am very unhappy about my brother. If you hear where he is then . . ."

"My orders are not to talk to the house women about outside." And then she saw in his face a genuine curiosity, which softened it. He came closer and said in a low voice, but not looking at her, "It is a strange thing when a brother gambles away his sister and the sister is not angry."

"I didn't say I am not angry. But he is my brother. If you hear . . ."

Now he did look at her, and said, "I have been in Mother Dalide's house for twenty years. She is good to me. I shall not go against her orders."

"Then tell me this: are there other women here who were gambled away in the Transit Eating House?"

"Yes."

"And was it Bergos who brought them here?"

But he shook his head at her and went out.

She was alone. She stood at the window and saw that in the garden the watchmen's fire was burning, and their shadows flickered over the earth and the shrubs as the flames danced. They were eating and the smell of food rose up to her and made her hungry. Her supper tray arrived, and she sat and ate and thought that already she took all this for granted: food, good food, better than anything she had eaten in her life. But the really strange thing was that she was not eating every mouthful with the thought, It is a miracle, a wonder, that this food should be here, and that I should be eating it, good food and clean water, as if it is a right, and I am entitled to all—I, Mara, who spent so many years watching every scrap of food and mouthful of water. And soon would she forget that Mara and see food without ever thinking about the hard work and the skills that had made it?

Where was Dann?

Again she stood at the window, mentally mapping out the house. A very big, square house, made of large, square bricks, not easy to dislodge or break through. The house was in two layers, rooms above rooms. In front was a street, and there was a guard there. At the back, the garden she was looking into—guarded. The rooms on the ground floor had thick wooden bars—not Dalide's, but all the others. This window was not barred, but if she jumped down she would break a limb, and the watchmen would stop her. All the servants, judging by Senghor, were devoted to Dalide. That meant, unbribable. And she could not let it be known that she had money, because Dalide would have it off her. So all that meant that if she was going to get news it must be from the men who came to the house.

Later that night she heard Senghor in argument with men outside her door: they were demanding to come in. The girls downstairs had talked about her to their customers.

Next day, but not till the afternoon, she went down to the big room. The women had just got up, and were lolling about, yawning. The little plump girl was sitting inside the arms of the tall white one, with her straight, pale hair; she was stroking and playing with the hair, but when she saw Mara, she reached out, took Mara's hands with little cries of pleasure, and pulled her down. So Mara was sitting within touching distance of this white female, who was so alien and so disturbing; and when the little girl said, "Talk to us, Mara, tell us something," she found it hard to compose herself. She told her story again, because what else could she tell them, when they were so curious about her? They took it as a tale, an invention, for what she said was so far from their experience, and this even though some were from the country regions of Bilma, sold by their parents to Dalide, because of hard times. None had known real hunger and could not conceive that there might not be water to drink. So Mara told her own tale and marvelled at it with them, particularly as she left out all references to the gold coins that had saved her and Dann. So the central thread of the story was not there and sometimes in the tale it sounded as if the brother and sister's successful flight had been due to supernatural interventions, instead of the slog of endurance backed by the little store of gold that had spent years hidden inside a battered floor candle.

She finished the tale as the customers were coming in, while the girls clamoured for her to come again tomorrow and tell them another tale. The girl, Crethis, who had been as close to her during the telling as she could, short of climbing inside her arms, now returned to sit on the lap of her pale friend, Leta, whom the others called the Albina. But immediately Crethis had to leave Leta, because in came a man who claimed her. He was a sensible looking, serious, pleasant man who seemed like a Mahondi—was he one? Yes, he was. He took a good, long look at Mara, nodded, smiled, but did not ask for her. He took Crethis off with him to a private room, and Mara went upstairs.

There she found that all her dresses had been washed and hung up. Her bag of coins had been put on the table.

She tried on the two gowns from Chelops. Well, these flounced, bright cottons had seemed fine enough, then. She put on the indestructible brown garment, and stood in front of the glass. It was short on her now, just to her knees, and seemed to float around her like a shadow. She was standing looking into the water-wall when Senghor came in with her supper tray and saw her. At once he pointed to what she wore and said, "What is that thing?" For he had tried to wash it.

"Once there was a civilisation that made things which were—they never wore out."

He shook his head: I don't understand.

"A people, long ago, hundreds of years . . ." She thought he had taken in the hundreds and tried, "Thousands of years ago, they found the secret of how to make things—houses, garments, pots, cans, that last for ever."

"What people? Who? Where?"

"Long ago. No one knows." He stared, his forehead puckering. "There were many peoples who lived and then vanished. No one knows why."

His face, as he stared at her, was sombre, awed, but also angry. Then he decided to laugh. "You must tell this story to the girls—they would like it," he said, and then dismissed all these difficult thoughts with an energetic shake of the head.

Next day, after the midday meal, when all the house and everyone in it was sleepy and heavy, the girls because sleep was their refuge from their lives, Mara went down again and found Crethis in her place in Leta's arms. This time Mara sat so close that Crethis did not have to move, but put out her hand to stroke Mara, or touch her hair, from inside Leta's protection.

Mara told them of the cities everywhere that had fallen into ruins, and the city she had seen that could never change or fall down; and then she began to tell them of the past of where they were now, the lands around Bilma. They listened, leaning forward, so interested they forgot their sweets and the poppy, and their yawns.

"From where we are to the Middle Sea was once only sand. The Middle Sea is called that because it was once a sea, but now it is only an enormous hollow in the earth where once a moon hit—it fell out of the sky and tore the earth open. Only sand. Imagine that a white streak of sand you see on the road grows and becomes everything you see—everything is sand everywhere you look . . ." Crethis's friend had come in and was listening. He signalled to Crethis to stay where she was, and not interrupt Mara. "Yet under this sand were once forests and fields where people grew corn. Forests and fields that fed people, and then for some reason the sand covered it all over. And then after many, many years"—she did not dare say hundreds, let alone thousands—"over the sand blew earth, and then seeds, and then again instead of sands were forests, deep forests. But people came to live in the forests, and they began to cut down the trees, and what you see now is that stage, people making towns among the forests and cutting trees and—everything always is a stage, one way of being changes into another."

The young women seemed troubled, or anxious, but not all. Some understood and leaned forward to listen, and Leta in particular followed every word.

"And when will the sands come back here?" asked one.

"Who knows? But perhaps it will all be sand again, where nothing can grow; but just when they think everything is dead, nothing will ever grow, the seasons will change and the rain is different and, instead of spreading, the sands go and there will be forests."

"As we have now," said Crethis, and she smiled over Leta's arm at the man who was listening.

"We have light forests now, and in them towns and great spaces where there are fields, and there the soil is blowing away and thinning. Deep under our feet are the sands of the time when all this was desert, sands as far as you could see."

Crethis's friend nodded, approving, which silenced the little sighs and exclamations of incredulity.

"Where did you learn all this?" he asked Mara.

"From Shabis in Charad. He taught me everything I know."

He looked hard at her, meaning her to mark it, and said, "I know Shabis."

"Do you know Darian?"

"Yes, I do know Darian."

That meant, he would know about Dann . . . He got up, signalled to Crethis to accompany him, and said to Senghor, "Mara will come with us."

"It is not permitted," said Senghor.

"I will answer for it to Mother Dalide."

The three went into a side room that had a table and cakes and a jug of juice, and even fruit, as well as the bed. Senghor tried to come in but had the door shut in his face.

Mara sat in the only chair, and the other two sat on the bed, where Crethis snuggled up to her friend, who put his arm around her, with an indulgent smile.

"My name is Daulis. I am one of the Council of Bilma."

"You don't look like the others."

"Thank you, Mara. I hope I am not like them—but not all are like the ones who spend their evenings here."

"I wish you spent all your evenings here," Crethis said, and pouted. This pout and the accompanying dimples were not something put on for work, but were how Crethis was, always—little smiles, and pats and pouts, and snuggles and strokes.

"Your brother is in danger, Mara. There is a big reward for bringing him back to Charad. And for Darian, too."

"I don't understand why Shabis couldn't—just bend the rules."

"Shabis is very much the odd man out among the Generals. Dann was his protégé. Darian was going to replace Dann. The other Generals criticised Shabis: they said Dann and Darian were too young. Shabis said they were both as competent as men twice their age. It is only a question of time before they are caught and taken back to Shari and a big show trial."

The tears were running down Mara's face. Little Crethis, from Daulis's lap, leaned forward to stroke them away.

"So, Dann and Darian have gone up to Kanaz."

"How?" But she knew.

"They were employed as coachmen. Pushing the coaches to Kanaz."

She could not prevent a despairing wail of laughter. "We joked that this might happen. But we said I would be riding in the coach."

"He will wait for you in Kanaz."

"And how am I going to get to Kanaz?" she said bitterly. "I am to be sold here."

He looked gently at her, and smiled, and she knew that this was the man to whom she would be sold. Meanwhile Crethis was smiling up at him and her hand was down inside the pocket of his robe. Mara knew that she had to leave. She got up, and saw how he looked at her, humorously, and like a friend. She went out, shut the door, and there was Senghor.

"I am sure it is all right," she said. "It seems that Daulis is a special friend of Mother Dalide's."

"Yes, they are friends. But it is forbidden, what has happened."

Back in her room, she sat down to think. Daulis was going to buy her, but meanwhile he was making love with Crethis. This made her sad. She hoped it wasn't jealousy, and knew she was foolish.

To be sold to Daulis, when she had seen what kind of man she might have been sold to—surely this was reason enough to be happy. And she was, if not happy, relieved, and realised that her breathing had been oppressed and shallow for days. She was breathing deeply again, from her diaphragm, and she did not feel as if there were knives in her eyes.

This man knew about Dann, knew about her, and wanted to help them. Why did he? He was a Mahondi, yes. There was something here, she knew, that should have been explained. Would it be explained? When Dalide came back, he would pay the old woman the sum of money for Mara and then—she would be out of here. But Dalide might be gone for days, for weeks. . . .

18

Mara was falling asleep, and she was thinking, not of Daulis but of Shabis. He loved her, so Dann had said, and she had never seen it or thought about it. Now she did think, seeing him standing there in her past, smiling at her, tall, kind, generous, but like a father, not a lover. Her heart was warm, thinking of him, but not as when she thought of Meryx, poor Meryx, who would never know he had fathered a child.

Mara's arms were full of a sweet warmth, small arms clung, and she felt a wet baby mouth open on her cheek and heard baby laughter . . . She woke, grieving, in the early morning. She had not allowed herself to think of the child disposed of by the wise women of Goidel, and she was not going to remember it now. Up she got, and washed and dressed and sat at the window, while the watchmen kicked aside the smoking logs of their night fire and went off yawning to their beds. Sunlight everywhere. A clear, cool sunlight, and she saw a little animal, a pet like her Shera, long ago, and it was frisking in some fallen leaves. It was so quiet here, in Mother Dalide's house. When Senghor brought her breakfast she thought he looked at her differently, but did not know what that meant. She sat at the window all morning, and nothing happened in that garden; and the guard yawning, and a small wind shaking a scarlet wall plant so that its shadows moved in patterns on the stone, were big events. Below her the women slept in their soiled beds. She knew they did not enjoy waking, often made themselves go back to sleep again, woke and slept, and got up only when they had to. At midday she heard their scolding, petulant voices, no laughter, and the big room was slowly filling, for there were sometimes afternoon customers, and the women lay around yawning and nibbling sweets and cakes, drinking juices. The weight of their sadness dragged the house down into it. The afternoons were always the worst time. Long, heavy, dragging afternoons, and the occasional customer was a diversion, and the quarrelling about who he—or they—would choose, was exaggerated to give them something to feel other than their griefs and grievances. Mara knew that in all her adventures, all her dangers, she had never known anything as bad as the hopeless dreaming that those poor women downstairs lived inside, like a poisonous air ... She was thinking of herself as apart from them, different, yet she was a house woman, with them, as Senghor reminded her. She could smell the cold, sweet, slow poppy smoke. Downstairs they were lighting their little stubby pipes, or the girls who did not were leaning closer to the ones who did, drawing in great breaths that had been in companion lungs. Second-poppy, they called this practice.

A knock. What was this? No one knocked, not Senghor; but it was Senghor, and he said, "The women want you to go down and tell them stories."

His manner was different. And when she went into the big room, she thought the girls looked at her differently, while they called, "Mara, talk to us," and the little one, Crethis, from Leta's lap, said, "Mara, start from the beginning again."

Now Mara began earlier than she had, which was the moment of running away from her parents' house into the dark, and started with her life as a small child—that wonderful, friendly, easy, indulged life where she woke every morning to the adventure of a child's discoveries, and to the expectation of *What did you see, Mara, what did you see?* And, as she talked, she remembered even more details, little things half forgotten: how the water in a stream ran over a shallow stone and made patterns; the soft flower smell of her mother when she came to say goodnight ... Mara talking, her mind a long way in her past, was looking at plump Crethis, with her baby face and wet pink lips, and she knew who was the infant she had been dreaming about. Crethis, lying inside a sheltering arm and looking out at Mara, was like a little girl. She was a little girl, even a baby, with her wandering hands, touching this, poking at the face just above her, and laughing. The face that was unlike all the others, with its heavy, green eyes and pale lashes, white, glistening white, and the heavy, pale hair that fell over Crethis's face so that she pulled it and laughed. But because Leta was so different, she never lacked customers, and a man came in and pointed at her, and she had to get up and go off into one of the little rooms with him. Crethis crawled to Mara and climbed inside her arms. Mara talked on, hearing in her voice undertones of longing, like a song, and thought, Yes, but I'm not telling them about how the dust piled up in the courtyards and the fountains were dry and the trees stood pining for water.

And now Crethis reached forward to touch Mara's face and said, "Princess Mara, and you lived in a palace."

Mara understood the new respect she was getting from Senghor, and the curiosity of the girls, and she said, "If I was a princess I didn't know it, and I'm not a princess now."

The evening's customers were coming in, and the girls got themselves out of their lazy poses, and sat about attractively and talking coquettishly to each other, with an eye on the door to see who would appear.

Daulis arrived. He looked worried, hurried, and at once signalled to Mara. Crethis got up but he shook his head—no. At this moment Leta came back and, seeing Daulis, went to him and talked urgently, in a low voice, holding his arm.

"Wait," he said. "Wait, Leta. Wait."

He and Mara went up to her room. Mara had time to see how Crethis cuddled up to another girl, not Leta, who was standing staring after Daulis. They did not sit down.

Daulis said, "Something bad. It is my fault. I am afraid I said something to Crethis about you . . ."

"A princess," said Mara. "A princess in a brothel."

He made a gesture—don't. And his face was miserable, all apology and anxiety. Seeing him thus she thought much less of him: he even seemed smaller, less impressive.

"So," said Mara, "she told the girls and the girls have told customers."

"I have the money to buy you out. It is partly mine and partly Shabis's money. But now some Council members want to buy you . . ."

"A princess prostitute?" said Mara.

"A Mahondi princess. It would be a feather in their caps. And they are going to offer Dalide double the price I settled on with her. I haven't got that much."

Mara thought, I've got it, here, on my body, but I'm not going to tell him. I might need it later even more than I do now.

"Luckily Mother Dalide is away. She wouldn't be able to resist, although she agreed on the price. I think you would soon find yourself in a much more unpleasant captivity than this one. And so we are going to move fast. I have made a statement before the chief magistrate, who is a good friend of mine, luckily, that the price was agreed between me and Dalide. It is legally binding, but I am sure Dalide and those crooks would find a way around it. I propose to take you up north with me to Kanaz immediately. And then when you have met up with Dann, we'll go on."

"Who controls the exit lines north from here?"

"The Council, of course. I am one of them. We have to leave before the others find out."

"And who is so keen to get this princess safely out of Bilma? Where am I supposed to be?"

He hesitated. "You'll soon know, Mara. I promise. You'll understand it all. Meanwhile, we must hurry."

She began putting her clothes into the sack, sad that these so beautifully washed and pressed dresses would be crushed up again.

Outside there were loud, arguing voices. Senghor and Leta. She came in, trying to shut the door on Senghor. He would not be shut out. Daulis had to push him back.

Leta said, "Daulis, why wouldn't you listen to me? I was trying to tell you. I've just been with the Chief of the Council, and he said that they are putting a guard on the north station."

Daulis sat down heavily on the bottom of the bed and put his head in his hands.

"But if you listen to me," said Leta, "Just listen. I know a way. You must marry Mara and then they can't stop you—well, you aren't married, are you?"

Daulis was silent, but a quick, almost furtive look at Mara said that he did not want to marry her.

"The marriage would not be legal outside the country of Bilma."

"Wouldn't it? How do you know?"

Leta laughed, angrily. "I know. I have spent years trying to think of ways to get out. I know about the laws. There isn't a man in Bilma with any kind of expertise who has been in my bed, that I haven't used. Information. I have been in this place ten years," she said. "Ten years." And Mara could hear the horror of it, in her voice, full of hate. "Take me out with you," she said. "I have saved some money. Mother Dalide lets us keep a little. I have had my price ready for two years now. I could buy myself free, here, but when I walked around Bilma I'd be looking into the faces of men I've had sex with. In Kanaz no one will know me."

"Surely if I took anyone it should be Crethis?" said Daulis.

Leta, Mara could see, was only just controlling impatience.

"I know you are fond of her," she said.

"Yes, I am," he insisted.

"Have you thought what you'd do with her? She's not like me, she's not independent. You'd have her on your hands."

"A pleasure," he said. But it was only to keep his end up—he was looking doubtful.

"There are women who hate this life," said Leta. "Like me. And there are some who like it. And Crethis is one." Daulis shook his head—shaking away the thought. "Crethis can have six men in a night and she often does, she's popular. And she will enjoy every minute of it." Daulis had got up and was staring out of the window where sparks from the watchmen's fire fled up into the dark. "If you took her out of this house she'd be back. It's her home. And if you took her to Kanaz she'd be back into the brothels in no time."

Silence from Daulis. He had his face turned well away but there were tears on his face.

"Yes, you love her. But she's a little girl. She was six years old when she came here—and began her life as a whore. She has never spent a night alone, except when she was ill last year with the lung disease."

"I promised her," said Daulis.

"What did you promise? A member of the Council couldn't have promised marriage to a whore out of Mother Dalide's brothel?"

"I promised her safety in my house."

"You're not the only one. Your friend the Chief of the Council took her out to his home, and she was back here six days later. This house is her home and Mother Dalide is her mother."

"All right, get your things," said Daulis.

Leta ran out, and as they heard her quick, light feet on the stairs, Senghor came in.

"Yes, I know," said Daulis. "It is not allowed; but I am Councillor Daulis of the Supreme Council and I am ordering you to stand aside." Senghor stood aside.

Mara and Daulis went downstairs, Mara carrying her sack, while the women not at work came out into the hall to watch. A few blew kisses, whether to Daulis or Mara it was hard to say.

Leta came with a little bag of her things in her hand, and then the three were out in the night streets of Bilma. They walked fast along side streets until they came to a big gate. The guard on it recognised Daulis and let them in. Daulis left the two women in a downstairs room while he went up to confer with his colleague and friend, the magistrate, and then they were summoned upstairs. In a few minutes Mara was married to Daulis, with Leta as the witness, by expedient law. It was a question of saying that they were both unmarried, and not promised to anybody else. Then Mara wrote her name beside Daulis's name in a great parchment book. She had not written, except for practising letters in the dust with a stick, since she was with Shabis. She was given a leather disc, on a thong, to hang around her neck, so the world would know she was married and the property of a man. And for this time she was pleased to have the protection.

Daulis asked the magistrate to send a message to the Council saying that Mara from Dalide's house was married and legally free to leave Bilma.

As they left, the magistrate asked Mara, "Are you the woman whose brother is wanted for treasonable desertion in Charad?"

"My brother has gone North. He is safe."

"With that price on his head he'd better shift himself. He's not going to be safe anywhere this side of Tundra."

And then she and Daulis and Leta were moving fast and secretly, always through lanes and side streets, to the hill overlooking the station where she had been with Dann, but skirted it, and were near the platform where a line of coaches stood waiting for the morning. They did not dare board a coach, in case there was a search for them, but saw a small shack or shed a little way off and went there. Soon they saw, in a dim moonlight, a couple of soldiers come around the hill, and then look through the coaches. They were going back, then one of them came towards the shack, peered through a cracked window, and came in.

Daulis stepped forward and said, "Do you know me?"

The soldier hesitated, and said, "I was told to arrest you."

"Where's your order?"

"There wasn't time for an order. The Chief of the Council sent us."

"Well I am giving you an order. I am Daulis, you know that, and I am going to Kanaz with my wife Mara. You have no legal right to stop me."

The soldier looked around the dusty interior of this old shed and was wondering: If it is legal, why are you hiding? But he was undecided, did not dare arrest Daulis. He went out, without saluting, and they could see the two soldiers conferring, by the coaches. They went off, slowly.

By now it was well after midnight. Leta produced some bread—she had snatched it from the kitchen as she left. They ate, hastily, wished there was water, and went out and found a fallen tree, with a lot of branches, and behind them they crouched, watching the coaches and the shack they had left, expecting a return of the soldiers. And just before dawn someone did come, but it was a tramp, and he might be more dangerous, because if he saw they were hiding, and therefore afraid of the law, he might go and report them hoping for a reward.

The sun rose. The station platform was filling. The three ran towards it, and then Mara saw the tramp standing staring at her. She knew him, could not think who it was ... went to him and with difficulty recognised Kulik, because he was so thin and in rags.

She was about to retreat when he came forward and grasped her arm, bringing that hated, scarred face close to hers, dirty teeth bared in a threat.

"Give me some money, Mara," he said.

"No."

"I'll take it."

The last thing she wanted was a fracas, a noisy incident, even loud voices. She gave him a handful of small coins, and as she turned away saw his triumphant face, and heard his low, "Where's your brother? Are you going to hide him?"

She joined the other two on the platform and they got on just as the coach began to move, pulled by the young men in front, pushed by the young men behind. And as the coach was already getting up speed, a couple of officers, not soldiers, came running on to the platform, looking after them.

"When will we be safe?" asked Mara.

"Not in Kanaz," said Leta. "But it is a big town, I hear, so we can hide."

And the two looked at her with respect, and believed her. Leta, now she was out of that place which so demeaned her, was an impressive woman, authoritative because of her knowledge of life, and handsome too. She wore a dark green garment which made her pale skin gleam, and her green eyes shine. Her pale hair was in a big knot. And who is the princess now? thought Mara, fascinated by this strange female who was like nothing she had ever known.

The three of them were clutching each other and clinging on where they could. This "coach" was a contraption of wood slats and lattices, like a cage, and it rattled and bounced and swayed—surely in danger of toppling? And quite soon a mess of splintered wood beside the track showed that these coaches indeed fell over, although they did not move very fast. A good runner could easily have kept up; runners were: the youths who pulled were loping along, and had plenty of breath to shout at each other as they ran. The youths who had pushed, had leaped on to the coach at the last minute and were waiting to replace the others, when they tired. But from their talk, it was apparent that there was a place ahead where the lines had fractured. That these breaks were not uncommon could be seen by the piles of rail sections at intervals along the tracks, pieces of the heaviest wood in the forests. Soon the coach was pulled to a halt by the ropes, and ahead workmen were replacing broken rails. The three did not have to confess their unease that they were stationary not more than a couple of hours from Bilma, and that a fast horse could easily catch up with them.

At first they had travelled through a light forest; but here was a grassy valley, rather like the ones Mara had seen so often in her journey north, across the wide, dry savannahs; but the grasses were different, and the trees too: lower, more compact and dense, not the airy, wide-branched trees of the forest south of Bilma. Beneath them, to the depth of—it was believed—twenty feet, still lay the old sands of the desert ancient people had called the Sahara. And Mara thought that in her sack were two striped robes called Sahar. While the sands far beneath them had been flooded—so they said—and pushed up forests, been swept by fire, and again and again, by floods, had been sands again ... While all this was going on, for thousands of years, one little word stubbornly kept an old sound, and people who did not know the names of their ancestors, or even that they had had them, could walk into a shop and say, "I want to see your Sahar robes."

On a parallel track to the lines appeared a stately procession of horses, donkeys, light carts, litters carried by—but they didn't have slaves in Bilma—and men and women walking. The people in the coach watched this caravan go by for a good half hour. Mara asked, "Then why the need for coaches?"

"A good question," said Daulis. "Some people want to end the coach service. But it takes one of those caravans a week to reach Kanaz, and it is a couple of days by coach. This is really used for urgent council work."

"And other things," said Leta, smiling at him, and he actually blushed.

"And other things," he agreed.

"This is also called the Love Trail," said Leta to Mara. "There are inns all along the route used for holidays and love." The word "love" when she used it sounded like a curse.

Daulis said to her, "Poor Leta. But soon it will all be different for you."

Her eyes filled with tears and she turned her face to look away from them. "Perhaps it will," she said at last. And then, "You are a good man, Daulis. We all of us know that." She was using the *we* of the brothel. "We know who are the swines." And again her voice shook.

Mara, sitting so close to Daulis, thought that she had not yet had a close look at him, and she did now, in the bright morning light. Yes, he was a good man. His face was one to trust—well, she had trusted him. But when she compared his face with another in her mind's eye, then he had to suffer from the comparison. Shabis was finer, and both stronger and more sensitive.

Mara asked, as the idea popped into her on some kind of prompting or instinct, "Do the Three Generals want me too, as well as Dann?"

"I wasn't going to tell you yet. But yes, they do."

"Are they offering money for me?"

"Not officially; but they have been in touch with our Council. They think you have Shabis's child."

"But that was just a bit of spite on the part of his wife."

"They think you had his child while you were with the Hennes. They plan to get rid of Shabis, and they don't want any child of his alive."

"There is a child of his alive."

"There was."

Mara thought of her life as a soldier, at the watchtowers, imagined a baby there, a child, and began to laugh. And laugh, while Leta and Daulis gravely watched her. She knew she sounded hysterical. She was tired, still frantic with anxiety because of Dann—and hysterical. "You don't know how funny it is," she said at last. "Well, the Three Generals can't know much about the Hennes. The Hennes planned to start a breeding programme, to improve their stock, using Shabis's child, if there was one, and to kidnap the Generals' children too."

"Exactly. Using Shabis's child to establish their claim over Agre. They planned to march into Agre with the child in front of their army."

"Then the Hennes don't know much about the Agre."

"And the Three Generals want the child. Because Shabis is so popular, they are afraid the soldiers will rally around Shabis and his child."

And now Mara sat silent, discouraged. She was afraid, too. Just a few spiteful words by an unhappy woman could get her, Mara, recaptured. Had caused so much fevered plotting and planning. Could have caused another war . . . But she was thinking too that she was to blame. How could she have been so blind and thoughtless, so blithely ignorant, living there with Shabis and not ever thinking that he had a wife who must be at the least suspicious. Though it turned out that she was poisoned by jealousy. Mara tried to imagine how she would have felt if, living with Meryx, she knew that he spent all his days with some captured woman, talking to her, teaching her, taking his midday meal with her.

"I have been very stupid," she said aloud, and told Leta and Daulis that part of her story.

Leta pronounced judgement. "Any of the house women could have told you what to expect."

"Yes, I know."

Daulis took her hand and, as she instinctively pulled away, teased her, "As my wife, Mara, you must allow me to hold your hand. If only to reassure me that you don't actually hate me."

"You know you don't want me as your wife."

She heard her voice, forlorn, sad, rough with tears. "Do you know what I keep thinking of? It's the baby I lost. The baby . . ." And she began to cry.

Leta said, "And I keep thinking of the baby I lost."

Here Mara and Daulis looked at her, surprised, and Leta explained, "Crethis. She was my baby. I never had a baby. And I can't help thinking of her."

"And I," confessed Daulis.

Leta said, "I've always looked after her. And now I'm gone. She loves Daulis—as much as she can. Mother Dalide is away. She must be in a bad state today."

"Are you feeling sad because you left? asked Daulis.

"You mean, do you think I should have stayed a house woman because Crethis will miss me?"

"No."

"Then what do you mean? Of course I feel sad. It's not only Crethis, but she is the most of it. The girls there are all I've known, as friends. But I've been trying to get out of that house from the day I found myself in it. And so—Crethis might die."

"Why die?" asked Daulis, quickly.

"You are sentimental," said Leta, "I don't respect that. If you do something that has consequences then accept them. Crethis has a weak chest. She nearly died. I nursed her. I was with her all the time. She would have died without me. Well, knowing Crethis, she's probably found someone else to cling on to already. But no one is going to sit by her bed day and night for weeks . . ." And now Leta wept too.

The rails were mended. The young men who had jumped on to the coach went forward to pull, replacing the others who took their place in the coach.

But they did not have to clutch and cling for long, because about an hour later they stopped where there was an inn, among the dark, sombre trees of this region. Some passengers got off, couples holding hands or with linked arms. Servants came from the inn to sell food to the passengers and they brought a jar of water.

Everyone drank in a way Mara recognised: they were afraid it would be some time before they got water again.

The young men who made the coach move changed again. Now they were all tired and were not shouting jokes and bits of gossip as they ran, and the ones in the coach waiting their turn to get out and push, or pull, were silent and apathetic.

The journey went on. They were shaken, rather sick, and Leta said she had a headache. Mara was glad to accept Daulis's offer of a steadying arm, and she sat against him, her head on his shoulder, and thought that her long, fierce independence had made it hard for her to be as simply affectionate as Crethis, who hugged and caressed and stroked and kissed as naturally as she breathed. She was thinking two contradictory things at the same time: one, that she was glad to be married to Daulis, for it made her feel safe; and then that she would shortly be free and herself again and married to no one.

When it got dark they had to stop because the coaches did not run at night over these fragile and so easily broken rails. There was an inn and they took a room together, the three of them, ate in the room, and locked the door from inside, and pushed a heavy table against it. Each had a bed, and they dozed and woke, and saw that the others were awake and watching and knew that this had to be one of the nights when the first light was a reprieve from enforced immobility. As soon as the square of the window showed some light they were up and dressed, and were down by the tracks waiting. It was a fresh clear morning, rather cold, and they sat on the benches provided for travellers and ate breakfast.

Mara told them about the flying machines down south that were grounded and had to be pushed by runners, and about Felice and her flying service. Leta was amazed, for she had not heard of such machines; but Daulis said that not long ago, in his father's lifetime, there had still been these machines in Bilma, but there was a coup, and possession of the machines was what was being fought over, and at the height of the fighting the rebels had set fire to the machines, all ten of them. Their remains could be seen in a forest north of the town, what was left of them, for they had been pulled apart over the years to make shacks and huts.

Mara asked, "Are you afraid of another coup?"

Leta laughed from surprise, but Daulis said seriously, "Yes, Mara, some of us are. But if there were a coup, it would be my friends who would make it. I don't know if we are more afraid of there being a coup, or not being. But it does seem as if the life of a rule, a period of peace, is never longer than a hundred years or so. And the last coup was a hundred and fifty years ago."

"And your Council is corrupt."

"Yes, some of us are corrupt."

"And there must be a lot of poor people in Bilma, otherwise you'd not have all these youths that look as if they need a square meal to push your coaches."

"Yes, there are poor people, and it is getting worse."

"Why worse?" asked Leta. She sounded threatened.

"It seems fairly clear that we are having another change of climate. They are saying up North that the Ice is retreating again."

"But there's always ice and snow up North," said Leta.

"Sometimes yes and sometimes no," said Mara. "Thousands of years of one, and then thousands of years of the other. Once, in a warm time, the sands stretched here from sea to sea. I have never seen the sea."

"Well, who has?" said Leta. "The traders talk about it, but that's all."

"I have," said Daulis. "When I was a child. But I can hardly remember it. It was rough water, crashing on rocks."

"Salt," said Mara. "Salt water."

"Why salt?" asked Leta "The traders say it is salt, but they tell us all kinds of tall stories, to see how much we will swallow."

Now the coachmen came down from their hostel, and soon the coach was off again. The shaking and rattling went on. They had to stop so the coachmen could change places, and once there was another break in the line. Because of the delay they did not reach the outskirts of Kanaz until it was nearly dark. They decided to stop at the last inn of the coach run for the night. Daulis was known there, as a member of the Council, and he dared to claim the privilege of a suite of rooms. Mara asked if any message had been left for her by one Dann, though Leta told her to be careful. "You'll be safe when you are in Tundra, and not till then."

"And you? What will you do?"

"I will get employment as a maid in one of the inns in the Centre. And if I fail, I'll go to Mother Dalide's house here."

"But you ran away from her," said Daulis.

"She was my mother. At least, I don't remember another one. She'll forgive me. And besides, my colour makes me a prize."

"Once everyone was your colour—where the Ice is now," said Mara.

Leta was astonished. "Everyone? When?"

"Oh, thousands of years ago," said Mara, laughing and thinking that soon she would be like Shabis, who, when teaching her, used thousands of years as one might say, last summer. "And then, later, there were colonies of refugees from the Ice in north Ifrik."

"There is still a colony," said Daulis.

"Perhaps I should go there?" said Leta.

"Then you'll lose your rarity value," said Mara. "Better stay with us."

"If you want to travel with us north, please do," said Daulis. His voice was much more than kind; and he put his hand on her shoulder, smiling. "Come on, take your chances with us."

Mara said, "I'd miss you, Leta."

And now Leta looked at them both, serious, grateful, her usually hard face soft, and said, "I'll think about it."

"At least if you fail in Kanaz, come up after us."

"Fail at being a housemaid? But I don't intend to stay a housemaid. I'm ambitious. But I'll remember what you said. But where could I find you up North?"

"People find each other," said Mara. "I'm waiting for Dann to find me."

Next day they moved into a caravanserai in the heart of Kanaz, to wait for Dann. This city was different from Bilma, that trading town so full of people from everywhere. Kanaz was not polyglot and busy. It was populated by a people with lean, flat bodies, and sharp features. Mara had seen them before, on the walls of the ruins near the Rock Village. And here they were, just as if thousands of years and many migrations had not come and gone. They were phlegmatic, slow moving, and all over the town were buildings with turrets and towers that were, Daulis said, places of worship.

"Of what?" Leta and Mara asked, at the same time.

And he told them they believed in a powerful, invisible Being who could be put into a good temper, a mood to help favour, by these fanciful, brightly coloured buildings, inhabited by men and women who wore special clothes, walked about the streets chanting and shouting the name of this Being, and were the rulers of the town.

"And Kanaz is not under the jurisdiction of Bilma?" asked Mara.

In theory yes, but in practice no. This was one of the reasons the more intelligent of the Council of Bilma believed in the imminent end of their rule. Bilma did not have the strength to bring insubordinate provinces to heel, and while harmony prevailed on the surface, the two cities watched each other, waited. So Daulis explained, and went into details of the situation which interested Mara, but Leta, not much.

But then Daulis said to Leta, "If you stay here you will have two disadvantages."

"One I already know. I shall not be such a novelty here as I am farther south. I am only a little paler than some of the people here. And the other?"

"You will have to learn the special language and customs of the priests and pretend to believe in them, because they are cruel to anyone who does not at least pay lip-service to their rule."

"And how does Mother Dalide manage to prosper here, with her brothel, in such a town?"

"She pays the priests here just as she pays us in Bilma."

Meanwhile they were all nervous. This was the biggest travellers' inn, and there were bound to be spies, both from Bilma and the rulers here. But this was where Dann was bound to look for them. The decided to stay that night, not move to a less well known place but eat their food in their room, well away from the enormous room that took up most of the ground floor, where food and drink was served.

Or perhaps they themselves should go from inn to inn around the town, asking for Dann? Mara had never told anyone about the coins hidden under Dann's scar, but she told these friends now, to explain why she did not know if he would be working in some low place, in order to eat, or if he would be decently lodged somewhere. Or—but she did not say this aloud, kept it to herself—perhaps in some place where he is smoking poppy again. For she feared this for him more than anything.

Late that night, when they had decided to sleep, and not wait any longer, there was a commotion outside the door. Mara rose straight to her feet—she recognised Dann's voice. Then he was standing there, in the doorway, and behind him the servant who had tried to bar the way of this poor coachman in his torn tunic, with his bare dusty feet. Which Dann was this?—Mara wondered, but saw in his eyes the responsible Dann, the grown up man, though his whole body seemed wrung with apology and with supplication. And the two were in each other's arms, hugging and weeping, "Oh Mara, forgive me," and Mara, "Oh Dann, you are here." The other two sat on their floor cushions and watched, silent, until brother and sister at last were able to let each other go and stand back, and look. Then Dann said, "Mara, it was the other me, not me." "I know," said Mara and thought that Dann had never before acknowledged his division. Now Dann took Mara's hands, and said, "Mara, it is easy for me to say now that it will never happen again—but you've got to help me."

"And what could I have said that would have stopped you going to the gambling room that night?"

His face seemed to crumple, and it was hard for him to look at her; and then he rallied and said, "Mara, all you have to do is to remind me that I gambled you away, and you are the most precious thing, the most . . ." And they embraced again.

This scene might have gone on, but there was another loud exchange of voices outside, the door opened, and Dalide came in, her hands full of travelling bundles and bags. These she set down, and then looked around the room, not the inn's best, with the supper trays still on the floor in a corner, the faded floor cushions, and in a corner a pile of shabby sleeping pallets.

"Well, Councillor Daulis, this is not exactly the kind of place one expects to find you." To Leta she said, "Pile up some of those," and Leta made a high seat with the bed pallets. On this Dalide carefully disposed herself, and then looked at each of them in turn. And they waited, apprehensively, for each had reason to fear her.

This powerful woman looked like some doll or puppet, with a voluminous red cotton garment, for the dust, over her tight leather travelling outfit, and her sharp, black button eyes, her dyed orange-coloured hair.

"Councillor, you owe me for Mara—and I hear that I could have got twice as much for her."

"Not legally," said Daulis, and took out a bag of coins and laid it beside him.

She made a gesture—wait until later. And turned to Leta there on her cushion, "Well, Leta? Have I really treated you badly?"

"No, Mother. But you know that I've always wanted to leave. And I have my quittance money."

Now Dalide turned to Mara. "I suppose you think that what you are going to find up in that Centre they talk about is going to be some kind of happy-ever-after? Well, I shouldn't count on it."

And now a long, very cold inspection of Dann, designed to shame him. He did manage to return her gaze, but they could all see he was not far off tears.

"Leta," Dalide said, "the woman who runs my house here wants to retire. Would you like to take her place?"

Leta did not seem able to take this in. She shifted about on her cushion, took her hand to her face in the beginnings of that gesture: It is all too much for me, dropped her hand, then she was sitting with both hands over her mouth, staring at Dalide. "You mean, stay here in Kanaz and run your Kanaz house?"

"That's what I said. You can do it. You are a clever woman. You know how I operate."

Daulis and Mara watched the struggle going on in Leta, and understood it. She had said she was ambitious, and the truth was that they could easily imagine her as the Mother Dalide of Kanaz.

"What makes you think I could deal with these praying people? I have no experience of them."

"They are just men. Like the Councillors. I have today paid them off for the coming year. And if there's trouble, I'm only a week away in Bilma. Or two days by coach."

"That means that yet again I'll not be able to walk about the streets without looking into the face of every man I meet to wonder if some time I've been his mattress."

"There's no need to sleep with them if you are running the place."

Leta was very still. Her eyes were fixed—staring inwards. And then she said, "Mother, I can't, I'm sorry. I think I'll go North with Mara and Daulis."

"And Dann," said Dalide. "Perhaps he'll gamble you away next."

Mara said, "Dalide, I gather you don't exactly discourage men from gambling away their women. And if you don't like Dann, then what about that little snake Bergos?"

"I don't have to like them for it," said Dalide. "Nor like Bergos. I'm a business woman. I see opportunities and I take them. And I'm not the only one who has agents in the Transit Eating House, to see what women are there to be bought or what men have got the gambling fever badly enough. Some of the Councillors, for instance—yes, Councillor Daulis?"

"I don't," he said.

"Some of your friends do." And now she said to Leta, "Give me your quittance price."

"Mother," said Leta, "it is all I have."

This time it was in Dalide that a struggle took place. Her eyes were on the bag that held the quittance price, and then her face softened and she said, "Very well, keep it."

And now Leta flung herself forward, embraced Dalide's knees, pressed her face into the scarlet folds, and sobbed.

The great knot of pale hair, which glistened in the lamplight, stood out over her neck, and Dalide took out the pins, and the hair flooded down, like sunlight. Dalide sat stroking the hair, fingering it, lifting strands, letting the light play on it. The face of the ugly, little black woman was a marvel of regret, sorrow, and bitter humour. "Ever since you came to my house as a little girl, I've longed to have hair like this." And she patted her own orange spikes in a way that was rueful, comic and self-critical. "Leta, if you don't do well up North, then come back to me. I'm fond of you—though I daresay you've sometimes wondered." She pushed Leta away, and said to Daulis, "Give me Mara's price now."

"May I give it to you in Bilma?"

"No. I need it to pay for two new girls I'm taking back with me."

Daulis gave her the bag with the money.

"At least with you I don't have to count it." She got to her feet. "And have you any messages for little Crethis?"

Daulis shook his head. "And you, Leta?"

"Tell her . . . tell her . . ."

"I know what to say. And are you coming back to Bilma, Councillor?"

"I suppose I am. When I've done what I have to do."

"When you've delivered these two Mahondis."

"Who are these girls, Mother?" asked Leta.

"Local girls. One of these precious priests asked me if I wanted them. He bought them from their parents, just as I bought you, Leta. They'll be a nice change for the men, in my Bilma house. What do you say, Councillor?"

Daulis shook his head: Leave me alone.

"How old are they?" asked Mara.

"They don't know how old they are. I would say ten or eleven. But they're underfed, so they look younger. I'll have them fed and prettied up in no time. Goodbye, Mara. You can't say you've done badly in my house. You've found a protector. Goodbye, Leta. Perhaps I'll see you again. I'll say goodbye to you, just in case, Councillor." She ignored Dann. And went out.

Leta ran to the window and they all crowded around her. Down in the street waited a carriage, with two mules. It was protected by a light awning, but they could see huddled together two little girls, who shrank away from Dalide when she got in and sat opposite them. Two frightened little faces: and they could hear the children's miserable sobbing.

Leta left the window, sank to a floor cushion, sat with her face in her hands, and swayed, back and forth, containing grief.

Daulis laid his hand on her shoulder and said, "That's all over for you, Leta." Then, "I'm going to sleep."

He threw a pallet into a corner, lay on it with his back to the room. Soon Leta did the same. Mara and Dann lay face to face on a single pallet and whispered to each other what had happened to them both in the last few days.

In the morning they sat around their breakfast trays, and made plans. How much money did each of them have?—was the main question.

Leta offered her quittance price, and Daulis said, "No, you keep it. We'd only use that as a last resort."

Dann said he had some change, but he was keeping it for an emergency.

"This situation not being emergency enough?" asked Daulis, and Dann laid out what he had, enough of the little coins for perhaps a day's lodging and a day's food.

What Daulis contributed was not much more: he had been counting on paying Dalide in Bilma.

Mara slipped her two hands up through her loose sleeves, untied her cord of coins and laid it down. "Eleven," she said.

"Treasures concealing treasures," said Daulis, and Leta looked sharply at him, while Dann said jealously, "I hear you are Mara's husband?"

"You may have noticed that I've not been insisting on my marital rights."

Dann apologised. Then he said, "I'm going to have to get out my coins."

"Oh no," said Mara, and untied a coin to give to him.

He went white. Really, she might have hit him. "I can't take your money after . . . after . . . "

"Don't be silly," said Mara.

Leta said, quickly, tactfully, so that Mara realised she had been too casual, insensitive, "Let me have a look, Dann. Mara's told us . . ."

Dann said, "I think one of them is just under the skin." He lifted his robe up. The scar showed white and glistening, and there were lumps under it. "Look," he said to Leta. "Feel that."

"I'm sure we could get that one out easily."

She took out a little leather bag, and from that a tiny knife, and some bundles of herbs. She wetted one of them and rubbed damp leaves on the place where the edge of the coin showed. "It will kill the pain," she said.

Mara watched, suffering. Leta saw this, and said, "I told you, I learned everything I could from the men who came to Mother's house. I've learned some medicine."

After about five minutes, she rubbed the little knife against another bunch of leaves, and made a tiny slit just above the scar and at once the coin was visible. Leta picked it out. Dann said, "It doesn't hurt," and she said, "Yes, but it will hurt a little soon."

"We should stay here until Dann is better," said Mara and Daulis said, "It's dangerous to stay."

Mara untied another coin, and said, "Go down and bribe them. It's not likely anyone is going to offer them more than this."

"Not in a year," said Daulis, and took the coin and went out.

When he came back he said he had booked the room for another day and he thought they would be safe.

Leta wrapped a cloth around her hair, to make herself unnoticed, and said she was going out to see the town. Mara wanted to go too but Daulis said she should stay. Dann asked Leta to buy him something to wear. He had only his soiled and torn coachman's garb.

Leta went, and then Mara asked, "Now, tell us about this Centre. Why are you taking us there?"

"All I can say is that they have plans for you both. Shabis told me, and it's not much more than he knows."

"But that 'not much more' is the point."

"Yes. But I'm not going to tell you more. Shabis said not. You'll find out. You've got some sort of choice to make."

"It's because we are Mahondis?"

"Yes."

"Where are all these Mahondis we were told are everywhere?"

"There are very few of us left."

"Does that matter?" said Mara, for now she had seen so many different kinds of people, in different regions, it was hard to think one was
better than another.

"I think there are people who dream of the time when Mahondis
ruled all Ifrik."

"All?"

"All."

"Did we rule well?"

Daulis laughed. "We ruled well from the point of view of the
Mahondis."

"So there are many people who do not remember Mahondi rule kindly?"

"You know, people forget quickly. This Mahondi empire was—let's
see—at its height about three hundred years ago."

"So recent. And there are still people who think it should come
back?"

"It is Leta who should come back. I'm getting worried."

And they were all three anxious, as the hours passed. Then Leta did
come back. She had bought all kinds of things useful for travelling: two
of the long black and white striped gowns, the Sahar robes, worn by
men. Then she inspected Dann's little wound and said it was almost
healed. She said she was glad she was leaving Kanaz, it was a horrible
town. The praying men were everywhere, and they had sticks, and if
someone was behaving improperly, in their view, they might hit buttocks, shoulders, or even heads. "Lucky I wrapped myself up well: they
beat women if they don't like the look of us."

Dann wanted to know how much money they would need to bribe
the frontier guards, to get into Tundra; but Daulis said, "Believe me, you
don't bribe these guards."

"That's unusual."

"It is the regime that is unusual, you'll see. It's quite new, and still vir-
tuous."

"How new?" asked Mara.

"Oh about a hundred years. So the usual rot will set in soon, I suppose. If it hasn't already."

After supper they each lay on a separate pallet, talking into the dark,
until one after another they fell asleep.

Next morning they had to choose between using a coach again, or a conveyance like Dalide's, a light carriage, with mules. They could not face another day of shaking, so chose the carriage, which would take two days to the frontier. It was as uncomfortable in the carriage as in the coach. The driver kept the mules at a steady pace, but the road was rough. They were all sick, the driver having to pull his mules up so they could get out. And they were cold. A thin, chilly cloud blew past above them and, on the higher parts of the road, came down low enough to hide the country they were travelling through. Leta seemed ill. When Mara said she hated the woolly whiteness hiding everything, Leta said she liked it, and confessed that the vastness of the landscape frightened her. "Too much space," she whispered, hiding her eyes as they came out again from the obscuring mists. The other three consulted with each other, but with their eyes. It was occurring to them that this woman had been sheltered inside Mother Dalide's house, had scarcely ever gone out, had been fed and kept warm, in a horrible and degrading safety, but safety. And here she was out in the world, with no idea at all of what would happen to her.

Mara put her arm around her, and felt her trembling.

Leta let her head fall on Mara's shoulder and whispered, "Mara, have I made a terrible mistake?"

The jolting and rattling were such that Mara had to say to the two men, sitting opposite, "Leta is afraid she has made a mistake in coming with us," and at once Daulis leaned forward and, all concern, took Leta's hands and said, "No, Leta, no, of course you must be feeling bad. It's our fault for not thinking about it."

"When you go back, please take me, Daulis, I don't think I can keep up with you, I really feel ill when I look and see . . . It goes on and on and it is so cold and so ugly."

This was an interval in the mist, and Mara thought that this great, sombre landscape had a beauty, though the chilly dampness of everything was not where she felt at home. Was this really Ifrik?—she had been thinking.

Daulis still held Leta's hands, and a jolt brought her forwards, and he lifted her. He said something to Dann, who precariously slid in beside Mara as Daulis settled Leta in beside him. There she clung to him and wept. This proud, strong woman with her lean, hawk face was at this moment not unlike her pet Crethis.

It was a long day, a bad one, the worst since Bilma. The inn the driver stopped at in the evening, was large, being on this main route North, but looked poor and shabby. It stood in the main street—the sole street of a village that had clearly come into being only because of the inn. When the four got out, the driver said he would come for them in the morning, and demanded payment for that day. Mara had already paid him. There was an argument, which caused interest among groups of people going into the inn. Dann said to Mara, "Don't draw attention." She gave the driver a little more money. He grumbled, but went off. And now there was no need to discuss what they must do next. There was a shop, of the kind that supplied travellers' needs, and in it was a whole wall hung with every sort of cloak, cape and shawl. They bought capes of the kind that has a hole in, for the head, and large enough to make bed coverings, for they had been cold at night. And they chose grey, not the bright or cleverly woven patterns, because they did not want to be noticed.

At the inn across the road, they were given a room without comment, and the innkeeper did not show any particular interest in them. But they were uneasy, and Dann said that this was the most dangerous part of their journey: tonight and tomorrow night. The daytime was probably safe, because pursuers would be looking for them on the coaches, would not expect them to risk themselves fully visible on almost empty roads. Besides, unless these pursuers were officials, they would not have money for a carriage. Which brought the four, hiding in their room with the door well barred, to the question, Which pursuers? Representing what, or whom? How could they be recognised? If the Bilma Councillors still hoped to sell Dann and Mara to Charad, then they would not send officials, but hired ruffians. If it was the long arm of Charad they had to fear, then, again, it would be disguised as a beggar, or a pickpocket or a thief. Or a gang of thieves. Or a servant in this inn . . . "So, what's new?" said Dann. "I'm frightened," said Mara.

They ate in their room. Leta dosed herself with potions from her medicine bag. She was apologetic and ashamed. She still trembled, though this could not now be from cold. They wrapped her well, and laid her on a pallet, and lay down themselves, to rest. They were not only fearful, expecting to hear a bang on the door, but badly affected by the days of being shaken and jolted. Without the fear of pursuers they would have walked, and tonight they would have been healthy and calm—themselves. Walking was best, they all agreed. After that, a boat—water. And lastly, the litters, the coaches, the chairs, the carriages, which shook you to bits and left you hardly able to think.

Daulis told them that once, thousands of years ago, there had been machines that whisked travellers over the distance it had taken Mara and Dann so long to cover, in a couple of hours. They could go around the world in a day. (With difficulty Mara forced her mind away from the shape of Ifrik to encompass hazy immensities.) There was every imaginable kind of vehicle, and some that they, descendants of those great ones, could not begin to imagine, for they were like the tales of flying dragons or talking birds told to children. Once, to travel from one country to another had been as comfortable as being transported sitting in a chair or lying in a comfortable bed.

Meanwhile, they had to get through this fearful night, and then there was another day of the carriage.

Dann said he would stay awake and on guard, and he did, with his knife beside him. Meanwhile Mara slept, and Daulis watched Leta. Then Daulis watched, and Dann lay down where Daulis had been. Leta slept heavily, and seemed chilly to the touch, so they piled on to her the inn's blankets. This alone told them how different a country they were approaching: all the inns farther south might provide no more than a thin cloth, or nothing at all, for bed coverings. Here there was a stack of thick blankets and the windows had heavy shutters. When they woke in the night, they heard the shutters shaking and rattling, and the coldness of the wind could be felt inside the room.

In the morning Leta lay limp under her heap of blankets, silent, looking at the ceiling. They all three knew what she was feeling. Daulis knelt by her and said, "Dear Leta, it's one more day, that's all. And then the worst will be over."

She did not at once respond, but then sat up, throwing off the blankets, and saying, "I think I know what to do. I don't know why I can't bear this ... horrible emptiness everywhere, but I can't. I'm going to wrap my head in a scarf and not look at it. And I'm going to give myself a dose that will calm me. If I sleep, then that will be best."

When the driver came with the carriage and the mules he demanded money. Mara again said she had paid him well before they started. Again it was a question of not being noticed. There were a lot of people coming out from the inn, to go to the rail coaches. And so the man was paid extra, when he did not deserve it. Mara said she was running low with money and must change another coin.

Daulis said there was no need to worry. Once over the frontier, changing money would be easy.

"And what is this paradise of a place? Dann and I have been worrying about changing money all the way from the Rock Village."

"No paradise, I can assure you. But—you'll see."

That day was worse than yesterday, but at least they had something to occupy them, looking after Leta. Through the gauzy veil she had wound around her head, it could be seen that this pale creature was white as . . . but what could that pallor be compared with? Her skin, which usually had a lustre or glow, was greenish and looked lifeless. She lay in Mara's arms until Mara's whole body had gone numb, and then in Daulis's and then in Dann's. She kept her eyes shut, and dozed, but was always shaken awake again. There was no mist today so it was as well that she did not look out at this country—like yesterday's, enormous expanses of dark earth, with gleams of water everywhere, and clumps of reeds that swayed almost to the ground in the wind.

The end of that day's journey was an inn a mile from the frontier with Tundra, standing alone by the road; and as soon as they were in the main entrance, it was evident that it had all the characteristics of a frontier inn. It was full of every kind of person; the proprietor observed them each, one by one, carefully, in case he would be asked to describe them, and there was no doubt that among this cram and crush of travellers would be spies and agents.

They were given a room at the end of an extension to the main building: an arm flung out, consisting of single rooms one after another with interconnecting doors that could be locked, with a narrow, covered pavement, because the ground was boggy. Daulis protested that they should be given a better room, was told the place was full. Meanwhile Leta was evidently longing for one thing only, to lie down. They all went to the room, put Leta to bed, and conferred. Dann said he hated this place, and Mara agreed. Brother and sister had never been more one than in their restless, unhappy prowling about this room, as if they were animals in a trap; and then Dann said that it would be madness for him to stay here, and Mara agreed.

Daulis did not like the two going off, to spend the night in the open. They said they were used to it. No, of course Leta could not be moved; of course Daulis must stay with her. Councillor Daulis was not enjoying being reminded that, in his own way, he had been as sheltered and comfortable as Leta. He contented himself with saying that after tomorrow everything would be better.

Dann and Mara took with them some food, but no water—this landscape hardly lacked water. It was dark, but a great yellow moon was up, and they could see everything. The trouble was that there were no buildings near they could shelter in, only sheds and stables belonging to the inn. They put themselves into the minds of possible pursuers and knew that these outhouses were where they would be looked for first. There seemed to be no trees anywhere. A big cluster of rocks, about half a mile from the inn, had the same disadvantage as the inn: it was an obvious hiding place. There were rushes, and some clumps of reeds. Reeds was what this landscape had most of, in the way of vegetation. And where would these imagined pursuers look for them, if not among the reeds?

Far away to the east was the shine of water and they went there, choosing their way carefully, through this marshy land. There was a little lake, and on it a boat, tied to a stump. They lay down side by side in the boat, knowing their grey blankets would disguise them. It was very still, the sounds of the inn out of earshot. The water was still, the moonlight poured down, moving the shadows of the reeds across the surface.

They did not dare to talk. "I've never been more scared," whispered Dann, and Mara agreed. "I know there's someone after us. I feel it in my bones."

It was cold, even wrapped tight in thick cloth.

The hours went past. Sometimes Mara dozed a little, then Dann.

The moon had gone out of the sky when they heard a squelch of feet. They were terribly tempted to leap up and run—but there was nowhere to run to. They lay still. Only one person—that was a surprise. Neither Charad nor Bilma would send one agent, much more likely several.

A man by himself came to stand above the boat, where the path descended through the reeds. He was staring across the lake. Then he looked down at the boat. It was so dark now that he could not see much, only a black boat on black water with something dimly grey in it. He stayed there some minutes, sometimes looking around behind him. Then a marsh bird screamed quite close, from some reeds, and the man gave a grunt of fear and ran off.

"That was Kulik," said Dann.

"I know."

They stayed where they were, hearing nothing. The bird screamed again, and they thought that might mean Kulik was coming back.

The sky lightened. They were stiff and cold. They crawled up out of the boat, through the reeds, and between them and the inn could see nothing. They went fast, not wanting to be observed. Around the inn all was animation, and people were already streaming off towards the frontier. The two went quietly into their room and found Daulis, sitting with his back against the stack of blankets, with Leta in his arms, leaning back against him. He was stroking her hair, and she seemed to be asleep.

Daulis said that in the night someone had tried to force the shutters, then the door. The two told their tale.

"Just let's get over that frontier," said Mara. "Let's go."

They roused Leta. They all ate a little. Daulis went to pay the bill, so the others would not be seen. They went with crowds of others towards the frontier post. This was a serious frontier, not like the casual, or invisible, ones of farther south. There was a heavy wooden beam across the road, in a fence that ran away on either side of it, out of sight. The fence was not like the ones Mara and Dann had seen, of heaped coils of rusty wire. This was not rusty. It was full of sharp points and it glittered.

On this side of the wooden beam were half a dozen soldiers who stood about yawning, and waving the line along; but on the other side were about forty men and women, in black overall uniforms, with black capes for warmth, and they were looking carefully at the people they let in, and counting them by sliding beads along a string. These strings were stretched in lines along wooden racks. When one rack was full, it was taken back to a shed where it was stacked with others. On this side, no one was counting who came through.

It was a bleak landscape, all right, with a few dark trees and a greyish look to the shrubs and grasses. Leta was not wearing her veil, but was forcing herself to look about her. Daulis was supporting her, just behind Dann and Mara, who had warned them that there might still be danger.

The waiting lines spoke in low voices, mostly Charad, but there was some Mahondi too. There were also dialects which at first they didn't recognise as Mahondi. The lines were made up of families, who were from Tundra, who had been visiting, and were going home. There were also groups of officials, and it was noticeable that people coming through from the northern side were let through at once if they were officials, but the officials from this side had to wait and go through the formalities. The different groups of people in the lines were wary, eyeing each other across the gaps they were careful to leave between them, so these lines were discontinuous and no one took any notice of the soldiers who tried to move them along. Those in front of the four kept glancing back at them, and the people behind noticed them and discussed them. Three tall Mahondis, handsome people, but there were other Mahondis in these enormous crowds. It was Leta they all looked at, this Alb woman whom they were treating as one of themselves, not as a servant. And Leta, now that she was feeling better, had regained her pale, gleaming beauty, and that hair of hers in its great smooth knot shone in the weak sunlight.

It was a wearying business, this waiting, moving forward so slowly; and just as Mara was thinking, we all look half asleep, she saw Dann being pulled out of the line by two men whose lower faces were covered by the ends of head cloths. One was Kulik. They had Dann by the arms, one on either side, and were trying to hustle him towards a waiting chair. Now Mara leaped out of the line and had her arm with the poisoned serpent on it, the knife released, around Kulik's throat.

"If you don't let go I'll use this."

Neither of the men recognised the snake, did not know their danger, looked at her face, then down at the tiny sliver of a knife, then back at her ... And Daulis was out of the line, with a knife in one hand and a dagger in the other. All this was happening so fast, the people in the lines had not yet noticed; but for Mara the pace was slow, every movement and gesture in a time of its own, so she was able to think, If I press this spring, Kulik will die, and then the soldiers will be forced to take notice, and there will be problems and ... The two men had loosened their hold on Dann and his knife was out and at the throat of the other man. One moment, and both these men could be dead. And Mara was remembering how long ago Dann had sworn that he would kill Kulik.

But not now. Mara let Kulik go. Dann removed his knife. Kulik's scarred face turned in the familiar bare-teethed, hated grin, for a last look, and then he was off into the chair, with his aide, and the runner in the chair had the shafts up and was off, going back fast to the inn.

The people in the front had not noticed what had happened. The

people behind, who must have seen, were staring ahead, their faces saying, We have seen nothing.

If Dann had been hustled off to the chair, not one of these people
would have intervened, or alerted the soldiers. What kind of people
were these, then? Probably they would only help someone in their own
immediate group. As for the soldiers, a couple were staring after the
chair, but not as if they had seen anything much.

Mara saw that Dann was energised by the danger: his eyes were bright
and he smiled at Mara, and put his arm around her. "Perhaps you should
sell that pretty snake of yours, for all the good it's done us."

"It's good for killing," said Mara. "So I'll not part with it yet."

And there it was on her arm, the deadly sting back in its groove, and
indeed it was a pretty little snake.

Soon they were at the front of the line, and were being waved on past
the beam, towards the Tundra soldiers, who were watching them come
forward.

Before Daulis could speak the officer in charge said, "We know about
you. But we were expecting three, not four."

Daulis said, "If the Centre had known I was bringing this woman
they would have made provision for her."

"They told us to have three horses for you."

"We need four."

"Horses are not to be had for the whistling for them," said the officer.
"As you must know."

The horses stood waiting. They were stout, stubby little beasts, and
certainly not able to carry two people. Besides, Mara had never been on
a horse. Nor had Leta. Dann had said he had, once, but it had been a
striped horse, different from these, well trained and mild. These horses
were anything but mild: they were kicking and bucking, and generally
making it clear that they did not enjoy their servitude.

All kinds of conveyances stood about waiting for customers. "We'll
find something," said Daulis to the officer.

"They're expecting you," was the reply, meaning, Don't waste time.

They walked slowly along the road, having a good look: there was
nothing like it in Bilma, nor in Charad—not since Chelops, where it
had been a solid surface of shining black—but this road seemed to be
surfaced by a grey spider-web, innumerable tiny lines, like scratches.
Daulis said the road had been made long ago, certainly hundreds of
years, and no one now knew the secret of this substance.

It was then mid-afternoon. Ahead was a town, and most of the travellers were making their way there. Daulis said he knew the town, a pretty and prosperous place, and well worth looking at. But they were all tired. The inn they chose was an affair of several storeys, with servants in uniforms, and the room was large, with real beds, not pallets on the floor, and fine hangings at the windows, and carpets.

They would have to pay for it. Mara changed two coins at the reception table, for their proper value. They lay down to recover. Then they went out to an eating house Daulis knew, and all of them, including Leta, ate very well. Neither Dann nor Mara had eaten this food or imagined it existed, and Dann said to her, "I told you it would get better all the time, didn't I?"

And Mara said, "I'll agree with you when I'm sure Kulik isn't following us."

"They wouldn't let him in," said Daulis. "No one comes into Tundra except for some good reason. Like being useful to Tundra."

"You don't know this man," said Mara. And she actually shuddered. She explained, "You see, you can't get rid of him, ever. It seems he has always been in my life—and Dann's. Why? It's as if he was born to torment us and chase after us, never letting us alone."

In the room they had to make decisions. To where they would catch a boat going North, would be two days if they took a carriage or carrying-chairs. The coaches did not run here on their rickety rails. If they walked, that would take nearly a week. With one voice, Leta and Mara and Dann averred they would rather die than ever again use a carriage, a carrying-chair, or a coach. Daulis said drily that they were lucky not to be officials, who had no choice.

"So we are lucky, we can walk if we choose," said Mara gaily, for her spirits were rising, and so were the others'.

"But we are supposed to be hurrying."

Daulis said, "Well, if you knew how long they've been waiting, I wouldn't worry about a day or so. Or even a week." And then he said to Mara, "Haven't we something to celebrate, you and I?"

"What?"

Leta laughed at her. "You are no longer married, not in Tundra. That ended at the frontier."

Mara had forgotten. She was surprised to feel a little sinking in her stomach, a giddiness. Regret. She was actually feeling sad, and she said to Daulis, "For a moment then I was really sorry. But don't be alarmed."

"I've enjoyed being married to you, Mara," said Daulis. "Though some aspects of married love seemed to be wanting. Better be careful never to go back into Bilma, though. Not if you don't want to be married to me."

"Oh but I might enjoy it, for a while."

This banter was upsetting Dann. Mara said, "If you are jealous about a convenience marriage, what are you going to be like when I am really married? If I ever am."

And Dann surprised them by thinking a while and then saying seriously, "I don't know what I will do. I know I won't like it."

This was an uncomfortable little moment, for Dann and Mara as well as for the others.

Next morning, when they got back on the big road, they saw a long procession winding out of town. It was a pilgrimage and it was going to visit a shrine. These new words having been explained by Daulis, they joined the end of the procession and were handed bunches of reeds that had been dyed black and dark red. The songs were doleful, and the people's garb was dark and sad, and all the faces wore looks of resigned suffering.

The shrine, Daulis said, housed a machine that was certainly many thousands of years old, of a metal now unknown, and it had survived vicissitudes, which included falling to earth like a leaf in a whirlwind, but into a swamp, which saved it. It was believed that Gods had descended to Ifrik in this machine, and the bones of two of these Gods had been sealed inside jars and set inside the machine. There were four pilgrimages every year to this ancient machine, which was guarded by priests, but of a different kind from the ones in Kanaz. The two different orders of priest despised each other, refused to let their followers have anything to do with each other, and had often fought vicious wars, in the past.

"But," enquired Mara, "why is walking to a place a sign of devotion to that place?"

"And why," asked Dann, "four times a year? Wouldn't once be enough?"

"And what," Leta wanted to know, "is the point of the bones?"

Daulis said that it would be better if questions like these were not asked aloud, because these people were of the sort that would set on critics and even kill them.

The procession went through more towns, each one prosperous, with well dressed people. What a contrast between the wild and desolate country they had walked through and these towns, which were like dreams of order and delightfulness. Except for police in their black uniforms, like the soldiers'; and several times the police stood on either side of the column of singing pilgrims, looking keenly into every face. At night most pilgrims slept in special pilgrim inns, but the four slipped away to the comfort of good hotels. They rejoined the procession in the mornings. It was tedious. Above all, Leta was getting tired. She was not used to walking, more than move from one bed to another in Mother Dalide's. She did not say this bitterly, as they had heard her speak in the past, but actually laughed. They decided to try the carrying-chairs, as the least uncomfortable way of going faster; and so, two people to a chair, Dann and Mara in one, Leta and Daulis in another, they felt they were covering ground. But it was an interrupted progress. The chair-runners, two behind and two in front—these chairs had no wheels—stopped at certain points, set down the chairs, and fell out, others taking their place. No matter how they were appealed to, the runners shook them about; and at a place where they stopped for a meal, Mara asked about those ancient times when travelling was always comfortable, and Daulis said that more than that, everyone in the world was constantly on the move, very fast and thought nothing of it.

"How do you know?" was the obvious question.

"You will soon find out how I know," said Daulis.

"But why were they always moving?"

"Because they could."

"Do you think we would if we could?"

"I would," said Dann.

And Mara said, "I would like so much—oh much more than I could tell you—to find a house, in a quiet place that had water, and live there with Dann. And my friends," she added.

"And your husband?" said Daulis.

"And I'll have . . ." Dann stopped.

"Dann will have Kira," said Mara, and was about to explain Kira, and how Dann had loved her, but Daulis said, "I know about Kira. Shabis has told me about it." And then seriously, to Dann, "I think you may find you'll catch up with her. I think I know where she might be . . . unless . . ."

"Unless she's found some man she likes along the way. Isn't that what you were going to say?"

19

On this last night before the river, Daulis said they should make the most of the comforts of the inn, because once they were on the boats, the river and lakeside inns would be a very different thing. And so they took care to wash well in the plentiful hot water, and to eat well, and to sleep soundly.

In the morning they walked along the road they had been following for days, and then they were standing on the edge of water where little waves ran up on to sandy verges and . . . *What did you see, Mara? What did you see?* "I saw the road I was on disappear into deep water." They could see it down there, black, clean, no weeds, and little fishes wagging their way across it. Boats of all kinds were drawn up on the shore. But the shore of what? This was not a river, for it did not flow and you could not see the other side, and it was not a lake, but channels between sandy or weedy shoals, and water that just covered shallows.

A man appeared from a waterside house where boatmen waited, and showed them a flat, wide boat with ample room for them and their bundles. Daulis bargained with him, and Mara parted with two more coins. Eight left. They took their places on piles of cushions on a flat bottom, through which they could hear fussing and lapping, and they looked over the boat edges at water they could touch, and trail their fingers through. Mara and Dann were thinking, water dragons; but the boatman said little fish might nibble their fingers, but that would be the worst. For a while the boatman seemed to be steering by the road they could still see, but then it descended even deeper.

Water had risen up, and covered the road and the land around it. When did that happen? The boatman said, a long time ago. He was tried with hundreds of years? Thousands?—but these words meant nothing to him. He said that his grandfather had told him there was a family tradition that all this, where water was now, had been frozen down to a depth nobody had been able to measure, but then the ice became water.

This was slow going, finding their way through marsh, then deep water, then marsh again. Sometimes the bottom was so close to the surface the boatman used a pole to push the boat along. Flowers floated on long, swaying stems. Birds ran over pads of leaves, and from a distance it looked as if they were running on the water. Big white birds sat on islands that were of massed weed, which dipped and swung with the ripples from the boat. There were no shores in sight but at evening they came to rest on a little promontory; and the boatman went off to his shelter, and they to an inn of the serviceable kind, and they ate food designed to satisfy hunger, and no more, and they sat about on their pallets talking, while the sunset died over the water. They lay down for the night covered with many blankets, and then there was another day of slow travelling. Mara felt that her thoughts had slowed, and all her life had become just this: sitting in a shallow boat just above water that smelled of weed, looking at Dann's face, at Leta's, at Daulis's, and thinking that she was so much part of them, and they of her, that she could not bear to think they could ever separate.

Days passed. It grew steadily colder and often cold mists crept about on the water and clung to their faces and hair. They sat wrapped in their grey blankets, even their heads covered. Mara sat dreaming in the water, that was what it felt like, as if she was in the water, in a shell; but what a difference from that other journey, down south, so hot, the water surfaces dazzling and flashing in her eyes, feeling sick, or not, but always the wet heat, the dangers from the water, where the dragons watched and waited and, always, the reminders along the banks of drought.

Mara saw beneath her a roof of red tiles, where bunches of weed swayed, and then another roof. The travellers were floating over a drowned town, and stretched down their arms to see if they could touch these roofs. The boatman said there had been many towns round about that had sunk down. Big towns. When the ice melted the earth grew soggy and could not hold the weight of the buildings, and they sank, and the water came up. He jested that if they were fishes they could swim for many days through drowned cities. And they certainly knew how to live, in those days, he said, look down there. Beneath them the water was deep and clear, with a white sand bottom, and there was a building grander than anything in the towns they had travelled through. Steps rose into a great arch of an entrance, which was set among white pillars, and there were stairs up to higher levels where terraces held figures of carved stone so lifelike it was easy to believe these were people they had known, or knew now; and the fine roofs, of many different coloured tiles, green and blue and red, had windows in them, and porches, and it seemed the easiest thing in the world to slide over the edge of the boat and land on a terrace and begin walking about there, live there, with friends; and then there will be children, Mara was muttering, there'll be big rivers of fast, fresh water and fountains full of water and little streams running into the house into basins of clear water ... Dann was shaking her by the arm, "Mara, Mara." The boatman had stilled the boat, an oar pushing at a tussock of muddy weed to hold them steady. He was looking carefully at Mara, then bent to feel the pulse in her throat. Then he did the same for Leta, who was staring at nothing and breathing badly. Then Daulis, whose eyes were shut, and grimacing as if in pain.

The boatman and Dann whispered together. Mara was aware of a slow rocking, through her whole body—yet the boat was still. And then knew they were moving again, towards a shore where there was a long building, low-built, roofed with reeds.

"The marsh sickness," said the boatman, and tied the boat up to a stump. He lifted Leta and carried her to the building and inside it. He came back and tried to prod Daulis into movement, but he was lying sprawled on his back, eyes shut. Dann and the boatman between them carried him up to the building, which was an inn. Mara must have slept, for the next thing was, she lay in the boatman's arms, being taken to the building; and then she glimpsed a tall, thin, worried woman, arguing with the boatman, saying she couldn't be responsible for three ill people. And then Mara was lying on a bed, a floor bed, in a big room, but it was a poor one, where the reeds above them were broken and needed repair, and on the edges of the gap in the roof hung water drops, which splashed down into a basin set under them. Across the room Leta lay on her pallet, very still, her arms flung out. Daulis was doubled up on his pallet, clutching his stomach and groaning. There was a horrible smell. Mara thought, Oh, I hope I haven't fouled myself; and that was the last she knew until she came to herself again and saw Dann's face just above her, wrenched with anxiety. He was wiping her face. Beyond Dann, the tall woman was kneeling by Leta, who was pointing at her bag where she kept her dried herbs. The woman spread out the herbs on a cloth and Leta pointed at one, saying "Boil it. Give it to us in water." And then she fell back into unconsciousness. Daulis was lying propped up, a rug pulled tight around him. He looked very bad. He's dying, Mara thought. And then, Perhaps I am dying. And Leta? But Dann, poor Dann, what will he do, all alone? Mara sank back into the dark but kept coming to herself, seeing little bright scenes she would remember. Leta, lying with arms flung out, that bright hair dull and soaked with sweat. Daulis, so very ill. The tall woman, taking pails out, but another time she was carrying them in. Dann, always Dann, bending over her, over Daulis, over Leta, and she heard his, "Mara, Mara, you mustn't die, please come back." She heard groaning, which she at first thought was hers, but it was Daulis. Sometimes it was full day, when she came drifting up, and the pale sun was shining down through the hole in the reeds, and there was sweat on Leta's face and on Daulis's; and sometimes it was dark and a lamp stood on the floor in a corner. Once she felt a weight and saw that Dann had fallen asleep where he sat by her, and his upper body was lying across hers. She was dreaming, oh, what dreams: she was running, running with enemies after her, always on the point of catching her; she was choking in dust storms; she was so hungry her stomach was like knives; and then she was conscious of the sweetest warmth, and her arms were full of a little boy, her little brother, Dann, who stroked her face and loved her; but then what was in her arms was not Dann but a baby, hers, and in her sleep she muttered and cried out that she had to go to her baby; and she held Crethis, the lovely girl who was a little child; and how sad Mara was, how sorrowful, when she momentarily came back to herself and saw that Dann was kneeling by Leta, holding a cup of something to her mouth, or that the tall woman knelt by Daulis, calling his name, to bring him back.

Sometimes when she woke she did not know whether she was in this wretched marsh-side inn, in a room where you could see the sky, or back in the Rock Village. And now she saw Daima across the room, sitting with her hands folded, smiling at Mara, and then holding out her arms so that Mara could run into them. "Daima," wept Mara, "I never thanked you, I never told you how I loved you, and yet without you I would have died a hundred times over." But it was Dann's face she saw, when she opened her eyes, "Don't cry Mara, don't, you've been having bad dreams, but it's all right. You are getting better. Look, drink this." Mara swallowed down a bitter liquid that made her stomach churn and rebel.

Then Leta was up on her feet, while the thin woman held her steady with an arm across her back, and the two walked slowly up and down the room. Leta was getting her strength back. But Daulis still lay like a corpse. Mara could see from Dann's face, as he ministered to Daulis, and the cool inspection the thin woman gave to Daulis, standing to look down at him, that they believed he was dying. And now Mara was grieving because of kind Daulis, who had rescued her: Why have I taken it for granted? Oh, oh, oh; and Dann came hurrying, "What is it Mara? Where is the pain?" But it was her heart that was hurting her, thinking of kind Daulis, dead.

He didn't die, though he was the last to recover. Leta and Mara were practising walking back and forth around the room, and then outside, until the cold from the marsh drove them back in, while he still lay unconscious. They began to eat, mostly the porridge prepared for them by their hostess, who was called Mavid, and was a widow, just surviving here on the rare customers the boatmen brought her—though usually the boats went past to the better inns farther on. She was very good to them. More than once she made Dann sleep, and herself sat up, because she was worried about him. Dann had become thin again, and Mara too. When they stood examining each other, like people who have not met for a while, they knew that yet again they mirrored each other: two tall, thin creatures with anxious eyes deep in their heads.

"Dann, please eat," urged Mara; and Dann said, "Mara, you must eat." And Mavid watched them and said she had had a brother, but he had died, and she thought of him every day of her life. Then she said that without Dann, Mara would have died. He was a wonder of a man, the way he nursed them all, but particularly his sister. There had been a night when she thought that all three of them were dying, and there was no way she could have managed without Dann. He hadn't slept for nights. He had eaten only when she reminded him he must. When it seemed Mara was slipping away, Dann wouldn't let her go; he made her come back, begging her, pleading with her; it positively gave her, Mavid, goose pimples to watch it, she had never seen anything like it—and so she went on.

When Daulis did open his eyes, he saw the three sitting by him, and his smile, his own real smile, not a grimace of pain, made their eyes fill. Leta wept and kissed his hands, and Daulis said, "Dear Leta," and closed his eyes. But next day he was up, and the day after began the tedious business of walking up and down, supported by Leta on one side and Dann or Mara on the other, willing strength back into his legs.

They were a month in that inn. Mavid said she felt that she had a family again. Mara gave her four gold coins. Mavid embraced her, then the others and said she could get her roof mended, and stock her store-room, and the boatmen would bring her customers. Their coming to her inn was the luckiest thing, and she would never forget them.

From her they learned about the history of the drowned cities. It was a long time ago, she said, and she spread her fingers, and set down her hands on the table, to make ten, ten times—and looked at them to say they understood. "One hundred," said Mara. She did it again. "Two hundred," said Leta. And again. "Three hundred," said Daulis. Three hundred years ago the frozen earth turned to swamp, and down sank the cities.

"You see," said Mavid, "the Ice is beginning to go again. When I was a little girl my parents took me to the northern edge of Ifrik. It isn't very far from here. They showed me the ice cliffs on the other side of the Middle Sea. And that is beginning to fill again. It has been dry, so they say for ... for ..." She looked at her hands, wondering whether to attempt setting them down, fingers spread, but again, and again and again, and gave up the idea, and concluded "a very long time. I mean, a *long* time."

Now they were going to travel in a boat with a sail, not in one low in the water, but tall, with a good deck and a cabin under it. The water would be deep, or at least have easily-followed deep channels, from here until their destination. Which is where they would start their walk to the Centre.

"And how is it you know all this, all the inns and the ways to travel?" said Dann.

Daulis smiled.

Mara said, "Because we Mahondis stick together, that's it, isn't it?"

"Yes. For better or for worse."

"I can see what you think."

"It's not as simple as that."

"But great plots and plans go on and Dann and I are part of it."

"You are the whole point of it all, I am afraid. I am not going to say any more, because you have to make up your own minds. Knowing you as well as I do now, I am pretty certain what you'll do—but let's leave it there. You'll understand."

The travelling now was much faster, because they sailed straight forward, with no need to dodge about among the shoals and sandbanks. Much deeper beneath them the cities stood on white sand, so Mara looked down, seeing them as birds must have done once. That was Sahara sand down there, the sands that long ago stretched from coast to coast. Cities were as temporary as dreams. Like people. And she thought of Meryx. But when I was sick and dreaming in that inn where you could see the sky through the roof, Meryx was never there. Not once. All the people I've loved—they've gone. There's only Dann now. Only my little brother.

This boatman said there was no need to stop at inns when night came; they could drop anchor and sleep on board. Which they did on the first night; but it was unpleasant, with thick, cold mists creeping about on the water, and lights flitting everywhere, which the local people believed were the eyes of the dead, but the boatman said were insects. The next night they stopped at an inn, a big one, where water was heated for them, and they ate well. Already they were getting strong again, but they needed good sleep and they needed good food. For four nights they stopped at inns, while the boatman grumbled and said they were wasting money: they could sleep for nothing on the boat. They must be rich, he said, and asked for more. All this, the boat and the inns, used up three of Mara's four remaining coins. One left. Leta had all her money: they wouldn't let her spend it. Daulis had nothing very much. Dann threatened to prise out his five, but they made him promise to wait.

When they left the last inn, in the morning, the man and woman who ran it said that a messenger had come very early to ask after them. "From the Centre," they said. "They seemed to think you were late." And they actually nervously looked about them, and spoke in low voices.

"They certainly seem to fear the Centre," said Leta.

"If only they knew the truth," said Daulis.

They stood watching the white sail of the boat fly back the way they had come, like a white bird that hardly notices what it is flying over. As for the boatman, he said he was so used to those old cities down there he seldom looked at them. What for? "Those are finer buildings than anyone can make now so why make ourselves miserable with the comparison?"

They were on a sandy track going north-west that made its way through a pale landscape of bogs and ponds and lakes under a sky where thin, white cloud showed like shreds and streaks of ice on chilly blue. Ice was in their minds because not two days' walk north from here were the shores of the Middle Sea, from where on a clear day they could look to the other side and see the ice mountains, the weight of ice, that Mara and Dann had seen on the ancient map in Chelops—the Ice that covered all the northern half of this world, which was like a ball floating in space. Which had on it crude outlines, one of them Ifrik. Shabis had said that the other similar mass, South Imrik, was a mystery: no one knew what went on there. Some said it had preserved all the old knowledge and was so far in advance of Ifrik it couldn't be bothered with this backward place; others that it was in the same state, too poor to care about anything but itself. All the information about South Imrik came from the past, so Shabis had said.

How much Mara had learned from Shabis, how much she owed him, she thought, putting one foot in front of another, not in dust, not in dryness, but skirting puddles and avoiding marshes. She believed she was dreaming of him, a kindly affectionate figure, and when she summoned him to her mind's eye, she saw a soldierly man, smiling at her. He had loved her, and all the time what she had felt was a flame of want, but for learning, for knowing more. What she felt now was mostly shame, for having been so awkward, and so blind; but her mind did keep returning to him, with a shy and a tender curiosity.

For the most part they walked in silence. This was partly because the cold greyness dismayed them, but there was a weight on them because of Daulis and Leta. Leta loved Daulis, and he loved her. There could be no future for them, Leta said. She had exclaimed more than once that she should have accepted Mother Dalide's offer, and Daulis said, "Nonsense, there are other possibilities." What one of these might be became clear when some people came towards them along the track, like pallid wraiths, to match the landscape. They were white, like Leta, with green or blue eyes, and their hair, what could be seen of it under their hoods, was pale too. Dann had actually reached for Mara's hand, for she had exclaimed in astonishment and fear, and Daulis said, "They are the Alb people. They live near here." The Albs stared at them, but then addressed Leta, first in their own tongue, and then, since Leta shook her head, in Charad, "Who are you? Where are you from?"

Leta said, "From Bilma," which made them stare even more; and one said, "We didn't know there were Albs in Bilma," and Leta said, "I was the only one."

Daulis asked how to get to the Alb settlement, and a woman replied by pointing north and saying, "This one will be welcome," meaning that the three Mahondis would not be.

"So you are going to leave me with the Albs?" said Leta, to Daulis.

"I think you should see it, that's all."

"The Albs seem as strange to me as they must to you."

But Mara was thinking that the Albs had a kind of beauty that went well with their frigid, colourless landscape. The blue eyes, like bits of sky, and the green eyes, like deep water, and the grey—well, like what they were walking through.

"Listen, Leta," said Daulis, sounding quite desperate. "Don't you see? You must know what your alternatives are."

"I see quite well. Councillor Daulis couldn't have me in his house in Bilma. I wouldn't be a little pet like Crethis . . ." And here Mara and Dann exchanged humorous glances at the idea of Leta's being a little pet. "And a common whore from Mother Dalide's couldn't be your wife. And besides, in Bilma you are married to Mara."

And she fell back, behind the other three, because she was crying. Mara fell back too, and put her arm around her. Leta was muttering. "A whore. That's all, a whore."

Daulis was wretched and did not attempt to hide it.

Their path went through and sometimes over water, on little bridges of planks; and then ahead was, astonishingly, not sheds and shacks and huts, but a solid town, as fine as the ones lying under the water. Some of the houses in the lower streets stood in water, but the higher parts of the town were dry and in good condition.

"This was a copy of a town in a northern part of Yerrup. Can you see how the roofs were made steep to let the snow slide off? Can you see the thick shutters, the thick walls?" He was instructing them on how to see this town, so different from anything they had known. "Once, long ago, when the Ice came down over Yerrup, they built towns here, and all along Ifrik's north coast, that matched the ones that were disappearing, so that there would be a record and a memory of that old civilisation. All the part near the northern coast was dry then, and the towns lasted for hundreds of years, perhaps much longer, because they were looked after so well; and then the ice up there suddenly got worse. It only took a few winters, and with that cold so close the earth here became half frozen, and the towns suffered. They began to crack and fall down. So a decision was taken to build the same towns, the same copies of the Yerrup towns, a bit farther south; and they lasted until things got a bit warmer and . . . Those were the towns we saw, under the water. This town, Alb, is one of few still inhabitable. There is ill feeling, because when this stretch of land was given to the Albs there were many towns, but now there are only a few and some people want to throw the Albs out and take this town back."

"You mean the Albs have no real right to be here?" asked Leta, and Daulis explained that when the Ice came down all over Yerrup, the white peoples were pushed down in front of it, and many wanted to live here in North Ifrik, and there were terrible wars. But the change of climate and the shortages of food killed many of the people in North Ifrik, and the pressure of population was less, and the Albs either took or were given certain definite places to live in. There were only two Alb settlements left and this was one of them.

They were in a fine street lined with pretty trees that had white trunks and light, graceful branches. Once, Daulis said, this kind of tree had covered most of the half of the world that was now under ice, and these could be seen as survivors from primeval forests.

He knocked at a house, a woman came out, and he conferred with her, indicating Leta. This woman had silvery hair piled up, and strong blue eyes. She was not young. She took a good, long look at Leta, and nodded.

Leta said to Daulis, "I may be an Alb, but I feel as alien here as you do." For all around the streets were full of white-skinned people, like bleached ghosts.

The Alb woman said to Leta, "I know how you feel, because I was working in a town to the south, and my family called me back when my mother died. I felt I had arrived in a place where everyone had a skin disease. But you'll get used to it."

Mara, and then Dann, embraced a stiff, unresponsive woman who was immobilised by grief. As for Daulis, he hesitated, and then held Leta close, and they were both weeping.

Then the Alb woman, whom Daulis called Donna, led Leta into the house.

"Why do we have to leave her here?" Dann demanded.

"She can't go to the Centre—it would not be appropriate. And she can't come with me now because I don't know what I'll find. I'm not going back to Bilma if I can help it. Not only because I couldn't take Leta. One way or another, things will turn out all right."

"How can they if she's not with you?" said Mara.

Now Daulis was grimly silent, and for quite a time. At last he said in a low voice, "There's something you two don't seem to take into account. Leta has known me as someone who has been coming to Dalide's for years. She must secretly think of me as one of the swines she talks about."

"You can't really think that," said Mara.

"I sometimes don't know what to think."

"I know what I think," said Dann. "Leta believes she isn't good enough for you, and you are afraid you aren't good enough for her."

"I suppose that's about it," said Daulis.

"So you ought to get on very well."

"First I've got to make sure of a place we could all get on in. That's what I'm going to arrange. And now, you two. The one thing you must not do is to think you have to choose the Centre because there is no alternative. Even without me I'm sure you two would manage—you've done well enough until now. But while you are there, I'm going to go on by myself to see if a place I know is still there. It is a house, with land. It belongs to an uncle of mine, but he must be pretty old by now. If he is still alive. Other people might already have got there—the house is part of what Mara calls the Mahondi network. But it has nothing to do with the Centre and it is important you remember that."

"I would much rather go on with you," said Dann. "I don't want to go to the Centre at all."

"Listen to me. What they are going to offer you is right, from their point of view. If I was in their place—well, I'd probably do the same. I'd have to. But I'm glad to say I'm not. And you have a big responsibility, you two. What you decide will decide—well, it's an important thing. I'm not going to say any more. But my advice to you is not to decide too quickly—if only because in the Centre you'll see things that are not seen anywhere else now, at least, not in Ifrik. So take your time. But if you decide to leave in a hurry, for any reason, you can go either to where Leta is—Donna is my friend, I've known her all my life—or to the next inn. That is, going west. I'll tell them you might be along. They'll see you're all right. And I'm going to buy a horse there, and get moving."

Dann was actually in tears. "I don't want to leave Leta. How do you know she'll be happy?"

"Happy," said Daulis. "I don't think that is a word she has used often in her life. And you don't understand. If it is possible, she can come home and live with—we'll see."

"She'll think you have abandoned her," said Mara.

"What's the good of making promises you can't keep? If the place I've told you about isn't possible, I'll be going back to Bilma. I don't know what I'm going to find. The old man might have died and people simply moved in. Once, if you said 'a Mahondi place,' people left it alone. Not now. Once, if you said 'The Centre,' they fell into line. They still do, in some places. Everyone around here knows that the Centre is . . . you'll see."

He took them to a low rise, and pointed. Ahead was a great wall that curved away on either side, enclosing a round or oval space. The wall was of stone. There had been not a stone, scarcely a pebble, for miles.

"All that stone came from the Middle Sea," said Daulis. "They needed a hundred years, and more, to get this place built."

And now Dann, then Mara, exclaimed and pointed. High on the wall was a shining disc, a sun trap, and there were others, at intervals. "We know those things," said Dann. "They provide power from the sun."

"They used to provide power from the sun," said Daulis. "The apparatus wore out. But a lot of people don't know they are dead and think they are spy machines. And now, go around the wall to the south and you'll find a gateway. Just go in. I wouldn't have been able to say that until recently—there were guards. Go straight into the central hall. I'm going around the wall to the north. Goodbye, and I do hope so very much that we'll see each other very soon." And off he strode, turning to wave to them before he went around the curve.

"So we're alone together again," said Dann. "I like that, Mara." And he put his arm around her.

"You're the only thing in my life that has always been there—well, most of the time."

"I'm frightened, Mara."

"I am very frightened, Dann."

"Are you as frightened as when we were in that place with the spiders and scorpions?"

"Yes. And are you as frightened as . . ." She was going to say, the Tower in Chelops, but could not say it; and he, gently, "You were going to say, that Tower where you rescued me; but no, I could never ever be as afraid as I was in that place. Never." He hugged her, so her head was on his shoulder, and added, "But I am as afraid as when we were fighting on that boat when Shabis's soldiers captured us."

"I wasn't frightened then because I was too busy stealing the old woman's money. Do you realise, if Han were still alive, she could probably make these sun traps work again?"

"Perhaps she was the last person to know the secret?"

The two stood there for quite a time, their arms around each other, talking. They could feel each other trembling.

At last Dann said, "Well, it can't possibly be as bad as all that. Let's go."

They went around the curve of the wall till they reached an enormous iron gate, designed to impress and oppress, and went in, and found the space between wall and inner wall almost as desolate as the tundra outside: it was greyish, lumpy, dried mud, with tussocks of marsh grass. Another imposing door, and they were in a high corridor that went on straight ahead, where there were big, painted doors, with faded pictures; and then they were in a very large room, circular, with pillars that supported a painted ceiling, which was cracked, and had flakes of plaster loose on it.

They waited. Mara clapped her hands. Nothing happened. Dann shouted, "Hallooo," and Mara too, "Hallooo."

They heard footsteps and on the opposite side of the round hall appeared two people. One was a woman, and she was a hurrying confusion of white and grey veils, and her face was first affronted, and then excited, while the man advanced in a calm, stately way. He wore some kind of uniform. He was serious, formal, silent, while she emitted little cries, "Oh, oh, my dears, oh how wonderful, oh at last, here you are." Then she was curtsying before Mara, "Oh Princess, we have been waiting so long for you," and before Dann, "Oh Prince, it has been so long." Meanwhile the man bowed stiffly from the waist, before Mara, and before Dann, and said, "Welcome to you both." Then the woman took a step back to look at them. She did not approve of what she saw, though her cries of pleasure and welcome broke out again, and now she embraced Mara, "Oh my dear Princess, Princess Shahana, oh, oh, oh." Mara, standing obediently inside those convulsive arms, knew she was muddy, unkempt and probably smelly. She knew too that the pressure of those arms meant, I shall take you in hand. And then the woman embraced Dann with, "Prince Shahmand." Her face wrinkled with distaste at the contact.

"I am sorry," said Mara. "I know we must disappoint you. You see, we have not been living like a prince and princess."

"Oh I know, I know," excitedly cried their hostess, who was so exquisite and clean and perfumed in her clouds of white and grey. "I know what a terrible, terrible time you have had, but now it's all over."

"Felissa," said the man at this point, "these two are clearly in need of food and some rest."

"Oh dear, oh dear, forgive me," and off she fluttered back into the depths of this Centre or Palace or whatever it was, while the man said,

"I am Felix, and you must forgive my wife. She has built up such hopes on you two, and of course so have I."

He led the way after Felissa, and they were in a smaller, pleasant room that had a low table, floor cushions, and a window that looked out on a vista of roofs, like a town, all inside the enclosing wall. "Please sit." They did so. He sat, and said, "Your mother was my mother's cousin. And your father was Felissa's mother's cousin. And you are the last of that family, the Royal House. But I expect you know all that."

"We don't know any of it," said Dann. He sounded grumpy, but— Mara noted—a little flattered.

"Well Shahana, well Shahmand . . ."

But here Mara interrupted. "I'd rather you called me Mara." And she looked at Dann, who saw her look, and said, "And I am Dann." But she thought he said it with reluctance.

"Mara and Dann? Well, for family use, if you like, but you'll have to use your real names, on formal occasions. At least, I do hope you'll agree to—well, to our plans for you."

Here Felissa came running back. "And there'll be food for you in just one moment." And now she sat opposite them and took her husband's hand and caressed it and said, "Felix, Felix, I had begun to believe this wonderful day would never happen."

"They want to be called Mara and Dann," he said to her, and Mara knew that she disliked him, from that moment, because though he smiled, it sounded like a sneer.

A hesitation, then, "We'll call them anything they like, poor dears."

And then in came an old man, with a large tray, and food. Nothing remarkable: they had eaten better at inns along the way. And Felissa said, "You must forgive our reduced style of living—but I'm sure that all that will change soon."

And she proceeded to tell them what Felix had already told, and the two marvelled that her style of fluttery, cooing, stroking—she had to keep fondling their hands or their faces—needed the whole meal to say what her husband had said in a few sentences.

Meanwhile Mara was thinking that for years she had secretly wondered about her name, her real name, the one she had been so effectively ordered to forget, and had believed, or half believed, that when she heard it a truth about herself would be revealed and she would have to cry out, Yes, that's it, at last, that's who I am. But now Shahana, and Princess, did not fit her, she could not pull the words over her, as she had dreamed she would, like a robe that had her name woven right through it. She did not want Shahana, nor Princess. They were for someone else. She was Mara. That was her name.

Through the window they could see how the light was fading. The same old man brought in lamps.

"He has prepared your rooms for you," Felissa said. "They are ready." And then, hesitating, "He has prepared your baths." And, hesitating again, to Mara, "There are clothes put out—if you like them." And she could not prevent a little grimace of dislike and disdain, as she looked at Mara's robe, the striped gown men wore in Bilma. It had mud around the hem.

"Perhaps my clothes could be washed?" suggested Mara, and Felissa said, "Of course, but these days we are short, so very short . . . There is the old man you saw, and his wife, who cooks, and a couple of Alb women come in to clean and do odd jobs."

"Then I'll wash them myself," said Mara.

This put Felissa into a real crisis of cries and protests. "Oh, Princess, how can you say that . . . Of course you must be looked after."

"Perhaps it would be better to call me Princess and Dann Prince only when there is a real need for it."

And now Felissa began to weep, her hands over her face. "Oh I hope that doesn't mean that you aren't going to agree . . . agree . . ." And they could see that if she was not old, she was getting on, for her hands were wrinkled, though delicate in shape. Her black hair was dyed. Her face was made up. Felix was elderly. He was quite good-looking, with the habit of pleasantness. But Mara was thinking, it's the same, wherever you see it, the Hadrons, or the Hennes, and—did she remember something of the sort in her own family, from her early childhood? Power. The ruthlessness, just hidden by smiles and courtesies. A coldness . . . And Shabis, he was strong and in command: no, that came from what he did, from his work, not from a belief in his superiority. That is what these people had. *How soon could she get out of here?*

"Oh please don't think we don't understand," wept Felissa. "You see we know everything, everything about you, we know everything about all Mahondis everywhere."

"Then perhaps you could tell us about the Kin in Chelops."

"Oh poor dear, yes, we know you had a child by Juba."

"I did not have a child by Juba."

This setback did not at all discompose Felissa. "Oh, then perhaps we do not always get all the truth but . . . There are so few of us left, and we do keep records about everyone."

"Then what happened to Meryx?"

"They all went to the East. But there was a war and we don't know who . . ."

So, she didn't know.

"There was the uprising in Chelops, and the terrible drought and big fires."

"We know about drought and fire and famine," said Dann, almost indifferently. Then, himself hearing how he sounded, said, "There was a time in our lives when Mara and I thought there wasn't anything any- where but drought and famine and fires."

"Oh dear," cooed Felissa, and stroked Mara's hands.

"I want to go to bed," said Dann, and again heard himself, his brusqueness. "I'm sorry. We aren't used to your kind of—fine living."

"I wouldn't call what we have now fine living," said Felix, polite, but cold.

Dann stood up, Mara stood up.

Felissa said, "We'll see you in the morning for breakfast."

Mara knew Dann was about to say, "We'll have breakfast in our room," as if he were in an inn, but her warning look stopped him.

They said goodnight. Mara knew that Felix did not like her, and knew she did not like him. It was an instant, instinctive antipathy. Felix's smile for Dann was affable, and could be thought of as kind. Mara hoped that Dann was not impressed by it.

The old servant led them through several empty rooms, all with flak- ing walls, mostly without furniture, to two pretty rooms, large, with floor-cushions and chairs and very large, low beds. It was a suite of rooms with a door between them, standing open. In each room a large, shallow bath of steaming water stood on the floor. The old man went off but not before seeing how Dann pushed his bath through the open door to be near Mara's. And he had stripped off his gown and was in the water, ducking his head; the water instantly turned brown. And Mara, who waited until the door shut, flung off her robe and was lying in the delicious hot water.

"What have we got ourselves into this time, Mara?" genially enquired Dann, rolling in his great basin like a fish. "Princess, are you listening?" For she had her head under water, and thought that water browned by so much travel dirt was hardly likely to leave them both clean.

"I don't like all this, I want to leave," said Mara. Out she got and, hiding herself with a drying cloth, tugged the bell pull. At once the old man came in—he must have been just outside the door. He was eavesdropping.

"Is there any more water?" she asked.

"It would take some time to heat, Princess."

"Then bring us some cold. And where can we throw this dirty water?"

Dann, who had not bothered to wrap himself, said, "I'll throw it out of the window."

"No, Prince," said the old man. "You should not do that." Now he pulled the bell pull and soon in came an old woman. She stood in the doorway taking in naked Dann, and just-covered Mara, with her bedraggled hair.

The two old people carried out one big basin, then the other.

"They shouldn't be carrying such heavy things," she said.

"Oh, they're used to it," said Dann. And now Mara was really apprehensive, hearing that jaunty selfishness.

The basins were brought back, put side by side on the floor, and a big jug was brought of cold water. Dann slid in, exclaiming and exaggeratedly shivering. "Look, clean water," he said to the staring old woman and laughed. He was over excited.

Mara waited till the two old people had gone, and got into her bath. The water was very cold. She ducked her head in it, again and again.

Then Dann was out and had dried and was looking at his enormous bed next door.

"I'll come in with you," he said, and came naked into her great bed.

"You know, Mara, there's something about all this that . . ."

But he fell asleep in mid-sentence. And in a moment she was in beside him and was asleep. She woke to see Felissa standing beside them, and her face was a mixture of shock, disapproval, and—Mara could have sworn it—triumphant pleasure too.

"Good morning," said Dann, sitting up, naked. "Good morning, Mara."

"Good morning to both of you," said Felissa. "It is very late. You must have been exhausted. We are waiting for you. Breakfast is waiting."

The crushed up clothes in Mara's sack had all but one been taken away. So while they slept the old man or woman had been in their room. One dress remained, the pretty gauzy one, but it was too light for this chilly place and Mara wrapped over it the blanket which of course was soiled from the journey. She could not wear it. What should she do? She took a covering from the bed, and wrapped that around her. Dann did the same.

In the room where they had been last night, Felissa and Felix sat on the floor cushions waiting. A meal was spread.

"Good morning, Prince, good morning, Princess," said Felix, signalling seriousness.

"What I saw this morning has made something easier," said Felissa.

"What did you see?" asked Dann. Innocently.

Felix and Felissa conferred, with their eyes, but Mara broke in with, "It is not what you think. Dann and I have shared beds, sometimes much narrower than your beds, a hundred times. And there was Daulis and Leta. We have all four shared beds."

"We know who Daulis is, but who is Leta?"

"She is a friend—an Alb."

"Oh, an Alb . . ." And that was the end of Leta, for them.

Felissa gushed, "There is something, a story . . . something fascinating . . . it is history . . . let me tell you both . . . you'll understand it all . . . you see, it is of the greatest importance . . ." Felix broke in with, "I shall tell them, otherwise we shall be here all day. Do you know the history of this part of Ifrik?" he asked the two.

"Not much," said Dann.

"A little," said Mara, thinking of Shabis and his lessons, which had all been in response to her questions—her ignorant questions, she knew now.

"Long ago, a very long time ago . . ."

"Thousands of years?"

"Exactly; before the Ice covered all the civilisations of Yerrup. Did you know that all those civilisations, all that history, happened in the twelve thousand years of a warm spell between periods of ice?"

"Yes," said Mara.

"No," said Dann.

"Twelve thousand years. They thought it would all go on for ever . . . But if I may be permitted a remark you may perhaps judge to be exaggerated, I think it is true that people always have a tendency to believe that what they have is going to continue for ever. However, that's as may be. About halfway through that warm interregnum between the ice ages, towards the east from here, at the mouth of the great river Nilus, which is still there, though not in the same position it was, was a successful dynasty of rulers. The royal family kept marriage inside itself. Brothers and sisters married."

Here Dann gave a loud laugh, and then apologised for interrupting.

"Yes. If you think about it, Prince, in turbulent times this guaranteed stability. When two families marry, or even two branches of a family, there is always conflict about inheritance, and sometimes wars. The offspring of siblings are more likely to want to keep an inheritance together."

Dann's face showed a mix of emotions. One could be described as a kind of jeer, an unvoiced raucousness. There was genuine interest in this old tale. And there was a hint of satisfaction, a puffing up that made his features seem swollen.

"How long did this dynasty last?" asked Mara.

"Hundreds of years, so they say," said Felix.

"With stability? Prosperity? Peace?"

He permitted himself a little look of irony, then a laugh, exactly prescribed, and then he made a little bow towards her. "You are asking too much, Princess. Hundreds of years—of peace? No. But the kingdom was able to fight off aggressions and attacks. There was no division inside the kingdom."

And now Felissa could not remain silent. "You two are the last, the very last. You are the only two Royals of the right age."

"Wouldn't any two young Mahondis do?"

"Real royalty. We need the Royal blood. Your child would revive the Royal house, the Royal family. When people know there is a Royal couple back in the Centre, and Royal children, then they would support us, as they did in the past."

"When Mahondis ruled all Ifrik?" said Mara.

"Exactly."

"And you are planning to rule all Ifrik again?" asked Dann.

"Why not? We did once."

"I don't know why you are so anxious to rule Ifrik," said Mara. "It is a desert of dust and death below the River Towns."

"Nothing stays the same," said Felix. "Now it is a time of dryness. But the drought will end. And we will be prepared. All the history of Ifrik has been that—swings of climate."

"The history of everywhere, from the sound of it," said Mara.

"Yes, but let us stick to our own—responsibilities. We believe we are in for another swing. The Ice is going again in Yerrup. There are signs . . .

The Middle Sea has been dry for thousands of years. There were cities built all along its bottom. But the oceans must be rising, because water is coming in from two different places: the Rocky Gates to the big ocean that once was called the Atlantic but now is the Western Ocean; and beyond the Nilus, to the east, there is a canal, which has been dry, but it is filling. There is a shallow lake now covering the cities at the bottom of the Middle Sea and the water is rising. It will be a sea again."

"In thousands of years?"

"Probably hundreds. But there are stages, and different levels of the ice and the melt. The Middle Sea has been filled to the brim between Ice Ages, and it has been half full, with cities along the shores. You two may live to see it filling so fast that shores you see on one visit may have disappeared on your next."

"And you think the dryness will soon disappear from Ifrik?"

"Why should it not?"

Dann was listening, and he was more intrigued than Mara liked.

She said, "You told us you know Daulis."

"Of course. He brings us news from the south," said Felissa.

"And he told us that you have wonderful things here in the Centre, and that we should see them."

"Yes, we have, and you should," said Felix. "We believe that what has happened will happen again. We are on the verge of another great age of discovery and invention. And in the Centre we have prototypes of the inventions of the past."

"Not everything," said Felissa. "You forgot a lot of it has been stolen."

"There have been raids," said Felix. "Robbers took some of the machines and inventions."

"We have seen them," said Mara. "May we see the Centre?"

"My dears, of course," said Felissa. "You'll find everything quite easy to understand, because it is all so carefully documented. Of course you won't see the original machines. Everything was copied, and then copied again, as long as any of the old skills were left, but then there came a time . . . oh, it is so sad."

"You will think about our plan," ordered Felix.

"We'll think about it," said Mara and stood up, and so did Dann, and they went to their rooms.

There Dann said, violently, "They want me as a stud, and you as a brood animal."

"That's about it," she said.

Then his mood changed and he said, "I rather fancy the idea of being married to you, Mara. And all our little ones running about."

"I would say they are a little insane," said Mara, "a little mad."

"Perhaps we shouldn't be too quick to see everything as mad." She did not know what to say; she felt apprehensive. "How old are they?" he went on. "Fifty? Suppose we had a child at once. They would be really old by the time it was ready to mate. Mate with whom? You or me. There would be another child. Ideally it should be not the same as the first. Imagine it, two old people, with two old servants, who'll be dead soon, and you and me. The Royal Family. Why should the locals put up with it? They don't necessarily remember Mahondi rule with pleasure, so I'm told."

And while he said all this, it was as if he were arguing with an invisible interlocutor.

Mara said quietly, "All the same, there is something in the idea you like."

He flung himself on the big bed and lay face down. He did not reply. She stood at the window and looked out over innumerable roofs, some as beautiful as those in the drowned cities. Some were crumbling, or had even fallen down.

"I want to walk around the whole place, along the wall," she said. At first he did not move, then got up, sullen now, angry about his thoughts; and they found the old woman cooking, and said they were going to walk around the wall: there must be a walkway of some kind. She said, not looking at them, so great was her disapproval, that there was a path just inside the top of the wall, and it was in good condition most of the way, but they should be careful, and it would take them the rest of the day. She gave them some food to take with them.

They set off, westwards. The wall was at the height of their waists. In some parts there were piles of sharp wire, now rusting. They knew where Chelops had got its wire fences.

"If I were ruling here, for a start all this wire would come down," said Dann.

"I see you are expecting a time of peace, Prince Dann?"

But he didn't laugh.

On one side of the wall could be seen only interminable wet earth and marshes, with paths through them, and sandy stretches, and rushes and reeds. It was a lumpy landscape that was more water than land. Inside the wall were what seemed like hundreds of every kind of building, for where some of the fine ones had fallen, reeds and mud replaced them. So this was where all the records of the great past were. The country was the same to the north, and they stopped to shelter on their little ledge of a path, from a sharp wind, crouching low to eat some bread. This wind had blown all the way from the ice fields and ice cliffs that covered Yerrup. If they could fly, as once people had flown anywhere they wished, to look down over the ice, would the great cities of those great civilisations be visible there? No, ice was not water, and so . . . They went on, chilled inside their thick wrappings. The eastern vistas were the same: this was where they had come, and so they knew that the marshes stretched for days of walking. All along the wall were the old sun traps. The metal of the arms had eroded, and some had disappeared, leaving the circlets of metal lying about on the wall; or they had fallen and lay on roofs or on the earth.

The light was going. Felissa and Felix had left a message that they would be served supper in their rooms, so that they could be alone to think about their decision.

"They don't like our manners," said Mara.

"When I am ruler," said Dann, and she interrupted with, "Dann, please stop it, even in joke. I'm afraid, don't you see . . ."

"What of, Mara?" He was defiant.

"I'm afraid of—*the other one*."

He stared, then deflated, and sat moodily on his floor cushion and was silent for a while. "You are right," he said. "But I'm going to see Felix and ask to hear more of these plans of theirs. Because there are things they haven't said. For one thing, they must be planning concubines. A baby takes nine months, and then at best a year before another. Not that I'd use you so badly, Mara."

"I had thought of concubines."

"And how exactly do they plan to live in the interval before there is another Mara and another Dann? They are obviously very poor."

"Another Shahana and another Shahmand."

"Do you know what? I keep thinking of Kira. I have dreams of her."

And she said softly, "And I am dreaming of Shabis."

"Are you, Mara? Well, we could start our own royal family, have you thought of that?"

"Please stop it, Dann."

He lay down on the big bed in her room, and then jumped up and went to his own bed in the next room. "I hate them," he said. "Curse them both. They've spoiled you and me."

Next morning Felissa accompanied them to the start of the Museum
Tour. That was what it had been called once, and she could remember
the lines of people stretching almost out of sight, waiting to get in to see
the marvels of the past.

In the entrance was a tall metal shape, like a shield, with coils of wire
behind it, and under it a button marked Press, in a dozen languages.
They pressed, but the machine was dead. Next to this shield, or plaque,
was another, and on it in the same languages, which included Mahondi
and Charad, the information on the metal sheet, writing which would
have come up in lights, had the thing still worked. This writing, on the
plaque, in elegant black and yellowish grey, once white, was faded, and
in some places illegible. Beside the plaque was a third attempt: a large
piece of black slate, and on it, written in coloured earth, the same information as on the other two, but in fewer languages, headed by Mahondi
and Charad.

"Start here for our tour through the ancient civilisations of The
Warm Interregnum. Some of the artefacts you will see were brought
from the museums of Yerrup while the first wave of the Ice was advancing. All the countries of Yerrup had innumerable museums of old artefacts. A replica of one of their museums will be found at Building 24.
The first wave of the Ice crushed and swallowed some cities, but the
ones on the edge of the Middle Sea were pushed over into it. There was
a period when parts of the Middle Sea were half filled with the remains
of the shoreline cities. The Middle Sea was already dry by then. It was
this material that was brought here to the shores of North Ifrik to make
the cities that copied those that had gone under the Ice. They, in their
turn, went the way of all cities, to ruin. And that material was used to
make other towns and cities. So some of the cities of Tundra are built of
material used by those ancient peoples to make theirs."

They made their way to Building 24. The first room showed people
dressed in skins, hunting, or sitting around fires. "These were the people
that preceded the ancient Yerrupeans from whom we descend. Observe
the shape of their heads. They lived for 140 thousand years. They
retreated before the ice waves of the Old Ice Age, and returned to
occupy sheltered valleys in the warmer interludes."

"They look rather like the Rock People," Dann said. He was disturbed. Mara felt the same—sad. It was painful, looking at a long
extinct people. "Why should we care about them?" Dann protested, but
they did, and moved on, holding hands, pleased the other was there.

The next room took them to the people who succeeded the Neanders. Again, people in skins, living in rough huts or thatched houses, hunting with knives and spears, and also with bows and arrows.

"I shall make one of those," said Dann. "Why don't we have them?"

Mara said she wouldn't have minded one of those spears at certain points during their travels.

"Well, Mara, are we being illuminated? I think not. We'd fit in very well here. Perhaps we could even teach them a thing or two about surviving."

And now at the entrance to a third room was a sign saying NO ENTRANCE, and the roof had fallen in. Peering past piles of plaster and tiles, they saw the walls were covered with scenes of wild looking people in boats that were longer and finer than any they had seen.

"So, we'll never know about the Peoples of the Sea," said Dann. For that was the description of this place.

And the next hall, a large one, The Age of Chivalry, was falling in. People encased in metal shells, with lances and spears of all kinds, with stuffed horses, had slid off them and the horses were bursting open and showing their shredded rag entrails.

It was now midday. Dann wanted to see the building described as Space Adventures, but Mara said she needed the continuity, she was already confused, and he said he didn't care about continuity. He was sounding angry as well as sad, and Mara too was angry, because of the futility of it all, a senselessness. Where these old people had lived the ice lay as thick as twice the height of the mountain that Daulis had said was where they would find the White Bird Inn. From their bedroom windows they could see it stretching up into the cold sky, and on its summit shone a cap of whiteness, snow and ice.

"I'm going to start crying, Mara, let's get out of here." And they began wandering about, lost, among this wilderness of buildings, and seeing a tall building, the tallest, went inside and stood limp with astonishment. They were surrounded by machines of a kind and complexity they could never have imagined, though it could be seen they were from the same time as the sun trap. These were not rooms, but halls, of machines once used for travelling between the stars—but stars was not a word they could any longer use as easily as they did, because all over the walls and ceilings were great maps of the sky, and there they saw the patterns of stars they had known all their lives shown as mere local manifestations, inside greater patterns. They saw that what they lived

on, this place called Earth, was one of a little sprinkle of planets travelling around a central bright star, their sun; but this was a very minor
star, that great pumping engine of heat that so directly ruled their lives,
a little star among so many that the words thousands, or even millions,
became irrelevant; and Ifrik, which they had learned to know with their
feet, putting one foot in front of another, was merely a shape among several on this little ball. And the moon, whose face they knew as well as
their own, was . . .

"Enough," said Mara, "I can't take it in."

"I don't think I like knowing what an ignorant lot of barbarians we
are," said Dann.

And they put their arms around each other, for comfort. They were
looking at a kind of metal box that had all sorts of projections and wires
and rods sticking out of it, that had gone to the planet farthest from the
sun and had sent back information . . . But why, and what for, and above
all, how? As they left this great building, a wall with writing on it
informed them that before this Ice Age had swallowed all the northern
parts of the Earth, machines had been sent into space as large as a big
town, and in them people were able to live, it was believed indefinitely;
and there were those that still believed that these machines existed,
travelling about up there. And might even return one day.

"Like that crashed machine the pilgrims were singing their songs to . . .
no Mara, let's go, I'm so sad I could . . ."

They returned to their rooms, hoping not to meet their hosts. Again
they were served a meal there, with the message that dear Mara and
dear Dann should make up their minds, because time was passing.

That night Dann went off to his room, looking rueful, and embarrassed, and even closed the door between them; but Mara woke in the
night to find him holding her, "What is it, Mara, what's wrong?" She
had been calling out to him in her sleep. She had dreamed of peoples
who emerged from a kind of mist, running and fighting, always fighting,
always looking over their shoulders for enemies; and then one wave
vanished and another appeared, dressed differently, of a different skin
colour, white or brown or black or yellow, and they too ran, and were
hunted, and disappeared, one after another; these long ago peoples had
appeared and died out and . . . She wept and he comforted her, and in
the morning he said he wanted to find Felix and ask him certain questions.

"I am sure those two are mad," she said.

"I suppose that depends on whether their plans succeed or not. If they do, then Felix and Felissa aren't mad."

And she said to him softly, "Dann, be careful. I am beginning to see that this dream of theirs can be a powerful poison."

He went to find Felix and she returned to the museums. What intricacies of invention, what cleverness, what seductive ways of living. She liked best some rooms calling themselves "A Day in the Life of . . ." A woman's life in a little island called Britain, in the middle of the eleventh millennium, and then in the twelfth millennium. A family at the end of the twelfth millennium, in an enormous city in North Imrik. A farmer in northern Yerrup at the end of the twelfth millennium. That was the period the makers of these museums liked best because of the crescendo of inventiveness of that time. But the end of the story in every building was war, and the ways of war became crueller and more terrible. In a room in a building that had only machines of war, was a wall that listed the ways it was thought these ancient peoples would have ended their civilisations even if the ice had not arrived. War was one. She could not understand the weapons: they were so difficult and so complicated. And even when the explanations were clear enough to understand she could not believe what she was reading. Projectiles that could carry diseases designed to kill all the people in a country or city? What were these ancient peoples, that they could do such things? "Bombs" that could . . . She did not understand the explanations.

There was a recklessness about the ways they used their soil and their water.

"These were peoples who had no interest in the results of their actions. They killed out the animals. They poisoned the fish in the sea. They cut down forests, so that country after country, once forested, became desert or arid. They spoiled everything they touched. There was probably something wrong with their brains. There are many historians who believe that these ancients richly deserved the punishment of the Ice."

And in another room: "The machines they invented were ever more subtle and complex, using techniques that no one has matched since. These machines it is now believed destroyed their minds, or altered their thinking so they became crazed. While this process was going on they were hardly aware of what was happening, though a few did know and tried to warn the others."

Shabis had told her that the people alive now were the same as those so clever, but so stupid, ancient peoples, and in Mara's mind was a little picture of what she had found in the Tower: Dann near death, one man with his throat cut and another nearly dead. Dann had killed that man, but he did not remember it. And there was another picture: of Kulik, with that teeth-bared, ugly grin, and his murderous heart.

When she got back to her room one day, she found Felissa looking with distaste at her old brown snake, or shadow, garment.

"We don't have this in our collections," she said. "Will you give us this one?"

"But Felissa, your museums are collapsing, they are falling into ruins."

"Oh my dear, yes, but that is why we need you and Dann so badly. We could soon get everything back to how it was."

"Felissa, I have to say this: I do truly believe that you and Felix are living inside some kind of impossible dream."

"Oh no, dearest Mara, you are wrong. Felix and Dann are talking, and I'm so glad." She stroked Mara's arms, and then her face, and murmured, in her intimate, caressing way, "Dear, dear Mara." And then, brisk and busy, "Dear Princess, you are such a lovely girl, I would so like to see you in . . ."

Spread over Mara's bed were gowns and robes that she had noticed hanging in the cupboard but, thinking they were Felissa's, had not touched them. She had walked through a hall full of clothes, from ancient times, but by then could not take in any more news from the past.

These clothes had been taken from the museum.

"Please, please, put this one on," entreated Felissa, and held up a sky-blue garment of shiny material that had a full skirt, and—this was something Mara had not seen or imagined—was tight about the hips and waist, and had bare shoulders and a bare back. "This was a dress they called a ball gown," said Felissa, "they danced in it."

"How is it these things haven't fallen apart from age?"

"Oh, these aren't the originals, of course not. They brought the originals here to Ifrik, when the ice began, to the museums they were making then, and as they faded and decayed they were always copied and replaced. Probably these are nothing like as wonderful as the originals, because we are not as wonderful as those old peoples."

"But we are as warlike," said Mara.

And now a quick, shrewd glance, far from the intimate, caressing style of her social self.

"Yes, warlike. I'm sorry to say that is true. But that is what dear Prince Shahmand—Dann—is discussing with my husband."

She held out the dress. Mara pulled off her robe and got the thing on somehow, but her waist was too thick for it and it gaped. She stood in front of a big glass that Felissa wheeled in from her own room and saw herself—and fell on the bed laughing.

"But you look beautiful, Mara," Felissa fussed.

Mara took it off.

Now, to her amazement, Felissa removed her garments that were composed of so many veils and draperies of grey and white, and stood revealed in long pink drawers, and a kind of harness for her breasts. "Yes, these are from the museum too. But they are beginning to rot and we do not have the means to replace them so I thought I might as well have the benefit."

She took from the cupboard a pink gown, all laces and frills, and put it on. She paraded up and down, glancing at herself in the looking-glass, and then at Mara, smiling. Mara saw she did this often: these clothes were not really here for Mara, Felissa wanted Mara to admire her.

And she was a pretty old thing, or perhaps not so old, quite slim still, but her limbs were hardly . . . And Mara could not prevent herself looking at her own smooth, fine, silky limbs.

Mara sat there while the modes and fashions of hundreds of years paraded in front of her. She had not heard of fashions, until now, and found the idea of it amazing and even absurd. From time to time Felissa cooed, "Oh, do try this on, Mara, it would suit you." But that was not the point of this little scene.

Mara sat on, smiling, and thought that nothing more ridiculous had ever happened to her than to watch an elderly brown-skinned woman parading about in clothes made for thousands-of-years-ago women—white women, who clearly had a very different shape, for not one of Felissa's experiments closed at the waist. Mara imagined these clothes on Leta, and found that hard too. That great bundle of fair, shining hair—yes, that would suit some of these dresses.

And so passed that afternoon. That night, when Dann came to their rooms, he went straight into his and shut the door. He did this as if casually, but it was a bad moment, and his conscious glance at her showed it. She wanted to know about his discussions with Felix, so she knocked, and there was no answer. She knocked louder. He came to open the door, and she knew who it was who stood there frowning.

"I don't like this place and I want to go," she said.

"Just a little bit longer."

"What does he want you to do?"

"He wants me to raise an army from the local youngsters. There are a great many, he says, that are dissatisfied and they want the Centre to be the way it once was. This place is like a fortress. He says I was General Dann and I should know about war. Well, I do know, Mara." And she saw his suddenly foolish, proud smile.

"And we would feed this army by stealing food from the farmers?"

"But they would benefit, because we would protect them."

"Protect them from what? This place has a good government, Daulis said so."

"The government would be on our side. They like the Centre."

"So why do the farmers need protection?"

"Oh, there are raids sometimes. Don't nag at me Mara. I need to know more before I tell you." And he shut the door in her face.

Mara spent some days in the museums. She was in a place where she could satisfy every hunger she had for knowledge, for information, to find out—learn. Some of the buildings were as good as hours of talking with Shabis. Even a wall, with a few lines of fading words, could tell her at a glance about things she had puzzled over all her life. She felt her brain was expanding. She felt she was soaking up new thoughts with every breath she took. And all the time she was thinking of Dann, with this Felix, whom she hardly saw, because he disliked and distrusted her and knew she was trying to persuade Dann to leave. This ruthless, cold man, with his social smiles and courtly manners, was not stupid. Felissa was stupid, because of a conceit of herself that made it impossible to discuss anything. Any conversation at once returned to Felissa. For instance, Mara asked her about the tombs in the sand that had held old books, old records, the city that had been found when the sands shifted; and Felissa at once said that she knew nothing about it. Mara persisted: she had been told about The City of the Sands.

"Who told you? It's nonsense. What sands?"

"Those leather books in the museum. There's a notice saying they were copied from books made of paper made from reeds."

"If there ever was a sand city I'd know about it. I've made it my business to know everything."

Now Felissa was meeting her as she came back from her days spent wandering through the things, and peoples, and tales of the ancient world, to clutch her hands, and stroke them, and murmur how happy she was that Dann and Felix were getting on so well, and how wonderful if would be if Mara could soon tell them she was pregnant.

Dann was silent, was morose, was very far from Mara, who watched him and Felix walking together, back and forth, in the great empty space between the outer fortress wall and the inner building. The good-looking, elegant Felix, and handsome Dann—they made a fine couple. Dann was deferring to Felix, perhaps not in words, but his demeanour was respectful, and the tones of his voice almost obsequious. And she knew only too well the rather foolish inflated look that was getting worse every day.

If she did not end this now it would be too late.

One night, when he shut the door between them, she knocked until he opened it. There he stood, *the other one*, and she heard without surprise, "Mara, I'm going to do it. There's everything here to make something wonderful. And look at me—everything that has happened to me, and my being a soldier, it all fits. Even you must see that." And he turned away, pulling the door to shut it, but she held the door and said, "Dann, I'm leaving tomorrow, by myself if I have to."

He whirled about, his face ugly with suspicion and with anger. "You can't leave. I won't let you."

"Your marvellous plans depend on one thing. On me. On my womb." And she tapped her stomach. "And I'm leaving."

He gripped her two arms and glared into her face.

"Dann," she said softly, "are you going to make me your prisoner?"

His hands did not lessen their grip, but they trembled, and she knew her words had reached him.

"Dann, are you going to rape me?" He furiously shook his head. "Dann, you once told me to remind you that when you were like this in Bilma, you gambled me away in a gambling den. I'm reminding you."

For a few moments he did not move. Then she saw *the other one* fade out of his eyes, and from his face, and his grip lessened, and he let her go. He turned away, breathing fast.

"Oh Mara," he said, and it was Dann himself talking, "I am so tempted to do it. I could you know. I could do it all so well."

"Well, I'm not stopping you. I couldn't, could I? Tell those two that a prince with his royal blood and a concubine are quite enough to start a dynasty. I'm sure it must have been done. But you mustn't stop me, Dann. I'm going tomorrow morning with or without you."

He flung himself down on his bed. "Very well. You know I wouldn't make you a prisoner."

"You wouldn't. But the other Dann would."

She shut the door, and in her room assembled the clothes she had brought with her, put them neatly in her old sack, and lay down on her bed to keep a vigil. She was afraid to sleep. After a night of quite dreadful anxiety, the door opened and Dann stood there with his sack.

They embraced, quickly and quietly let themselves out of their rooms, went down the long empty passages, into the central hall, and then out of the big building, through the empty space between the walls, and found the big gate locked. Dann took up a stone and hit the lock and it fell into pieces.

20

It was only just light. They were walking east, returning to Leta. There had been no need even to discuss if this was what they should do. It was cold, and they were bundled in their old grey blankets. The sky was low and grey. Here they were, Mara and Dann, with scarcely more between them than they had had when they first set out far away down in the south. They saw the tears running down their faces, and then they were in each other's arms, comforting, stroking, holding hot cheeks together; and this passion of protectiveness became a very different passion and their lips were together in a way that had never happened before. They kissed, like lovers, and clung, like lovers, and what they felt announced how dangerous and powerful a thing this love was. They staggered apart, and now Dann's gaze at Mara, and Mara's at Dann, were wild and almost angry, because of their situation. Then Dann stood with his arms up in the air and howled, "Oh, Mara," and Mara stood, eyes shut, rocking slightly, in her grief, arms tight across her chest, and she was gasping, "Dann, oh Dann, oh Dann." Then both were silent, and turned away from each other, to recover. On the same impulse they set off again, but with a distance between them, and they were both thinking that if they had stayed with the two in the Centre this was what they could have had, a passionate love that was approved, permitted, encouraged. They were in a pit of loss and longing.

Dann said, "Why Mara, why are brothers and sisters not allowed to love each other? Why not?"

"They make too many defective children. I saw why in the Museum. There was a whole room about it."

Her voice was stopped by grief and he was crying, and so they walked, well apart from each other, stumbling, and sobbing; and then Dann began swearing, cursing his way out of his misery, and Mara, seeing what anger was doing for him, began cursing and swearing too, the worst words she knew; and the two went faster now, fuelled by anger, swearing at each other and at the world, until they saw the Alb settlement in front of them. A doleful singing was coming from there, the saddest chant imaginable. Soon they could hear the words.

> *The Ice comes*
> *The Ice goes*
> *We go*
> *As the Ice flows.*

They arrived at Donna's door, knocked; she came out, and said at once, "If you've come for Leta, she left not more than an hour ago."

She was staring past them at a crowd of Albs dancing and singing, their robes flying in a chilly wind. To the two Mahondis it really was like seeing an assembly of prancing, whirling ghosts.

"Where was she going?"

"To find you. But who else she hoped to find—that's another thing. But she could never fit in here. She's seen the world and the Albs here live as if no one but themselves exists."

"You mean, you don't fit in either?"

"No, I don't. They don't accept those born here who then spend time outside. Like me. They see it as treachery. As a criticism of them. They are small-minded people. They have only one thought, that their grand-children or great-grandchildren will return to Yerrup when the ice melts. And it is going at last, so it is said."

> *The Ice will go*
> *Then we shall go*

Where the Ice has been
Will be fresh and green.

So chanted the dancers.

"We have been singing that or something like it for—well, they say it is fifteen thousand years. Who knows how long? The first refugees from the ice made a rule that these songs should be taught to every child and sung every day. They say there was a time when the songs spread all over Ifrik and became children's games. And they didn't even know what ice was."

When the Ice has gone
We'll build our homes
Where wait for us
Our forebears' bones

"Poor fools," said Donna. And then, "I'm going to miss Leta. Though she left partly to save me trouble." She sounded so sad Mara put her arms around her. "You are good people," Donna said. "Sometimes I don't know how I shall stand it, this eternal wailing about a life that was lived thousands of years ago. Or what will happen in another thousand. And now, you'd better hurry. I don't like to think of Leta alone. She's gone on the road north of the Centre. And, by the way, is it as sad a place as they say?"

"Sad and old and falling to pieces."

"Once it was the pride of the North Lands. Everyone took their education there."

"You too?"

"Oh no, not me. My grandparents' generation was the last. They were educated, you may say, above their needs. That was a great time though. The Centre ruled all the North—and ruled well, for autocrats. But now there is an administration that rules in the name of the Centre, and most people don't know the Centre is an old dog with no teeth."

They said goodbye, and the two set off westwards again. They heard Donna call after them, "Remember me. If there's a place for me where you're going, I'll come running."

When the wall of the Centre appeared they began a wide detour northwards. They were walking slowly, as if they were very tired, or even ill, Mara thought, watching how Dann stumbled along, stopped, went on. And she had to force her dragging feet. She was so sad, and knew he was too. She wanted to put her arms around him, her little brother, as she would have done before the scene at the Centre, but was afraid. He stopped walking, so did she, and they stood side by side. Without looking at her, he took her hand. She felt the strength of that hand, of his life, and thought, We'll soon be all right. He'll feel better, and so will I. Meanwhile she was so heavy with grief she could have lain down and . . . but where? Pools and marshes surrounded them and mud oozed around their feet.

He said, "Do you know, I'm sorry for those two. Poor old Felix and Felissa. For years and years they've been dreaming of their little prince and little princess, and then what did they get? Us." He was trying to sound humorous, but failed.

"Their dream came to an end, with us."

They were standing very close, just linked, and very cold under their capes. A cold wind blew from the north. Was blowing, they knew, off mountains of ice.

"And what about our dream, Mara? We couldn't get more north than this. This is north of north, the northern edge of the Ifrik North Lands."

They looked around them, and saw the interminable, grey, wet marshes, dark water, pale rushes and reeds, a low, dark, hurrying sky. Harsh cries of birds, the dismal sounds of frogs, like the voices of the marsh itself. And the wind, the cold, cold wind that whined over the waters.

"This is what we have been travelling to reach, Mara."

"No, it isn't."

"It's what I am feeling now."

She dared to put her hand around his wrist, warm and tight, and he cried out, "There's that too. Now I feel like an orphan. Now I really am alone."

She did not take her hand away but kept it there, consoling and close, though she felt as bereft as he did.

"Do you think those two will send someone after us? To get us back?"

"No," she said. "We were such a disappointment to them—no, I don't. Do you know what I think will happen? They'll die soon, of broken hearts. They've got nothing to live for now."

"Why do I feel so afraid then?" He was looking around again. There was nothing: in all that endless grey and black marsh and water—nothing, not a soul.

"I know. I am afraid too. It is because there is nowhere to hide."

"Not unless we pretend we are water rats."

He was trying to sound brave, and to make her laugh, but instead their eyes met and what they both saw was only grief.

"We must go on," said Mara. "Daulis said so. And there's Leta."

They went slowly on through that day looking ahead for Leta, and behind them for possible pursuers, and actually joked that if they ever did reach safety it would be hard to lose the habit of looking over their shoulders. Above them the clouds were hurrying westwards, as if to remind them to walk faster. The big mountain at first did not change, but at last it was towering over them, with its cold white snowcap, and there was a track going off with a sign saying, The White Bird Inn. The bird was no poetic fancy, for tall, slim, white birds stood about in dark water, their reflections making two birds of every one of them, and flew about over the marshes, letting out cries that the two could not help hearing as warnings. It was dusk when they reached the inn, which was not much more than a large house. They had scarcely knocked when the door opened and a man emerged who took them by the arms and hurried them to the back of the inn. "I'm sorry," he said, "but you mustn't be seen. There's someone after you." The two heard this as if there was nothing else they could have heard: their feelings of apprehension had deepened with every hour of walking. "I didn't like the look of him," said the innkeeper. "He was in the uniform of the border guards, but that's a trick we've seen before. There's many in that guards' uniform the guards would slit the throats of if they caught them."

"Did he have a scar?"

"A nasty one."

"Then we know who he is."

"He said he was looking for runaway slaves." And now this new friend—he was that, they could see—examined them closely, first Dann, then Mara, waiting.

"We haven't committed any crime," said Dann.

"Then I'll ask no questions," said the innkeeper. And they both heard what he had not in fact said: And hear no lies.

"There's a price on our heads. From Charad."

"That's a long way off."

"Not if he can get us to the border with Bilma. He has accomplices there."

"It's a long way from here to the border." He was thinking hard, and on their behalf, they could see. "I've done my best to put him off. He's been several times in the last week or so."

"Why should be come here?"

The man laughed and there was pride in it: the pride of a lifetime was in his face. "This is the only inn between here and for miles beyond the Centre going east, and for miles west, and that's only a farm that puts up travellers. Everyone comes to me for news. He would have to come here. Roads meet here. I sent him south, but that road ends in water, and he came back. The road ahead west ends in the sea—you'll find your friends along there. I told him that along that road he would find only well-defended farms, and that genuine guards patrol there, and if they saw him in their uniform that would be the end for him. There are no guards, but he's not to know that. I sent him off into the marshes on the marsh tracks, saying he might find you there. I thought he might fall into a quick-marsh and drown. I know when I'm looking at a man the world would be better without. But he was back, all right. He knows there's a track up the mountain but I told him the hut up there was swept away by an avalanche. I hope he believed me. Your friend Leta is up there. Daulis told me to look after her. I wanted her to stay here till he came, or you did, but she was anxious to see snow. I told her that if she'd seen as much of it as I have she wouldn't be in any hurry to see more. She'll be pleased to see you. If you don't mind my saying so, I don't think she's suited to rough travelling." He stopped, and Mara finished for him, "Not like us."

"No, not like you. Daulis told me you two could look after yourselves. I can see he was right. But be careful, be on your guard." He went inside, came out with two heavy cloaks, twice the weight of the ones they had brought for cold, thinking they were thick enough to keep off any cold they could meet with, and handed them a bag of food. "There's some matches. Try not to need a fire. You can melt snow for water over a candle—I've put one in. There'll be a moon in a few minutes." And as they thanked him and moved off, they heard, "Be careful, you two." And then, when they had gone a few paces, "Don't come down too soon. Give that fellow a chance to get away. Keep a watch. It's three hours to the hut."

"It sounds to me as if this path up the mountain is the only place left for Kulik to look for us."

"Yes, and our friend the innkeeper knows that." But Dann was alive again, danger was invigorating him. And she felt better too, leaving the dank weight of the water-filled marshes behind.

The way led up through boulders of all sizes, which seemed in the dim light like crouching enemies; but the moon came up and showed the track, and struck little flashes of light off the boulders: crystals, embedded in the rock. A mist was gathering below them, and soon they were leaving behind a sea of white, lit by the moon, and they could see their shadows down there, like long fingers pointing to the east, moving with them. It was cold. Without the innkeeper's cloaks they would have done badly. Up they went, until they saw ahead a large hut, with beyond it the white of the snow that lay over the summit of the mountain. They were in a white world, the mist shining below, and above them snow and the big white moon shining on it. They ran past the hut to gather a little snow and taste it and marvel at it, for they had never seen the stuff before. The edges of the snowcap were little white fringes and lacy crusts on grass that crunched under their feet, and sent the cold striking up into their legs. Down they went to the hut, and knocked, afraid of what they might see, but when the door opened it was Leta and she was alone. They shut the door against the cold and embraced, the three of them tight against each other. They could see she had been frightened, alone, and how glad she was to see them. If she had known, she had said, she would never have come up, but she thought she would just touch the snow, and taste it, and then go down, but the dark came . . . "I'm sorry," she said, "but I'm not like you. I don't know how to judge dangers—or distances." Inside the hut it was not much warmer than it was out. Leta had lit a floor candle, a little one, and had melted some snow to drink. They huddled on the floor inside layers of wool. Leta had a cloak from the innkeeper too. Even so they were clenched, trying not to shiver, and they ate the food, and huddled close, talking late, about the Centre, and what Mara and Dann had been offered. Dann was making a ridiculous story out of the old people's plans, and their long wait for their royal children, and the more he talked the funnier it got, until his eyes met Mara's and he faltered and stopped. "The truth is," he said, seriously, "if Mara and I had been different people, perhaps it could have worked. After all, everyone seems to think the Centre is a wonderful place, and they would believe what they heard."

"Everyone except those who know the truth," said Mara.

"Very few of those, still," said Dann.

Leta said, "We all heard about the Centre down in Bilma. We would have believed anything we were told."

"Even that a brother and a sister were making a new royal family?"

Leta laughed and said that if they knew what went on in Mother Dalide's, brothers and sisters making assignations, then Dann and Mara would not have been so surprised at Felix and Felissa.

And now they were so tired and chilled that when Mara and Dann lay down on the floor with Leta, as close as they could, spreading the woollen folds into three thicknesses, to cover all three, there was no danger in the closeness, only a need to shiver themselves into warmth. Dann said, "Don't you think we should keep awake and watch?" and Mara said, "Yes," and then they had fallen asleep. They woke in the morning stiff and chilly, and pushed open the door and saw that the mist still lay low below, but only for a certain distance. Beyond the edge of the mist the ground broke abruptly into a great chasm or canyon that stretched west and east as far as they could see. Once the Middle Sea had filled it: a warm, blue, lively sea that had bred civilisation after civilisation—whose artefacts and pictures crammed many halls in the Centre—and where ships had made great and dangerous journeys; but now all they could see were rocky declivities. But if they looked across the canyon, this enormous hole in the earth, there far away was a line of white, which they knew was not clouds, but the edges of the ocean of ice that had engulfed Yerrup. The three stood in that white landscape of mist and snow and stared at the faraway white, the bright sun making the sky sparkle; and they went back inside the hut and shut the door, to huddle there, feeling themselves to be nothing, their sense of themselves diminished by the white immensities, and above all by knowing how close they were to the terrible enemy, Ice.

But should they go down into the mist? It was so thick they could not see the path. They decided to stay up in the hut that day, although it was so cold and they dared not light a fire.

And now Dann pulled up his robe, so that Leta could see how well the scar had healed where she had taken out the coin, and said that since they had nothing better to do, and since he was so cold anyway he wouldn't be able to feel a thing, she might as well take out the rest.

"They have worked their way to the surface," he said: and there they were, five little rounds just under the skin.

Out came Leta's bag of healer's tools and herbs and she had rubbed the place with the herb that numbs, and had nicked out the first coin with her sharp little knife before Dann knew it.

"Are we sure we aren't going to need to keep them hidden?" asked Mara, and Dann said, "We'll be with Daulis soon."

"Why are you so sure of that?" asked Leta, and they could see her love and her anxiety.

"Because he'll want to find us," said Dann.

"And now don't look," said Leta, and Dann lay back and gazed at the roof of the hut: reeds from the marshes. She took her knife, rubbed herbs on to it, and cut. She eased out, easily, the four coins, and staunched the beads of blood as they welled up. Soon the bleeding stopped. The long scar was mostly white, like a very old wound, and the new raw bits would soon be the same. Leta went out, fetched a handful of snow, and spread it over the wound. She told him to lie still and soon he would forget he had ever had those coins in him. And so Dann lay, on his back, with a wool cape covering the bottom part of him, to the scar, and brought around to cover his chest and shoulders; and Mara and Leta squatted under the other cape, and they chatted and from time to time looked out to see if the mist had lifted. It had not. The coins, five of them, lay on a strip of cloth, shining, perfect, beautiful little things, with their tiny, incised pictures, back and front, of people who had lived so long ago.

"Is there any other metal that could have lived inside flesh for—how long Mara? . . . well, it's years now—and never change or get poisonous?" said Dann.

"Silver," said Leta, "but it's not worth much."

"Gold has always been like nothing else," said Mara. "I saw that in the Centre . . ." and she stopped. She was saying, it seemed in every other breath, "I saw it in the Centre." She was already earning amused looks, but probably these looks would soon be impatient, even irritated. She said quietly, "I wish I could spend my life there, just learning, Leta. You have no idea, no idea at all, of how wonderful those ancient times were, what the Ice destroyed."

And Leta questioned her about the medicines and plants she had seen in the museums, and Mara explained what she had seen, and so they entertained themselves that day. At evening Dann sprang up and said his scar was as good as healed. "And now, what are we going to do with the coins?"

Leta said, "You could put them with my money. I still have my quittance money almost intact."

"No, Leta. It is in a bag, and a bag is easily snatched away," said Dann. "We must each of us have something, in case we are separated. Mara has her gold coin and some small money. Where am I going to put mine? If feel as if I'm back in that horrible Tower, knowing that I would be killed if anyone suspected I had even one gold coin."

"I think you should put them in your knife pocket," said Mara. "It's long and narrow."

"Which is the first place any thief would look, apart from the other obvious place."

Mara cried out, "Do you realise this is the same discussion we have had over and over again, all the way up Ifrik?"

Leta said, "Daulis will find us soon. He must." She was tearful, then apologetic because of it. "I'm only going to feel safe with him," she said. "I'm afraid of being single. In the Alb settlement they were gathering outside Donna's house and shouting, 'Where is the Bilma whore?'—no, they didn't know that I had been one, but if you are a single woman, you are a whore. They wanted to get at Donna, so it was 'the Bilma whore.'"

Dann and Mara reassured her, held her, comforted her; but when she said she did not know why but she was so frightened, they had to agree. "I don't know why I feel uneasy," said Dann. "Has the mist cleared?"

It had not.

"We must keep guard tonight," said Mara. Leta said she would watch with them, but she wasn't used to it, and fell asleep. Mara and Dann sat on either side of the door, both with their knives out and ready. Listening to every sound, the silence became full of noises, which turned out to be snow shifting on a slope, or the wind tugging at a broken roof reed. They went out to see how the mist was doing, because of the pressure of their anxiety, which made it hard to sit still. The many boulders were appearing and then going again, as the mist blew across the slopes. They thought one moved . . . decided they were mistaken, tried to fix the pattern of the boulders in their minds, failed because of the shifting mist, stood peering and staring, their hearts pounding. Then the mist cleared, and not far below them the boulder they thought had moved, did move, and a man's shape was visible for a moment before it disappeared behind a large rock.

There was a thin, wet moonlight.

"Give me your snake," said Dann, very low.

"We can't have a corpse up here. They'd know it was us."

"If it is a poison, no one would think it was anything but cold, he died of cold. A knife wound would have guards after us."

She slipped off the snake and he sprang the knife and was off down the slope. Mara, her knife in her hand, went quickly after him. One minute she was in mist, the next, the wind had driven it off. She could not see Dann, could not see Kulik.

Kulik, always Kulik. How strange it was that again and again all through her life there was Kulik, the danger in a place, or in a group of people—her enemy and Dann's too. Now she thought, I'm going to kill him. I want him dead. This is the time and this is the place. And then never again will I be looking over my shoulder, or see someone I seem to know, and he turns his head and I see Kulik . . . Meanwhile she could see neither Dann nor Kulik.

Then, while the mist swirled, she heard loud breathing, and the sounds of feet slipping about and scuffling on stones. The mist parted and she saw Dann and Kulik, wrestling. This was a deadly life-and-death fight, and Dann's face—but she had never seen that face—and Kulik's showed they both knew it. Kulik had Dann's hand, with the snake knife in it, held up well over both their heads, and his other hand was pushing Dann away from him, while Dann was gripping that hand at the wrist, and had his nails deep in the flesh—Kulik's face was tortured with the pain of it. Their breathing laboured and groaned. And then Kulik tore his wrist free of Dann's grasp—Mara saw the blood from Dann's nails running down—and there was a knife in his hand. Mara shouted, "Kulik," and he let go Dann's hand that held the snake, and had turned to run, because he had seen her there, with her knife, not more than half a dozen paces away. Two of them against one, and it was clear he knew now that the little snake gleaming silvery in the moonlight was a deadly thing, because he kept his eyes on it, as the main enemy. That face! That scarred face! The bared teeth! The cold, ugly eyes!—Mara was so full of hatred that she could have rushed at him with bare hands, but she threw her knife, aiming at his neck. It struck his shoulder and fell clattering. Kulik came straight at Mara, who was now defenceless. She could see that he was as full of murder as she was. Kulik was within striking distance—all this was taking seconds, the time of a breath. The blood was pouring off his shoulder, and from a wrist. He had his knife in his right hand. Dann leaped to intervene, and was between Mara and Kulik; and now the little snake flashed, just as the mist swirled up, half hiding Kulik, who went stumbling off down into the thick mist.

"I felt it touch," said Dann.

"Him, or his clothes?"

"Flesh—I think."

"Then we'd better move fast," said Mara.

They woke Leta, gathered their belongings, and left the hut. It was by then well after midnight. Soon they left the brilliance of the sky and moon and snow behind, and were descending in thick mist, watching their feet on the path, afraid of falling, of losing the path, and perhaps of stumbling over Kulik's body.

By the time they reached the bottom of the mountain the mist had gone and the sun was rising. At the inn they knocked at the back door and handed back their thick capes. The innkeeper said they were honest people but he expected no less of Daulis's friends. Then he said he thought he had seen someone going up the mountain early in the night, but the mist was thick. Dann and Mara conferred, with their eyes, and then Dann told what had happened. He said the poisoned knife had only just touched flesh, but probably that was enough to kill. "And," he added, "I hope he dies. If you think that I have no pity for him—no, I haven't. It's not a runaway slave he's after, but a runaway general, and if he did manage to get me into Bilma it would be the end of me, and of my sister too."

The innkeeper stood silent. He did not like what he heard, that was clear. Then he said, "If anyone asks, then I won't know about any fight. And if he turns up here asking for help I'll turn him away."

"There's probably a dead man on the mountain," said Mara.

"If so the snow eagles will dispose of him. And dry bones don't tell any tales."

Off they went on the road west, and before long they saw Daulis coming towards them. Leta stood waiting, and her face was such that Mara and Dann reached for each other's hands, but what their eyes told each other made them look away quickly and back to Leta, who was in Daulis's arms.

The four walked briskly on, leaving the low, wet lands behind, because the road was climbing into hills and fresh airs and breezes. That night they slept, all together, in a room in a house where Daulis knew the people; and before they dropped off, Daulis said this was the last time they would share a room together, because next day they would arrive at—but they must wait and see.

In the middle of the next day they stopped as they reached the top of a hill, stunned, silenced. In front lay a vast blue, which went on and on until it met the paler blue of the sky. This blue was flecked with little, white, moving crests. On their faces was a salty wind, and salt was on their lips.

Daulis stood by, smiling with pleasure, and watching how Leta and Dann and Mara stared and looked at each other to share their astonishment, and stared again, until he said, "You'll be seeing the Western Sea every day of your lives now."

They went on, with the sea at their right, for they had turned south to climb a long rise towards a large, low spreading house, of red brick, with verandahs and pillars. Two dogs came down to greet Daulis—big beasts, friendly, licking the hands of three newcomers as if to say there was no need to be afraid of them.

Friendly, handsome, well fed dogs: this was a new thing for them all, and told them that times of famine or even hardship were behind them.

And now it could be seen that on the verandah of the house were two people, and Dann ran forward shouting, "Kira!" and he bounded up white steps and stopped, staring, at the fresh, pretty woman, who was smiling at him from where she reclined in a chair.

Mara heard her say, "Well, Dann, you've taken your time," and then he was kneeling beside Kira and kissing her hands and then her cheeks, and then they were in an embrace.

Mara was looking beyond the two at a tall figure, a man, thinking, But I know him; and saw it was Shabis. She had never seen him out of his soldier's garb before. He stood leaning forward a little, smiling at her and, it seemed, waiting. She took some steps towards him, and stopped. Her heart was thudding and she was afraid her breathing would stop. He came forward, took her hands and kissed them, and said in a low voice, so only she could hear, "This time, Mara, are you going to promise to notice that I love you?" She had to laugh, and then . . . But he did not kiss her, only held her and said, "Mara, I've thought of you every minute of the day and night."

A likely story, thought Mara wildly, summoning commonsense to her aid; but then she was in his embrace, knowing that these were arms she had dreamed of, or perhaps remembered, and that, as she stood there, her face against his shoulder, his face on her hair, she was at home.

Kira said, "So here we all are at last. We are a family. We are a Kin. Just like Chelops."

"You are forgetting me," said Leta, and Daulis said, "No, Leta, we could never do that."

Kira said, "Aren't you going to introduce Leta and me?" And held out her hand. Leta took it. They all looked at the two hands, the brown one, covered with what seemed like a hundred rings, and the other pale one, roughened, reddened, grubby.

"Are we two going to get on, do you think, Leta?" said Kira.

"Why shouldn't we?"

Kira said laughing, "I'm easy to get on with provided I always get my own way."

At this Dann said, "I'm not going to let you be a bully again, Kira, and don't you think it."

Kira, seeing they were surprised at this brisk marital tone so soon after they had met again, said "Oh Dann is such a boy. You're such a boy, Dann." Then, as Dann turned away, frowning, she said quickly, "Dann, you know me, come here." He did, but sat down only close enough for her to put out her hand to touch his arm. "Dann," she coaxed. Slowly he softened, and smiled, and they could see how hopelessly he was fascinated by her.

Soon they were sitting around a big table in a room where windows overlooked the Western Sea, where the sounds of the sea accompanied their talk, and from where they could see a little spring that became a stream and rushed and bounded down the hill past the house, widening into pools, narrowing again, finally bursting down a low cliff into the sea: water into water.

On the table was not much more than bread, vegetables and cheese.

This was their situation. The house was large, and in good repair—the recently dead uncle had kept it so. Squatters had moved in, but left amicably when Shabis arrived. There was enough food in the storerooms to keep them going till the harvest. There would be a time, not of hardship, but of being careful, till the farm could be brought back to what it had been. The fields grew maize and corn, barley and cotton, sunflowers, melons and squashes; grew, too, grapes; and there was a grove of ancient olive trees that supplied the oil that stood in a big jar on the table. There were goats, the minikin relatives of the enormous milk beasts of the south. Soon they would have fowls, for eggs and for the table, and when there was enough money, would buy a couple of horses.

Now there was a general accounting.

Mara slid her hand under her gown and brought out the cord that had on it one gold coin, which she laid on the table. Dann set out his five gold pieces. Leta fetched her bag of coins from her sack, and said, "My quittance money." Shabis said that he had arrived with very little, and laid out a handful of small money. Daulis said that his contribution was the farm. And now they looked at Kira, with her heavy gold earrings, bracelets, rings. She was about to take off her bracelets, but Shabis said, "Keep them, we'll know where to come when we are short."

Kira smiled, her lids lowered.

And now, the weapons.

Dann showed his knife, and Daulis produced a knife and a dagger. Shabis had his General's sword and small gun, which he said did not work but frightened people. Leta had a knife. Kira shrugged and said she relied on other people to defend her. Mara showed her knife and slid the poisoned serpent from her upper arm, and it lay glittering on the table as if it wanted to be admired for its workmanship.

Then she said, most passionately, "I shall never wear that again. I never want to see knives and daggers and weapons again."

"My dear Mara," said Shabis, "what sort of time do you think you are living in?"

She slid back the snake.

"So what dangers may we expect now?" asked Dann.

"At the moment, probably nothing much. But as the Centre weakens and dies, the authority of the Tundra government will weaken too. Already we see lawlessness in places where people have learned that the Centre is—what it is."

Now Daulis showed them a big room full of weapons of all kinds— not merely knives and daggers, but swords and lances, and the bows and arrows that had intrigued Dann, axes, and many different kinds of guns, which Mara recognised from the Centre.

"All stolen from the Centre," said Daulis. "In the last hundred years or so the things pilfered from the Centre have found their way all over Ifrik."

Dann said, "Pilfer is a funny little word for stealing sky skimmers and road hoppers and guns and sun traps!"

Mara said that what she wanted from the Centre was to go there, spend time there, and learn.

Shabis said, "But Mara, you have farming skills and they are needed here."

"And besides," said Daulis, "you two had better keep your distance from the Centre, at least for a time."

"But every day it crumbles a little more, it is disappearing. As soon as I can I'm going there. I am. I must."

"Meanwhile we must all know how to use at least some of these weapons. There are always madmen and thieves and people who enjoy killing to be reckoned with."

Mara looked at Dann. He was looking at her. Both were thinking, they knew, of Kulik, who might not be dead. And Mara was thinking that now, just as often before, vague and possible dangers were taking a definite shape—Kulik, who was going to haunt them both—because of their uncertainty. Into her mind's eye came a picture: a skull among the boulders on the mountain, rocking or tumbling as the winds blew or as crows trod the bones looking to see if they had missed something; the skull turned its face to her and she saw the terrible teeth-bared grin that had been in her childhood nightmares.

She said, "Do you think we should have some kind of guard?"

"Yes," said Dann. "I'd feel easier."

"The dogs," said Daulis. "That's what they're trained for."

Next, they had to bring each other up to date with their stories.

Shabis, seeing that it was only a question of time before the other three generals arrested him on some charge or other, fled from Agre, and made his way North, in the same way the others had.

Shabis did not know how it had been with Mara, except in the barest outline, from Daulis; and having had this outline confirmed, said he wanted to know more later. "Everything," he said. "I want to know everything about you. Just to set my imagination at rest. You have no idea the horrible things I was imagining, when you were with the Hennes."

Daulis said that they all knew his story.

Dann told Shabis and Kira what had happened to him.

Now it was Kira's turn. She had run into Shabis in Kanaz, and he had looked after her on the journey here. Kira did not say much, but her eyes were on Shabis, and told Mara that it was not Dann Kira wanted, but Shabis. Mara felt this as a stab to her heart, and she thought that loving someone meant that a look, a touch, a sigh in the dark, could flood you with happiness or doubt. She had done better, she thought, when she had had a heart like a stone. She saw Shabis was smiling at her, knowing what she was thinking, wanting to reassure her. And Leta too, who always picked up the slightest nuances of feeling, was smiling at her, *It's all right, Mara.*

And Mara was reassured, she knew Shabis loved her. But she could not prevent a bitter little thought: You don't know what Kira is like. She glanced at Dann to see what he had caught of this little play of looks, thoughts, feelings, and he was looking at Kira and then, thought-fully, at Shabis.

When the night came, they had not finished all they had to tell each other, but next day would do. "And next week, and next month, and next year," said Shabis, "but now it's bedtime."

Kira and Dann went off together—"Just like an old married couple," said Kira, with a flirtatious look that included them all, but lingered on Shabis. Then Leta and Daulis went, but shyly.

Mara and Shabis sat on.

Shabis said, "And now I must tell you about the Chelops people." His manner had changed, as if he, Shabis, had withdrawn himself, leaving a formal, almost cold voice and eyes where she could see only a man doing his duty.

From his spies, and from travellers, he had pieced together a story which he believed was more or less accurate. When the townspeople attacked the eastern suburbs, the slaves repelled them. Then the slaves rioted and most of the Hadrons were killed. The Kin collected together a company of themselves, including some babies and children, and slaves who were ready to go with them, and went east, meaning to reach the coast where there was a Mahondi Kin. They did not know a war was being fought in the area between Chelops and the coast. Some were killed, but some escaped, including a woman called Orphne and the head man, Juba. At this point Shabis hesitated, but went on, "Orphne is living with Meryx, and they have a child. They reached the coast."

Mara was so strongly back, in imagination, in Chelops that, thinking of the people dead, she wept. And then, happy about Orphne, and both happy and unhappy about Meryx, she felt for the second time that day a pang of jealousy so sharp that she got up, staggered blindly to a couch, flung herself down and sobbed. Shabis came after her and, no longer withdrawn into a correctness that was meant to reassure her he did not want her to repudiate her old lover, put his arms around her and she clung to him. Soon he led her off to the bedroom that would be theirs.

This was not a busy time on the farm. The harvest had been taken in, the fields replanted, and the animals were inside good fences and needed only to be fed and milked. Mara undertook this work, and taught Leta how to do it.

The big house, spreading over a hill where you could hear the sea booming or sighing all day, all night, was like the end of tales she had seen in an ancient book in the Centre: "And so we all lived happily ever after." But Mara's heart, which these days in no way resembled a cold stone, told her otherwise.

One night she was lying in Shabis's arms, listening to the sea, when she heard what she thought were the complaining voices of sea birds, but then knew it was Kira's voice, shouting at Dann.

Mara quietly got up, and went into the room where they so often all sat about, talking, and as she did so Dann came in from the other side. He was white, and angry. He flung himself down on floor cushions, hands behind his head, and Mara sat by him, and took his hand, which gripped hers then fell away.

"She doesn't love me," he said, and Mara said nothing. Then he turned to her, put his arms around her and said, "Mara, why can't we be together? We ought to be together . . . But now you've got Shabis." And his arms seemed to go cold, and withdrew.

Mara said, "It's going to be hard for both of us, loving other people."

"I haven't noticed you have any difficulty loving Shabis."

She sat by Dann, close, in the dark room where a sky full of stars showed through a big square window, with the so familiar feel of him, the smell of him, her little brother, her companion through so much; and she knew that she loved Shabis but she always would love Dann more and nothing could change that.

"Who made these laws in the first place?"

She said, "I told you, Nature made them. I saw it all in the Centre."

"The Centre, the Centre—suppose I don't care about children and posterity?"

Mara sat silent, allowing herself to think of the happiness of loving Dann; and then this dream dissolved with the coldest of reminders, because from nowhere, or from deep inside her, came the words, "You'd kill me, Dann, if we loved each other. It would be so—violent."

"Why do you say that?"

She could only say, "I just think something like that would happen."

He stroked her face, "I love you so much, Mara."

"And I you."

"Am I really such a violent person?"

"Yes. And I am too. We have been made violent. And if we fought— it wouldn't be with words."

"You are sure of that, Mara?"

"I'm not sure of anything."

He began playing with her hair, long black hair, and she stroked his, so like hers. She put her arm under his head and her arm over his shoulders. So they reclined beside each other, as they had so often, and then she felt his hand fall, slide down her shoulder, and to his side. His eyes were shut; he had gone to sleep.

She sat holding him for a long time, and then saw a light move on the floor, looked up and Shabis was there, with a lamp which he set in a corner on the floor. He settled himself opposite them. He nodded to Mara: It's all right.

The big room was a different place, with the lamp spreading around it an intimate circle of yellow light. The square of starlit night in the wall, the sound of the sea, seemed to have retreated. A wildness had gone. Dann sighed, but it was more like a moan. Mara saw that his face was stained with tears, and then that Shabis had opened his arms to her and was waiting. After a moment—she could do nothing else—she gently slid away from Dann, went to Shabis, and was beside him as she had been by Dann.

"Mara," he said softly, "there isn't anything you can do."

Soon she fell asleep, inside the comfort of his arms. And then Shabis, too, fell asleep.

It was cold. Dann started up, staring around him as he usually did on waking, for a possible enemy. He saw he was safe, and then that Mara was asleep in Shabis's arms.

He stood looking down at them. Mara seemed to shrink and shiver as through the window came a cold blast from the stars. He took a blanket and laid it gently over his sister. He hesitated, frowned, and spread it to cover Shabis as well. He went out, not into the room he shared with Kira, but into the night and down to the sea, the dogs at his heels.

Next morning at breakfast he announced that all this hanging about was driving him mad. He wanted to see for himself how the water from the Western Sea was splashing through the Rocky Gates into the Middle Sea, and then go north until he stood right under the ice mountains to find out if it was true they were melting. He wanted to walk down the dry side of the Middle Sea until he reached the water at the bottom and then walk all around the water line till he got back to where he started. He wanted to raid the Centre for things they could use here on the farm.

These excursions were vetoed because the farm work would soon be starting. Then Leta suggested that when the weather was better he should go and fetch Donna, whom they had agreed would be invited to live here. Daulis said it would not be dangerous, if Dann travelled at night and kept well clear of the Centre.

They could all see that Dann was on the point of demanding Mara should go with him, but he stopped himself.

"Five Mahondis and two Albs," said Kira. "A new kind of Kin."

"You are going to like Donna," said Daulis.

"I didn't say I wouldn't. I like Leta, don't I?"

"Do you?" said Leta, laughing.

Mara said, "I think quite soon there won't be any Mahondis. I saw that in the Centre. Tribes—different kinds of people—they just die out."

"Soon?" said Kira.

"Well," said Mara laughing, "a hundred years."

"Not thousands, then?"

Mara was teased by them because *thousands* appeared in her talk as often as *The Centre*.

"I don't want to wait until the weather is better," said Dann. "Why not now? And there's another thing: we are always talking about the next season, the next year. Suddenly, I'm a farmer. Being a soldier suited me better."

Daulis said gently, you could say coaxingly, smiling at Dann—the others joked that if Shabis was Dann's father, then Daulis was his big brother—"I wouldn't be surprised if there wasn't fighting to be done one of these days, General Dann."

"I agree," said Shabis.

"Well, Daulis, well General Shabis, defending a farm is not the same thing as defending a country."

"Perhaps it will feel the same when you've worked on it and made it your own," said Mara, intending to sound calm, and calming. She knew the others were anxious about Dann, his restlessness, his discontent. She felt differently. Here in this place, this one place, were two men, two Mahondis. Two men had haunted Dann all his life, the good one and the bad one, sometimes merging into one, always a threat. These two men, Daulis and Shabis, were good men, had absorbed that past, and Dann was for the first time in his life feeling safe. Besides, a very bad man lay dead on the mountain, and Dann had killed him, as long ago he said he would. Or believed that he had killed him, at least most of the time. He felt safe: and that is why he permitted himself petulance and complaint. Probably this was what it was like being a parent, knowing why a child was like this or that, because of some event or incident, even a little thing, that the child had forgotten; but you couldn't say to the child, who was growing up to be a person, doing his best to forget the bad things, "This is why you do this," "I know why you do that."

Kira said, "And what about me when Dann goes off?"

"It'll give you a rest from my impossible behaviour."

"You mustn't go for long, because there's going to be a lot of work, as I know, from Chelops. But we had slaves there to help."

Here Dann and Mara protested, "But Kira, we were slaves too," and, "You were a slave, Kira."

"What? Nonsense." And she went on protesting. She had decided to remember, as her truth, that she had had slaves to do her bidding—true to a point—and that she had not been one.

Mara insisted, "We were the Hadrons' slaves."

"Then how was it we lived so well and had everything we wanted? How was it we ran everything?"

"Did you run everything for the Hadrons?" Shabis asked.

"Most things. But we were their slaves. They had got so fat and lazy and disgusting . . ." And now Mara cried out, remembering, "We must not let ourselves get like that, it frightens me even thinking about it."

"Better slaves than be like Hadrons," said Dann.

"I don't see what's wrong with having slaves," said Kira, "not if you treat them well."

"We aren't going to have slaves," said Dann.

"Then there'll be a lot of work, even for seven people."

There was another little scene, equally suggestive of the possible developments in the lives of our travellers.

After a week of storms, of crashing and roaring seas, the sun shone and the sea lay quiet. For the first time in days they were all on the verandah, stretching themselves in the warmth. The two big dogs were there too, asleep, the sun hot on their fur. They were so peaceful there, these great animals, so harmless, just as if, at nights, their growls, or a sudden outbreak of barks at some threat they saw or heard, did not often alert the nerves of the people in the house, so that they got up and stood at a window to see the dangerous beasts outlined black against the sea or sky, staring out, motionless, watching.

On the warm brick of a pillar were two little lizards, bright green, with blue heads and yellow eyes.

"Oh they're so pretty," said Kira. "I do love them so."

Mara and Dann grimaced at each other, and Kira saw it and said, "More songs without words. What is it this time, do tell us?"

"We told you about the big lizards," said Dann. "And anyway, I'm getting sick of it. We've been sitting here day after day talking about what we've done. I'd rather talk about the future."

"Good," said Shabis, "because we really must have a serious talk about our plans for the season after next. We need to allocate work."

"Well don't allocate any to me," said Kira. "I think I'm pregnant."

"Oh thanks for telling me," said Dann. "Well, congratulations."

"I was going to wait a day or so to be sure, but this seemed to be a good time." And she was genuinely surprised that he was hurt. "Oh, Dann, you're so touchy."

"I think I might be pregnant," said Mara.

"I suppose you did bother to tell Shabis," said Dann.

Leta said, "I'm not pregnant, but whores don't get pregnant so easily."

When she struck this note, all of them criticised her, as now. "Oh Leta, do stop it." "Leta, you know you must forget all that." And, from Daulis, "Please, Leta, don't."

"Anyway," said Kira, with the casual honesty that was the nicest thing about her, "I wouldn't have got anywhere without men. But I'm not going to call myself a whore."

"Could we just stop talking about the past?" said Dann.

"Very well," said Shabis. "You start, Dann. What kind of work do you think you'd be good at, on the farm?"

Dann ignored him, looked straight at his sister, and said, "Mara, tell me honestly, no, truthfully, the real truth: when you wake up in the morning, isn't it the first thing you think of—how far you're going to go today, one foot after another, another little bit of the way up Ifrik? And the two of us together? Even if the thing you think about after that is Shabis?"

Mara took her time, smiling at him, eyes full of tears. "Yes," she said, "yes, it's true, but . . . "

"I just wanted to hear you say it," said Dann.

The End